Fallen Angels

Guardian Series, Book 3

Andrew P. Weston

Pagan Writers Press

Houston, Texas

ISBN: 978-1-938397-86-8

Published by Pagan Writers Press, Houston

Edited by Rosa Sophia
Cover by Christie A. C. Gucker
Typeset by Angelique Mroczka

Printed in the United States of America

Fallen Angel

A watcher

An attendant or ministering spirit

An angel that has sinned and fallen from heaven into a darkened spiritual state

A demon

"And the angels that did not keep their original position but forsook their own proper dwelling place he has reserved with eternal bonds under dense darkness for judgment on the great day."

(Jude 6)

"Certainly if God did not hold back from punishing the angels that sinned, but, by throwing them into Tartarus, delivered them to pits of dense darkness to be reserved for judgment…"

(2 Peter 2:4)

Tartarus

From the Greek–tar.ta-ro'o

The lowest condition of abasement

A darkened mental and spiritual condition

Acknowledgements

As always, I'd like to say 'thank you' to everyone who has made the continuing journey possible. To my wife, Annette, for her ongoing support. To Marty, who must have a real-life Guardian Angel looking over him. His positive attitude in the face of continued ill health has been a great source of inspiration. And—as usual—a special 'thank you' goes to Angie and the team at Pagan Writers Press for their ever-present faith in the concept.

As always, this book is dedicated to the real life heroes of our emergency services, without whom, the world would be a poorer, and much more dangerous place.

—Andrew P. Weston

Contents

Prologue

Feeling returned first. That and spatial awareness.

His perceptions were confused. A jumbled maelstrom of conflicting thoughts and energies that were only matched by the gut-churning, bile-inducing plummet of fearful proportions he knew was occurring. And yet, although the plunge dominated his world, he felt detached somehow—indistinct—as if those sensations were an echo belonging to another entity. Any moment now, he hoped he would awake to find himself partaking of the Bliss in utmost tranquility.

But no! This horror was real. It was happening now!

As he regained consciousness, the terrible, endless fall seemed to afflict his very atoms with an overwhelming compression, as if he were being squeezed out of existence.

Sight returned, along with a giddy, kaleidoscopic rush of chaotic impressions. Then sound! A deafening roar swamped him, overpowering his ability to form a coherent thought. He fought to establish some form of equilibrium, and exercised his draining capabilities in an effort of heroic proportions.

Yes! The others were here too, all around him. Silent participants of this sickeningly endless descent! Over and over they tumbled. Darkening the further they fell from the Source. He could sense their diminishing life-force and the shift in their spectral brilliance as the Flame was leeched from their essences.

One by one, they too gained a measure of awareness as they approached the geodesic curvature between realities. Their rising panic flared neon-red amid the chaos, marking their positions like beacons.

BRACE YOURSEVES! He called, as they approached the nexus of actuality.

This was going to hurt!

Silent screams filled the ether as the esoteric grip increased, crushing their fragile sensibilities even further. He himself felt as if he had been fastened to a torture rack where he was now being stretched to the point of rupturing.

An eternity of pure agony—where he was pierced by a blade of the darkest anguish imaginable—and then he was through! The grey limbo of quasi-dimensional subspace replaced the overwhelming surge of light and sound that had threatened to squash him out of existence, bringing with it a welcome respite.

He felt a presence behind them.

Casting his diminished senses backwards, he recognized Heim-dhal-riel, Guardian of the Crossing. He was already in position to bar the way back to those who might retain sufficient puissance to create a bridge.

How did I miss him?

He was about to send a mental query, when a voice of thunder suppressed him, and indeed, the rest of the Fallen into silence.

IN YOUR DEBASED CONDITION, YOU ARE FORBIDDEN TO INTERACT WITH THOSE WHO ARE UNTAINTED. YOU ARE FORBIDDEN TO REVEAL THIS JUDGMENT TO ANY WHO'S ORIGIN IS NOT OF THE HOST. ONLY THE TRULY PENITENT MAY ONE DAY HOPE TO ACHIEVE CONSOLATION. GO NOW AND REFLECT ON THE ACTIONS THAT LED TO YOUR JUST PROSCRIPTION.

With that, Heim-dhal-riel raised his flaming sword. A blazing shockwave raged forth and a tau-field formed within the grey limbo, creating an irresistible pull that swept them all away in its merciless grip.

Psychic disorientation increased. The vortex swallowed them whole, ripping yet more of their vitality from them as they were forced through the celestial arch. The pulse of ambient life became muted, less fluid, more frangible and somehow more insubstantial than it was before.

Sachael-Za-Ad'hem sensed his own diminishing life-force as he crashed through. He felt as if he had solidified in some way, and darkened. *More* than he thought would be possible!

Within moments they were ejected from the cosmic axis and found themselves within the physical/mortal plane. One of the first to recover, he scanned their position within a huge void at the center of an immense galaxy. A galaxy now bereft of its anchor because of their banishment.

So! THIS is what Tartarus feels like?

The energy shift was more pronounced here. So palpable, that he could taste and feel it with every molecule of his remaining complexus. His analysis was interrupted by a query from Sariel-Jeh'oel: *Sachael-Za-Ad'hem?*

Yes my friend?

Sariel-Jeh'oel's attention was also turned inwards, scrutinizing, assessing. It took a moment for him to continue: *I am...we are...enveloped by corruption! WE, who were of the Primary Echelon, are now debased. Why were we so harshly judged?*

Sachael-Za-Ad'hem directed his most intimate friend's attention to their already squabbling brothers and sisters scattered about them. He said: *It would appear those who fomented rebellion still insist on justifying their actions and fulfilling their perverted desires. They covet that which belongs to someone else. We should not have tried to speak for them in the deliberation of their judgment.*

But we took no part in the rebellion! We only expressed our doubt as to the wisdom of banishing them from their proper dwelling place among the Host. Such action must surely reflect poorly against the Source?

Directing Sariel-Jeh'oel's attention to one of the largest groups, Sachael-Za-Ad'hem replied: *Ah, but in expressing doubt we inadvertently raised a challenge against the wisdom and validity of His judgment. We allied ourselves with these, the moment we expressed those doubts. Because of our station, an example had to be made.*

They looked across to where Psi-edon-ijah and his cohorts– Menoetius, Ares-tartus, Porphyries, Mnemosyne, Bael-zebad, Hesta'n-ea, Hadez'ekiel, Xeno-Dionysus and Oph-aestus, were already trying to justify their actions to the others crowding in on them.

Although not of the Primary Echelon, their former glory as members of the Median–or Secondary Echelon–had been corrupted over time. In an effort to gain themselves positions of power and influence, it was these in particular, who had started to intervene in the affairs of the lower realms. They wanted to be worshipped as gods. Something they felt was their right as superior/higher life-forms and members of the Host. Those of the Exterior Echelon, who had been swayed by their higher brethrens arguments into joining the insurrection, were now questioning the wisdom of their leadership.

Psi-edon-ijah was the most vocal: *I tell you we can turn this abasement to our advantage. If you'd all just listen, we can establish our dominance...*

You call THIS an advantage? Selene interjected.

Her reference to their darkened and degraded condition was not lost on the majority. She continued: *No matter what our station within the Host, we were glorious. Look at us now! Are you seriously trying to suggest we fall even further by continuing this madness?*

Psi-edon-ijah's puppet and most avid supporter, Menoetius, cut in: *You are a fool, Selene, if you think we shouldn't seize control of the mortals inhabiting this realm. Yes! We can all feel the effects of our exclusion, but our grandeur still far exceeds anything they possess.*

Psi-edon-ijah's aura flared in approval: *Menoetius is correct. This venture has cost us our true standing, so it is only fitting they worship us, as is our rightful due.*

A score of others blazed in support.

Marking them, a warning thought passed between Sachael-Za-Ad'hem and Sariel-Jeh'oel. The latter reacted instantly. Storm loud, his mind cut across the chatter: *FITTING? OUR RIGHTFUL DUE! Have you been sleeping during recent events?*

Silence!

He continued: *Your corruption sinks deeper than I thought. Tell me, Psi-edon-ijah, is mental derangement a prerequisite of joining this little faction of yours?*

A menacing undertone began to coalesce amongst Psi-edon-ijah's most ardent followers.

Hadez'ekiel said: *Brother, guard your opinion! Psi-edon-ijah's assessment is sound. Yes, we have fallen from grace because of the strength of our convictions. So would it not be a course of wisdom to capitalize on the situation we now find ourselves in?*

Murmurs of support echoed forth, along with a deeper nuance of stubborn defiance.

Sachael-Za-Ad'hem moved closer to his friend, darkening slightly in warning. The gesture was not lost on the majority. The former Avenging Destroyer of the Host would still be a formidable adversary, Fallen or no.

Hadez'ekiel continued: *We are cut off, there is no way back. So where is the harm in making the best of our circumstances? The beings of this realm are fleshly. They are beneath us. And Fallen or not we are superior to them.*

Sariel-Jeh'oel's mind whispered: *Strange that you would forget Heim-dhal-riel's words so easily. I fear that for those like you, there is indeed no way to return.*

Intent formed within Psi-edon-ijah's mind. Quickly insinuating itself into the thoughts of others like him, it gained in both strength and purpose.

Sariel-Jeh'oel continued: *Tell me Hadez'ekiel, what would you and those in your faction do for these 'lesser' beings?*

Do for them? Are you mad? They are beneath us, Brother. We should be considering what THEY *can do for us. They owe us their servitude. Their worship! We could reign supreme here!*

Menoetius, Hay-yel, Mnemosyne and Porphyries began fanning out, their auras darkening to scarlet, betraying their intent.

Acknowledging their posturing, Sariel-Jeh'oel said: *It would appear Sachael-Za-Ad'hem and I made a grave error in speaking out on your behalf. I did not realize the depth of your depravity, nor indeed how corrupted you have become.* Turning to Sachael-Za-Ad'hem, he admitted: *We were fools to forget that the Source would know the true extent of their iniquity from the outset! What have we done?*

Sending a signal to their faction, Menoetius began to meld with over a dozen of the more volatile entities. He snarled: *Fools indeed! Especially if you think to oppose us now!*

Before the harmonic link could be established and before any of them could react, four coherent beams of devastating energy stabbed out. The containment thresholds of Menoetius, Hay-yel,

Mnemosyne and Porphyries were breached within seconds. For a moment they hung there–impaled and in agony–before they ruptured, their atoms shredded into a million pieces.

All minds turned to the originator of the lethal blasts. Sachael-Za-Ad'hem! His spectral brilliance hadn't shifted once during his attack.

Subsuming the essences of the would-be murderers into his already mighty complexus, he then seized the rest of Psi-edon-ijah's cohorts within a vice-like mind grip. All of them rippled and heaved with the utmost anguish for just a micro-second, before his hold abruptly cut off.

An echo of that grasp then returned only moments later. Settling gently over each of them, they automatically shied away, tensing in terror and anticipation.

Sachael-Za-Ad'hem merely hung there, silently.

Eventually, he said: *It would appear Sariel-Jeh'oel and I retain an echo of our former capacities as members of the Primary Echelon. Remember that, should you be inclined to further foolishness…or scheme treachery in the future.*

The point was well made. Already a number of the Fallen were gravitating towards Sachael-Za-Ad'hem and Sariel Jeh'oel, especially those who were regretful of the wrong they had committed.

Sachael-Za-Ad'hem continued: *Do you not appreciate the reality of our situation? We are now afflicted by a Tartarus condition! A disorder we were never meant to have! I cannot believe I stood for you before the Assembly of our Brothers and Sisters, advocating a more lenient form of correction for your errors. I see now I was wrong. Your corruption runs core deep. If you do not make a choice to leave that error behind…well…you have no future.*

Psi-edon-ijah asked: *So what would you have us do, Brother? Ignore them?*

Sachael-Za-Ad'hem looked toward Sariel-Jeh'oel. A buzz of mental activity spurted back and forth between them at lightning speed. An accord was reached.

Sachael-Za-Ad'hem replied: *Listen, everyone. Listen!*

He enfolded their minds within his vast nexus and ranged for billions upon billions of miles in all directions. Searching out the faint sparks of newborn sentience, still so recent in this universal plane, he continued: *This new life needs our help. They need to be nurtured, guided. Can't you hear? Can't you perceive their potential? Although fleshly, they contain an echo of the divine spark within them. When it matures—maybe thousands upon thousands of their cycles from now into the future—they will have an opportunity to bring glory to the Source in their own unique way.*

A number of them flared at that idea. Some in hope! But sadly, more in rejection.

Psi-edon-ijah looked bewildered, confused. He whispered: *What? You would have us serve...them?*

Sariel-Jeh'oel interjected: *Why not? Who understands the true depth and scope of the Source? Perhaps our banishment here can be turned to our advantage? Merely in a different way than you originally intended. Who knows, perhaps our service may facilitate an eventual return?*

Psi-edon-ijah replied: *But how will serving them, serve us?*

Sariel-Jeh'oel looked to Sachael-Za-Ad'hem and said: *Our fall was due in part to our presumptuousness. A number of us thought too highly of our own opinion. Others craved that which does not belong to us. Whatever the reason, service will require humility. A quality that some clearly need more than others! Perhaps our exclusion to this realm may serve the Source's purposes if we but put our mind to the task?*

He scanned the throng about them as they considered his thoughts. Some were obviously keen to accept the challenge. Of these, Sariel-Hera'nai, Cassiel, Selene, Za-Hermesiah, Raphael and

Din'athinae were to the fore. Others cogitated more deeply, troubled that they had been led into turmoil so easily.

A few, led by Mae'loch and Bael-zebad of the Median Echelon, were still determined to remain inflexible. Sachael-Za-Ad'hem delivering a blunt warning as they edged away: *Persist on that path if you must! The choice is yours. But be aware of a simple fact. If you seek to dominate any of the beings inhabiting this realm, I will ensure you face the consequences of your error. Even reduced as I am, you will find me a fearsome adversary.*

His remark was accepted with a grudging acknowledgement.

One by one, each span their own respective hyper-translation field and departed in solitude, brooding as to what might have been.

Sariel-Jch'oel turned to Sachael-Za-Ad'hem: *My friend, out of all of us here your precognitive sight is the strongest. Please. Reveal the way forward to us so we may better decide the right course to take.*

Sachael-Za-Ad'hem softened his aura and began gathering the potential of his immense faculty. Gently, soothingly, he separated the causational probability nodes saturating sub-space, and sent an almost insubstantial pulse along each one.

A multitude of filaments bloomed instantly into scarlet and black fragments. Glowing briefly, they quickly died in implosions of hopelessness. Discarding these, he sent another, deeper throb of power along the remaining chords.

Most of these also expired, flaring into brilliance for a moment, before fading like glittering dust into nothingness.

Again and again Sachael-Za-Ad'hem exerted his will. Every attempt became more refined and precise. Softly, he drew music from the remaining strands, coaxing their hopeful notes into a melody of exquisite beauty and possibility. They began to gleam, their brilliance creating pinpoints of light about them. Each a source of potential joy in itself.

A mere seven burst into an argent radiance, their clean silver lights creating tones of the purest majesty. Quickly, these were gathered together and caressed with a finesse that the others could only appreciate from a distance.

Among their kind, only the Source and the First surpassed his skill in this area. In silence, they watched, awestruck as he extended his faculty along each node. Weaving his will through and around each filament, he urged them toward the probability apogees every single one of those prospects would encompass.

Finally ready, Sachael-Za-Ad'hem opened his mind to them.

Intricate triple helixes hung in the darkness. Whirling multi-colored petals, fluttering around the preeminent course of action that needed to be followed over the centuries to ensure each example was given the chance to become reality. Projecting them all forward into the distant future, only four eventually solidified and remained stable.

Sachael-Za-Ad'hem said: *It would appear we have a choice before us.*

Sariel-Jeh'oel asked him: *Which offers the best outcome for the mortals of this realm?*

It depends on how many of the Host actually joins us on this venture. Each must play their part...observe! Sachael-Za-Ad'hem then highlighted the variances and complexities involved within each strand. The specific obstacles that needed to be overcome and the victories and defeats they would have to face as the years passed. He also stressed what would be required of *them*.

Sariel-Jeh'oel sighed: *Who is with us?*

Immediately, Gaur-el, Sariel-Hera'nai, Cassiel, Selene, Za-Hermesiah, Raphael and Din'athinae moved to their side. They looked back to the remaining Fallen.

Some were obviously deliberating the matter. Others couldn't seem to decide.

Sariel-Jeh'oel said: *Why do you hold back from the course of wisdom?*

Hesta'n-ea was appalled: *Is there no other way? MUST we adopt a restrictive lesser form? Is guiding these…these insects not enough?*

Sachael-Za-Ad'hem interjected: *The alpha probability indicates the best results will be achieved by walking amongst them as humans. Shepherds and guides must be approachable. Our current form, although darkened, would result in them attempting to worship us. THAT must be avoided at all costs.*

Psi-edon-ijah looked to his remaining advocates, Ares-tartus, Hesta'n-ea, Hadez'ekiel, Xeno-Dionysus and Oph-aestus. They were joined by Liwet and Xaph-ean.

A multitude of thoughts then began flashing back and forth between them. By the extent of the scarlet flares splitting the darkness, the debate was obviously heated.

As they argued, the rest of the Fallen gravitated away slightly…just in case.

Eventually, Psi-edon-ijah spoke for his group: *While we question the wisdom of this charade, we feel that perhaps it would be a course of prudence to at least make the attempt. If only to see how long it lasts?*

The dark seeds of ill-concealed malice burned deeply within Psi-edon-ijah's complexus. Sadly, that same attitude was prevalent amongst his supporters too—especially Ares-tartus, Hesta'n-ea and Hadez'ekiel—who seemed incapable of repressing their true feelings sufficiently to hide them.

Sachael-Za-Ad'hem's warning, addressed along Sariel-Jeh'oel's intimate mode, was urgent: *We need to watch them closely, Brother! Even if it takes millennia, they will seek to turn this situation to their own advantage.*

Sariel-Jeh'oel's mental overlay revealed his fatigue: *No, Brother! YOU will have to watch them. After what we've been through, I don't have the stomach to play nanny to these idiots as well as shepherd the younger race towards enlightenment.*

Sensing Sachael-Za-Ad'hem's shock, Sariel-Jeh'oel continued: *Oh don't worry too much. I wouldn't leave you totally alone with such a vital task ahead of you. I'll wait until after we initialize the intervention before I begin my own personal penance.*

Indicating the huge void around them he suggested: *I was thinking that perhaps here would be as good a place as any?*

Sachael-Za-Ad'hem scanned the abyss around them. It was evident their arrival had caused a major catastrophe by destroying the resident black hole that had anchored this galaxy in place. Without it, the entire star-whorl would gradually slow, diminish and die.

He said: *What? You intend to fulfill the function of a singularity?*

It will be a good place to start. Who knows? It might even work! If you read between the lines, I think Heim-dhal-riel was trying to give us a hope as we were cast down…

…I'd like to think so anyway.

Sachael-Za-Ad'hem didn't appear convinced.

Directing his attention toward the more responsive of the Fallen, Sariel-Jeh'oel said: *And to be honest, I don't think you'll face the task alone! There are enough Median Echelon members there to help you keep our wayward kin in check without having to play the Destroyer.*

Sachael-Za-Ad'hem noted that nearly a score of the remaining Fallen—all of the Exterior Echelon in fact—were still unwilling to join them. Of those, almost all were contrite, obviously crushed and overwhelmed by the events that had led to their ostracism. Their auras revealed no hint of malice. Projecting his question towards them in particular, he said: *What will YOU do?*

Gaia-le'el was the first to answer. She said: *I, for one, need to be alone. Seclusion will give me time to reflect as I travel. If we are to nurture the infants of this plane, then perhaps I may go ahead and determine how many worlds are suitable for life. Perhaps my manipulations of their planetary essences will help prepare them for future habitation?*

Both Sachael-Za-Ad'hem and Sariel-Jeh'oel radiated approval. It would be a worthy task, stretching across the eons. Other minds were quick to add their support.

As she began to spin her hyper-spatial matrix, she was joined by Azala-Jophiel, Aslan-di'el, Ocean-az'el, Sachael-Yao-teth and Olinda.

Ocean-az'el said: *We would come with you, Sister…if you don't mind the company to begin with? Your proposal will give us added impetus to begin our own efforts along a similar course. I assure you, it will not be for long. But perhaps we can determine where best to direct our respective endeavors as we go our separate ways?*

You are welcome, Brothers and Sisters. Come. Let us depart in haste so we may begin to soothe the burning heat of our discontent.

And with that, they winked out of existence.

Sariel-Jeh'oel turned his attention to the others: *And you? Have you determined a course to follow?*

No one answered at first, although the mental chatter between them increased. Eventually a thought became predominant.

Sariel-Jeh'oel said: *You have a question Gazad-riel?*

Gazad-riel was hesitant: *Are we worthy to join you? We are the least of these, our Brothers and Sisters and are concerned our scant efforts would be unequal to the task.*

Glancing towards Sachael-Za-Ad'hem, Sariel-Jeh'oel projected feelings of support and comradeship towards their lower brethren. He replied: *Be in no doubt, your assistance would be greatly appreciated and sorely needed. The task ahead of us is vast, and your contributions will no doubt be vital to the success of our endeavors…*

…Sachael-Za-Ad'hem?

Sachael-Za-Ad'hem stilled his mind, concentrating. Weaving the influence the remaining members of the Fallen would generate into the matrix, he manipulated each of the enduring four probability nodes. At last, one blazed into a miniature golden sun, surrounded by a myriad of rainbow filaments.

His mind sighed: *There! This is the course we must take to ensure the fulfillment of our purposes.*

His vast mind opened to them again. Weaving a rich tapestry of circumstances and events, he displayed what would have to take place across thousands of years should they stay true to the proposal. It was a grand initiative, majestic in its scope and purpose. But it required change!

A price some were unwilling to pay!

The midnight of space was suddenly thrown back as Gau-re'el and Elphaesus triggered their self-immolation. The brightness of their sacrifice caused all present to throw up hasty shields. All except Sachael-Za-Ad'hem, who swiftly subsumed their ruptured energies into his own potential!

Before anyone could question him, he flatly stated: *You know my cardinal attribute. NOW, is not the time to waste vital strength on futile gestures!* He activated the probability strand again, assessing if any permanent damage had been caused to that timeline.

Thankfully, after a momentary ripple, the node remained steady and golden, indicating its potential was still a vital quasi-reality. Satisfied, he turned to Sariel-Jeh'oel: *You were generated before me, Brother, so it is fitting that you should shoulder the burden of leadership in this commission. Please, let us all join in harmonic union. I need to reveal our path in its fullness and demonstrate how we may empty ourselves of our Divine nature to assume a human form.*

Sariel-Jeh'oel consented, and they came together in a state of utmost intimacy.

For more than five days they stayed locked in position like an orbiting cluster of miniature stars. During that time, their path and their undertaking was revealed in all its glory. When it ended, they were content to float quietly in the vastness of space, ruminating privately on the future...and the parts that they would individually play in it.

Eventually, Sariel-Jeh'oel said: *Shall we?*

And with that, the darkness of the void flared briefly as the Fallen began their immense journey towards a small planet lying so very, very far away. Their ministrations there—although due to come to fruition only after thousands and thousands of years had passed—would nevertheless yield everlasting results.

IF all went to plan!

Chapter One
Close Call

Grand Master Hex-aka Moonlight, watched her class with professional scrutiny. They were attempting something that had always been very dear to her heart. Tracking!

Of Dakotan Indian descent, she had grown up in the Swan Lake area of Manitoba, Canada. Indeed, many of her family still lived on the Reserve there, proud bearers of a noble and prolific heritage.

Her own name, Hex-aka—Hexa for short—was Dakotan for, *deer*, an apt title in her case. Even when she was a child she could run like the wind over most terrains. And no matter how fast she ran, she always had a keen sense of where she was. She could always find her way home and she could track better than anyone they had ever known.

Of course, Hexa's family had discovered why it was she was so gifted in the days leading up to her twelfth birthday. That was when her latent psychic abilities had manifested.

She was highly telepathic and powerful in all of her ultra-senses. She was also capable of generating a shield of impressive integrity and could manipulate the light medium in all sorts of startling and delightful ways.

Indeed, as her abilities broke through, people from her tribe would often see her running through the forests surrounding the reservation at breakneck speed. Always laughing and shining like the sun, she was looked upon as a good omen. Her kinfolk's legends contained a great deal of history regarding the life and times of characters called *Sun* and *Moon* and *Falling-Star*. It was inevitable her gifts would attract a comparison.

Of course, her expansion into psychic infancy–some fifty years ago–had also attracted the attention of another group of very special people. And now, Hexa's life was devoted to serving others, and helping *them* discover the delights of their gifts.

Although rising to the rank of Grand Master, Hexa had never lost the skills she had honed during her early years, and was delighted to find that her expertise in this area was much in demand. The Guardians had always ensured their members were as thoroughly trained as possible, both physically and psychically. Whatever the environment or conditions, they liked to be prepared.

Earlier today, she had been with a group of fifth year students in a lunar canyon close to the Florey Basin, a few miles from the Training Academy. Fortunately, many in the class were able to generate a shield of sufficient strength to protect themselves from the effects of the lunar vacuum. However, they carried the additional protection of belt-mounted mitigator shields...just in case!

She had laid a number of increasingly difficult to follow trails across the lunar landscape. The students were then divided into teams, and allocated a diminishing amount of time to follow those tracks, retrieve a hidden object, and return.

They had done well! As such, Hexa had made the task more difficult by moving their position to the rugged canyons close to the magnetic north pole. To try and confuse them, she had added a little surprise to the final exercise. Instead of leading to a series of hidden locator orbs and then back to the RV point, the final stages of the "Rapid Ravine Race" as she had christened it, led back here. She had selected a spot just outside the Academy's impressive shield ring. It added an extra seven miles to their route and she was keen to see how the students would react to the change in location and distance.

Hexa had observed the class with her far-sight as each respective group had reached the return point, only to discover that the trail continued along an unexpected path. Commendably, the majority had immediately followed the tracks. They had obviously remembered she was well known for pulling such stunts in an effort to baffle her students.

Only two teams had vacillated.

Checking back along their presumed return rout, they had travelled for nearly a mile before realizing their error. Needless to say, they had expended themselves mightily since then, getting back on course.

Hexa watched closely as all five groups approached, less than five minutes apart. The last two had caught up admirably and were sweating heavily for their efforts. As usual, the lunar dust was caking their uniforms in an ash-like film. It always amazed her, how the damned stuff always seemed to filter through the mechanically generated mitigator shields. But at least it was entertaining. The powdery soil made the students look like aboriginal hunters engaged on a dream-quest.

That'll teach them!

Smiling with satisfaction at the small personal victory of catching yet another class of students out, Hexa had to admit. This bunch—due to graduate next month—had been a pleasure to teach. As they arrived, she began handing out bottles of water so they could refresh their parched throats. Speaking mentally because of the vacuum, she said: *Well done! Take a break over there by the shield generator while we wait for the others to come in.*

The environs of the Guardian Headquarters and Academy were protected by a three-tiered, reactive, shield system. Just having her students back and close to its shelter helped Hexa to relax her guard a little.

The inner shield—a hard barrier—was always operating. It not only formed an impervious but transparent line of defense against solar radiation and meteoroids, but it also confined the air bubble to a specific one hundred feet radius from the furthest reaches of the base.

The outer shield, generated to a distance of a full mile, was invisible and reactive. Operating on an oscillating pulse frequency, it incorporated empathic, AI awareness software. It was actually capable of identifying unknown threats within a fraction of a second. If a danger *was* detected, that barrier would transmute into a viscous medium. It would also simultaneously *tag* the objective while it triggered the intermediate buffer.

Once activated, the aggressive median shields would deliver a psi-tronically amplified electrostatic/psychic shock to the indicated target, thereby neutralizing it.

At this moment, Hexa's third team was about a hundred yards out. Suddenly, the Academy's defensive screens bloomed to life. In an instant, her skin began to tingle and her extremities began swelling alarmingly. Within moments, everyone was slammed to the ground. The force of the impact knocked the air from their lungs.

Hexa felt her teeth begin to throb as the shields did their work, delivering a stunning charge to whatever they had targeted. She was getting to her feet, when she was bowled over by a second, more powerful surge of energy that sent a static discharge dancing crazily up and down her spine.

Knocked momentarily unconscious, Hexa came-to in a panic. She was experiencing the most awful discomfort in her chest and eyeballs. They felt like they were exploding.

Instinctively, she raised her own shields and the pain cut off, dramatically.

A tremor shook the ground! She tensed, expecting another surge…which never came. Looking around, Hexa saw several of her students writhing on the floor before they too thought to raise their own shields.

The penny dropped!

The potency of the instillations safeguards, amplified by psi-tronic energy, had overloaded the personal mitigators they were wearing.

Quickly, she scanned out toward the remaining three teams who had not yet returned: *RAISE SHIELDS! RAISE SHIELDS! THE DEFENSIVE PROTOCOL HAS SHORTED OUT THE MITIGATORS, RAISE YOUR SHIELDS NOW!*

Turning toward the base, Hexa activated her locator beacon and calmly said: *Emergency Standby Teams, home in on my signal. We have casualties.*

Suddenly, the air in front of her contorted. She was treated to the sight of Team Three—Robin Johns and Emma Boucher—each carrying a pair of candidates from the final two groups.

Both Robin and Emma were, fortunately, very strong shielders. Emma also possessed Grand Master Class teleportation abilities. Having been a paramedic before entering the Guardians training program, Emma was well used to keeping her head in a crisis. It was evident she had been able to quickly assessed the danger.

Because they were further away from the generators, Robin and Emma had remained conscious when the mitigators blew out, and had reacted instinctively by raising their own defenses. Emma had then teleported them both out to Team Four. Dropping Robin off there to protect their classmates with his own shields, she had then jumped again. This time out to where the Team Five were fighting off the effects of asphyxiation!

Snatching them out of the vacuum, Emma had then leapfrogged back through her teammate's position, before unceremoniously dumping everyone at the feet of their instructor.

Impressed, Hexa now watched Emma begin to treat her stricken classmates as the first Emergency Standby Team arrived. *That girl has one hell of a positive attitude. Won't be long before she's leading teams of her own!*

Turning to the Team Leader, Guardian Master Mark Smith, Hexa said: *Mark! What the hell happened?*

I don't know Hexa! One moment things were quieter than a morgue, and then all hell broke loose. Next thing I know, the Shadow Lord turns up—literally within seconds of the activation—closely followed by the Lord Inquisitor! They politely told the Protection Team to basically, "Get lost", and began looking into it themselves. They're still there now! Stuff me if I know what it's all about?

I'm sure we'll find out what we need to know later. In any event, thanks for getting her so quickly Mark! This was a close call. If Emma and Robin hadn't been here, I think you'd have had far worse to deal with.

That's the great thing about fifth year students, Hexa. They're almost ready to be unleashed on the world and are a little bit easier to look after. So I'm told!

Grinning, he teleported his team away and Hexa got to work, helping to prepare the casualties for the brief hop back to the medical wing. She had to admit, although things had turned out well, it *had* been a close call!

God knows how I'm going to explain my injured students to Lord Marshall Suresh!

***

Andrew exited the emergency transport field and thundered into the lunar surface. Mind blazing, his plasma baton was drawn and he was ready for battle. The ground shook from the force of his arrival, feeling to bystanders like a moonquake.

It was still less than ten seconds after the first activation of the protective measures. Locating the position of the tag, he quickly jumped to the quivering halo of power that marked the focal point of the defensive bolts. Their esoteric vibrations throbbed wanly in the ether.

Then Victoria arrived.

As she materialized, she delivered a psychic pulse designed to locate and paralyze her target. Descending like a shrieking meteor toward the bruised shielding, she pulled up short: *What have we got?*

Manipulating and assessing the tagged medium, Andrew replied: *I'm just getting the results now, sis. Although I've got a feeling we already know.*

A few seconds later, he had his answer.

Before he could speak, a full Protection Squad jumped into the location. Arrayed in a tactical formation about them, their shields were already up, and batons charged and deployed.

The team leader, High Grand Master Designate Tamari Singh, was surprised to find the two Lords already in attendance. She said: *Sir! Ma'am! Do you wish for me to take over?*

Victoria turned to her subordinate and replied: *Thank you, Tamari, but we'll be handling this. You can all go now!*

If she was surprised by the bluntness of the dismissal, Tamari didn't show it. Turning, she signaled for her team to leave. Once they had departed, Tamari scanned the area herself. Satisfied there were no further intrusions to worry about, she too disappeared without a further word.

Once they were alone again, Andrew said: *Take a look at this Vic!*

Moving to one side slightly, he displayed the results mentally in the air between them.

Victoria digested the data and read the AI's tag-log herself: *Well screw me blind! It worked! It recognized the binary signature and generated sufficient wattage to almost capture them!*

ALMOST being the point! They're obviously stronger than we thought, and are still employing an amazingly sophisticated means of escape. A pyramid pod of all things! But now we know! So we can zap them as soon as they dare make another appearance...

A calculating look crossed his face. He added: *I think I may also add a little surprise for the next time.*

You think there'll be a next time?

Well, they didn't get what they came for! So, who knows?

Victoria had to concede, it was sound reasoning: *Can we tell who it was exactly?*

Andrew deftly completed his manipulation of the data: *Hang on...*

...Yup! Here we go! It was Ares/Johnson. And from what I'm reading here, he only just managed to escape. Damn!

Why do you think he was here? You don't think he was snooping around the hyper-jump gate do you? It's almost completed and security around it is tight. If he could screw that up, it would cause a disaster!

Andrew's own face became a mirror image to that of his twin: *I don't know Vic. That would be too obvious...*

He had a thought: *Hey, what about their hosts? They've been our patients now for over five years and are only just coming out of their comas. Who knows what their conscious, reintegrated minds will tell us?*

Victoria looked at her brother and opened her mind. Her look said it all. Prepare for every eventuality–*even* those they hadn't thought of yet! She said: *So! How do we prepare for the unexpected?*

Andrew chewed his lip for a moment before receiving unexpected inspiration: *Yes! Where's father? I've just had a brainwave!*

Guess! He's near to completing his preparations. Why?

Let's just say…I think we're definitely going to need his help on this.

Victoria was intrigued: *What have you thought of? Come on, spill!*

She watched as Andrew formulated his strategy, his thoughts actually meshing into a foolproof plan of action as they spoke. He was doing that more and more often recently! And she had to admit, she was fascinated. Her older brother–by one minute–was getting annoyingly proficient.

Sensing her thoughts, Andrew grinned. Holding his sister around her shoulder, he said: *I think I can say for a fact…If we adjust the output of the psi-tronic crystal, it should easily be able to nullify their potential and hold them here. Yes?*

Yeeees.

But that won't do any of the orbital stations, ships or earth-side facilities any long-term good will it?

What are you thinking?

It's just a thought, but…what if we could somehow splice some of the crystal shards together with fragments of the moon rock from around the Reflection Chamber? Think about it! If we could suppress their capabilities and render what's left dormant, we'd have them over a barrel!

Victoria was impressed!

Unexpectedly hugging her brother for just a moment to spare his blushes, she added: *AND we would be able to protect every other facility we have, no matter how small. Wow! Talk about, SURPRISE! Brilliant!*

Andrew hadn't finished: *Also, what if we could somehow negate the effects of their pyramid escape pods?*

What do you mean…negate?

Well, as you know, once initiated, the escape pod generates two gates. One real and the other bogus! They in turn generate four gates, then eight, then sixteen, and so on. The more levels they incorporate, the more false trails they leave. It makes tracking their true path extremely difficult.

Yes, I know. So?

So…if we COULD rig something up that either tagged the real escape route, or corrupted it, they'd fall right into our grasp! Andrew replied, clenching his fingers together for emphasis: *The final materialization point would be at a location of OUR choosing.*

A tingle ran down Victoria's spine.

Andrew was definitely getting more and more like their father every day. She didn't know if she liked that. He was losing the childish good humor that had always made him such a pleasure to be around. Grudgingly, she admitted: *Andy. If you could do that, I would be uber-impressed!*

Unable to resist the opening, Andrew replied: *Well, it comes naturally, as you know. Pity you came out second, otherwise you'd have been the one unfairly blessed with a vastly superior intellect.*

Grinning, Victoria punched him on the arm: *I'll contact father. We've got to get this sorted. Fast!*

Beginning her ultra long-range call, she became haloed in astral flame.

Unbelievably, Andrew still wasn't happy. He had a nagging feeling he was missing something. Something obvious! He tried to think of things from another perspective.

What would I look for if I wanted something valuable from here?

A few moments later, his jaw dropped open.

Victoria, ending her far-call, caught the look on her brother's face: *A-ah! There's the witless look I know so well. What made you revert back to normal, caveman?*

What if they were after the crystal itself?

Her mood sobered instantly!

Andrew continued: *Remember? At the time, Hestia was second only to father in her understanding and use of a psi-tronic crystal. She maintained the Flame for goodness sake! Just imagine what she could do if she got her hands on this new one! It's many times more powerful than the source that protected old Kalliste.*

They looked at each other mutely. Then Victoria got a crafty look in her eye: *Unless we made it easy for them?*

What do you mean? Now it was Andrew's turn to be hooked.

I was just thinking of letting them have enough rope to go and hang themselves.

What? A booby-trap?

Precisely, older Brother! I think Father's going to enjoy setting this up. We've waited so long for them to slip up. It would be a pity to have to waste another opportunity.

Andrew's eyes got a faraway look.

Victoria said: *What?*

Yes. We have had to wait a very long time for them to try anything, haven't we? It's almost as if they'd disappeared of the face of the earth. Now they've shown up again and know their transcended forms will give us a heads-up, they'll be very careful.

So we'll have to give them an incentive wont we? Victoria interjected: *And make sure we're fully prepared for the next time they show their faces.*

Nodding in agreement, Andrew replied: *Whether we like to admit it or not, today was a close call. So, why did they act after all this time? It's not like they've been busy, is it?*

***

Ares/Harry Johnson exited his final escape nexus in human form, and breathed a huge sigh of relief. *THAT was too close for comfort! How on earth did they discover me so quickly? I wasn't radiating anything hard, being aggressive or confrontational. In fact, I was only concentrating on remaining mute and invisible. So how did they..?*

He replayed the events leading up to his capture within his impressive psyche.

Dissecting those moments and the effort that had been required to escape, he examined, and then reexamined the split-second the base's defenses were triggered. Slowing down each rerun considerably, he studied the event in minute detail.

There! Sneaky bastards!

Appalled and yet clearly impressed at the finesse of the shielding measures employed around the facility, he had to admit. He'd almost made a grave error. *I should have remembered! Those damned Guardians notified Yeung over five years ago now that they'd recovered his former employee's from Antarctica. Trapped as they were within our old forms, they were transferred to the hospital wing of the Academy. Our friends have obviously been busy since then.*

Thinking more deeply about where their former bodies now resided, he realized. *Of course! They would have been able to decipher our new binary mind signatures from them. They're unique! They must have entered our psi-dents into the AI mainframe. Damn! That's going to make it difficult to get the intel we need for the next phase of the plan.*

Mulling things over for a while, he suddenly brightened. *Aha! Unless we make it appear they were the target and that we ARE actually trying to reclaim our bodies. Now that could work! Especially if we add in a new filter to change our signatures again! Or use some of Esther's toys to create false readings.*

Suddenly, Harry's more positive frame of mind vanished!

He would still have to face the others with the pathetic results of his supposed intelligence gathering mission. *Ah hell! At least my snooping revealed how progressed their defensive measures have become. A little stronger and they'd have had me. Lucky for us they don't know how much feeding we've done since our revelation, nor the work we've accomplished.*

Shaking his head, he steeled himself for the ordeal ahead. *Ah well, I'd better get back and share the joy. This should be interesting!*

And with that, he initiated a shielded, slow-time teleport jump. One that would take him home in a transference stretching across twenty mind-numbing seconds. The pain of creating such a slow translation was considerable. But it was far better than the alternative!

The things we do to stay under the radar.

Chapter Two
That's Given Me an Idea

Rio de Janero, Brazil — January 15, 2023

Rio de Janero was the principal city of Brazil for nearly two centuries, before the honor was claimed by Brasilia in 1960. It remains, however, the capital of the state of the same name. As the second largest city in the country, Rio—as she is known—along with her eight and a half million residents, play an active role in the continuing drive Brazil had begun as an emerging industrial light from the turn of the century.

Rio has always been the most visited city in the south Americas. And you can appreciate why. Spread along a south facing coastal plain—Guanabara Bay—and split by the granite majesty of the spur of Serra do Mar Mountains, it is an area of outstanding natural beauty. The city is also blessed with several impressive *must see* attractions: Christ the Redeemer, atop Corcovado Mountain. Sugarloaf Mountain, along with its cable car. The Sambodromo Parade Avenue—famous for its carnival. And finally, Maracana Stadium, one of the largest football stadiums ever built.

Additionally, you would find the shining cosmopolitan sprawl of the coast is contrasted sharply by the breathtaking majesty of the Brazilian Highlands to the rear. Those witnessing the view for the first time from the air, are so struck by the impressive green and white fresco that it leaves an impression they will never forget.

However, there were other values to be found in the city besides its beauty.

Not only was it the headquarters of four major Brazilian companies, but, in more recent years, it had also become home to two global conglomerates. Sigma-Sat Systems—a media based offshoot of Yeung Technologies—and, Yeung-Tec, a research and development branch of the same commercial technologies giant.

These two companies had boosted the economic growth of Brazil by over seventy percent. Now, they were a major employer throughout the city. Ninety percent of their fourteen thousand workforces were local residents.

Indeed, Yeung's commitment to the region had been demonstrated only five years previously when he had moved a large portion of his global operations to the outskirts of the city. Stating it was part of a logistical, restructuring program, he had assured city officials the relocation would help facilitate the regeneration of the South Americas economy.

Needless to say, that step had been warmly received. Especially by the citizens of Rio, who went out of their way to make the new corporation and its executives feel welcome. It was also a major factor in the newly established enterprise being extended a great deal of leeway when proposals for their relocation had been presented to city officials.

Because of the obvious economic and social benefits his company would bring, Yeung had been allowed to purchase over two hundred acres of pristine government owned land to the north of the city. At the time of acquisition, the authorities were assured that no industrial facilities would be operating from that area. Laboratories would be located underground, within the mountain, and all research undertaken there would be devoted to the enhancement of recently released Artificial Lung technology.

Yeung also went to great lengths to emphasize that the exquisite nature of the region would not be marred in any way. He promised that any benefits derived by his companies' research, would be devoted to the environment in this locality first, as a "thank you" to the people of Brazil. Needless to say, that had sealed the deal, and turned him into a local hero at the same time.

However, he did fail to mention something.

One of the major factors in his choosing that site was its strategic value. This area of Brazil drew literally millions of visitors each year. The carnivals, pageants, nightlife, beaches and areas of pristine splendor, guaranteed an overabundance of outsiders passing through the city almost every day.

Excellent when you wanted to hide in plain sight.

Additionally, the complex structure found within the mountains, provided a natural geological filter against many forms of intrusive surveillance, including the telepathic kind. The dense composition of granite, together with its naturally occurring radioactivity, made it very difficult to scan through without a great deal of concentration by all but the strongest telepaths.

That was even better when you had something *specific* to conceal.

***

"Well this is just fan-fucking-tastic! Idiot! Are you insane? What on earth possessed you to make such a stupid attempt? Moron! You could have blown everything we've been planning for!"

The furniture was literally dancing across the floor in response to the esoteric undercurrent saturating the room. Lei Yeung winced under the vehemence of the onslaught, being very pleased *he* was not on the receiving end of it. He honestly thought his hair was singeing and felt a genuine pang of empathy for Harry Johnson, as Esther Perry let him have it…with both barrels.

Turning purple, she continued, "I thought you were a warrior for Christ's sake. Not some human simpleton with an IQ of a fuck-wit! You're supposed to think of things like, tactics, ambushes and planning *before* you go jumping in and fucking things up like some…some brainless retard who can't think further than the end of his dick!"

Yeung was impressed. Esther's grasp of cursing with all of its subtle nuances was coming along nicely. Especially regarding the use of one vulgarity in particular! When she expanded beyond it and mixed it up a little, she'd soon be classed as an expert and blend in perfectly with the residents of just about any city in the world.

Harry was angry himself, shouting back, "Well what do you expect? You get to play with your toys and experimenting on humans while I have nothing to do. I only thought to…"

"That's just it," she cut in, "you didn't think! Psi…Simon told us to stay well away until our plans were nearer to completion! But oh no! *You* have to play the prize prick and go sticking your nose in where you shouldn't, creating a nightmare of a balls-up that could come back and bite us in the ass. He'll be furious."

Then she noticed Yeung was smiling and turned the heat of her anger on him. "And what do *you* think is so funny, you insignificant sack of skin?"

Raising his hands in an effort to placate her, Yeung replied, "Although I am a mere infant in your eyes, being only eighty years old, it would nevertheless appear that I possess the greatest maturity of anyone here."

Esther was taken by surprise. Catching her next outburst in her throat, she growled, "What do you mean?" The menacing undercurrent increased dramatically.

Ignoring it, Yeung continued, "If I may start with Harry first?

"Yes! He did make an error of judgment today. A big one! However, there are positives to be gained from the experience…"

"Positives?" she hissed, "from a monumental fuck up like that! Are you…"

"Yes, Esther! I'm talking about a definite benefit arising from today's unpleasant surprise. Do you want to find out or not?"

Swallowing her anger, she replied, "Enlighten me then...*human.*"

Standing up, Yeung began to pace back and forth between them. He said, "Whatever the reason Harry chose to go snooping is irrelevant. He did. He nearly got caught and although we're not happy with that, we gained valuable intelligence..."

"That's precisely what I was trying to say!" Harry whined. Biting off his next words, he tried to score points. "But *someone* didn't give me the chance."

Exercising patience, Yeung turned to Harry, took a deep breath and said, "What do you feel we actually *gained* from your near capture then?"

Pausing for a moment to collect his thoughts, Harry replayed the event over in his mind. Eventually, he replied, "Well firstly, we didn't know their defensive capabilities were so formidable. We mustn't forget—as I admit, I did today—that their technology is very, very advanced. Beyond even what *we* have assisted you to develop..." Glancing towards Esther, he added, "...With Esther's most valuable guidance of course!"

The compliment had the desired effect. The heat of her anger dropped considerably.

Continuing, Harry said, "In addition, we discovered the obvious advantage they have gained from *your* former employees."

Yeung looked momentarily puzzled, so Harry emphasized, "The ones whose bodies we now possess. Remember, in swapping forms with them, we each had to adopt part of their corresponding original complexi. We now carry an echo of their original mental signatures within us. They, likewise, carry part of ours in them."

Esther's eyes bulged! "And who else on this planet carries a unique binary signature like ours…or theirs?"

"Precisely!" Harry replied, satisfaction written all over his face.

Yeung was confused. "So, this is different to when you subsume someone's essence?"

"Very different!" Esther replied. "If we subsume someone, we consume everything about that person. There's nothing left except their vitality, which we add to our own."

Harry took over, "But when we assumed *these* forms, we had to graft part of our corresponding identities onto each complexi to prevent psychic rejection." Tapping himself on the chest, he continued, "Remember, this isn't *my* body, It's Harry Johnson's. Although my personality and psychic nexus are now dominant, the body itself is not naturally meshed to me. If we didn't add the splicing component, it would reject my essence, or die."

Amazed, Yeung said, "So you're talking about a psychic personality transplant? And the grafting program acts as an immunosuppressive filter–preventing rejection?"

Both Esther and Harry were delighted by the speed with which Yeung grasped the concept.

They were about to be even more impressed.

Yeung continued, "So! They obviously identified the hybrid signatures generated by the meshing of your natural bodies with the personas of the real Simon Cooper, Esther Perry and Harry Johnson? Yes?"

"Exactly!" Harry replied. "Then they clearly incorporated their findings into their AI defensive systems. Which, as I discovered today, have been enhanced to capture us alive! Not destroy us."

Esther gasped, "Those sneaky bastards! We knew they would identify us if we ever adopted our true forms. But I never suspected they could pinpoint us just by our psychic nexus alone. They'd be all over us in seconds."

Yeung cautioned, "And don't forget. After this little escapade, I bet they're tweaking everything they've got as we speak…"

Turning to Esther, Yeung asked, "Esther. Is there anything you can do to mitigate the signature you emit when in purely human form? Even if it's only temporary! Or add a false layer so you become a trinity instead of a duality?"

"I like your thinking."

Glancing towards Harry, she couldn't resist the urge to tease, "I'll just go and play with my *toys* and get onto that right away."

Yeung said, "Before you do, you've just given me an idea. Can you also give some thought to a mechanical means of reproducing your idents as they currently are? I was just thinking. Wouldn't it be fun to have our adversaries running around, say, in the middle of the African continent, while we get on with *our* business elsewhere? It would be nice to be able to work without having to worry about avenging angels breathing down our necks."

"Now *that* I know I can do! Well done! Perhaps you're not such a useless sack of skin after all."

Chuckling, Yeung replied, "You see, this infant *does* have his uses. I may only be an eighty year old man—who looks sixty because of your wonderful *toys*, as Harry likes to call them—but I'm quite grown up for my age."

They all burst out laughing at his self-mockery.

Their revelry was cut short by the appearance of a hyper-spatial translation creeper. Slowly, torturously, it phased into potency and began squeezing its traveler through the inter-space medium toward them.

Thirty seconds later, Simon began congealing in the air before his co-conspirators. Pouring out of the vortex like a gooey soup, he solidified from the feet up. Once manifested, he shook his head to clear his thoughts, "No matter how adept I'm getting at doing that, it hurts like hell."

Yeung acknowledged, "Impressive that you've managed to slow the process down even further. That took thirty seconds to complete. No one would be able to detect such a jump. You must instruct me in its operation now that I've been enhanced with such ability. It's such a shame my frail old body couldn't accommodate more than two additional artificial enhancements. I would so love to fly as well."

Simon was stunned. He replied, "If you're sure you wish to subject yourself to such unnecessary pain, be my guest. We can start later today if you wish?"

"That would be excellent. However, I fear we may have some news you will wish to digest first." Pausing, Yeung mentally transferred the earlier events from the Guardian Headquarters, ensuring to add the benefits that had fortuitously arisen from the near fiasco.

They waited, expecting some display of anger.

When none was forthcoming, they were obviously intrigued. Eventually, Harry couldn't take it any longer. Holding up his hands, he sighed, "If you're going to rip my ears off, just get on with it will you."

Simon ruminated for a few moments more, and then replied, "I don't think berating you further will achieve anything. Do you? As Yeung has already pointed out, certain benefits have accrued from you error, which will give the advantage to *us* when we eventually decide to act."

Turning to Esther, Simon continued, "Do you think you can achieve what Yeung suggested?"

"Regarding the techno-identities? Certainly. And quickly too! Why?"

"Check with me before you make things *too* refined. We don't want to tip our hand before we can gain maximum advantage, do we?"

Yeung was quick on the uptake, "What? Are you thinking, a rudimentary test to check their efficiency? Make sure we can trigger a response without having to be *too* precise?"

"Exactly! There are a number of stages to our strategy. Each requires specific things being in place to guarantee the success of the next phase. As you are always urging my friend, prudence and patience will guarantee the realization of our goals."

Yeung smiled. "It's a philosophy that has kept me alive in an unfriendly world until now. I intend to make sure it stays that way."

Chuckling in agreement, Simon changed the subject. "Has Angelika returned from Los Angeles yet?"

Esther replied, "No, although she far-spoke me about an hour ago."

Suddenly, everyone became more focused.

Yeung said, "And?"

"The results are better than we'd hoped for. She's still retrieving the latest data, but from what she's gathered so far, we have determined the sites of three major and five minor asperities along the Pacific and North American coast."

Yeung wanted clarification, "What *exactly* has she managed to recover?"

"She has everything from our integrated orbital and Californian GPS network. Creep meter, tilt meter and magnometer results have also been collected. She's just retrieving the final strain meter measurements, and then she'll be returning here."

Yeung deliberated for a moment. Finally, he said, "This is very good news my friends. With that much energy building up, we won't need as many people on the ground. That will make our task so much easier to execute."

Each of them bristled with anticipation. They liked that word…*execute*.

Looking to Simon, Harry asked, "If we are successful, do you think you'll be able to pull your end of the plan off?"

"*That* my longtime friend remains to be seen!"

***

Guardian Headquarters and Training Academy — January 16, 2023

Anil Suresh, Lord Marshall of the Guardians, drummed his fingers on the desk, impatient for the conference to begin.

In the five years he had held this position, he had rarely felt as aggravated as he did now. The murderers of his oldest and dearest friend were scum he would dearly like to obliterate with the fire his own mind. It irked him, greatly, to think they were still at large. And the fact they had showed their faces again after so long could only spell trouble.

All Ultra Class Guardians were in attendance today, including those now displaying the potential for transcension. Anil was eager to find out why this meeting had been called at such short notice.

Looking around the table as he waited, it amazed him to witness firsthand the fruits of the Earth's incredible psychomaturation. Joshua Drake and Becky Selleck were at the far end. Fast approaching their twelfth and thirteenth birthdays respectively, they had only recently begun their pre-Guardian internships. It astonished him to think that they were already beyond High Grand Master Class in strength!

The staggering Ultra-Mitigator Program, revealed to them only five years ago by the Overlord, was allowing a greater than ever number of newer candidates with the potential for transcension to be recognized. Additionally, it also ensured such aspirants received the early stimulus that would guarantee the emergence of their Ultra Class abilities. For safety reasons, this was normally delayed until after they had achieved physical and psychic maturity.

However, as soon as their capacity for expansion was recognized, an ingenious adaptation of the compressor training used on all Guardians—was implemented. This modification allowed the candidates to access their expanded capabilities long before the metamorphosis actually triggered.

The effects of this had been mind-blowing! As demonstrated by the first ever subject to partially undergo the process, Deputy Marshall Anatt Yasin. Having transcended less than six years previously, she was already stronger than everyone else, except for Andrew, Victoria...and the Overlord of course!

It was a shame their latest transcended brother and sister, Ultra Grand Master Aaron De-Ville—an astonishingly gifted healer—and Ultra Master Felicity Dobson—a shielding genius—had missed the opportunity to undergo the new system fully. They had transcended just over four years ago, before the program was wholly incorporated.

However, soon they would witness the full impact of the new system. The first Guardian due to undergo the full Mita/Com expansion was Aaron's partner, Charlie Savage. Charlie was a thirty-two year old telekinetic/teleportation prodigy. He was scheduled to magnify next month, as the esoteric and mental barriers incorporated within his super-energized cerebrum began their structured collapse.

Everyone was eager to see the results, especially as they had been designed and implemented by the Lord Healer, Corrine Jackson. She had been the first Guardian to receive specific instruction in the program's incredible finesse and scope from the Overlord himself.

Looking across the table, Anil counted off in his head the other candidates who had the priceless psych-ware embedded within them. Each individually tuned to their host, to ensure the uncannily accurate cascade failure that would trigger their augmentation:

Madison Mozdure, an elemental tigress of American/French decent, blessed with a preternatural control of molecules and subspace…March.

Pieter Schmidt, an ultra-sensing giant from the small Swiss town of Altdorf…April.

Rosa Fairbanks, a future Lord Inquisitor if ever there was one. Her aggressive, intuitive and empathic mental capacities had earned her the nickname, *Venus Flytrap* in Guardian circles. You might go in, but she would never let you out…May.

Finally, there was The Adjutant Marshall herself, Naomi Cruiz. Out of all of them, she would have undergone the Mita/Comp the longest, having received the primary stimulus over five years ago. Due to receive her triggering sequence in June, it would be fascinating to see just how strongly she manifested. Interestingly,

Victoria had volunteered for the Shepherds role during Naomi's ceremony, and Anil was itching to find out why.

Regardless, much debate still raged as to who her Supporter would be. Evidently, the list of volunteers was a mile long!

Anil's incredibly analytical mind marveled at the implications, coming back yet again to Becky and Joshua. Somehow, the wonders of the compressive design would prevent the triggering of their transmogrification for over sixteen years. Sixteen years!

What the hell will they become?

In these children in particular, the results had already been astounding in other ways. Gone were the precocious little monsters of several years ago. They had been replaced by children who were polite, patient and levelheaded. They displayed a maturity that was, quite frankly…freakish. It was if a miniature Yoda had been miraculously transplanted into their egos and let loose!

And the good news didn't stop there!

The world now had the luxury of Psychic Emergency Service Personnel. Certified and registered, there were fire and rescue teams, police officers, lawyers and judges, together with an ever expanding number of doctors, nurses and therapists. Later in the year, the new Global Marshal's service was also due to go into operation. It was delightful that so many people were coming forward to offer their skills and abilities to the growing pool of experts. Public expectations had never been so high!

Of course, the Psychic Law & Order Bill had gone a long way in facilitating this change. Smoothing out and accelerating the transition whereby gifted individuals were recognized, it offered guidance, protection, training and encouragement for all those who volunteered.

The knock-on effect this program was having on the Guardians workload was already being felt. Such were the professional standards each psychic operative brought to the collective table, safety standards around the world had been elevated exponentially!

Yeung Technologies were a prime example in this regard. Over thirty-four percent of their employees were psychic. Their inclusion in the advancement and implementation of progressive science had been as innovative as it was outstanding.

Thanks to them, the understanding of mitigator and mirror shield applications had been stunning. Progress toward a viable, working, atmospheric scrubber had almost been completed. Their breakthroughs in the fields of advanced medical diagnostic and assessment regimens were spectacular, as were their AI applications in the Human Genome project. Anil was particularly looking forward to their latest findings regarding the early detection and evaluation of children with latent psychic abilities. Having discussed their results with Corrine, it was hoped they might incorporate their discoveries into maternity wards globally within the next two years.

Lately, Yeng-Tec had also been turning their interests to such innovations as quantum levitation and micro aqua-cell power sources. Simply brilliant!

Such a lot of progress, in such a short period of time!

But still Anil fumed!

Out of everyone present, only *he* was old enough to remember the uphill struggle mankind had endured over thousands of years to make it this far. As indeed, Earl had been.

If we're not very careful, those bastards could put it all in jeopardy…

…God, I want them dead!

His musing was interrupted by the arrival of both the Overlord and Shadow Lord.

An expectant hush settled over the room as Andrew erected a privacy barrier about them. Adjusting it for a few moments until he was satisfied, he nodded once to the Overlord.

The Overlord began, "Thank you for coming at such short notice. Although I'm sure you all know the reason why I've called you here, *this* is the gist of it."

He played out a concise, full sensory replay of the attempt to infiltrate the facility by their mystery intruder.

Resuming, he said, "The murderers of the former Lord Marshall have remained quiet and elusive until now. We are going to find out why."

Pausing, he opened his mind to them, and displayed a set of strange hybrid mental signatures. As they studied the proffered information, he continued, "These are the unique binary idents of our enemies. Absorb them. Memorize them. And program instinctive aggressive and defensive measures into your psyches. Whatever you do, do *not* face them alone, even if you encounter only one of them! They may have the talent to employ some form of warped mirror/mitigator ability to neutralize your capacity. As they did with Earl! We suspect this capability may be technologically enhanced. Be wary. If you think you have isolated such a signature, call myself, the Shadow Lord, Lord Inquisitor or the Deputy Marshall…"

As he spoke, the Overlord sent a lightning-quick private message to his Lord Marshall: *Sorry Anil, no offence. Anatt IS stronger than you are. And these bastards have the muscle to screw you over!*

Anil nodded once: *I'm well aware of Anatt's capacity old friend. Don't worry, I'm far too old to be throwing teddy out of the pram.*

The corner of the Overlord's mouth twitched in a miniscule smile, the only outward sign he'd noted the Lord Marshall's comments. He paused as if collecting his thoughts and continued addressing the room. "...That being said, we have a plan."

He waited and suddenly, they were interrupted by the arrival of the Lord Inquisitor, along with two other people. One was immediately recognizable, his six feet, seven inch frame and wide grin seemed to fill the room.

Marty Mays waved a hand, "Howdy y'all. Miss me?"

The other person was unknown to them. A diminutive young woman with long mousey hair down to her waist, she wore stylish glasses and an equally huge smile.

Victoria said, "Allow me to introduce you to Sharon Dyer. Although you might not know *her* yet, you're certainly aware of her father. Doctor Peter Dyer, of Yeung Technologies fame! You'll be glad to know, Sharon is blessed with even stronger abilities than her father...telepathically speaking. Her *additional* forte lies in the fact that she has a powerfully developed deep-sight capability. So powerful in fact, that she can discern the inherent nature or symmetry of the object or person she scans.

"We are very fortunate, in that her gift has an unusual twist. Sharon can *invert* her sight to supply a reverse or opposite evaluation. Simply put, it means she is able to discern what would naturally negate the target she is scanning."

Most people looked quite stunned at the revelation of such an unusual—and dangerous—gift. Sharon merely nodded at the simplicity of the explanation, but kept silent.

The Overlord took over, "As I said, we have a plan. Andrew will now explain our strategy, as he came up with an ingenious way to gain the upper hand."

Andrew nodded and stepped forward. "As you now know from Earl's death, our targets employed a new style of Mirror/Mitigator technology. Those emitters, combined with the harmonic union of three extremely powerful individuals, were sufficient to prevent Earl from being able to assume his transcended state. While in his human condition, he was helpless to prevent his obliteration and subsumption.

"Although those generators self-destructed, we were able to analyze sufficient debris at the scene to retrograde their Tec. With Marty's help, we uncovered the frequency signatures they used. Indeed, the shields surrounding this facility now incorporate such a design, and were nearly successful in capturing our surprise visitor. I say *nearly*, because our adversaries are obviously growing in potential. The shield should have been strong enough to capture them. It wasn't, revealing that, if you're powerful enough, you can overcome the emitter...*IF* you're powerful enough! So...it gave me an idea!

"Who is the expert at naturally reading and meshing with all known forms of energy?"

Holding out his hand toward their imposing guest, Andrew continued "Marty is! Added to that, is the *ace* that Sharon can now bring to the table. Sharon has been working with Marty for the past five months and they have discovered something which is great news for us! When they combine their talents in harmonic union, Sharon can not only piggy-back Marty's ability to distinguish different forms of energy, but she can also evaluate its direct *opposite*. So, having identified the specific measures needed to negate the target, Marty can then generate the appropriate frequency wave and cancel it out!

"In a nutshell, our new team is going to help us come up with a mechanical equivalent to their combined natural skills. We are going to develop and install Inverse readers/emitters at all our facilities that will not only recognize our enemy, but produce a field that will completely nullify them!"

Shock ran through the room.

Holding up his hand, Andrew continued, "Now, we don't know how long it's going to take, but both Marty and Sharon are willing to get right into the project today. And, once we have the particular method weighed off by which their incredible gifts function, we're going to do our best to devise a mental program to embed that sequence within our own psyches. One way or another, we'll soon have a natural barrier against such machinations in future.

"I'm going to get them settled in. In the meantime, the Overlord has a few defensive procedures we have already devised to share with you that will ensure you survive long enough for us to get there."

A buoyant mood emanated around the room as Andrew began ushering the guests out.

Smiling, Marty asked, "Hey Andy. Is there any chance we can stop off at your canteen on the way? I told Sharon about the steak and eggs you have here and can't wait to show her I wasn't exaggerating."

Grinning, Andrew replied, "Certainly. In fact, I'll join you! I've had a busy morning and feel like I could eat a cow."

He paused momentarily as his father spoke to him subliminally: *Andrew, once Marty and Sharon are settled, get yourself back here. Your plans have given me another idea as to how we can lay out some irresistible bait!*

Really! How?

Think Marty! Think Sharon! Then combine it with the null-strata around the Crystal Chamber. Oh! And a conveniently timed set of upgrades requiring installation.

What? Leaving handy gaps in the shield grid they can exploit?

A mind-smile swept across Andrew's cerebrum: *You've got it, but I'll explain in full when you're back. How long will you be?*

Andrew replied: *With steak and eggs? Is half an hour okay?*

See you then.

As he walked from the room, Andrew was unaware he was being scrutinized by a very sharp mind. A penetrating gaze flicked backwards and forwards between the Overlord and Shadow Lord several times.

Anil Suresh murmured to himself. "They're becoming more and more alike each passing day. I wonder…?"

Chapter Three
Graduation

Chest swelling with pride, Ali Omar Biixi, watched through night vision binoculars as his fifteen year old son, Assad Ali Omar, navigated his craft with professional skill and flair through the inky black waters.

A tenth generation fisherman, Ali had begun taking Assad with him on the family's daily expeditions out into the Indian Ocean, as soon as the boy could stand. As was their custom, Assad would watch closely as the crew went about their business. Day after day and month after month, this process was repeated. As time went by, Assad was gradually allowed to assist with the many chores involved in managing a fishing boat at sea.

Thus, in an age old custom practiced around the world, son was trained by father in the skills required to earn a living and feed his family.

Coming as they did from the Galmudug region of Somalia, it was more difficult than people realized. Although the advent of the Guardians had done much to quell the unrest caused by old civil wars, their presence had also curtailed another source of revenue his family had been particularly skilled in. Piracy!

In the past, Ali had trained with his father too, learning the secrets of their very particular trade. Then, one day when Ali was judged mature enough, he had been invited to accompany the men of his clan on a raid against a Greek registered tanker. It was during that time—when international maritime patrols were increasing—that Ali had been labeled with the nickname that would stay with him for life. Thinker!

As was the custom, most Somalian pirates would attack vulnerable ships during daylight if they came too close to their waters. Approaching from the rear, they would threaten the sailors on board with their Russian made RPG's and machine guns, and then force them to stop.

Once boarded, the vessels would be held to ransom, and huge amounts of cash demanded for the safe release of the crew, cargo and of course, the craft itself. Most of the time, their demands were met and everyone went their separate ways. Sometimes—thankfully rarely—things ended in bloodshed, and the wrath of the global community was brought to bear. As such, the presence of international maritime patrols became commonplace.

This in turn, not only led to the inevitable drop in revenue, but weapons too, as they would have to ditch them overboard in a hurry before being apprehended. As costly as this was, however, it was preferable to the alternative. Under international law, any and all vessels involved in attacks on shipping were always confiscated. As such, on the rare occasions people *were* caught in the act of piracy, it meant the loss of their livelihoods and certain poverty.

As a boy, Ali often wondered why his elders stubbornly stuck to old ways. They were increasingly hazardous, unprofitable and very *hit and miss* at best.

One day when they were out fishing, Ali had complained to his father, Omar, so much about this, that his father had said, "If you are so clever and you think you know better than generations of your elders, tell me! What would *you* do?"

Without pausing to gather his thoughts, Ali had replied, "Father! If the old ways are flawed, does sticking rigidly to them make them right?"

Omar had been surprised by the depth of feeling in that reply. Several of the deck hands had also stopped to listen. Intrigued, Omar had said, "Go on, what would you do?"

"Father, because *we* have been blessed and have been more fortunate than our brothers, we must be careful not to waste that good fortune. We must spend money to make money. So many of the families continue to raid in the daytime! This is dangerous. They can not only be seen on radar, but by sight too! The warships they send have helicopters. We can't outrun them if we are too far from national waters, so we need to change..."

By *that* time, everyone else was listening as well!

Ali had continued, "...If I were a father, I would buy a very good computer. They can do all sorts of things now, and provide much information about shipping and destinations. We could check to see *what* vessels are going *where*. What are they carrying? Where are their crews from? We could choose our targets more accurately. If some of the family was sent north to the Gulf of Aden, they could see which private yachts came through and find out which way they were heading. We could be waiting, fishing and earning our bread until they came. Choosing those who are vulnerable would provide many riches for little risk. I would buy better engines for this boat so we could move faster. I'd buy other smaller craft, to sail close to us when making the approach to our targets. That would fool the radar the authorities now use. Instead of buying more guns and rockets, we need to purchase the goggles that can see in the night—and radar of our own! Then *we* could work when no others dare, and reduce the hazards of being caught. I would time our attack with the rest of the family fishing nearby. If the big military ships come, we can escape with better engines, or confuse their radar by mixing with the other boats. We could even form a blockade! Remember, the other countries have to follow the law and will not be allowed to sink simple fishermen, even if they do hinder their pursuit."

Omar had been stunned! Although speaking quickly and in an embarrassed garble, the commonsense in his son's words had been evident. On their return home later that day, Ali had been required to repeat his ideas in front of the elders.

That meeting resulted in Ali's nickname being changed to "Thinker" forever. Additionally, his village went on to become exceedingly successful in their *alternative* livelihood. So successful, that they even managed to remain active after the arrival of the Guardians, simply by changing their strategy. Following Ali's good advice, they began targeting smaller, private vessels instead of the larger cargo ships.

So, it was with pride that Ali watched his son, Assad, completing his drills. The exercises were part of a new regime Ali had instituted himself when he took his own father's place as head of the family.

Everyone who wanted to be part of the "White Sails" was required to complete at least a year's probation. During that time, they were granted ever growing responsibilities–*if*–they passed an increasingly difficult set of trials. Some of those tests involved: seamanship, navigation, reacting to authority figures, being tested under mock–yet realistic–interrogation conditions, weapons handling and radio procedures.

Training and familiarity was a key to success. Knowing how the other reacted under stressful conditions had helped each of them operate much more efficiently as a team.

Ali had trained his son well. Taking Assad fishing from an early age had revealed the natural sailor in him, and exposed his aptitude for piloting craft of all sizes. No matter what it was, Assad could drive it, steer it and maneuver it through the tightest, most impossible gaps or courses imaginable. It didn't matter what cargo was on board, or if his boat was considerably slower than those about him. Assad could out-turn, out-run and out-play just about everyone else by the time he was twelve.

Obviously, the *Thinker* in Ali wanted to put those skills to use in the *other* side of the family business as quickly as possible. Interestingly, it was around that time that Assad's additional skills began to manifest.

At first they thought it was luck! Every time they took Assad along on a raid–merely as an observer of course–they enjoyed a rousing success. Yes! Usually, they only ever attacked at night now. Their targets were softer than in previous years. However, those victims could still present difficulties, especially if the private yachts or motor launches involved had an alert crew, security teams, or the latest GPS radar/alert technology to call for help.

Nevertheless, once Assad began accompanying them, they somehow always managed to get nearer to their objective before rousing suspicion and were able to escape with an ease never before witnessed.

They looked on him as a lucky charm. Until the raid, only a year ago, when they realized there was more to young Assad than met the eye!

They had completed yet another successful attack. Their target had been a private yacht owned by a wealthy banker sailing from Egypt towards the Maldives, with his wife and two young daughters on board. The family had so many possessions, that Ali and the crew had stayed far longer than intended. Making their escape only thirty minutes before dawn, they developed engine trouble when only several miles from their own territorial waters.

Unfortunately for them, an experienced and usually competent crewmember, Bahdoon, had failed to render the ship-to-shore radio inoperative. A fact they were unaware of, until forty-five minutes after their departure. *That's* when they found themselves bobbing helplessly along in the ever increasing daylight with a Canadian Warship bearing down on them!

Sitting ducks!

Ali had been forced to ditch thousands of dollars worth of weapons and contraband over the side in an effort to avoid arrest.

However, he needn't have bothered.

Stunned, they had watched as the frigate sailed past in a hurry, seeming to be searching for another target entirely. Then the helicopter had been launched. Flying backwards and forwards, it too appeared intent on another purpose, actually swooping directly over them twice!

The crew had looked at each other in wide-eyed amazement. Not daring to breathe, they had then settled in to watch the entertainment.

When Rashid, their engineer, managed to get the engines cleared at last, they had set off for home at full speed. Whooping with delight and relief, they had kept their eyes fixed on the ship and its encircling helicopter until they were mere dots on the horizon.

Relaxing at last, they suddenly realized Assad had been sitting quietly at the prow during the entire episode. Head bent, staring down into the water in quiet concentration. When Ali had checked on him, he was horrified to discover his son's pupils had apparently expanded to fill the whole socket, and were giving off whorls of mist!

The movement seemed to bring Assad out of his trance. Suddenly, he shook his head, and his eyes reverted back to normal. As they did so, a distinctive shimmer ran along the boat from stem to stern. So pronounced was that curtain, everyone noticed it.

Startled, Ali had said, "What was that?"

Letting out a huge sigh, Assad replied, "It was me Father. It's something I've been able to do for a while now."

Ali was confused, "What do you mean? *WHAT* have you been able to do for a while?"

"Hide us."

"Hide us? My son, how could you possibly do that?"

Shrugging his shoulders, Assad had quietly replied, "I don't know Father. I can only say…when I concentrate, we remain hidden from sight. And I'm beginning to think from their radar too!"

Sure enough, when Ali tested that theory with several of their own boats over the following days, they discovered it was true! Assad would take various vessels out to sea and, at a signal from his father, activate his ability. No matter what craft he was aboard, or how big, it would suddenly disappear from radar.

They brought him closer to shore and asked him to repeat his trick, this time having a clear line of sight. As soon as Assad exerted himself, a shimmering haze rippled across the water, very similar in appearance to a cold water mirage on the sea. Whatever crafts the boy was piloting at the time, simply *folded* out of view, blending into the haze as if they didn't exist.

Needless to say, Assad's nickname came to reflect his ability–Shadow!

And now, as his son completed the final tests, Ali's heart swelled with pride. The boy was talented, both in the ways of the sea and with psychic ability. Assad's graduation to "White Sheet" signified his full entrance, as a man, into the White Sails. An apt name for their pirate clan really, as it signified their amazing record of making clean getaways.

Assad brought the skiff back to shore where the elders waited, his silent approach a testimony to his skill and maturity. Leaping lightly from the prow, he came up to his father to receive the mark of a member.

Removing the knife from the fire, Ali carved their sigil into his son's forearm. Assad remained silent as his flesh sizzled to the blistering kiss of the blade.

One by one, the elders approached to offer their congratulations.

Finally, his father said, "Well done, Shadow. Soon we will mark your graduation with your very own first raid, but tonight, we celebrate.

***

Guardian Institute of Scientific Research (Former Site of Headquarters on Earth), Pacific Ocean—February 10, 2023

Joshua Drake reached down to absentmindedly scratch behind an ear that wasn't there. His actions didn't go unnoticed. Becky's mind said: *Missing someone?*

A crooked smile lifted the corner of Joshua's mouth, but he didn't take his eyes of the Graduation Ceremony taking place in front of him. He replied: *Looks like it. I don't realize how much I do it.*

He'd let you fuss him all day long if you were stupid enough. You do know he's subliminally compelling you?

Of course! All felines do. Just because String is as big as a house doesn't alter his nature. He's telepathic. He's a cat. And he loves being scratched.

Becky giggled at the mere mention of the huge predator's name. When he was a cub, String's mother used to regularly bring him—

along with his brothers and sisters—to meet the small humans who had befriended her.

Although the size of a snack to them, none of the big cats ever viewed the children as a tasty morsel. Instead, they had been fascinated by the toy's Becky and Joshua would bring for them to play with.

In particular, String was the cub most mesmerized by the rope Joshua always seemed to carry with him. Within seconds of it being offered, he would pounce on it. Then, in a display of frenzied feline ferociousness—and much spitting and hissing—he would claw the cord to shreds. Once accomplished, String would writhe on his back like an upended squirrel, in absolute ecstasy at vanquishing his imaginary foe.

From an early age, Joshua had begun scratching him behind the ears as they played. It always made Joshua laugh, the way the huge cub would suddenly turn to stone at his first touch. Head frozen to one side, String would begin radiating huge waves of cosmic pleasure. If Joshua dared stop, the cub would whine and butt his head against the boy, knocking Joshua over while demanding he continue his ministrations.

Needless to say, one of the most deadly predators on Kalliste was doomed to a name denoting novelty for the rest of his life.

As String grew larger, Joshua began playing telepathic games with the Veran. This not only bonded them together, but also had the amazing side effect of increasing the animal's natural psychic capacity. Alarmingly so!

That fact had been noted, and currently, studies were being conducted as to how far those abilities could be enhanced. A great opportunity, especially as the Verans were now adapting to the presence of humans amongst them. With the colonization program moving forward apace, settlers would need time to adjust to life in an initially strange and hostile environment. Because of the predatory nature of some of the larger species, they would be dependent upon near invincible "guard dogs" to protect them. It was looking as if the Verans might be just the thing to fulfill that role!

At nearly six years old, String was approaching adolescence. Already six feet tall, he was only a shadow of the beast he would one day become. So, it made it all the more amusing when Joshua projected an image into Becky's mind of the powerful animal lying on his back, kicking all four legs in the air in wanton abandon, as he shredded yet another medicine ball from the gymnasium. Joshua said: *Yes! I do miss him! And he doesn't like it when I'm gone. I can feel his anxiety.*

Becky was surprised. "What? You can sense him from here?"

For the first time, Joshua turned to look at her. Shrugging his shoulders, he murmured, "Like I said. He doesn't like it when we're apart…Even when I project feelings of comfort!"

Becky didn't argue.

She knew they were different. For Joshua, his empathic abilities were unmatched…apart, perhaps, from their favorite aunt and uncles. Somehow, he was able to taste and influence the true emotions and feelings of individuals across vast distances. They were beginning to suspect his ability may even be able to manipulate the probability lattices, as Joshua's precognitive function was also massively developed. He seemed able to *feel* the right course that needed to be taken to achieve the most beneficial results. As such, the Overlord had personally been training him over the past year in some very advanced techniques to enhance his natural flair for a very rare gift.

Becky had received similar attention herself. Victoria was widely regarded as having the most finely attuned ultrasenses amongst the

Guardians. She had been instructing Becky in some astounding long-range, hyper-scanning and calling techniques that were already way beyond what most of the Lords could achieve.

Suddenly, Becky grunted!

Joshua's mind said: *What?*

She pointed to the graduating class of 2023. The new group of fully trained, qualified Protectors was leading the way. Marching smartly along in their crisp, new, distinguishing black uniforms, they were closely followed by the class of 2021. The more senior group was here today to be confirmed as fully fledged Guardians.

Becky said: *That will be us in the not too far distant future. We're already stronger than most people here. Yet, for all our differences, we still need to complete the training that will raise our physical and mental dexterity sufficiently to begin closing the gap on our psychic freakiness. How do you think we'll fit in?*

Surprise showed on Joshua's face. Already, his features were beginning to change, revealing a hint of the man he would one day become: *Do you know, I hadn't really thought about that. I know a few noses will be put out of joint because of our ages. Up until now, the youngest candidates to enter the Academy have been sixteen. So just imaging the joy the 'grownups' will feel at having a couple of snot-nose kids pulling at their skirts for five years. Especially as we're already stronger than they will ever be?*

Becky stifled another snort: *We're already getting a little taste of THAT on the Pre-Course! Thank god it's broken down into phases over the year so we can get a break.*

Joshua's mind echoed: *And I can get to see String…*

Suddenly, he sat up: *…Hey! Do you think they'll let me take him to the Academy?*

Giving Joshua an incredulous look, Becky replied: *Seriously? God! You are! Josh, if you want to improve your chances from 'nil' to 'when hell freezes over', I think you'd better start working on them now...don't you?*

Sighing, Joshua noticed the display had just ended. He said: *You're probably right! Didn't you want to go and congratulate Robin? He was at that same place they rescued you from wasn't he?*

Yes he was. That'll be nice. Let's go mingle shall we?

***

Jose Calderon couldn't believe he'd actually done it!

Looking at the freshly added bronze ring at the end of each sleeve, he beamed with pride. The Cheshire cat grin adorning his face, added a softness that had been sorely lacking when he was younger.

A blunt and highly compulsive individual with a powerful self-healing faculty, Jose had originally been a career hood, carving out a little empire for himself in Huston, Texas. Growing up alone and always having to look out for himself, he was a naturally secretive and insular person. However, after a number of *successful* hits on him had mysteriously failed, he had been exposed as a person with psychic capabilities to the authorities.

The CIA had subsequently tracked him down and incarcerated him within the ultra-secure facilities of the Angel Project, at Langley. Fortunately for him, he was one of a number of people held there illegally, and had been rescued by the Guardians themselves just over seven years ago.

That incident had changed his life.

For the first time ever, people had treated him with respect and granted him all sorts of responsibilities. And he hadn't let his instructors down!

Here he was, seven years later, clutching his authorization documents to his first posting. Inquisitor Wing, Section 1, South Americas Sector. He was a Guardian cop, with compulsive and healing abilities currently assessed at Grand Master level. And to top it all, it was thought the additional self-healing aspect to his gift was going to be even stronger by the time his maturation had run its course.

The irony of it all still hadn't sunk in and made him smile even now. His appointment meant he would be stationed at the underground Zone facility in the Mato Grosso do Sul district of Brazil. That would please his new girlfriend immensely, as her company had recently relocated her to Rio de Janero. Being so close together would mean they could take their time getting to know one another properly.

Excellent!

Some of his classmates came over to make sure Jose was going to the photo lines. If they didn't get there fast enough, the best seats at the Graduation Dinner Gala would be taken.

He was about to join them, when he saw someone he knew from the Langley facility.

It can't be!

Pushing his way through the crowd, Jose came up behind his quarry. His victim was chatting to an attractive looking, female blonde Protector from another class. Jose grinned at her and winked as he covered his target's eyes with his hands. In a false gangster voice, he said, "Stickemup fuckwit! Guess who?"

Robin Johns face immediately lit up with a broad smile.

Despite the huge paws covering his eyes, Robin still managed to assume a thoughtful posture. Tapping his chin with one finger, he said, "Hang on a minute, no clues! Let me see! Let me see! Smooth girly hands with a very weak grip. Now, that indicates either a complete weakling or someone with a penchant for self-abuse. Or both!

"The casual use of vulgarity highlights my aggressor has an exceedingly low IQ, most likely equal to that of a three week old turd! The smell of body odor combined with vomit tells me, *that someone* is so ugly, even the sight of their own reflection causes a reflex hurl. They also dare to put their grubby paws all over my handsome face. Goodness only knows what disgusting bodily orifices those fingers have been scratching or delving into? Although from the stench, I can guess! Mmmh, only one person I can think of has somehow managed to wheedle his way through Guardian training with such appallingly low standards. Probably playing on the mental disability quotient employers are forced to adhere to…

"Did you manage to dress yourself today Jose?"

Spinning Robin around to face him, Jose embraced his friend in a huge bear hug. He said, "How're you doing, you pig-ugly retard? Long time no see!"

Nodding to his blonde companion, Robin replied, "Oh you know, overcoming further huge hurdles on the long road to recovery…and saving lives with my classmate here."

Looking impressed, Jose said, "Jesus! I heard about that! Lucky you guys were there then by all accounts."

Shrugging his Shoulders, Robin replied, "Yes and no. I throw up a pretty mean shield, but it was Emm's here who really saved the day with her teleport function. They'd have been dead by the time I'd jogged to them, even with Moon gravity being what it is."

Jose replied, "Good point! Get out of the way you useless fucking moron, so I can speak to a real hero."

Roughly pushing Robin aside, Jose began advancing on Emma Boucher.

Emma looked aghast, until both men suddenly paused to embrace each other again. Amid a further stream of exchanged curses and vulgarities, they burst out laughing.

Emma relaxed.

Men!

Their manner clearly suggested such insults were their normal means of communicating their deep affection for each other.

Suddenly, Robin looked embarrassed. Turning to Emma, he said, "Where are my manners? Emma, this is Guardian Jose Calderon. Sorry about him, he's a twat that isn't getting used often enough…by men *or* women…or any form of mutation known to mankind. One time criminal thug and hit-man, now–believe it or not–destined to blaze a trail of self destruction within the Inquisitor ranks! God help us…

"…Twat! This is Protector Emma Boucher. She's far too nice a lady for you to even look at. So…just grunt and go take your club and play with the sand on the beach. About two miles out should do it…Don't bother holding your breath."

Emma was astounded at the bluntness of their humor. Her jaw dropped open.

Using his finger to lift her chin, Jose ignored the jibe and said, "Hi, Emma. It's nice to meet a *real* hero who doesn't still wet the bed at night."

She began to reply, "Nice to mee…"

"I've told you, dickhead!" Robin shot back, "I only ever do *that* when we're in bunk beds and you're on the bottom…"

Looking theatrically at Emma, Robin added, "…I don't know *how* my body can hold that much liquid! It's like I'm blessed with an additional ability."

Jose continued ignoring Robin and pushed him even further out of the way, "Anyway! It *is* nice to meet you Emma, even if your choice in monkeys leaves much to be desired."

Struggling to keep a straight face, she replied, "Good to meet you–at last! He's always going on about you, you know."

Without missing a beat, Jose replied, "All bad, I'm sure. We're getting engaged next month. The wedding's due as soon as I get him heavily insured. Needless to say, soon after, he'll suffer a needless, painful accident. Twice…just to make sure! I'll mourn his heartrending loss for a healthy period of about, five minutes…" He paused to look directly at her, "…then *we* can run off together to Vegas. Sound Good?"

Emma burst out laughing. Fortunately, she was spared further displays of testosterone, as Jose suddenly blinked. He was on the sharp end of a curt mental reminder from one of his fellow graduates: *Hey, big man! Haul ass! You'll lose your place in the line if you don't shift it!*

Suddenly looking apologetic and beginning to push his way back through the crowd, Jose shouted, "Sorry guys, you enjoy your own celebrations. Well done by the way! I'm late for the class photographs we're having done. I promised Angelika I'd get her a few portraits for her bedside cabinet."

He raised his eyebrows as he projected a lurid mental image of himself naked, in a typical male model catalogue pose.

Emma began choking on her punch!

Robin was on Jose like a rash. He shouted, "Angelika? Who's Angelika? Surely you can't be alluding to someone with an actual pulse?"

"Oh, a great girl I met on a night out in Rio a few months back."

Jose was getting a bit far away, so Robin reverted to mental speech. He called: *Are you sure she's a woman? Was it dark? I've heard the transvestites from that part of the world are particularly alluring?*

Well, you'd know!

Is she blind?

Boring!

Is she retarded?

Prick!

Is she a moose? She is, isn't she? A certified double bagger!

Raising a middle finger, so the young upstart could clearly see it across the throng, Jose projected: *Twist on this, spindle dick…*

…No! Cancel my last thought. You'd DEFINITELY get a kick out of that!

Jose cut off further conversation as he met up with his fellow classmates.

As he was led through the throng, Jose smiled to himself.

It was REALLY nice to see him again. He's an entirely new kid now that his mind's sorted out.

Thinking of his girlfriend's voluptuous body, Jose had an even better idea.

I think I'll have to introduce him to Angelika. When he sees what she looks like for real, he'll be sooo pissed! I'll be able to wind him up with it for years!

Chapter Four
An Echo in the Night

Andrew entered normal space/time with his shields fully raised. The scarlet flashes coursing through his essence revealed his readiness for battle! He was over fifteen billion light years from earth, in an area of the universe that was ancient and therefore, sparsely populated.

He emitted a huge seeker-pulse. Throbbing potently, it sizzled out into the vast inky blackness surrounding him, sensitive to any anomaly that might reveal the presence of the *other* that had caught his attention just moments ago.

Andrew had been busy, exploring the immeasurable reaches of the cosmos for future, viable colonization candidates. His vast senses had been finely tuned to the very precise ethereal and geo/physical spectrum required for human life to exist. Jumping from one focal point–(F/p)–to another in grids, he was employing an arcane program of the utmost complexity. It allowed him to scan for a distance of over a hundred million lights years in every direction as he travelled along the hyper-spatial ellipse.

Only thirty seconds previously, he had been traversing the outer reaches of Abel 18351k1916. As one of the outermost galaxies yet detected by mankind, it was a region of space that should have been deserted. And yet, his mental alarm had notified him of the presence of another sentient transcended life form.

Because of the current threat, none of the other Guardians had been assigned this far out. Victoria was on Earth, overseeing the amalgamation of her new staff from the previous week's graduation. Anatt was on Kalliste. And the Overlord was busy again, attuning himself to the galactic hub in preparation for the role he would undertake in the near future.

That considerably narrowed the margin down as to who the mysterious entity might be.

I wouldn't put it past them though! The renegades are onto the fact their transcended complexi would ring like the proverbial bell to other higher beings if they were close enough. But out past the galactic rim? That would be a different matter! We would have to be specifically scanning for them, with all manner of filters phased in, to stand a chance of locking onto their binary idents. Especially with the amount of celestial white noise and background radiation that exists along the spur…

He looked around his current location again.

…Perhaps that was why my mystery guest dropped their guard? They weren't expecting me here!

Being thankful for the absence of the esoteric frequencies that would encroach on his ultra-fine senses, Andrew altered his perception. Subtlety, he began to blend with the dark matter that was so prevalent in old space. Sending out a probe…he waited and listened.

Nothing!

…Well, nothing that can be termed, unnatural or a threat.

Andrew stretched himself again.

Merging with the cosmic chains that bound space/time together, he became one with the deep melodic tone of their pitch. Vibrating his complexus to the exact same key, he sent out a further query.

Still nothing!

Absorbing energy from the subspace matrix pervading the void about him, he exerted himself to the point of agony. Over and over he pulsed, repeatedly straining to listen…ever further, ever deeper.

There!

At the very threshold of his capacity he discerned an echo, achingly familiar–and yet–hauntingly alien in some way.

What the hell is that?

Spinning a hasty teleport field, Andrew punched through hyperspace in pursuit. As he did so, he suddenly felt his potential swell alarmingly! Emerging into normal space moments later, he discovered that he'd travelled over four billion light years in one jump!

Overflowing with never before experienced power, Andrew gasped as his psi-well and nexus expanded, resonating to repeated ethereal discharges.

The unexpected phenomenon brought him up dead.

How on earth did I do that?

Checking his coordinates, Andrew had the presence of mind to scan for the elusive echo. He caught it, winking out of existence along an entirely different course. Discarding it–for now–he assessed his position for a third time.

I've just jumped half again as far as I've ever managed to do in one attempt!

He altered his perspective so he could look down on himself.

Wow!

His transcended threshold had now grown to nearly twelve feet in height. His spectral brilliance was numbing, even to someone in ascended glory.

Realization hit him.

I've just experienced a maturation phase! I'm almost as strong as father now and....

Abruptly, his whole complexus throbbed in esoteric sympathy!

Shifting through an entire spectrum of scintillating colors, he felt a familiar mind, far, far away, undergoing a similar growth spurt. Without knowing how or why, Andrew understood he had just experienced his twin sister–back on Earth–undergoing the same augmentation.

An urgent voice suddenly entered his mind: *Andrew? Andrew? Are you there?*

Yes Vic, are you okay?

I was just going to...did you? Did we... just...grow?

It looks like it! I was in mid-teleport too. It boosted me four billion light years in one jump!

Victoria's mind betrayed her surprised: *Four billion! That's, that's...*

Bloody incredible! He cut in, finishing her sentence for her: *I know. Look, when I've finished here, we've got to talk. I'm at...* (Squeezed data containing precise coordinates)...

What are you doing all the way out there? She interrupted: *I thought you were on Star Search?*

I was! I am! I came across something and when I began to pursue, it just jumped away from me before I could lock-on properly.

Astonished, she said: *What? Jumped away from you? Who besides father can do that?*

That's what I'd like to know Vic. You don't think they've somehow enhanced themselves again, artificially do you?

There was no need to clarify who *they* were.

Hell, I don't know Andrew. Finish up there and we'll get Father to examine the data with us. Perhaps he can shed some light on this.

Sending an image of himself nodding, Andrew said: *Will do. Catch you...WHOA!*

He came up short!

Immediately sensing his shock, Victoria cried: *What?*

Andrew checked his position once more, doing so easily within moments. He said: *Sis, how far am I from you?*

Here on Earth? Hang on! At your current location, you are precisely...fourteen billion eight hundred million m...Fuck!

Vic, I know you're better at this than me, but do you have to strain to maintain this connection over such a vast distance?

No, not at all! Jeesh Andrew! Is this what father was hinting at when he talked about us maturing into something never seen before?

Numbed, Andrew replied: *I can't say for sure! But I've got a feeling this is just an echo, a taste of what's to come...*

That brought him back to the reason he was there. He continued: *...Talking of which, I'll catch you later. There's something I've got to look into...now!*

Breaking the link, Andrew concentrated again on the last heading the mysterious entity had taken. He decided to follow with caution, and began a series of short teleport skips at a tangent to that last trajectory. This allowed him to adopt a similar course, while maintaining full tactical readiness.

On his fifteenth hop, he emerged from hyper-space...and was stunned!

There before him—plain as day—was a small solar system containing three planets. The star at the center was a main sequence, G2V yellow-white dwarf, slightly larger than Earth's own sun.

The inner planet was only seventy million miles out. Therefore it would be too hot to sustain life. However, the outer two, orbiting at ninety-seven million miles and one hundred and seventeen million miles respectively, were an entirely different kettle of fish. For this class of star, they were smack-bang within the sweet zone!

Andrew swooped in on the second planet. Assessing it closely, he discovered it to be about ten percent again as big as Earth. Casting his astral vision about the orbital plane, he also saw it was ideally placed and protected within its local family group. It had no moon, and the beautiful blue/white vista indicated a high probability of an eco-friendly environment.

He scanned the surface. Land mass accounted for forty percent of its total area. Seasonal variation was clearly evident and would warrant further scrutiny. The oceans were comprised of water, albeit with nowhere near the amount of sodium found in Earth's seas.

Jumping into the thermosphere, Andrew examined the oceans more closely. They were teeming with life. Magnesium, sodium, sulfur, potassium, calcium and fluorine were plentiful. So were beneficial levels of sulfates, bicarbonates and borates.

In fact, the entire planet seemed to subliminally radiate health of the highest quality.

A tingle ran through Andrew's essence. It was almost as if the Earth had a slightly younger sister that had somehow been scrubbed clean and transported through space and positioned here.

He tasted the atmosphere. The predominant gases were nitrogen and oxygen—both at tolerable levels—and the remainder was comprised of Carbon Dioxide, Helium, Argon, Hydrogen and Ammonia. Trace elements were plentiful, ozone was good.

This is bloody spooky!

As there were no moons, Andrew couldn't easily read the tidal variation. That would require a deeper study of the planet's interaction with its sun and neighbors. Nonetheless, by skimming across the four major continents, he was able to discern areas of coastal erosion and accretion. Additionally, he discovered two zones of volcanic activity where continental plates infringed upon its neighbor.

He scrutinized them for a while.

Hmm, nothing we can't deal with at a later date. They're localized to two of the landmasses, giving us room to maneuver and prepare on the others.

Gravity was fractionally higher than that on Earth, and the rotational variant indicated the days here would be twenty-five and a half standard Earth hours long.

Andrew lightly sounded the planet's surface and oceans to get a better indication of the range of bio-diversity. He jumped in shock as he received multiple instant responses to his telepathic probes!

Instinctively he broke the link.

However, after quickly replaying the event in his mind, he couldn't discern any danger. Gently, cautiously, he extended the invitation of his thoughts again.

Wave upon wave of eager naivety and innocence immediately replied!

Holding his ground this time, he gauged the emotions behind those queries, and quickly determined no threat was present.

What the…?

Measuring them, Andrew realized he was receiving millions upon millions of responses! Inquisitive, curious and vastly different in their composition! Despite their diversity, they were achingly united, conjoined in questioning this new shining mind from above. He recognized the beginnings of a crude harmonic union as they increased their efforts to find an answer.

In wonder, Andrew descended further into the atmosphere.

He was astonished to discover an amazingly balanced and self sustaining ecosystem. The multitudes of living organisms surrounding him were not only intimately attuned to each other, but also to the nature of their environment too.

They were so *different* to the life forms he was used to or had witnessed elsewhere amongst the vast reaches of the cosmos. Yet, here they all were! Subconsciously working and thriving together to concisely manipulate the bionetwork and ensure everything was more conducive to the life-force of the planet.

Andrew re-tuned his perception to the entire globe...

...and was flabbergasted!

Although primitive, the *mind* of this world was so incredibly rich in essence, it was almost sentient!

How?

...Bloody hell!

He couldn't help it.

Andrew was so dumbfounded, he couldn't think straight.

Then he heard it...an echo from out of the darkness!

Andrew flung his mind after that resonance...and came up short! His search over before it began. The last planet out in this system—only twenty million miles away—was calling out in response to its sister's excitement!

I've got to see this!

Quickly spinning a crude tau-field, Andrew bore himself through the interplanetary medium and materialized above his next object of astonishment.

Wow!

It was immediately apparent conditions here were *very* different!

This final world was much larger than its sibling. At just over a hundred and seventeen million miles out from its sun, it should also have been unable to support humanoid life. However, there appeared to be some form of obscure link between the two bodies. That bond was causing subliminal frequencies to resonate from within the heart of the larger planet. Those vibrations were, in turn, directly manipulating the planetary core, and altering its electromagnetic field. This effectively resulted in a decreased rate of axial spin and gravity.

Andrew guestimated its rotational frequency as lying between seventy-three to seventy-four standard Earth hours. Incredibly, that was *exactly* what was required to warm the thick soupy atmosphere and surface sufficiently for human life to thrive.

Piercing the vale with his mind, Andrew was greeted by a melody of the sweetest angelic purity!

I don't believe this…it's…

Emotions fluttered unbidden, from one end of his complexus to the other. Had he been in human form, tears would now be rolling down his cheeks.

She…they…*IT*…was beyond beauty. And breathtaking to behold!

Dragging his perceptions away from the wonders below, Andrew scanned about him, and deep into the vast regions of local space. From Earth, this planetary system would appear behind the constellation of Leo. If he had followed his current search pattern, it would have remained undiscovered for nearly two thousand years.

A sudden realization caused a thrill to shoot through him.

I was led here! He thought, *but by who?*

Andrew replayed the events over and over again in his mind. Whatever—whoever—that echo was, it displayed no overt signs of aggression.

And its mental signature...

Although unknown, there was something about it that was achingly familiar. Not only was it most adept in its use of higher functions, but it had guided him here as if it was showing him an example of its work.

Now that's a point!

Pausing, Andrew meshed with the harmonic frequency emitted by the two outer planets and let the music pull his mind along in the current. The flow led him directly to the star at the center of the group. He was stunned to discover it was generating an amazingly intricate network of arcane filaments. Although natural—in that they employed the interrelated gravity and particles this system was comprised of—what they were feeding was not!

Over what must have been eons and eons of time, someone—or something—had taken this groups natural arrangement, and gradually and painstakingly enhanced it at its most basic level. Whereas before this solar system had been mute, now it flared with an awareness that connected each of its members in an almost perceptive way! The matrix was guaranteeing the optimum conditions for transcendent life were not only being achieved, but maintained *and* improved with each passing day.

Andrew looked to the first planet again, this time through new eyes.

The patient manipulations that were terra-forming its hostile conditions into a friendlier environment were now evident. He could clearly see that, one day in the far distant future, this world would be overflowing with life. Sentient life!

A familiarity within this obscure arrangement called to him. Subconsciously, Andrew meshed with one of the esoteric strands, and sent a feeling of welcoming consonance to the already existing life forms on the outer two planets.

The filament somehow recognized and obeyed his nature without hesitation. In an instant, his expression of love and fellowship was amplified and transferred to everything capable of understanding the sentiment.

Within seconds, the entire system throbbed in response! The harmonic echo that came bounding back sent a shock of delight surging along his synapses.

The others have got to see this! Of course, we'll have to quarantine the damn place until we can be sure we won't harm it. What a shame if the human mindset is too aggressive to settle here...unless?

A thrill ran through him.

Would this arrangement actually enhance humans as well? Remove their natural inclination to destroy and speed up their maturation?

...Well screw me blind!

Without realizing what he was doing at first, Andrew began running through suitable names in his head. It was something he had always loved to do when unearthing new discoveries.

Smiling, he let the mood of the place guide him.

Hmm...Latin might be appropriate on this occasion.

Looking first to the sun, he acknowledged, she certainly *was* a life giver to the astonishingly developing mind here. It came almost immediately... *Veritasu.*

The first planet was also an easy choice. The hope this incredible arrangement gave to future life there would be wonderful to behold... *Speratus.*

The strangely fascinating third planet came next. Beautiful for all her differences! But of course, it was so simple when beauty was involved... *Decorus.*

Finally, he turned his attention to the magnificent second planet and let his emotions guide him.

You certainly are a wondrous place, he thought. *So many people will love to experience the essence you have to offer.*

Chuckling, he admitted, *yes! You certainly are wonderful! Mirari it is...*

He couldn't wait to tell others about this new find.

Then remembered what it was that had led him here... Literally! In his augmented state, he also saw *why* the mystery entity had managed to elude him. An infinitely faint network of pathways crisscrossed a little-known layer of the subspace medium.

A stable wormhole system!

Seeing the extent and complexity of the grid, Andrew realized it was too structured to have been caused randomly.

What has father 'forgotten' to mention to us THIS time I wonder?

Resisting the urge to intrude, Andrew opened his mind to every single frequency he could think of, and sent out an extremely powerful, but gentle thought: *Thank you, whoever/whatever you are! I will personally ensure this cherished gift is not squandered.*

He waited... radiating feelings of welcome and camaraderie.

Nothing!

In sad resignation, he checked his position in relation to his target. Within moments he had located Earth and had spun the vast hyper-translation field that would take him the unimaginable distance home in only three jumps.

Then he was gone, leaving the strangely hypnotic, little star system in peace.

***

A short while later, something peeled back a hitherto unknown layer of subspace and peeked out. Tasting the essence of the stranger, the entity decided the surprise visitor was neither *known* nor *unknown*, but something in between.

Impossible! How can such an anomaly exist? It thought.

This stranger presented a puzzle it was neither equipped nor enlightened enough to understand. The entity decided it might be best to consult the others.

It will mean rousing them from consulate bliss, but they have been dormant long enough. Cogitation will provide a stimulating change after an age spent contemplating our errors…and our reduced place within the cosmic all.

Then it had another, more disturbing thought.

No! It couldn't be…could it?

Already?

Chapter Five
Surprises

The Reception Dais of the Headquarters transportation hub glowed faintly as Jade Heung, Lord Evaluator of the Guardians, materialized. The scarlet flashes rippling through her aura betrayed her obvious excitement to the security detail stationed there. Ignoring the looks of surprise her unannounced arrival had generated, she swiftly made her way toward the main elevator pads.

Jade rarely displayed emotion in front of others. So, for her to be telegraphing her feelings now, was giving the game away that *something* was up!

It wouldn't cause any harm, of course, but she berated herself nonetheless. *Switch on Jade! You're acting like a first year student who's just managed to levitate her first chair!*

She clutched the reason for her elation tightly in her hand. The message crystal, detailing the latest results of the *Negater Program* they had been working on for only two weeks. Two weeks! And already they were preparing to go live…

…*If* she gave her blessing!

Summarizing the contents of the report again as she hurried along, Jade cursed the fact that headquarters etiquette required everyone to walk about the complex as opposed to teleporting. And of course, the mere fact *she* was the Lord Evaluator, meant she had to set an example.

Bah!

A few moments later, and she'd reached the pad. Snorting to herself as it began to descend, she had to admit. The walk was helping her restore the usual glacial veneer she liked to adopt in front of others! But boy! Was it difficult!

Everyone had been on edge since the attempt to infiltrate the facility had become public knowledge. Herself included! So, the fact her people had already come up with a solution to the immediate threat, would give everybody the boost they needed. A boost and something positive to focus on!

In fact, it had surprised Jade how easily Marty and Sharon had pointed the rest of the team in the right direction.

They had wired Marty up to a converted HaSP scanner, courtesy of Yeung Technologies. Making use of its multidimensional holographic interface, they had then begun to measure and catalogue each and every single psychic capability the Guardians had at their disposal.

As they were already aware, each faculty generated its own unique energy signature. By using the HaSP, they had since been able to transpose those esoteric frequencies into a quantifiable mundane form.

Marty had then demonstrated what actually happened when he deployed his mirroring capability. Being able to watch the mechanics of the process as they took place, had allowed the Guardian scientists to accurately quantify the precise wavelengths Marty employed on each occasion. Using the data collected, they then reproduced those same effects artificially.

Next, they had asked Sharon to demonstrate her particular gift.

It had been amazing to watch how Sharon's skill inverted the wavelengths. Unlike Marty, she didn't just reflect the exact same frequency back to create a barrier. She actually nullified them, cancelling them out entirely!

And they'd been able to mimic the process using technology.

If the report was correct, the procedure was still a little slow. The scanners took a few moments to accurately read the signature of the incoming talent, before inversing it. But that didn't matter. Accuracy was essential. Speed could be enhanced later by upgrading the sensitivity of the targeting nodes.

All in all, very encouraging news!

However, *that* wasn't what had excited Jade so much.

No! What had Jade doing mental back-flips, was the fact that once the unique tonal signature of each inverse capability had been absorbed mentally, that was it! Any competent operator would be able to embed the program within their Psi-Well.

Of course, their individual strength would then be an obvious factor as to whether they would be puissant enough to negate their opponent. But that wasn't the point. In developing a mechanical means of defense, they had stumbled upon a psychic one too!

And if today went well, they would see a successful demonstration against targeted psi-dents!

Still mulling things over, Jade swept into the main laboratory. Suddenly, she found herself frozen in mid-step and enclosed within a crawling skein of power. A faint buzz also announced the fact that the internal security countermeasures had locked onto her. She was about react, when she recognized the absence of any threat.

Everyone was staring at her, professional interest or concern written across their faces. All, that is, except for Marty Mays, who was sat behind a command consul and grinning from ear to ear.

The penny dropped.

"I see you've managed to adapt the Negater technology to psi-dents as well?"

"It would appear so, little lady!" Marty replied, maintaining his Cheshire Cat smile.

Little lady?

He added, "I hope you don't mind. But, seeing as we needed your approval, I thought you'd be the perfect guinea-pig to try it out on. Minus the psychic stun element...of course."

"Of course!"

Everyone quickly went back to work, while Marty continued tinkering about for a few moments, making minute adjustments.

As he did so, Jade discovered that no matter how hard she tried, she couldn't get her muscles to work. So she attempted to move herself with telekinesis.

A miniscule vibration ran through her body, and then, *something* simply cancelled out the consequence her will *before* it evolved into motion.

Intrigued, she tried to teleport.

Again, she felt the instant manifestation of her purpose begin to coalesce, before it...*stopped!* It was almost as if her capability would begin responding, only to flutter away from her mental grasp. Once absent, it remained elusive and beyond her ability to recall.

Jade was impressed...and somewhat disturbed. Calling out to Marty, she said, "Can I have my foot back now, please? I'm beginning to feel a little ridiculous standing here like a frozen cartoon character."

"What? Oh yes, of course!"

A faint hum coincided with the restoration of her motor functions.

Walking across to Marty's consul, she held out the message crystal. "So! You weren't exaggerating when you said we were ready to go live across the board."

Shrugging, he replied, "I aim to please. But you *really* need to be thanking that pretty lady over there…"

Pointing towards Sharon Dyer, he continued, "…Sharon came up with the idea of incorporating the HaSP's holo-displays into the equation. They say a picture paints a thousand words? Well, her idea jumped us forward a thousand-fold. Once I could *see* what was needed, it was a simple matter to replicate the ideal conditions. After that, we simply forged ahead."

Looking across to the diminutive young woman who was now engrossed in the circuitry of a cerebral enhancer, Jade though, *Hmmmh! She's full of surprises. I really must make the effort to get to know her better.*

Out loud, she mused, "Marty, what's she doing now?"

Glancing across, Marty's eyes narrowed for a moment. "Ah! She also had the idea of trying to incorporate the new Tec into the scanners used aboard your orbiting stations. A major part of the problem appears to be pinpointing the murdering scumbags when they're keeping their heads down. We've seen how elusive they are when they choose to be. But, if she manages to splice the new readers into the sensitive targeting nodes of the cerebro-energizers…well, it'll be game over!

"We've run into some hurdles, true. But she's working on them."

Jade looked more closely at the young woman.

Yes! FULL of surprises! I'm definitely going to get to know her better…Starting now!

***

Like the finest particles saturating the interstellar medium, the ionized dust cloud drifted sedately across the northern polar region of the moon. Blending perfectly with its ambient surroundings, it was careful to act as naturally as possible. Diffused as it was to the uttermost limits, it became almost indistinguishable to any form of scan. The pain of the effort was considerable. But the entity was used to discomfort. It seemed to be the only way he could safely get about lately.

And safety was a priority now. Especially after Harry nearly got himself caught!

Oh, it was tempting to try Esther's new toys out. But there was always a risk involved in any new venture. And he wasn't willing to dip his toe into the water just yet…not until they'd finished *seeding*.

The entity now known as Simon Cooper smiled within himself.

Yeung had come up with that term the week previously, when they had been discussing their options. Esther had completed the new sub-dermal emitters and was keen to incorporate her findings into their new trinary psi-dents. As always, Yeung had urged for caution. He had suggested that, perhaps it would be beneficial to sow the seeds of doubt *before* using the devices on themselves. His idea to scatter examples of the technology amongst the unsuspecting populace was as surprising as it was brilliant.

Getting Esther to replicate fifteen of the prototypes, Yeung then incorporated them into a set of biodegradable chips. Those chips were then seeded among random families in France, Moscow, Hong Kong, Mexico and Australia. Designed to disintegrate less than a minute after initiation, they would lay dormant within their unsuspecting hosts until activated.

Just as well.

Over the past week, they had triggered three of the five clusters. The fact they worked was evidenced by the speedy response of the freaks and their minions.

On the first occasion, the infernal twins had reacted in less than sixty seconds. On the second, they'd cut their response time to only forty-three seconds. On the last attempt, in Australia, it was down to thirty-eight! And they'd brought an Inquisitor team with them, armed to the teeth with all sorts of lethal looking gadgets and weaponry!

Valuable intelligence indeed!

The stakes had changed! They all knew now, without a shadow of doubt, that if they were ever captured, they were dead! Unless…

As light as a smattering of moon dust, Simon allowed his consciousness to drift idly across the base below.

What are you up to in there?

Yearning to get any hint he could as to the way his ancient foes might turn this latest development to their advantage, he tried to penetrate various parts of the complex with his rarified vision.

Nothing!

For over two weeks now, there'd been a deathly hush in the air. An expectancy that something was going to happen! The urge to scream was very tempting.

After several more hours of fruitless scanning, he decided enough was enough! Yeung would be back with the results of his latest move within the hour, and he was eager to see how things had gone.

Simon thought for a moment about his fellow conspirator.

For a human, Yeung was surprisingly resourceful and innovative. He displayed a wisdom that was as insightful as it was revealing. His counsel had repeatedly steered them away from suspicion and saved them from tragedy on a number of occasions where mistakes had been made.

He's been more use to me than my own people! Pity he's so temporary! Still, I must confess…he doesn't cease to surprise me. If there was only some way to raise him up…

Subconsciously, Simon cast his senses upwards. They came to rest on the Hyper Jump Gate instillation and its protective Star Base.

He didn't have to look too closely to recognize the unknown enhancements across the defensive/scanning grid. They were the same kind as had been deployed around the Headquarters. And every other Guardian facility come to that!

Hmmmh?

Checking to ensure his composition was as dispersed as possible, Simon drifted closer. Something tugged at an ancient memory in the deepest recesses of his mind. A familiarity that was…

…His attention returned to the gateway.

A thrill ran through him as he was suddenly hit by a powerful feeling of recognition.

The Monolith Gate! They're using a similar principle to the old system around Kalliste. And…

Risking closer scrutiny, he focused more precisely on the bridge generators. A musical tone from the long distant past confirmed his suspicions.

…and they're using a polarized pair of shards from the old psi-tronic crystal! Well, well, well! Esther WILL pleased. I think she'd love to take a closer look at this!

Gathering purpose, Simon made his slow departure. He waited until the solar winds had swept him over a hundred thousand miles from the area, before beginning the torturously slow process of pouring himself through the subspace medium toward home.

As he squeezed out of existence, he had a thought.

What have they got on the other side of the gate?

***

The motor launch wallowed calmly at anchor, a picture of muted serenity in the moonlight that cut across the still waters of the Indian Ocean. So quiet was the surrounding sea that the occasional *twang* of cable-guides rang for nearly half a mile out into the night.

A gentle mist caressed the graceful hull, its fingers eagerly probing every nook and cranny with the intimacy of a lover.

Gradually, the vapor thickened. Within a few minutes, it had become a fog, gleaming with a silver iridescence that complimented the radiance of the light shining from above. Suddenly, several other craft materialized around the lone traveler, as if out of nowhere. The silence of the night was thrown back by the sound of repeated orders, barked in a tone that expected swift compliance.

Shadowed figures swarmed onto the motor launch, each reacting with a practiced familiarity to the drill. In moments it was over.

An older man approached a teenager who had appeared on the stern of the captured vessel. Surprisingly, it was the younger individual who appeared to be in charge! "The boat is taken my Son. Your orders?"

Assad Ali Omar—Shadow, to the rest of the White Sails surrounding him—paused to consider his options. He said, "Check again. Make sure no one is hiding. Disable the sat/nav and radio systems. If they are serviceable to our needs, remove them.

"Support boats, return to the water. Patrol out from this position for at least a mile. Raid teams, you are to begin a thorough search. Stem to stern, all decks. Father, Sylvester, Jagpal…you're with me. Let's go and say 'hello' to our…host."

Ali's heart swelled with pride. His son was not only a highly skilled sailor, and gifted with preternatural abilities, but it would appear he was a natural born leader too. Just what his men would need in the future.

Swiftly, they all made their way below decks. As they neared the galley, they were met by several members of their team. All had shocked faces!

"What's the matter?" Assad enquired.

"Look for yourself…" muttered Nevadan, a veteran White Sheet with over twelve years experience. Nevadan paused to listen to another message over his handheld radio, and appeared puzzled by what he heard.

Shaking his head, and pointing into the kitchen, Nevadan continued, "…From what we know, the guy in there would appear to be all alone. There's no one else here…"

"Then keep looking," Assad interrupted, "Something's not right. Search more thoroughly. And have the third Support Team extend their range out for another mile, just to be safe!"

His father at his side, Assad strode forward to take a look for himself.

A man of European origins was sat at the galley's only table. Although open, his eyes were rolled into the back of his head. At first, Assad thought the guy's hands were resting upon a heavy rock on the surface in front of him. But he was wrong. It took him a moment to realize what he was actually seeing. The man's fingers were, in fact, sunk into the stone itself, as if he were clutching it in a death grip.

How?

Ali cautiously touched the unknown occupant on the shoulder.

Their host suddenly started, and took a deep, shuddering breath. Then in perfect Somali, he said, "On behalf of distant friends who admire your work, please accept this fine vessel—and its entire contents—as a token of our esteem. Within the forward cabins, you will discover equipment you will no doubt cherish for many years to come. However, within the rear cabin lays the price for this craft. Your cooperation! Do not be alarmed, for the cost should involve no danger to yourselves, considering the skills of the young man in your midst…"

Ali's gaze snapped to Assad.

Whoever this person was, he represented people who clearly knew about his son *and* what he could do.

The man continued, "…The instructions are clear and concise. Your acceptance of these terms will be signaled by computer, and the fact you take the vessel into your possession. Please be aware, this craft is sanitized, and is not registered to any person or corporation. If you refuse, you will not hear from us again. You may, however, keep the contents of the forward compartments."

As if on cue, a muffled voice intruded from the bow. "Come! Come and have a look at this! You won't believe it…"

Everyone rushed forward, crowding around the two cabin doors which were now ajar. Both rooms were overflowing with weapons and equipment. Rocket propelled grenades, flash-bangs, Kalashnikov assault rifles still in their wax papers, telescopic and night sights. All Soviet made, all without serial numbers. Mixed in among them were the latest sat/nav hand-held GPS systems, radio scanners and jammers, walkie-talkies, boat engines, first aid and resuscitation kits. It was an Aladdin's cave of goodies!

They stared at each other for a long time. Here was a treasure trove they could never hope to amass in their own lifetimes.

Ali watched his son closely. The boy was muttering to himself under his breath.

"You have something to say?"

Without taking his eyes off the fortune in front of them, Assad replied, "Father. While tempting…especially if this vessel is included in the prize…should we not first assess the cost of our cooperation? Whoever these people are, they are not to be crossed. They know about us. They know about me! If we accept, I have a feeling we will be bound to something we can't back out of."

Heads were nodding in agreement.

Excellent! Thought Ali, *he is earning their trust.*

Aloud, Ali said, "A wise choice, my Son. Come. Let us see what the price entails."

Slowly, they made their way aft, only to find another group of shocked White Sheets, staring bug eyed into the spacious cabin. Although many of the team couldn't read, they were well aware of the international symbol for radioactive materials. They were looking at a number of such emblems now, emblazoned in several places along the outer casing of two devices.

Between them, sat a strange looking computer!

Pressing the play button, they watched for the next five minutes as their *price* was spelled out in crystal clear clarity.

At the end, everyone fell silent. All eyes looked to Ali. Although Assad had been leading the teams for this specific raid, *this* new decision affected the entire clan.

Ali ruminated for a while before asking the opinion of his trusted friends. "What do you think? The instructions are as simple as they are specific. They–whoever they are–have chosen their target. Because of the nature of its cargo, it will be travelling in secrecy and without escort. We will be furnished with specific details on the day of the attack, so as not to jeopardize security. When we receive confirmation, we are approach the craft under cover of Assad's ability. Once there, we will secrete these devices among others already stored within its hold, and withdraw. If we proceed with caution, we will not draw attention to ourselves in any way…AND will benefit from the services of this vessel and its gifts for many years to come."

He looked slowly around the circle.

Everybody nodded once.

Tentatively, Ali reached out and pressed the accept key, sending their response.

Within moments the computer sputtered and sparked, before bursting into flames. Assad reacted quickly. Swiping it to the floor, he doused the fire with a blanket. As he extinguished the blaze, the sound of running feet and shouting could be heard from further along the motor launch.

What? Ali thought.

As one, they raced through the craft, eager to discover the cause of the commotion.

The disturbance was moving up onto the main deck.

The sounds of a struggle grew louder. There was more shouting, followed by a distinctive *splash* and cries of alarm!

Charging up onto the bridge, Ali was shocked to discover over half a dozen of his men looking over the railing and into the sea. Three more were in the water!

"What the hell's going on?" he demanded.

"He jumped in!" one replied.

"What do you mean he jumped in?"

"The man with the rock! When we tried to stop him, he used some kind of invisible force to knock us down. Neel and the guys tried to tackle him round the legs, but he just vaulted in with them wrapped around his ankles. He sank like a stone!"

Ali was too shocked to laugh at the pun!

Surprised, he thought. *They obviously appreciate their anonymity more than we do. I hope I haven't bitten off more than we can chew.*

Looking around one last time, Ali could see dawn approaching on the horizon. Turning to Assad, he placed an arm around his shoulder and said, "Well done Son! An unexpected and fruitful success! Round things up and get us home. If you don't mind, I'll drive this beauty home. You can play with it once we've discovered exactly what's on board!"

Smiling, Assad turned to follow his father's instructions.

Watching his men move with practiced ease, Ali still couldn't help feeling uneasy.

Who are these people? How did they know about us, and especially about Assad? And what the hell have I gotten us into?

Chapter Six
Progress

Sighing, Deputy Marshall Anatt Yasin eased back into her seat and looked out of the shuttle's viewport. The spectacularly rare sunset bathed her face in warm radiance, despite the filters, and helped her to relax.

A great deal had been accomplished over the last five years, so she had every right to feel contented. Smiling, she reviewed their progress as her brief journey got underway.

The infrastructure for colonization was now in place. What headquarters had assessed would take ten years to complete, *she* had achieved in five. Beta site—now called Helios because of its elevated position—was fully equipped and ready to go. As the least dangerous zone, it would serve as a temporary capital/reception area until settlers decided for themselves where they would like to establish their primary city.

By positioning the main Teleport Hub at that location, Anatt had ensured that each of the thirteen settlements scattered throughout the three main continents could be accessed with relative ease.

At Naomi's suggestion, they had also incorporated a central reception area on each of the major landmasses. Doing so would ease the sheer volume of traffic through one point as things got busier, and allow explorers to access the various sites within each zone via their own local network. Extensive shuttle ports and storage facilities had also been incorporated into each settlement.

I can't believe I almost threw a spanner in the works over that issue! I was so sure it was all too excessive and would slow us down. Thank goodness Naomi had the spine to stand up to me.

Thinking back to that heated discussion, Anatt remembered how Naomi had stood nose to nose with her, and reminded her of the nature of initial traffic…

…'Although scientist and terraformers will no doubt form the bulk of the earliest travelers, that will change as time goes by. Each outpost will eventually become established. As they do, they will need room to expand. Properly and safely!

By looking ahead now, and viewing those settlements as a future township— or even a city—we will ensure the right facilities are in place from the word go. Thereafter, we won't have to worry when heavy plant or agricultural equipment and machinery is needed to complete subsequent modifications. It'll already be there! Each location will be able to expand into its own area of economic specialty at their own pace, and in their own way!'…

Anatt giggled at the memory. *It was radical thinking! And spot on too! Thank god she had the guts to force the issue.*

Although initially slow, Naomi's recommendations had proven a great boon to the accelerated development of each site. It didn't matter whether a region was earmarked for agricultural, harvesting or industrial use. The huge undertaking was now set to take off, and capable of sustaining future growth for the next ten years at least.

Soon, the first civilian colonists would be invited to attend.

I can't wait! The cream of the world's scientists is bound to bring a fresh infusion of skills that will bring this place to life. It'll be refreshing to work with some new blood, completing the final stages of our preparations for the ones who really matter. The general populace!

Because of the nature/temperament of the flora and fauna, Anatt was aiming for a fifty/fifty balance. Psychic and specialist.

Living and working side by side. She hoped such a blending of colonists would encourage them to bring out the best from themselves and their unique environment!

Overcoming differences is still a hot potato back on Earth! Like it or not, international political agenda still exercises a lot of influence over public opinion. If we're successful here, we'll be able to hold Kalliste up as a beacon to mankind. Maturation of the human mind will take a major leap forward and pave the way for even grander colonization projects in the future.

A thrill ran along Anatt's spine as she thought about that prospect. She knew better than most that one day, the human race would be united. Psychic and transcended! She'd seen it clearly within the Overlord's mind during their private sessions together.

But that was a long way off. For now, they were still dipping their toes into a very big pond, and anything that made the water more inviting was to be welcomed

I just hope the template we're offering will be enough.

The shuttle had circled the southern tip of Nerada twice, and was now heading toward Viridian, the westernmost continent. The humidity of the vast jungles covering that zone was evidenced by the density of the vapors rising high into the already thickened atmosphere.

Watching those mists ascend the slopes of the majestic mountains that formed the spine of Nerada, Anatt was reminded as to why they had been called the Vulcan Range. The rapidly rising warmer air, combined with the colder ionized clouds at high altitude, gave the horizon a decidedly ruddy glow. It looked as if the whole land was burning.

However, on rare occasions like this, when there was a break in the actual clouds, you caught sight of its full glory! The brilliant indigo-blue glare of the setting sun was enhanced by the shimmering violet and orange vapors rising past the peaks. The mirage produced a living-flame effect that made it look as if the mountain tops were on fire.

It would literally take your breath away…and your sight too, if the protective filters weren't in place. That's why they had to be so careful here. Kalliste was certainly beautiful, but she was also dangerous.

Just as well I've got an Adjutant Marshall who never leaves anything to chance!

Thinking about Naomi again, caused Anatt to cast her mental sight backwards.

She'd only dropped the young woman off at Aeralon–their original Alpha Site–five minutes ago, but already she could see her aide was hard at work. From the look of it, preparing the schedules that would ensure the Star Base and its extended facilities would be completed on time.

It had become Naomi's latest pet project, and Anatt had to agree, it was an excellent idea. New arrivals would spend their first couple of weeks acclimatizing to this system aboard the orbiting base. There, they would be educated as to the conditions and the environment they could expect, and indoctrinated with the necessary safety drills. Then, when they were considered competent, they would be allowed to complete the final phase's planet side.

Very clever!

And of course, things would only get better later in the year when Naomi finally underwent transcension.

Roll on the day! I can't wait to see what she becomes. Probably Deputy Marshall knowing my luck!

Yes, Anatt Yasin had every reason to feel satisfied.

They were well ahead of schedule, everything was going to plan, and she was determined things would stay that way.

***

Esther Perry loved to keep herself occupied.

And fortunately for her, the past five years had been very busy indeed, thanks in particular to one person, Lei Yeung!

Looking back through her computer files, she could see exactly *why* it was she'd changed her opinion about him.

The years constrained to a human body had disturbed Esther deeply. She found the fleshly *condition* to be most unnerving. It made you weak and susceptible to external influences! Even if you were blessed with higher mind functions, you were still temporary at best…unless you were fortunate enough to be among the elite of course! Then, the strange aberration that caused the metamorphosis would change you into something closer to a more natural, godlier personification!

But even so, etiquette would require you to restrict yourself to a most disconcerting form in your day to day dealings with the insects that still infested this world.

And yet, for all its inherent drawbacks, being fleshly has never seemed to hold Lei Yeung back…

…He's resourceful, wily, surprisingly strong willed, and absolutely ruthless when it comes to achieving his goals and protecting his assets. Despite being limited by his temporary condition, Yeung has still gone on to become one of the most powerful and influential individuals on the planet.

Esther reflected more deeply on this remarkable man.

When he was younger, he not only rose through the ranks of the criminal underworld, but cunningly created the perfect façade to hide his true—psychic self— behind. Nothing goes on, commercially, without his knowing about it. His iron grip within the advanced technologies and medical fields in particular, is as insidiously concealed as it is complete…

…And yet, for all his caution, Yeung never feels complacent. He always plans ahead for the unexpected. Wheels within wheels!

Esther liked that about him.

Flicking through her document library, she highlighted a number of his projects and press releases.

Just look at where it's got him!

Known to humanity as one of their greatest ambassadors for peace, Yeung had led the way in integrating both the psychic and normal communities together. Molding them into a united, cohesive force had made him an attractive prospect to the world's military, who now courted his influence with open arms.

Publicly, he had engendered a benevolent profile. He was on record as stating he would be happy to consider martial projects, only so long as their aims remained focused on a global quest for the ultimate *planetary* defensive capability.

Behind the scenes, however, Yeung had ensured his satellite companies had pounced on those invitations like a starving cat on a mouse, regardless of the objectives.

Brilliant!

Esther had never thought it would be possible for her to look on a human as a friend.

But I do! And I can see now, why.

Because of Yeung, she had been able to devote her considerable talents to a multitude of worthwhile projects. Tasks that had helped to keep her focused. Keep her sane! Schemes that not only ensured Yeung Industries remained in control of the global markets, but ones that also ensured their more *personal* agendas were well served too!

Esther brought up the specs on the new generation of Wave Readers as an example.

Designed to provide an invaluable security screen around sensitive venues, they contained an ingenious modification, hidden away within their software. Controlled by thought, they could be triggered to gain access to the minds of both 'mundanes' and operant psychics. An invaluable tool for the amassing of information!

With deep satisfaction, she looked at the results of her enhancements.

With my help, we've also managed to add a compulsive element to the penetration matrix. This has guaranteed we are in the enviable position of being able to exert the most subliminal of influences over those we view as a threat…or as useful to our machinations.

Scrolling down the list, Esther picked out another example she found to be particularly gratifying. The upgraded Mita/Emu implants!

Only last year, Esther had been dabbling with Bio-Tec augmentation. During some of her tests, she had recalled how versatile the latest generation of HaSP readers had become.

That had given her an idea!

Esther had required each of the Apostles of the Council to undergo a full molecular scan. Using the results of those readings as a template, she was able to assess by what margin their physical bodies could undergo modification without surgery. By adding an additional component to the micro-technology already implanted within their systems, she discovered she was able to influence the elasticity and efficiency of the major muscle groups and organs.

The simple pleasure of those amazing results brought a smile to her face, even now!

On average, muscle mass had been improved by thirty-two percent. Reactions, stamina, hand-eye coordination and balance by over twenty-seven percent. Additionally, by entering the correct code sequence, it was possible to stimulate the nanobots saturating their bodies to restructure their profiles.

So startling was the contrast, that in some cases it was as if they were looking at another person entirely!

Obviously, age was a major factor affecting the flexibility of this innovation. While Yeung himself could only manage one such adaptation, his younger Apostles could store up to four profiles within their implants.

Another handy tool to our growing arsenal! She thought. *Especially with the little extras I've thrown in.*

Most of her toys incorporated a backdoor system. And Esther had devised some nasty surprises for anyone foolish enough to try and steal or replicate her handiwork. She purred with self-satisfaction as she looked through some of them now. For each barbaric trap had been motivated by her deep-seated and long abiding hatred of the lesser beings she still viewed at insects.

Well, mostly!

Because, as she reviewed several of her latest assignments, she was reminded of some of the lessons she had learned from one human *insect* in particular. One who was now a friend!

The psi-dent issue sprang to mind. Especially as Esther had now solved that issue!

Once activated, neither she nor her Fallen comrades would be distinguishable any more. The new trinary signatures would see to that.

But, as eager as she was to implement them, Yeung had counseled patience, stating...

... 'Our latest venture will cause a huge backlash if successful. Needless to say, THAT will be the optimum time to activate the new identities.'...

On reflection, Esther had to concede, *he was right! But how can someone who's only eighty years old be so damned quick and wise all the time?*

Then there was the quantum levitation program!

Esther had shown Yeung the solution over two years ago.

True to form, when she had actually presented a working model to him, Yeung had asked for patience, and suggested an alternate and more profitable course. He stressed that, by siphoning their *breakthroughs* through in a number of subtle stages, they would be able to secure a massive amount of funding and support from commercial, transport and energy companies alike.

And that's exactly what had happened!

Lining the Council's coffers directly from the profits, Yeung had kept his sponsors happy during the intervening months by edging ever closer to the ideal of their dreams. Dreams that would soon be a reality, for the next year would bring the long awaited *discovery* they had been waiting for.

Or so they thought!

Because, that revelation would only involve a poor copy of the original archetype Esther had thrown together! A prototype that would inevitably be prone to malfunctions! Malfunctions that could only be rectified by further funding.

Smiling at the thought, Esther mused, *for someone who isn't precognitive; he's an astute little bugger! And annoyingly clever!*

Needless to say, the enhanced and fully operating system would remain the property of the Council, and be used to further their purposes until they had moved onto something better.

The same was true for the new Satellite Orbital Defense Systems.

Invited to contribute, along with a number of other leading companies, it came as no surprise when Yeung Tec had forged ahead in the development and refinement of a particle beam accelerator. Thanks to Esther, their concept was so innovative, that it left all other offerings behind and was snapped up by eager sponsors. A little tinkering saw the newly patented system ready to go, and incorporated into the firing platforms now arrayed about the Earth and due to go live in the New Year. In fact, it was that move in particular, which had secured the numerous military invitations that had flooded in since.

Regardless, they were still only presented with Esther's cast-offs.

What the world at large didn't realize was, in each case, these supposedly advanced and groundbreaking concepts were a poor man's version. A stop-gap to please the public! The Council always kept their most sophisticated models for themselves…just in case.

And Esther loved the fact that Yeung would always put *their* interests first.

Only recently, he'd finalized the activation of his latest ghost company. Separate and sanitized from his other holdings, it was an entity through which the Council could survive if anything ever endangered their livelihoods.

In tandem with this project, he had asked Esther to take the lead in establishing a number of covert command bunkers.

Of course, the term, *bunker*, was rather a loose one.

Highlighting the blueprints now, Esther could plainly see the structures were more like miniature palaces. Underground, armored and bristling with the most sophisticated weaponry and technology on the planet, true! But palaces nonetheless.

It had taken her six months. But it had been well worth it, because now they had a number of ultra secure facilities secreted away around the world that no one knew about. From each of those locations, they had an extensive software network that would allow them to manipulate the worlds markets...and more!

Much more! She giggled!

Opening a restricted folder, Esther looked over the designs of the Specter Protocol System she had incorporated into each site. Installed as failsafe should anything ever go drastically wrong, they would be able to remotely commandeer a large number of the new orbital defense facilities circling the Earth, to protect themselves.

Esther had already factored in the inevitable countermeasures that would be launched against them. She had seeded a number of additional, mobile, and heavily shielded platforms throughout the system, which would only respond to their commands. Separate from the main grid, they would remain cloaked until called upon.

Of course, once the Guardians started to play, they wouldn't last for long. But they would serve their purpose, and allow them to escape under cover of their new, genetically altered states...until the next time.

It had been great fun, and Esther had to admit...she'd enjoyed exercising her creative talents more than she'd realized.

And it's all thanks to Yeung! A human!

But having completed these assignments, she had been left wondering what on earth she could turn her talents to next.

Then, out of the blue, Simon told her about some *old* toys he'd recently discovered that were currently being used to power the latest Guardian Hyper Jump Gates!

Perfect!

Opening a new folder, Esther paused to consider what she would call her new pet project.

***

Although she wouldn't say it out loud, Naomi Cruiz sometimes thought that being the Adjutant Marshall was a crock of shit!

Instead of being out and about, exploring this still magnificently fresh and wonderful world, she was stuck here, in Aeralon, doing what was expected of her. Completing reports!

Lucky me!

What made it worse was the fact that she was very good at it. Her ability to compartmentalize multiple scenarios at the same time made her a natural organizer and planner. She was able to complete more, faster, than just about anyone else she knew. And sadly, instead of furnishing her with the free time she craved, her ability only ever seemed to guarantee yet *more* work!

Glancing across her latest report, she decided to add the amendment she had thought of only this morning.

> *'…As Helan 1 Star Base will be completed and fully functional at least one month prior to the arrival of the first settlers, (as per appendix A—attached), I propose the following revision of the reception itinerary for newly arrived travelers/colonists:*
>
> *The initial two week reception phase is to be altered to just one week.*

This module is an essential educational package. Arrivals must be indoctrinated as early as possible as to the dangers incumbent within this system. In particular, the elevated UV hazard and the long-term consequences of ignoring safety protocols. Once apprised of the risks, colonists must then pass a number of written tests to confirm that, in theory at least, they are aware of the conditions they will face on the surface.

Although essential, I feel this phase can be reduced as colonists will be better served by the real-life conditions presented on the planet itself. Therefore, at this stage, I propose the sealing of a written and verbal waver in the presence of two witnesses.

The planned 'groundside/development' module should then be extended into two parts.

Part A: Helios.

This two week period within the prime arrivals center will allow colonists the opportunity to experience ambient conditions firsthand. Extensive gym/cardio-vascular work is to be undertaken, so that individuals can familiarize themselves with the effects of the elevated gravity and alternate atmosphere.

Mild cases of euphoria/dizziness and/or dyspepsia are expected.

More severe cases will be rare. However, such suffers will have the opportunity afforded by the extensive medical center, to assist them in acclimatizing.

Part B: Localized.

(This addendum has been added to enhance safety).

I feel new arrivals will be better served by 'real life' experience in a controlled setting. Therefore, the week taken from phase

1, is to be added here. Once colonists have gained a degree of familiarity with their new environment, they will be expected to put what they have learned into practice within their assigned settlements. This will take place under the watchful eye of our own people initially, and more experienced colonists as numbers increase...'

Yes, that makes much more sense! By pruning a week from the primary module, the safety of the colonists will be improved in the long run. There's no substitute for 'real life' experience, and everyone will benefit from it...

She was interrupted from her musing by a deep, throaty growl from Lucifer, her pet Quincha.

She had rescued him as a cub from the Paladian Sea just four years previously. Although young, he had already developed his perpetually bad temper, and had attempted to tackle a fully grown Grylar. Looking like an unholy alliance between a polar and grizzly bear, Gylars were to be treated with respect. And all the more so by foul tempered feline cubs with a bad attitude.

Fully grown Quinchas were no slouch in a fight either. Appearing like a tiger/cheetah/hyena cross, they were the size of a fully grown male lion. And their size belied their speed, as they could cruse at seventy miles per hour and sprint for short distances in excess of one hundred and ten!

But that was an adult...

Lucifer had been a mere cub.

Because of his temper, Lucifer had attempted to scare a female Grylar away from a carcass she was feasting on down at the Silver Cliffs. Not taking her warning growls as a hint, the sparky little ball of fluff, claws and fangs had stalked right up to the beast and stood toe to toe, challenging her.

The Grylar had put up with his petulant attitude for all of three seconds, before smashing the upstart from her sight with one swipe of her huge paws. Lucifer had sailed over the cliff edge, and plunged two hundred feet into the raging sea below.

Fortunately for him, Naomi had heard his pathetic telepathic bleating just before he succumbed to exhaustion. Bonding to her from that moment on, she was the only one he never showed the slightest inclination toward eating.

Even the Deputy Marshall had to stay on her toes around him!

Lucifer had been asleep, curled up, and filling one of the corners of the room with his considerable bulk. Now, his head was leveled straight at the door and his eyes had the *black eyed stare* of a predator about to pounce.

Skimming his mind, Naomi saw the object of his fixation and giggled. "Now! Now! Lucifer...Down boy! I keep telling you, Grand Master Williams doesn't like to be looked on as food. Or a claw post!"

Lucifer's ears twitched and swiveled toward her, the only sign he had listened to his mistress.

Lucifer! She repeated mentally.

Reluctantly, he lowered his head onto his paws.

A brief rapping came from the door as Ben Williams entered, "Hi Naomi, how's things in the world of the great and mighty?"

Snorting, she gestured to the pile of documents in front of her, and replied, "Oh! Just great! This little lot will ensure I never ruin my skin by too much UV exposure. Talk about house arrest!"

Grinning, Ben subconsciously went to pat Lucifer on the head. The deep, resonating, warning grumble issuing from the corner made him think twice about it. Altering course, he plunked himself down in the chair next to Naomi and said, "How'd you like to help me out on something? *Something* that would get you out of the office!"

Grabbing his face in both hands, she squeezed him and shrieked, "If you could do that...I'd be *eternally* grateful."

Ben felt momentarily embarrassed. He didn't have a lot of experience with women, so to think someone as bright and vivacious as the Adjutant Marshall would be in his debt, was a little overwhelming, to say the least.

Sensing his discomfort, Naomi quickly changed tack. "And to show you how grateful I was...I...I just *might* have to slip you the name of a demure young scientist who thinks you're the best thing since sliced bread was invented."

Suddenly perking up, Ben gasped, "What? Who? Where?"

"Whoa! Slow down big boy! This is priceless information we're talking about here," Naomi teased. "I need to see the goods you're offering are worth what I have to tell you. But to oil the works, I'm talking about someone very quiet and reserved, like yourself. Like you, she's a student of theoretical and quantum physics. And like you, she finds gazing at the stars all night better than food itself!"

"Heaven!" Ben gasped.

Deflating with a sigh, he added, "Where would I find a girl like that, who's interested in me?"

Shrugging, Naomi replied, "Do you know, I appear to have forgotten! What on earth would help me remember?"

"Okay! You win!" Ben exclaimed.

Inching forward, he continued, "I was tasked to implement the latest security upgrades. You know...the ones that were recommended at the meeting you attended at Moon Base last month."

"What? The neutralizing emitters! To prevent snooping by transcended beings?"

"Yes, that's right! We have the prototypes already, and to tell the truth, the actual installation should be quite straightforward."

"So why do you need my help?"

Looking a little embarrassed, Ben replied, "Because they have to be positioned tactically...and I'm totally useless at that type of thing! You know me. Ask me to build a quantum gateway out of a toothpick and the contents of a woman's purse, and I'd beat MacGyver any day! But thinking tactically? The closest I can get to *that* is chess."

Naomi was intrigued. "So what do you need?"

"At the moment, we only have a limited number of prototypes. I've got sixteen orbital platforms to play with in total. Eight targeting scanners and eight emitters. I thought you might like to take a look *upstairs* and personally assess how they could best be deployed."

Naomi's eyes widened. *Upstairs! Off planet! Out of the office...*

...Thank God!

Patting Ben on the knee, Naomi whispered, "Now we're making progress. You've just earned yourself a deal." Solemnly, she projected the identity of a recently arrived Guardian Master, assigned to Shadow operations, directly into his mind.

Ben's eyes popped open in shocked disbelief. "What! She's interested in me? Are you sure?"

"Oh yes, Ben! So sure, I've already selected the dress I'm going to wear at your wedding!

"Anyway, about this visit...upstairs..."

***

At forty-one years old, Angelika Papadakos was still a striking woman. A healthy, active lifestyle and diet had helped her stay young. People looking at her often mistook her age, thinking her to be in her early thirties at most.

But she had to face facts. While she had always been at ease working undercover, this latest task would have been beyond even her, were it not for the upgraded nanobots she carried within her body. Tec that allowed her to modify her appearance into four different profiles!

On this setting, she had opted for simplicity.

Glancing at her reflection in the display cases and she breezed along, Angelika smiled.

Hello you!

A striking young woman, appearing in her early twenties smiled back.

She giggled!

The mirror image reciprocated.

It was as simple a charade as it was elegant. Because it drained less energy from her nexus, Angelika could maintain this representation for over a week before having to rest. It also explained why she was able to stalk the halls of Cambridge University so easily. She blended with her environment perfectly. No one gave her a second glance.

Well, apart from admiring ones from both men and women alike!

And Angelika had made sure to use her obvious allure to make remarkable progress in the two weeks she had been here.

Her target was a young German under graduate, twenty-three year old Annika Pahmeyer, from Dusseldorf. A scientific genius, Annika favored biology and chemistry over the other disciplines. She was also a strong psychic, being blessed with telepathy, and an extremely refined far-sight and healing faculty.

Angelika had discovered that Annika had been attracted to Cambridge because of the university's work on behavioral modification. Evidently, the young woman had lost her own parents to Alzheimer's and Parkinson's just five years previously. However, the debilitating affects those diseases had upon their minds, had eaten her parent away long before their inevitable deaths.

It had left Annika with a very cynical view on life. And a determination to put things right! Although great strides were being made in combating such diseases, Annika didn't feel they were moving fast enough. And her strong gifts, personal experience, and startling insight into the human mind were speeding developments along considerably.

Following her lead, the University was now close to producing their first working prototype of a Docilator, a remarkable piece of nano-engineering that could directly influence cognitive function.

Needless to say, Annika's efforts had come to the attention of the Council.

As such, Angelika had breezed into her life only two weeks ago, and suddenly, Annika found herself with a new dorm-mate. Someone who was rapidly turning into something more!

When they had met for the first time, the bitterness in the girl's heart was all too apparent! Of course, skilled operative that she was, Angelika had seized upon that weakness and shamelessly exploited it. And she didn't feel the slightest remorse at what she was doing.

The Council's objectives were of paramount importance. Their schemes were forging ahead nicely. But, to continue doing so, they needed information. In particular, the knowledge locked away inside the head of Angelika's new boyfriend, Jose.

Being a newly qualified Guardian Inquisitor of considerable strength, they were sure he would have access to certain codes and psi-dent keys that would make their ambitions, so much easier to execute...

...*If* they could just get at them!

The trouble had been gaining that information without suspicion.

Subconsciously, Angelika gritted her teeth in frustration at the mere thought of this latest hurdle. *My problem stems from the fact that he's a highly compulsive individual with a strong self-healing aspect to his psyche. No matter how subtle my methods, I can't seem to break through the firewall that will make him want to share his deepest secrets with me. Bastard!*

Even when he's asleep, or distracted by sex, his mind remains shielded. Aware in some arcane fashion of any attempt to manipulate his thoughts or desires!

Entering her room, Angelika prepared to take a shower.

Thinking back to her earlier efforts to try and get Jose to demonstrate the functioning of one of the latest Wave Reader's, she became frustrated all over again.

If I could just get him to put the damned helmet on, I'd have him! After all, my own capabilities are technologically enhanced now with a highly compulsive element. Last time Esther calibrated them, they were close to Grand Master Class in strength. The additional coercive matrix within the Reader should allow me to crack Jose open like a nut.

But for some reason, Jose had refused play along, muttering instead about his concerns over his new position and status.

Men and their preoccupation with image! Is it a dick thing?

This had posed a problem.

Angelika's natural abilities had also been augmented because of the implant. On the last assessment, her telepathic, remote viewing and energy-draining functions had been measured at High Grand Master Class.

If push comes to shove, I could just kill Jose and take the information I need from his ruined skull. But the backlash doesn't bare thinking about. He IS a Guardian cop after all. Thank goodness there's still time for this alternate plan.

Annika and behavioral modification!

It's taking slightly longer, but, if I'm successful, it will have been worth the wait. The intelligence will benefit the Council as a whole. I'll be able to use what I've learned against Jose, and refine it as I go along. Then, once the niggles have been ironed out, Yeung will no doubt seize the opportunity to saturate the world with behaviorally modified sleeper agents. He'll love having an army at his disposal that won't have a clue they're working for us. Perfect!

Well, it will be, she thought, *if I can get the bloody secrets out of Annika in time.*

Showering, Angelika prepared herself for the young woman's eventual return.

Wiping away the steam that had condensed across the mirror, she looked herself up and down and thought, *one way or another, I'm going to get a result tonight!*

Chapter Seven
Ready or Not

It's always darkest before the dawn!

For some reason, Yeung couldn't get that well known saying out of his head as he watched his co-conspirators prepare for their latest mission. A task that involved the greatest danger they had ever faced since forming their coalition, for they were venturing deep into the heart of enemy territory.

Just thinking about today's venture caused Yeung to breathe more deeply and his heart to beat that little bit faster.

Several weeks had passed while they waited for Angelika to get the information they required at Cambridge. When the result came, only a few days ago, it had been even better than they'd hoped for! Annika Pahmeyer's proposals for the new technology's development were as radical as they were brilliant. She'd even managed to progress the program further than they had anticipated.

Esther had been driven to absolute raptures by the implications.

However, that result had come too late to help them now!

It's going to take at least a few more weeks for Esther to be able to retrograde the Tec, so I can patent it under the auspices of my own companies. And a few more after that to get it ready for Angelika to test on her Guardian boyfriend! No! Ready or not we have to proceed now, without the benefits of the key codes or psi-dents.

For some reason, that filled Yeung with an enduring sense of foreboding.

In an effort to shake off the darkness, he had devised a cunning strategy for the mission and scheduled what he hoped would be a rousing pep-talk.

In honor of the fabled weapon wielded by Neptune, (Psi-edon's namesake in Roman mythology), Yeung had proposed they adopt a three-pronged, or trident attack.

By approaching each of the targets simultaneously, he stressed they would not only spread their enemy's resources, but reduce the chances of a concerted response. In the confusion such an attack would generate, it was hoped they may be afforded opportunities that would not otherwise occur, and which they could turn to their advantage.

His accomplices had responded enthusiastically to that idea!

It had been decided that Simon, as the most powerfully skilled of the three, should attempt the patients residing within the Healers Wing of the Academy. He possessed the greatest finesse when it came to mental dexterity. As such, Simon would be in a better position to trigger the aneurism in each of their former hosts, which would kill them without arousing suspicion.

As the foremost expert on psi-tronic crystals, Esther had been the obvious choice to approach the hyper-gate. The shards energizing the gateway were pieces of the old power source from original Kalliste. And she knew them with an intimacy, bettered only by the Guardian Overlord himself. Although they were housed within a formidable security screen, Esther had assured Yeung, she felt confident of being able to gain access without trouble.

Yeung himself knew all about the extraordinary origins of his accomplices. They had been revealingly honest about their fall from grace and the repercussions their errors had caused. They had also been remarkably frank about one of their greatest concerns!

The Crystal Chamber!

So, while Simon and Esther had vital roles to play in this day's venture, it fell to Harry, the former warrior, to tackle what was felt to be *the* most dangerous phase.

As they had discussed the various options open to them, Simon had related something Yeung had never realized. With a haunted expression on his face, Simon had said...

'*...As Fallen, we are attuned to higher forms of sentient life. Even when interred, our ultrasenses had been left operative. Because of that, we were able to distinguish the expansion of each human into a higher life form every time it occurred over the centuries. Something about the ascension process called to the divine spark still burning within us. It appalled us, for humanity was evolving before our eyes and there was nothing we could do. When we realized the shards of the old crystal were being used to enhance the process, we knew our plans were doomed. For in accelerating mankind's development, it speeded the day of our own demise. When we arrived on this plane, our adversary foretold the ascension of mankind. How you would become a force that would not only rival our glory, but surpass us!*

And now he has an even more powerful crystal. You have seen for yourself the increase taking place in recent years. That potential is not only a threat to us, as Fallen, but to you too, my human friend, for it facilitates the change of insects into beings capable of challenging us. Soon there may be nowhere left to hide...'

Simon's simple admission had made Yeung's blood run cold!

That Chamber and the damned crystal inside it must be destroyed!

Turning to Harry, Yeung had said, "It's up to you to gain the intelligence we need to bring about its eventual destruction, Harry. So, although I can't be there in person with you today, I will nevertheless, play a part. After all, our futures are united now...and success is dependent upon precision."

Addressing the room, Yeung had continued, "Normally, it would be an easy matter for you to mesh minds and coordinate the timing of your attack, so it begins at the exact same moment in each of the three areas. That isn't an option today. Nothing can be allowed to give away your positions, and especially not a stray thought from the binary psi-dents you still possess. So, I have devised a simple solution.

"Today also sees the first test firing of the orbital platforms that now encircle the Earth. As the leading benefactor of that project, I have been invited—along with a number of other dignitaries—aboard one of the Guardian space stations to witness that operation. The exercise will involve the discharge of all one hundred photon cannons. They will be brought online, primed to twenty percent strength, and aimed at targets arranged about the local system. Some of those targets had been positioned past lunar orbit!

"As mental speech might give your positions away, your signal to *go* will be the very first beam to cut across the path of the moon. As that happens, I will ensure to trigger the false identities seeded within one of their remaining families. This will enhance our surprise, because our unsuspecting host's will suddenly find themselves very busy indeed.

"Think about it! Not only will they be providing targets for some very powerful weapons to shoot at, but they will also have to be on guard for any stray discharges that may go amiss. They will be focused, on edge, and keen for everything to go smoothly. Just the time for three of their *most wanted* to suddenly pop up out of the blue. They will react, and react decisively, only to find they've been chasing ghosts. That will unnerve them! Throw them off guard. When will you *ever* have a better time to launch a simultaneous attack?"

Sure enough, Yeung's outlining of his strategy had done the trick! Their moods had improved considerably, and everyone had left the meeting energized and in a more positive frame of mind.

However, that was four hours ago now. Waiting had only ensured the return of Yeung's dark mood. Looking across to his friends, he saw their usually impervious shields were tinged with anxiety and stray thoughts of doubt.

That just won't do...Time for that pep-talk!

***

Simon didn't dare to hope...yet!

His approach, although prolonged, had been surprisingly incident free. Together with Esther and Harry, he had made his slow and painful way to the far side of the sun. Once there, they had masked the transcension process, by blending with the thermonuclear reactions of the star itself.

It had worked like a dream.

Once transformed, they had simply meshed their essences to the billions of tons of energetic matter being thrown out every second, and allowed themselves to be swept towards their targets on the solar winds.

Thus concealed, they had advanced upon the moon.

Because the Hyper-Jump Gate had been positioned above the Guardian Headquarters, Esther had ensured her plasma disguise had flowed toward the northern polar area. Simon and Harry made sure to approach from the opposite end. Their concerns were within the complex, and they had thought of a novel method to breach its defenses.

Through the very moon itself!

Without bidding goodbye to his friends, Simon had allowed the cohesion binding his nexus together to become so diffuse, that it was on the verge of dissolution. He had then sunk down into the surface and began traversing the lunar medium.

It had taken hours, almost as long as the journey from the sun. But it had been well worth it, for he now found himself at the outer barrier.

Allowing his rarified senses to wash across the energy field, he tensed in anticipation, awaiting the dreaded response.

Nothing!

Casting the minutest of queries forward, Simon couldn't believe his luck! The shield was flaring intermittently while repairs or upgrades were being undertaken.

Perfect!

As gently and as guardedly as possible, he cast his net wider. Scanning for the distinctive binary signatures he knew so well, while keeping a careful watch for danger.

There!

That's where they're keeping them! All together?

He thought it a gross display of negligence on the Guardians part to put all their eggs in one basket. But then again, why would they do anything else? They'd had their patients with them for over five years now. Five years! In which time they'd gradually nursed them back to health. By all accounts, there was a possibility of them waking up soon…

Or so they think!

***

Esther had been ultra cautious.

As soon as she was within a hundred miles of the gate complex, she knew exactly where the crystals were. They called to her with an intimacy that made her want to rush to their side and crush them to her bosom.

But of course, she couldn't do that.

Thank goodness they sang on a level few could ever begin to comprehend fully.

Not even the transcended lowlife of this plane would fully understand the connection. Why would they? They were beneath her. Lesser beings, for all their unimaginable power! If they survived the coming cleansing, it would take them an age to even begin to scratch the surface of the intricacies she commanded.

Insects!

Expanding herself beyond anything she'd ever attempted before, Esther had divided her essence. Using the atoms existing within the interplanetary medium, and the Hyper-Gate complex itself, she had been very careful to stay away from the crystals. The temptation to do something would be too great.

That being said, she'd not been idle while she waited for her friends to get into position. In the four hours she had been here, Esther's attention kept being drawn to the subliminal energy field that thrummed across the invisible plane of the stable wormhole before her. Something kept tugging at her mind…

…Something familiar!

Psi-tronic crystals were extremely rare. Although she was an expert in their use, she'd never seen one formed, nor did she know where they came from. Only their nemesis knew that. But what she *did* know for certain was that they contained eighteen, instead of the usual fourteen Bravaias Lattices always found in crystals. Their long range symmetry was so arcane, that they generated a dual polarity field that gave them an inordinate amount of power. A capability that was virtually limitless.

Then Esther remembered something else about polarization!

Somehow, that arrangement could push them through the temporal barriers and into the fourth dimension.

So that should mean...

Cautiously, Esther extended her will and caressed the quantum plane with the most refined probe she could muster. Although it was closed, the grey void blanketing the bridge between worlds rippled to an unseen current.

Snatching her mind back, she almost crowed in triumph. *Something's at the other end! Something important! Something that houses a further set of matching crystals that are anchoring a geodesic tunnel in place!*

So what the hell's is it?

и и и

Muted and invisible, Harry finally allowed himself to coalesce just inside the armored doors leading down to the chamber. He was glad that he had erred on the side of caution. By the time he had walked just a few hundred yards, he could feel a strange elasticity pulling at his consciousness.

It felt as if an unseen hand was reaching into his mind and swirling his psyche round and around. As it flowed past, intangible fingers would then try and pluck abilities from his skull. It was most disconcerting. But he had to remember, this was a natural phenomenon here.

Harry was surrounded on all sides by the unique strata that could only be found in this one location. The crusty black walls of the tunnel appeared fragile, as if they'd be brittle to the touch.

However, that was only an optical illusion, as try as he might, Harry couldn't break any of the protruding flakes free.

He also found he could see where he was going quite clearly. Veins of iridescent orange plasma threaded throughout the rock glowed dimly in the darkness. Those seams vibrated to a regular rhythm, like a heartbeat, hinting at unfathomable energies hidden just out of reach. Each pulse caused the light to glare brighter, and caused a sympathetic throb of power to swell inside his head. It felt to Harry like his scalp would catch fire at any moment.

I wonder what would have happened if I'd try to jump in? Or phased through the rock? Subconsciously he shivered. The picture in his mind was as graphic as it was accurate.

As if I couldn't guess! No wonder they bring their candidates here. It must act as a psychic suppressant until their safely within the chamber itself. Very clever!

Fortunately, he was a warrior. He appreciated this environment would even the field. And he'd brought more than enough toys with him to gain the advantage in a hand to hand fight.

Not that it'll come to that. This place is deserted.

Carrying on for what seemed like an age, Harry eventually rounded a boulder and discovered the tunnel widened out abruptly. He found himself at the edge of an open cave filled with the same pulsing rocks as were in the corridor. In front of him stood a sophisticated robot sentry station, behind which, lay a chasm at least a hundred yards wide. From where he was standing, the gorge stretched off into the distance in either direction.

I bet it's deep too!

Peering across to the far wall, he espied another sentinel, positioned outside a set of impressively armored doors.

Stumped, he retreated to the edge of the tunnel and began to cogitate.

C'mon Harry! Think!

Now…I already have sufficient intelligence to plan for another attempt. What I've learned will be very useful. But that will waste the golden opportunity we have today, to hit them hard from all three sides.

He paused to check through his equipment.

If it comes down to it, I'm sure I could use the disruptor to take out the sentries. The anti-grav belt will get me across the chasm, no problem. But then there are the doors!

He looked at the antimatter crystals dubiously.

Their size belied the strength of the devastation they could unleash. But, he'd still have preferred to detonate all three within the chamber itself, instead of wasting one to get inside.

Of course, if I do that…they'll come running!

Harry looked around the cavern as he tried to select a viable option. Then his gaze returned to the strangely glowing rock face. His face brightened in hope.

Of course! That's just it! They WILL have to run…literally! And while they're sweating their merry way all the way down here, I can set the mines and use the short range matter transmitter to haul my sorry ass outa here! Once they detonate, the crystal will amplify the energies unleashed, and take out a huge chunk of the lunar surface!

He looked at the band around his wrist.

Although this thing will only get me as far as the surface, that won't matter. Pursuing ME will be the last thing on their minds while they're trying to save what's left of their precious base!

Snorting in satisfaction, Harry sat back against the wall.

Now all I have to do is wait for the signal!

He looked at the transport band again.

I hope this damned thing works!

Suddenly, Harry found himself thinking back to another subterranean chamber from long, long ago. One in which his dreams had been shattered and where one of his dearest friends had died!

An evil smile crept crossed his face.

This time, it's going to be MY turn!

Chapter Eight
Trident

Simon Cooper had been waiting patiently for the moment to arrive.

He'd contented himself by silently drifting about the extensive healing faculty and watching the students and staff at work. Although alert for the beacon that would signal the attack, he'd become quite absorbed in several of the classes being conducted here, especially those concerning the manipulation of the mind. It was a subject very dear to his heart!

However, try as he might, he hadn't been able to resist taking a long hard look at his targets. After all, his hosts were making things easy for him!

They had been grouped together within a purpose built ward. Only, this wasn't like any treatment room he'd ever seen before. No beds. No obtrusive equipment that he could discern. Just three patients, spaced equally apart, suspended in midair within a glowing tau-field.

A special kind of lens in the ceiling emitted three beams of light. One fell on each casualty, enveloping their foreheads in a soft scarlet nimbus. The atmosphere created was one of the utmost tranquility. Of course…he'd wanted to take a closer look.

He had stared at his own form for what seemed like an age. Still robust and finely muscled, his body's self-rejuvenating capacity was obviously still working. He missed the benefits his original fleshly coil had brought him with all its strength and vitality.

How easy it would be, he thought, *to just slip back in and let the fool reap the consequences of his own mortality…*

Simon was disturbed from his thoughts by a sudden burst of activity from out in the reception area. Drifting back into the corridor, he noticed someone had turned on a huge view screen above the main desk.

Ah! They're watching the live firing exercise. Excellent! Not long to go then.

He was about to drift toward the group, when three, extremely powerful individuals walked into the lobby. He recognized the adult straight away. It was the one they called the Lord Healer. The two children with her, however, caused him to freeze on the spot!

They were definitely human. That much was clear. But something about their auras was causing his defensive matrix to skitter about in alarm. Adjusting his perspective, he saw why.

Although they could only have been thirteen or fourteen at most, they radiated with overwhelming might. He hadn't witnessed such power in a long, long time. Royal blue and golden bands of scintillating energy coiled around the silver and white core of their nimbuses. Like electric eels on acid, those strands throbbed and pulsed with staggering energy! It appeared as if some monstrous capacity was being restrained within them, and held at bay until the moment was ripe to unleash it, in all its fury.

He had only ever seen auras like that on transcended entities.

But…they're children! Human children!

He was stunned! So much so, he thought he *must* have misread their idents. Scanning more closely, he subconsciously drifted toward them. Too late, Simon realized his error.

The young boy in front of him suddenly stiffened in alarm.

Turning, the child looked back and forth across the room for a few moments, before his gaze fell on the exact spot Simon occupied.

***

She had been taking advantage of the long wait by relaxing.

In her prime location, it was Esther's responsibility to alert everyone of the moment they would act. Soon, the golden beam of energy that would signal the start of the mayhem would cut across the path of the moon. Then people would begin to die.

Smiling within herself, she imagined the confusion that would ensue.

If only I could be there to watch.

The Guardians would be all cozy, safely ensconced within their control rooms. Maneuvering their toys like a swarm of asteroids, they would be keeping a watchful eye out for stray energy beams, and staying alert for any other possible dangers. Then, out of the blue, they'd find them!

Young would activate the microchips hidden among one of the unsuspecting families, and the top three individuals on the Guardians *Most Wanted* list would pop up and say *'hello'*.

She had no doubts the freaks would be onto the signatures like a rash, only to discover their error! The totally bemused family would be traumatized beyond belief. After all, the sight of two of the most powerful Guardians in existence suddenly appearing in front of them, together with an armed execution squad, would be enough to give anyone a heart attack.

In any event, the Council's major opponents would be out of the equation, trying to deflect the ensuing media storm!

Meanwhile, Harry would have detonated his mines.

The combination of antimatter and psi-tronic energy would cause a colossal explosion. Esther was positive that most of the facility would be consumed in the blast and cave-in that would follow. Hopefully, many of their antagonists would also die in that bold move, or be taken out of the picture.

In any event, the margin for error was slim.

That's why Simon had to be quick to act. They couldn't hope the base's destruction would rid them of their former bodies. No! He had to deprive their enemies of the only source from which they might gain further intelligence about them in the future.

And he'd better be quick about it!

If he was successful, it would look as if the disaster had triggered a fatal aneurism that was impossible to treat in time. Shame! She would have *so* loved to get her own figure back. Although it was only a shell, she had worn it for such a long time that she had gotten used to the advantages it had over these *inferior* models.

Turning her attention back to the gateway and its delicious crystal shards, she ruminated once more as to her own options.

What am I going to do?

She was still in two minds.

Smash and grab, or simple explosion?

The inky backdrop suddenly ignited into a frenzied crisscross of lights as the photon cannons opened fire. One blazed a trail very near to her position.

She was just about to send the signal, when a flare of alarm stabbed into her consciousness. Simon's mind was filled with the image of a triangle and he was screaming the word: *THREE!*

Reacting, she triggered the attack and responded: *Watch out! Heads up!*

Turning toward the gate, she thought, *option 'A' it is then!*

***

The vibration against Harry's wrist brought him out of his doze.

Damn! Time already?

A typical warrior, he had been repeatedly running through a number of scenarios in his head, trying to cater for every eventuality and circumstance he might come across.

Of course, the dim lighting, the steady heartbeat of the surrounding rock, and his purely mental efforts had lulled him off to sleep. But he wasn't too bothered. The place was deserted, so he'd only have to remove the obstacle presented by the sentries before unleashing a world of woe on the unsuspecting idiots above.

Standing, Harry primed the disruptor and began creeping forward. He didn't know what security protocols the sentinels were equipped with, so he thought it best to take them out quickly.

It'll probably drain the weapon, but so what? It's not like I'll need it again.

Calmly, he edged into position and took aim.

No sooner had he raised the gun, than a crackling discharge burst forth from the nearest sentry. Arching through the air, it caught the disruptor full on, and sheathed it in a network of living lightning.

Pain overloaded Harry's nerve receptors, and he fell heavily to the floor, stunned.

A concussion punched through the air moments later as the weapon blew apart, and for a moment, all went still.

***

The hairs on the back of Joshua's neck prickled.

What?

Spinning, he turned away from the screens and faced the isolation wards. Although Corrine and Becky seemed oblivious to the danger, Joshua knew better. His intuitive skills were already far more sensitive than just about anyone else's, and especially when something was happening close to him.

As it was now!

"Bex! Corrine…" he began.

Employing his refined senses, Joshua conducted a thorough sweep of the room. Suddenly, his attention was drawn to one section of the lobby just outside Iso-3. Although it appeared nothing was there, he kept getting a huge sense of foreboding every time his astral sight crossed that point.

His anxiety alerted others in the room to a possible threat.

Pointing, Joshua continued, "…there's something…*someone*, over there."

People instantly began fanning out. One or two brandished hidden plasma staffs. Corrine herself advanced forward a few paces and threw up a strong barrier. She too began an aggressive scan.

"I see it!" a voice said.

"Over there! By ward three." said another.

A security klaxon activated, its two-tone warble cutting the air like a knife.

Corrine's mental command brought everyone together: *TO ME!*

Instantly, over a dozen powerful minds meshed in harmonic union, using the Lord Healer as their prime focus.

Joshua added his potential to the matrix, and got a sudden *hit* from his precognitive ability. "He's after the doppelgangers!

Quickly!" His thoughts also revealed the precise spot where the intruder was hovering.

Corrine adjusted the focus of her attack. Splitting the potential in two, she sent out a glittering web of crimson energy toward the area Joshua had highlighted. At the same time, she formed a barrier around the very special patients within the isolation room.

The net descended and began to tighten around an invisible entity. Sadly, only moments later, it fractured into a million pieces. Everyone was treated to a glimpse of a roughly humanoid outline cocooned in scarlet radiance.

It's got to be one of them! Joshua shouted.

Becky's mind blared: *Use the new program! Use the new program! Now!*

There was a pause as Corrine adjusted the harmonics of the mind-meld. In only two seconds, she was ready to go. Instantly, she reinforced the shield around the ward, and created a hard wall in front of her own party. Then they began to advance.

All of them felt a sudden strain. The force field around the casualties in Iso-3 rippled in response to an extremely powerful and sustained attack. The colossal pressure kept mounting, higher and higher...

Corrine employed the new defense.

...And then it was gone. Squelching out of existence like a burst bubble in the wind!

Without pausing, Corrine began to mould a lethal ball of plasma in the air in front of her. Addressing their unknown attacker both mentally and verbally, she said, "As you can see, we now know how to neutralize your cowardly attacks. Please! Just stay where you are for a moment and I'll be glad to give you a taste of your own medicine."

The air shimmered. It looked as if their assailant had attempted to teleport and discovered the hidden countermeasures incorporated around the base.

Smiling, Corrine called out, "Surprised?"

The entity flared in alarm. It began contracting and swelling repeatedly, breaking forth in a myriad of rainbow lights. Its brilliance shifted through the spectrum in ever increasing cycles.

As Corrine brought the potential of her focus to bear, their unknown visitor solidified momentarily, and radiated a blinding light into the room. As the flare died, the entity projected a triangular symbol into the ether, and with a deafening roar, yelled the word, "THREE!"

Moments later, it was gone, evading the new security measures with surprising alacrity.

A pregnant pause followed. Everyone stared at each other in disbelief. Then Corrine began issuing orders. "Sammie, liaise with control. Find out if this was isolated or if it's part of a larger attack. Helen, take your team and check every ward. Make sure patients and staff are all accounted for. Christos, take Marc and Sonia and go through every store, every nook and cranny we have. Make sure no one's lurking where they shouldn't be. Use *this* defensive program, (compressed psychic data), report back to me once…"

Corrine paused as she received mental updates from around the base.

A slight tremor ran through the structure beneath their feet.

"…It would appear we've had *other* uninvited guests!"

Looking toward Becky and Joshua, she sighed, "Let's go check on our patients. Thanks to you two, they're still alive."

***

Blazing plasma beams sizzled across the sky as the test firing sequence began to advance into the next stage of the exercise.

Three? What in hell's name does he mean by...

...Whoa!

Suddenly, Esther became aware of two energy spikes focusing on her exact coordinates. At the same time, she was able to distinguish an almost invisible skein of power swooping down toward her.

Goddamit!

Unleashing a surge of arcane potency, she skipped to the far side of the gate.

Was this a setup all along?

The dazzling chaos about her increased as nearer targets began exploding, blinding in their death throes. Trying to cut out the distraction, Esther concentrated.

She noticed the energy net had condensed around her former position. It had solidified into a coruscating cocoon that would have held her frozen in place. Two beams stabbed out from the gate instillation, searing that area with an unusual form of energy.

It was a trap! But how di...

She felt a tingle as the seeker beacons began to lock onto her once more.

Shit! They've made us! But...

...THREE! THAT'S what he meant!

Abandoning any pretence for stealth, Esther jumped again! Then again, trying to stay ahead of the target locators.

The fuckers have worked out how to spot us. Simon must have...

She aborted her next maneuver at the last second.

A horrendously concussive blast radiated outwards from a point close to where she had intended to teleport. Had she been there, it would have rendered her senseless.

The AI sentinels are anticipating my moves!

Thinking as fast as she could, Esther tried to fathom a solution.

YES!

Forming several jump points at once, Esther began to flow toward them, only to snap back at the last second to phase in the opposite direction. Sure enough, the defensive measures responded, peppering the original vicinity with a multitude of lethal discharges.

Using her telekinesis, Esther morphed her old Emu emitter through her complexus. Taking it, she formed another tau-field, and displayed a clear intention to teleport. As she crossed the plane of dissolution, Esther flung the emitter forwards, and allowed it to be projected along the pathway she had chosen. She followed right behind. However, no sooner had she entered the stream, than she punched through the geodesic medium at a tangent.

Instantly, Esther called forth her new identity, and prepared it for activation.

Her plan worked like a dream.

Emerging above the gateway generators, she watched as a blinding halo of light radiated outwards from the point of a massive explosion. She didn't have time to gloat. Meshing with the familiar signature of the crystal shards, Esther initiated a psi-tronic back surge which blew out the gravity containment field and melted the vacuum shields.

Within moments, the AI measures were locking onto her.

All of them!

Nows the moment of truth...

Holding her ethereal breath, Esther scooped the shards toward her and, using them to amplify her power, began creating a huge teleport nexus.

The batteries locked on.

But nothing happened.

Not wanting to push her luck, Esther completed her preparations.

It worked! They won't fire while I'm meshed to the crystals for fear of the backwash taking out the instillation.

Feeling smug, she threw herself through the event horizon and made her escape, initializing her new tri-dent signature as she went.

Then she remembered!

Oh no!

What about Harry! Would he have heard Simon's warning down there?

***

Shaking his head, Harry fought to clear the avalanche taking place within his mind.

Jesus! That hurt! What the...

Three persons were stood in front of the sentinel.

Oh fuck!

The freaks and...

"I remember you!" Harry gasped, "You were some kind of shaman they discovered on an eastern continent." Wracking his brains, a faded memory struggled to the fore, "Aniless? Anilese Surinesh? Or something like that wasn't it?"

"Just Anil will do," replied a very, very furious man, "Although *you* get to call me, Lord Marshall! As you're well aware, it's a title I was forced to inherit after the last holder–a very dear friend of mine, by the way–was murdered by a bunch of cowardly scumbags."

Edging backwards, Harry's fingers began to creep toward his teleport band. "Well, it's been nice talking to you. Sorry if I've got to…"

As Harry slammed his palm against the activation button, Victoria made the barest of gestures. Instantly, the bracelet about Harry's wrist began to spark and fizz as a powerful coil of astral lightning played across its surface.

The telltale hum of an overload in progress gave him the scant opportunity he needed to wrest it from his arm and fling it into the chasm. Moments later, it exploded.

Harry was shocked. "How the…I thought this place muted…"

"Don't leave just yet," Victoria cut in, "We've got such a lot of catching up to do."

Turning on his heels, Harry sprinted for the corridor.

He'd only managed to take half a dozen steps before he was unceremoniously yanked backwards by an invisible grip to his throat and mercilessly slammed into the floor before Andrew's feet.

Winded and gasping for breath, Harry looked up.

Andrew stooped down beside him. Grabbing a fistful of clothing, he lifted Harry into the air and easily held him off the floor. Eyes as black as death, Andrew murmured, "As you've correctly surmised, we *freaks* no longer seem to be affected by the unusual geology of this place. Good news for us. Bad news for you!"

Harry refused to cower. "So, what are you…"

He was silenced by a vicious punch to the face that instantly broke his nose and sent him spinning backwards through the air. Landing heavily, Harry was aware Andrew was upon him in an instant, and dragging him back toward the robot sentry.

Throwing him to the floor in front of Anil and Victoria, Andrew growled, "You're probably wondering if I'm going to kill you now?"

Spitting out blood, Harry raised himself up slightly and slowly looked from face to face. He found no mercy in their eyes.

"Well, *I* won't be." Andrew continued. Nodding toward Anil, he added, "*He* will!"

Anil removed a blackened plasma staff from within a fold of his robes. A gentler, softer glint entered his eyes for the briefest moment as his gaze wandered up and down the scorched metal of the weapon.

Intuitively, Harry guessed who that staff had belonged to. Surprisingly, he chuckled.

"Is something amusing you?" Anil asked, hatred returning to his face once more.

Snorting, Harry replied, "You forget what I am…human. *That* may inflict damage on this mortal frame, but it will be unable to destroy my divine essence."

Anil looked puzzled.

Andrew was quick to intercede. "Ah! My dear unfortunate friend! What you are failing to take into account are the unique harmonics of this place."

Gesturing around them, Andrew emphasized, "We haven't quite fathomed out why, yet! But in *this* place, unless you possess the puissance of a primary echelon entity, you're screwed! Something about the way the atomic structure of the rocks combine with the solar resonance mitigates the essences of both divine and transcended natures…unless you're a freak like Victoria and I of course."

Harry's face turned white. Spitting out another mouthful of blood, he got slowly to his feet. "So I *can* die here eh? At least I won't be alone…"

Deftly, Harry activated all three of the antimatter gems on his belt.

Before anyone else could react, Andrew made a scooping motion with his hands. Instantly, the mines were transmuted through the air and into his grasp. As Andrew sheathed himself in astral flame, the crystals exploded.

White light blinded them, and the ground heaved in response to the colossal detonation. Harry and Anil were thrown to the floor. Rocks and dust, dislodged by the pressure wave, fell from high above, only to bounce off an invisible shield.

As the light receded, they all caught a momentary glimpse of an angelic apparition nearly twelve feet high, hovering before them. Then it was gone.

Andrew remained, untouched and unblemished. His eyes had become wells of midnight. He gestured, and Harry flew into his outstretched hand like a magnetized lump of metal. Slamming into the terrible grip, Harry writhed in agony as Andrew began pouring an arcane amount of energy into him.

Harry screamed! His spine on the verge of shattering.

Drawing him closer, Andrew hissed, "Father always said you were a coward."

Glancing toward Anil, Andrew commanded, "Do it!"

A thrumming sound was heard at the same moment a glaring arc of royal blue light cut through the air. A brief hiss announced the moment that blade bit into flesh. A dull thud followed as the head hit the floor. Its eyes were still wide open in shock from the moment of death.

Andrew maintained his grip on the torso as he imbued its titanic strength and essence. He continued draining it utterly, until the remains crumbled to ash.

Looking at her brother, Victoria noticed his complexus had swollen. Addressing him on his intimate mode, she said: *Andy, are you okay? You look…you FEEL…different.*

Smiling, Andrew took a moment to assess himself: *Hmm! It was…IT IS…strangely enlightening.*

What do you mean? Was the process successful?

Oh yes! And then some! Look, Vic, we can't really discuss it…here. Do you mind if I tell you about it later?

Victoria didn't miss the hint toward their present company. *No problems! I've got a feeling I'm gonna love what you have to say.*

They broke contact, only to discover they hadn't been as discreet as they'd thought.

Anil was staring at them both, casually tossing Earl Foster's old plasma baton over and over in his hand. His sharp mind hadn't missed a thing! Eventually, he took a deep breath, and sighed, "I don't suppose you'd care to enlighten me, would you, on certain references that scumbag alluded to before his death?"

The twins remained silent.

Anil continued, "In particular, I'm keen to understand what he meant by the words, *divine, freak,* and *father.* Oh, and not forgetting, *primary echelon* of course. As you can imagine, I've got my suspicions…but I'd love to hear it from *your* lips."

When Andrew and Victoria continued to stare mutely back for a few minutes longer, he sheathed the baton, and walked up to them.

Looking them both in the eye, he whispered, "You should know, I'm not going to let this go. My door is always open. Feel free to drop by for a chat…when you're ready."

Chapter Nine
Aftermath

As a VIP, Lei Yeung had been invited onto the command deck aboard Guardian Observation Station 2, to enjoy a birds-eye view of the orbital defense trials.

When they had gotten underway, he had ensured to carefully watch out for the first of the salvos to be aimed at targets close to, and beyond the lunar orbit. Having successfully initiated the false psi-dents, Yeung then relaxed, confident in both his planning of the operation and the team's ability to execute their individual roles.

However, having worked very closely with those special individuals over the years, some form of bond had obviously been forged between them. He hadn't been aware how strong that link was, until an overwhelming *absence* suddenly filled his mind.

What the hell? Someone's gone!

Yeung wasn't quite sure who, but he knew without a shred of a doubt that one of his Fallen friends was unaccounted for.

Are they hiding? Using the warped physics of the moon rock to block their presence from pursuers? Have they teleported through the escape pods they prepared in advance? Jumping so far out, that they're now beyond the range of scans? Are they stuck somewhere? Hidden, cloaked, and waiting for the opportunity to flee?

Yeung couldn't say for sure. He only knew for certain that a cold knot of dread was clawing its way along his spine. With growing trepidation, he returned home and put his vast intelligence network into action.

The first indicator that something may have gone terribly wrong had come from a surprising source. Angelika!

Not three hours ago, she had contacted Yeung to ask if anything unusual was *occurring*.

When questioned *why* she was asking, Angelika had informed him of the fact that her Inquisitor boyfriend, Jose Calderon, had suddenly been recalled to duty. Evidently, he'd mentioned he was required to assist with *an attempt* against the Moon Base and one of its orbiting facilities. Angelika hadn't been able to gain any further information from Jose before he'd left, but she had been alarmed to sense an overwhelming *impression* of victory or success emanating from his mind.

Victory or success over what? Yeung had thought. *Oh God! I hope it's not linked!*

Soon after that, Yeung had received a rather intriguing communiqué from one of his Apostles in China, Chang Xi.

Xi had revealed that a European family, holidaying in the area, had been the focus of a great deal of media attention at China's Great Wall. Apparently, they had been in one of the attraction's cafeterias, when an armed squad of Guardians had arrived. The team had surrounded that family, and—much to everyone's alarm—had stunned them! Once unconscious, each member was subjected to some form of intrusive examination.

Whatever it was the Guardians were looking for wasn't revealed. In any event, they didn't find it. After apologizing profusely to the outraged family and promising that someone from the Concilliator's office would be in touch, they had left empty handed.

Videos of that incident were already circulating on various social networking sites, and Xi had included several of them for Yeung to look at.

When Yeung had pressed for details, he discovered there was more to the story than originally met the eye.

By now, the Lord Inquisitor and the Shadow Lord had gained something of a celebrity status. Although they shunned the limelight, it had become common knowledge that they were among the most powerful Guardians in existence. When Yeung had sought clarification as to the descriptions and ranks of the Inquisitors attending the Great Wall, it was clear neither of them had been there. Indeed, by looking at some of recordings Xi had provided of that incident, Yeung was able to confirm this was, in fact, true!

That had set alarm bells ringing in his mind!

So why didn't they feel the need to respond on this occasion? I don't like this!

He was still mulling that point over a few hours later, when Angelika called again.

"Lei, I know it's not my area, but do we have any candidates lined up for a special project with the Guardians in the near future? Something that might involve them going off world?"

Yeung was forced to think for a moment before replying. He had been very cautious in his dealing with the Guardians in recent years. Anyone involved in joint *special* projects, were initially squeaky clean. He'd been careful to include only a handful of sleeper agents across the board. All highly trained, and loaded with nano-technology to both enhance their capabilities and render them impervious to scanning.

Eventually, he'd recalled something earmarked for the future.

"We do have a contingency now you mention it, Angelika. Nothing solid at this stage! Just a list of specialists' in botany, zoology and certain life sciences who may be called upon to form a shortlist of candidates. They haven't revealed what they'll be required for, yet.

"Why do you ask?"

"I'm not sure. But Jose got back a few minutes ago, and *then* had to go straight to his command center at Mato Grosso. Before he left, he muttered something about, and I quote,

… The damage to the hyper-gate will delay the off-world project by at least a month while they refocus the new generating anchors'…

As soon as I heard those terms, I thought I'd better let you know."

Puzzled, Yeung deliberated for a moment, *Is there a connection, perhaps?*

Out loud he replied, "Thank you, Angelika. I'll look into that.

"By the way, your boyfriend sounds as if he's becoming a font of knowledge? Getting along well, are you?"

"Oh, we are, Lei, believe me," she'd replied, chuckling. "Esther's been showing me how I can recalibrate the Docilator to stimulate different emotions. I think I'm starting to strike the right balance. He's been very keen to *share* lately."

"Excellent work! Keep it up. I've got a feeling we may need his…insights more often in the future."

Ending the call, Yeung had then sat back to try and make sense out of what he had learned so far. The pieces of the jigsaw lay before him. Now all he had to do was fit them together while he waited for what was left of the team to get back.

***

Yeung was appalled. He'd never seen his associates so unsettled before.

Initially, he had breathed a huge sigh of relief when, just fifteen minutes ago, Simon had at last made his appearance. However, that relief quickly turned to concern, because since then, his friend had continued sitting there without moving. Ashen faced, silent and unresponsive.

Esther had followed him in only five minutes later. She too had turned to stone, a look of shocked disbelief on her face.

Yeung had fussed about like a mother hen at first, offering them refreshments, trying to get them comfy. But through it all, they had remained completely mute.

Finally, Yeung reached the end of his patience. *This is taking too long! There's too much I need to know.*

"ENOUGH!"He roared, stamping his foot at the same time.

Simon and Esther both jumped.

"For goodness sake, snap out of it! Something has obviously happened to Harry. Are you going to tell me what it is, so we can *do* something about it?"

Esther was the first to respond. Turning crimson, her temper flared. Rising, she flew forward and began, "How dare yo…"

"HOW DARE I?" Yeung cut in, shouting loudly.

Marching up to her, he went nose to nose, "I dare, young lady, because *you* are obviously forgetting something… for all your power and antiquity! You ought to be ashamed!"

His boldness took the wind right out of her sails.

Jabbing her in the chest, Yeung continued, "I only knew Harry for five years. Five, short, human, years! That's nothing compared to you. But *I'm* going to do something about this…this, *whatever* it is, to honor his memory. We are clearly at war. And like it or not, there are always casualties in war. *Always!* Or don't you think the rules apply to you?"

As Simon came to stand beside her, Esther managed to clamp her jaws shut. Shaking from barely restrained grief, she continued flexing and clenching her fists for a few moments until Simon grasped her firmly by the shoulders and began to steer her back toward the couch.

Yeung followed them.

They all sat, and in a calmer voice, Yeung said, "Right! Tell me, what the hell happened to you out there?"

Esther ignored him. Glancing toward Simon, she gasped, "Did you feel it?"

Tapping his heart, Simon nodded. "I felt it clearly. In here! The moment he...Even though he was obviously still inside that...it...

More gently, Yeung repeated, "Simon. What happened?"

"It was all going to plan," Simon replied, eyes vacant, "I was right in the ward, waiting for the signal to start. Then those damned children walked in."

"Children?"

"Yes, children. Teenagers. They…they were unlike anything I've ever seen before!"

Yeung was confused. "What? Like the freaks?"

"No, no, no, nothing like them! These kids were fully human. Just not in a way I've ever witnessed…"

Pausing, Simon projected an image of two psychic complexi into the air between them. "…I mean, look at them! They shouldn't still be capable of retaining their corporeal forms. But they are."

They all looked in astonishment upon the monstrous capability each child possessed. A potential that contradicted the fragile flesh in which they were housed!

Yeung had been doing his homework on such things. But what he saw confused him. Leaning toward Esther, he whispered,

"Esther, you're the expert. Am I reading this right? It looks to me as if these youngsters should have transcended by now, yes?"

"Yes, you're quite correct." She replied, lost in the mesmerizing vision before them.

"Can you enlarge the image?" Yeung continued. Gesturing, he added, "In particular, these quadrants, here, here, and…there?"

Esther did so. As the portions expanded, the brilliance of the cerebral tapestry threatened to overwhelm them. Suddenly, Esther gasped!

"What?" The men asked in unison.

Pointing to the areas under scrutiny, Esther replied, "Yeung, were you indicating those sites there? The ones that appear to have something that looks like a cluster of miniature black holes positioned at the junctures of the major power bands with the silver chords?"

"Yes I was. I'm no specialist, but they don't look natural to me like the rest of their matrix does. I was wondering what function those black spots would serve?"

"Nothing that I know of! Hang on…"

Leaning closer, Esther added, "…Although I can see they appear to mitigate the flow of transcendent energy in some way. I'd have to make a closer study, but…I wonder?"

Turning to Simon, she asked, "Tell me. Did they sense you before you had a chance to kill your targets?"

Cutting the projection, Simon replied, "Yes they bloody well did! Why?"

"Well, I'm not sure…but I've got a sneaking suspicion we're looking at some form of advance Mitigator program. Somehow, it's delaying their ascension, but allowing them to access their superior functions."

Simon appeared horrified. "But why on earth would they do that?"

"I've no idea. I can only surmise that they don't want ascended juveniles running around. Perhaps it's something that holds off their transformation until they're mature? Whatever the reason, those kids have some of the most powerful attributes I've ever seen."

Snorting, Simon replied, "Tell me about it! My screens were at maximum and my resolution was at its most refined. With the enhancements we've made, I should have been indistinguishable from the surrounding environment. And yet, the boy in particular, zeroed in on me as if I was standing there smothered in luminous paint and standing under black lighting! No sooner had he pinged my location, than he also fathomed exactly *why* I was there. Imagine my deep joy when I then discovered they were able to counter my initial efforts to zap both them, and our three friends! They were on the verge of capturing me until I thought to dump my psi-dent and initialize the new tri-nary one."

"I knew it!" Esther spat. Punching Simon in the arm, she shook her head in gratitude. "You saved my ass up there! *That's* why you projected the triangle and the word *three*, isn't it?"

"Yes! They'd obviously developed some form of enhancements to neutralize us, so I tried to think of a warning only *we* would understand. One that would counter them! Why?"

"Hell! That was close. You wouldn't know this, but you were discovered only seconds before I gave the signal to go. In those few seconds, they'd obviously broadcast some form of alert and almost netted me alive. Well, netted me alive, just so they could roast me to death where I hung. Bastards!"

Yeung cut in on the conversation. "So, because of his proximity to the Crystal Chamber, Harry would have been unaware of this? There's no way a psychic signal would have gotten through? And Esther couldn't update him of anything through the teleport band?"

"That's right," Simon replied, "Why do you ask?"

Yeung then told them about the false psi-dent incident at the Great Wall in China.

Concluding, he said, "This confirms my suspicions. Firstly, they appear to have developed something that mitigates your special enhancements. That's why they felt it was safe to dispatch an Inquisitor Team without the twins being present.

"Bearing that in mind, I feel confident in expressing my second misgiving. I strongly suspect the twins were there to intercept Harry. That's why he died!"

Simon appeared unconvinced, "How can you be so sure?"

"Just putting two and two together. Listen! We know that area acts as a dampening field in relation to psychic abilities, yes? That's why they take transcension candidates there. The special geological conditions reduce the risk of catastrophic danger should an aspirant go novae. So, if Harry had been intercepted by just anyone, well, his chances of getting away would have been high. Put yourself in his position...

"...You're a trained warrior. You're armed. You're equipped with the latest Tec to help you do your job in an environment that mutes psychic ability. That equipment will also aid you in getting away. So! Why did *you* die when the odds were all in your favor?"

Esther's eyes almost popped as the sudden realization hit her. "Because someone was there who was capable of stopping me! Someone, with the ability to nullify both my training and experience! Someone, who could not only counter my superior strength, but the advantages my equipment, gave me as well!"

"*Someone*," Yeung added, "Who obviously wasn't hampered by the dampening field like you or I or just about any other transcended being we know of, would be! C'mon, who do *you* know of who might have the capability to function within that kind of environment? I can only guess at three."

Simon and Esther stared at each other, aghast.

Simon muttered to himself, "I've underestimate him often enough in the past. But I've got no doubt he'd easily be able to work his diabolical schemes in there. He was Primary Echelon for goodness sake, third only to the Source and the First. But we've had no sighting of him for months. So that only leaves the…"

"The twins!" Esther interjected, finishing his sentence for him. "Shit! What are we going to do?"

Suddenly standing, Yeung announced, "Do? What are we going to do? Why, my dear lady, we're going to strike back! We're going to hit them where it hurts. And what's more, we're going to do it when they least expect it.

"They think we'll be licking our wounds. Well, we can do *that* at the same time we're making them pay, dearly, for their affront. Interested?"

"Of course we are," Simon replied, "But how do you propose we even begin to start?"

"Well, if you're asking my opinion, I'd probably start with those!"

Pointing to a long cylindrical tube laying beside Esther, Yeung continued, "From the emanations coming from within that package, I can guess what's inside. Am I correct in assuming those are the shards?"

Glancing beside her, Esther replied, "Yes, they are. You have to be careful what stimulus you expose them to. Otherwise you could end up vaporizing a small town."

"What? They could do that? Just those two pieces!"

"Yes, that's why I was so long getting back. I had to ensure they were encased within a gravity conduit. Although *I've* built up an affinity to them, others won't share that bond. They have to remain isolated from outside stimulation. Otherwise they could absorb it, amplify it, and release it as undirected energy."

Sitting beside Esther, Yeung said. "May I ask? What did you use the original crystal for?"

"It was mostly used as an energy reserve, for both arcane and mundane power. We'd all regularly contribute, and then use its potential to assist us in performing terra-forming operations, or atmosphere and weather modifications. It can also absorb the effects of earthquakes, hurricanes and thunderstorms and so on…"

"And don't forget the Monolith Gates," Simon cut in, "Or the shields!"

"…Oh yes," Esther replied, "The original crystal was configured to automatically maintain the shields around the entire island. We'd positioned the capital above an active volcano and the site of the convergence of three tectonic plates. It provided a constant source of energy for the crystal you see, and allowed us to modify the flora and fauna throughout the region. As Simon said, it also allowed us to power the Monolith Gates."

"Monolith Gates? What were they?" Yeung asked, fascinated by his glimpse into the real past of Earth's long hidden history.

"You'd call them teleport gates, a much smaller version of that hyper-gate up in lunar orbit. It allowed our subjects virtually instantaneous travel between all the major cities of the

Protectorate." Esther's face momentarily brightened. She added, "I designed them actually. They were one of my more…pleasing efforts!"

Yeung appeared fit to burst. He beamed, "Well there you go! I think I know how we can proceed. Tell me Esther. Can you tinker with these pieces safely?"

"I should be able to. Once I've rearranged the lab. Why?"

"I'd like to put your former tools to use if I may?"

When Esther didn't reply immediately, Yeung continued, "You won't be aware of this, but while I was awaiting your return, I had a very interesting chat with Angelika. She's been fine tuning the Docilator to get better results out of her current *assignment*, Jose Calderon. I'll have you know, you caused quite a panic, blowing out the Hyper-Gate generators. How did she say Jose put it, *'the damage to the hyper-gate will delay the off-world project by at least a month while they refocus the new generating anchors'*. Can I ask you, when the Guardian was referring to *the anchors*, I take it he meant those crystals?"

"Yes he did," Esther replied. "These shards were positioned at one end of a geodesic pathway, and their corresponding twins would have been placed at the other end. The mated harmonics counter the effects of galactic drift by keeping the two materialization points locked onto each other. Without these ones anchoring the gate this end, they'll have to replace the entire system. Why?"

"I was just thinking ahead. Would I be right in assuming that a teleport band powered by a fleck of one of those crystals would be far more powerful and effective than the ones we currently use?"

"Yes they would."

"And would you have to use much of the shard to do that? Say, for a dozen or so bands."

Esther thought for a moment, before replying, "If I cut carefully, I imagine I'd only need to use about one quarter of a single piece. That would give a band sufficient strength to teleport the wearer around the Earth a number of times before it would need to be recharged."

Yeung's eyes narrowed as he worked things through in his head. "May I offer a new set of proposals, ones that will advance our cause as they help us to strike back?"

Simon and Esther moved forwards on their seats. "Please do!" they said.

Yeung began, "Simon. Esther. I suggest we formulate a fresh Trident Strategy. Our new line of attack will involve three major steps against three major targets.

"Phase one will now be concentrated on the Hyper-Jump Gate. From what you tell me, the crystals powering that system have to be replaced. This will afford us an excellent opportunity to do two things. One! Gain intelligence as to what lies on the far side of the hyper-tunnel. And two! Gain possession of the old crystal shards from the other end.

"We don't have to rush with this stage. Part of my conversation with Angelika revealed that the Guardians plan some form of joint operation with civilian scientists in the near future. Whatever the specifics are, they will involve zoologists, botanists, and certain life science experts and..."

"Colonization!" Simon said flatly. "It can't be anything else. Part of Adam's original grand plan involved seeding humanity throughout the stars. I'll bet my balls they've already found a suitable planet."

"I agree with your assessment," Yeung replied, "I was looking over the list of the candidates the Lord Marshall's office had me compile, while awaiting your return. Needless to say, in view of our current…*strategy*, I'll be making several adjustments to ensure the right people are in the right place to seize any opportunities that come our way. They will form a nucleus of our phase two operations. Whatever *is* on the other side, I want in on it! I'm hoping both of *you* will also put yourselves forward. You're both respected scientists. You're psychic. And as far as the world is concerned, you're squeaky clean and work for Yeung Technologies. Just imagine the hassle we can avoid by having you *invited* there, as opposed to having to sneak through!"

Despite their heavy hearts, both Simon and Esther couldn't help but smile at Yeung's audacity.

In keeping with their mood, he added, "Actually, I'm trying to get myself on the list too! I know it's cheeky, but after all. My staff will provide the bulk of the initial teams sent there—wherever *there* is—and I'm sure they'll extend me the courtesy of a little tour at least!"

Everyone burst out laughing!

Yeung concluded, "I'm glad you're getting in the spirit of things, because we need to forge ahead and prepare phase three, now. Our original goal will continue as planned against Los Angeles. All data has now been collated, and we can put the final stages of that idea into operation with one additional bonus. The antimatter mines can now be upgraded with any surplus flecks left over from Esther's upgrades to the teleport bands. The additional energy that will add to the blasts is sure to break the spine of the entire fault line.

"Once again, the Guardians will be exposed as unable to save those they profess to serve. Only *this* time, the casualty rate will be far, far higher…especially with the distraction we have planned across in Somalia."

Yeung could taste solidarity of purpose suddenly manifesting within the room. Walking across to stand in front of his friends, he placed a hand on each of their shoulders. Quietly, he said, "Never forget. We *are* at war! They bit us in the ass today, and we were forced to take casualties. But we didn't just lie there waiting to be finished off. No! We've regrouped, devised a new strategy, and we'll come back even stronger than before.

"Just imagine their horror as LA goes sliding into the sea. It won't be anywhere near as grand as the huge slide *they'll* take in the popularity polls, I can tell you. And of course, if we plan things well…we won't just be screwing things up for them on one planet, will we? There's a whole new world out there for us to manipulate!"

Yeung sauntered across to his private bar to pour some celebratory champagne. As he returned—drinks in hand—he could see both Simon and Esther were deep in animated, mental conversation. Intrigued, he said, "More ideas to bring to the table?"

They turned to him, and Simon said, "Actually…yes! We've been here so long now that…well. We sometimes forget that not all of us came to Earth."

Yeung nearly knocked the drinks over as he placed them on the table. "What? What do you mean by *all* of you?"

"Us! The Fallen. Not everyone agreed or had the stomach to begin such a vast undertaking. We've been so wrapped up by what happened leading up to the rebellion on Kalliste that we've failed to consider the others like us."

"How many *others* are we talking about?"

Simon and Esther looked toward each other again. Mental images began flashing back and forth. A few minutes later, Simon nodded and replied, "We think there might be up to a dozen Lower Echelon members, and one or two Median entities still out there who'd respond to the call. They didn't wish to join us at the time. But that was because of certain leadership and policy issues. Now…who knows?"

Yeung was stunned at the implications.

Tentatively, he said, "And would they answer your call? Could you even reach them?"

"I haven't got a clue," Simon replied, shrugging. "Space is so incredibly vast, that they could be scattered far beyond our ability to reach. But it's got to be worth a try."

Chapter Ten
I Remember Now

Do you appreciate now, why I roused you from you slumber? Gaia-le'el asked, profound hope and sorrow emanating in equal measure from her essence.

She continued: *This is the third such system I have nurtured within this reality. Although I do concede, it is the furthest out from the point of Original Causality.*

Aslan-di'el looked on in wonder, his mind ranging back and forth along the esoteric strands. As he examined the structure of her creation, he easily managed to coax a million eager responses from among the blaze of life forms burgeoning below him.

Eventually tiring of play, he sighed: *It is a truly rewarding feat, Sister. You have managed to foment a matrix conducive to harmony in all its fragile nuances. But if what you say is true, then its very nature may be in jeopardy!*

It IS my Brother. I'm sure of it!

Pausing, Gaia-le'el replayed the incident through again in their minds, allowing Aslan-di'el to gauge the strength and scope of the visitor. She said: *When I first encountered him traversing the mundane medium of hyper-space, I must admit, I was misled. His essence burned with such fearful intensity, I felt sure it was Sachael-Za-Ad'hem himself come to pay his respects at long last! But I felt unworthy. Unfit to darken his grace with my depleted condition. So I led him here, thinking to show him the results of my latest efforts. Hoping to prove my hands have not been idle!*

But it wasn't him?

Alas, no! She opened her mind wider and allowed her companion to savor the precise signature of the entity: *Can you see why I was mistaken? His whal is so similar he can only be a product OF Sachael-Za-Ad'hem himself. But that is a contradiction! Such a thing was never envisaged. Nor should it be possible. He represents a huge risk!*

And yet…he exists. AND he displays a puissance reminiscent of his father, Stated Aslan-di'el with the obvious logic that made him so annoying sometimes.

However, before his sister's mood darkened, he added: *Though I can appreciate why you hid yourself within fold space. You were surprised. However, I sense no malice within this entity. Look how the strings responded to his skilled caress. Taste the love and camaraderie of his invitation toward the life forms he had so newly met. Revel in their eager response toward him.*

Gaia-le'el still radiated uncertainty.

Aslan-di'el concluded: *And don't forget, Sister. Your sensory replay reveals some very positive aspects about his nature too. When he discovered the geodesic tau system, he maintained a respectful distance. He also ruminated loudly as to his concerns for this gift. He obviously seeks to protect and nurture…while those in his care reach out to the stars to fulfill their destiny, as his mighty father envisaged.*

Reluctantly, Gaia-le'el admitted: *Yes! I remember now. I've been alone so long! I sometimes forget that events would unfold about me, whether or not I partook. You don't really think that time's upon us already do you?*

A feeling of warm fellowship flooded her system.

Aslan-di'el replied: *The time? No, I doubt that. As mighty as Sachael-Za-Ad'hem was, not even he could bring about such a maturation so quickly. However, I do think we may be at the dawning of a new age. Unification may be approaching faster than any of us ever imagined.*

Or thought possible! Gaia-le'el quietly added.

Turning fully to her closest friend, she asked: *Aslan, are any of the others actually coming to commune with us this day?*

I hope so, Gaia. I hope so. Jophiel, Ocean, and Yao-teth have lived in seclusion for so long now, that they've almost succumbed to eternal petrifaction. They comprehended the call. Whether they heed it or not will be another thing.

And what of Olinda, and Gazad-riel?

Ah! Now THEY were keen to see the results of your handiwork. They still love the wonder of discovering new things. I was hoping they would have been here by now. Shall we travel the network together to ascertain their whereabouts?

Accepting the invitation, Gaia-le'el followed Aslan-di'el across the threshold, eagerness saturating her psyche for the first time in a millennium.

***

Do you see what I mean Vic? Andrew Gushed: *Isn't it wonderful? The sheer scope of the work being undertaken here is breathtaking! Out of this world! Pun intended! It's…*

Magnificent! Victoria's mind cut in: *THIS is something to commit to! And truly lose yourself in.*

I know! If we didn't have to deal with all that crap back home, I could easily come here and just drift along the filaments generated by the nurturing matrix and…and…well. Just drink it all in…

…Listen to this! Melding with his sister, Andrew sent out a fair-spoken invitation of welcome. Within moments, the essences of millions of sentient life forms washed over them, rushing out in their eagerness to say hello and enquire who the new shining star-minds were. Tellingly, interspaced within those responses were alarmingly coherent queries from more evolved entities whose souls registered heightened perceptions.

They recognize me! Andrew exclaimed. *I only touched them briefly on my last visit. And yet they've remembered my signature!*

So why aren't they hiding? Victoria teased: *Poor things probably thought they'd had a lucky escape last time. And now you're traumatizing them all over again.*

Victoria's attempt to wind her brother up was wasted. He was lost to the obvious delights before him. She thought, *damn! He's getting more and more like father every day!*

Sending a flare of static energy along the filaments of her brother's complexus, she complained: *Hey! Mr. Boring! If you can't be bothered to play along with your sister anymore, I'm gonna start thinking you don't love me!*

Sincere and intimate affection washed over her. Andrew replied: *Ah! Is my widdle sister getting all insecure? Of course I wuv you! I'm your brother, and sadly, it's my job! I don't want to, but as you know it's part of the burden I bear. A particularly heavy one in my case, because you're an immortal wuss! Capable of plaguing my happiness for all eternity!*

THAT's more like it! Victoria thought. Mentally, she continued: *Thank god I won't have to seek a legal separation from you just yet then. But I will you know, AND I'll want custody of the X-Box!*

Noooo! Andrew screamed in mock horror.

They both erupted into a fit of giggles. Suddenly, Andrew started, and said: *Hey! I almost forgot. Do you want to see something else just as impressive?*

Seriously! As impressive as this?

Oh yeah! Altering the subspace medium, Andrew began peeling back the fabric of reality to expose the quantum travel network cunningly arrayed about them: *What do you think of that?*

Victoria was too stunned to utter a single thought.

Andrew could sense his sister was already employing the strengths of her alpha ability, and was ranging for light years in all directions. Assessing, scrutinizing, measuring and determining the scope of the construct before her.

Eventually, she thought: *Andrew, this is extremely sophisticated and complex. Who the hell constructed it?*

Damned if I know Vic! Seriously! But whoever it was, displayed a refinement and level of understanding I've only ever glimpsed within…

They were interrupted by a power spike of unimaginable proportions.

Abruptly, a fourteen foot angelic apparition materialized before them, shining with luminosity so bright that it threatened to counter the star at the center of the system.

Father! They cried.

Glad you could join us! Andrew said. Extending an ethereal hand toward the delights below them, he crowed: *Do you see what I mean? I'd like to have said I found it all by myself. But that couldn't be further from the truth.*

Adam scanned the system from end to end in moments, fully comprehending the extent and capacity of the machinations arrayed before him. It rang with a familiarity that lifted his heart, as it made him sigh with relief.

Andrew continued: *That's why I called you. THIS is a significant discovery. It would be a marvelous aide to the outworking of our long-term strategy. But it's just too important to squander by rash decisions hastily made. We need your input.*

A smile crept over the mental façade of the titan before them.

Yes! I remember now. Well done. VERY well done! You've discovered something more important than you realize and…

Without warning, Adam detected the minutest of probe's washing across them. So sophisticated, so delicately attuned to an ancient and long-disused mental signature, he almost missed it.

...Andrew. Victoria. May I ask for your forbearance? I'll explain later why this discovery is so vital, but first, I need to reacquaint myself with some old...friends.

Comprehension flared throughout Andrew's aura. Somehow, he had also picked up an undercurrent nearby. Turning to his sister, he quickly opened a gateway and said: *C'mon Vic! I'll help you excise the new fragments from the crystal. We might as well get it over and done with. The sooner we get the Kalliste project back on-line, the better. I'll update you about...all this...on the way!*

Victoria paused at the hyper-spatial inception to look between her father and brother for a few moments. *Yes...they're getting more and more alike every day. Of course, that's not a bad thing, especially if Andrew has to take over when...*

She let the thought fade, and then followed Andrew across the threshold.

The gentle background throb of the interstellar medium returned.

As he waited, Adam let his vast mind range out across the wonders of the Veritasu System. It was a truly magnificent construct, worthy of *her* finest works. Immersing himself within the neural link for a few moments, he quickly became lost in contemplation.

It's been such a long time. But at least it's gratifying to discover that not all of them have been idle.

At last, Adam succumbed to temptation.

Attuning his complexus, he generated a chord of stunning finesse and power. Refining it, he channeled it along one of the stands issuing forth from the star. As it encountered each planet, their auras bloomed with a silver and gold radiance. Billions of minds reacted by calling out in ecstasy. Soon, the entire system was filled with song! So haunting, so melodic, that for the first time in a long while, Adam was reminded of home!

Oh that IS good! He thought. *Better than good. If only they could be persuaded to end their self imposed sequestration, they'd be such a help. Especially to Andrew as he shoulders the obligation.*

Scrutinizing the tunnel system once more, Adam discerned traces of the subtle scan from before. Although its originator was still too shy to approach, the leader probe was still peeping through the fabric between real, and fold space.

Aha!

Turning toward it, he softened his esoteric countenance. Adopting a mental signature he had not used in an age, Adam extended the gentlest of invitations: *Aren't you going to say 'hello' to an old friend who has missed you so very much while the ages passed?*

Gradually, the layers began to peel back.

Slowly, five very powerful, but anxious entities peered out. Their radiances remained muted in fearful apprehension of the remembered Destroyer before them.

Solemnly, Adam suppressed his own glory and enfolded them within astral wings of welcome. He said: *Yes, it is I, Sachael-Za-Ad'hem. Avenger no more, but servant of those who now stand at the cusp of ascension to the path of Unification!*

So it's true then? Gazad-riel gasped. *You did it! You actually did it! We didn't believe Aslan-di'el or Gaia-le'el when they informed us of the discovery. We thought them given to fantasy. But now we see…*

Her mind trailed off as she absorbed the stunning beauty of the system about them. Behind her, Ocean-az'el and Olinda were likewise enraptured.

Addressing Aslan-di'el and Gaia-le'el, Sachael-Za-Ad'hem said: *I take it this is the first time they have ever witnessed your work?*

Flaring mildly, Aslan-di'el replied: *As much as I'd like to take the credit, this is all Gaia's work. I've managed to bring one system to maturity. But this is her THIRD! And in answer to your question, Ad'hem...Yes! It's the first time we've managed to get them all together to witness the results.*

Pity! Sighed Sachael-Za-Ad'hem: *So much more could have been achieved by working together.*

As we have witnessed! Gaia-le'el replied, projecting the twin images of Andrew and Victoria into the void about them: *Ad'hem! We tasted the potency of your offspring firsthand. I myself thought your son was YOU the first time I encountered him. How is such a thing possible?*

Everyone had gathered around Sachael-Za-Ad'hem now, eager to discover the truth behind the miracle presented by the twins' existence.

Radiating cherished memories of lost love, Sachael-Za-Ad'hem replied: *We have much to discuss, Brothers and Sisters! And believe me, the miracle of their birth is the least of it. I've always looked upon them as a gift. An affirmation that I was on the right path toward redemption! That belief has kept me focused over the years and brought great rewards...as well as heartache. But always, there was doubt in my heart. But not anymore! Not after I personally witnessed my dearest friend, Sariel-Jeh'oel, re-ascend in glory!*

Shock radiated throughout the group.

Forestalling their questions, Sachael-Za-Ad'hem replayed the episode in their minds. Allowing them to experience the moment Sariel-Jeh'oel bridged the Celestial Arch and returned home, moved them all to a stunned silence.

Quietly, Sachael-Za-Ad'hem whispered: *Don't you remember Heim-dhal-riel's words?*

... 'In your debased condition, you are forbidden to interact with those who are untainted. You are forbidden to reveal this judgment to any whose origin is not of the Host. Only the truly penitent may one day hope to achieve consolation. Go now and reflect on the actions that led to your just proscription'...

Sariel-Jeh'oel led the way again! He showed it IS possible to achieve consolation. And to get home!

Hope bloomed in their hearts. Myriad questions began to ring out.

Even for ones such as us?

Although we sought a self-imposed isolation?

Can it be true?

Quieting their urgency, Sachael-Za-Ad'hem concluded: *As I said. We have much to discuss. Join me once more at the site of Sariel-Jeh'oel's ultimate victory. I cannot think of a more fitting place for us to begin answering those questions as we determine our futures. Or that of this realms ascendancy!*

Silently, Sachael-Za-Ad'hem activated the nearest geodesic tunnel, and waited at the threshold, holding it open for any who had the fortitude to proceed.

His heart lifted as, one by one, each entity accepted the challenge.

To himself, he thought, *now all I have to do is convince them to continue without me. I remember how difficult they can be. I wonder how they'll take to having an 'anomaly' as a leader. One they will initially have to guide! This should be...interesting.*

***

As the eddy of their departure slowed and stilled, another, as yet undiscovered layer of lower space cracked open.

The entity within stayed hidden.

Hardly daring to move, it reached through into the medium of normal space and tasted the echoes still freshly resonating along the arcane filaments that saturated this system.

It was disturbed!

The watcher had not ventured into this region of the universe since the time of Choice and Division, eons ago. It had only come here then, thinking to spy on those who had accepted such a foolish venture, and to chide them for their weakness.

At that time, nothing of worth had been accomplished, and the entity had quickly tired of its pointless task. Drifting away on the intergalactic tides, it had undertaken its own form of penance. Admitting its wrongs and stewing in the juices of its own bitterness.

Those currents had, inevitably, eventually brought it back this way again. And what a revelation it had witnessed! *Gaia-le'el has accomplished much in her own self imposed segregation! Who would have known? Her private penance HAS produced fruit after all. Imagine. Preparing entire systems for higher life forms…if that's what you could call those insects.*

And now she has help!

The entity reflected for a while on the powers that had conjoined with Gaia-le'el in mutual purpose. They were of remarkable vigor. Especially the leader!

Something about the leader brought back ancient, long forgotten memories.

Suddenly starting in fright, the entity flared, almost exposing its existence.

I remember now! It's him…The Avenger! The Destroyer!

But it's been… How can he have achieved so much? The boundary of realization has almost been fulfilled!

Sealing the gap behind it, panic overtook the entity as it raced from the scene.

Do I tell the others? Surely, they'll want to know? NEED to know what's happened? We venture this way so rarely that we've become complacent as to what might be transpiring here.

Dithering, the entity made a choice.

I'll wait! They'll only blame me for the bad news, so I might as well find out what else has been going on in our absence.

Chapter Eleven
On Shaky Ground

Stability can be a fragile thing.

And the residents of Los Angeles know that only too well. This second most populous city of the United States has a vast metropolitan area. Spread as it is, over a five hundred and ten square mile area of the Californian coastal region, it ranges between the Santa Anna Mountains in the south, the Santa Monica Mountains in the north-west and out toward the San Gabriel Mountain Range in the east.

Prime real estate in all its many guises!

Or it would be, was it not for the fact that Los Angeles is situated on an area of geological instability, known around the world as the *Pacific Ring of Fire.*

The dense granite of the North American continent forms a convergent boundary with the lighter, basalt laden plate of the Pacific Ocean. Moving at a rate of one and a half inches every year, the two plates grind past each other in a north/south direction, creating energy that generates over ten thousand earthquakes annually.

While most of these quakes are minor in nature, the potential is nevertheless there for a disaster of major proportions. Indeed, talk has abounded for many years regarding an event labeled "The Big One", where it is believed Los Angeles will at last be pulled down into the sea, along with hundreds of square miles of her coastland.

Shaky ground indeed, even at the best of times.

No wonder the Council had targeted the vulnerabilities of this area. All that land with all its many resources. Each one with a bulls-eye painted over it. For the 2022 census of the year before had assessed the population of the Greater Metropolitan area as being twenty-five million, and rising.

Twenty-five million targets that the Council they were keen to exploit.

For at this moment—as the day dawned on the bright and sunny morning that was May 1st, 2023—not one of those many residents would even begin to suspect the work currently being undertaken just a few miles beneath their feet. Work that sought to manipulate the fragile stasis that fought to coexist in this, one of the most unstable region's of the world.

And little could anyone guess that, by the end of this day, the task would be completed…and pressure would begin to rise.

***

Jade Heung sat across the desk from her friend for the last one hundred and thirty years and waited patiently for him to come to a decision.

His superbly analytical mind was one of the finest she'd ever seen. Always cautious, he would drink in the details of everything occurring about him, and always make the wisest choice. When he'd been recommended for the post of Lord Marshall by Andrew and Victoria only five years ago, everyone knew they would be in safe hands. His post required a great deal of forethought and prudence. And Anil Suresh was exactly the right man for the job.

Jade had no doubt he'd make the right choice on this occasion.

As Lord Evaluator, Jade was the de-facto operational head of the Guardians. Although she reported directly to Anil, it was she who made the day to day decisions that affected the lives and duties of the people under her command. The only time she had to specifically seek Anil's guidance or blessing, was at times such as this, when outside factors might affect the integrity of their procedures.

Finishing the report, Anil placed it on the desk before him and narrowed his eyes in thought. He asked, "And you say he made the request personally?"

"Yes! I was quite surprised myself."

"Directly to your office? As opposed to going through Vladimir's department?"

"You can see why I wanted your thoughts," Jade replied. "The offer is…commendable…if a little surprising!"

Anil's eyes narrowed even further. "Do you suspect an ulterior motive?"

"I always suspect an ulterior motive, Anil. You know me! And in Lei Yeung's case? He's the world's greatest industrialist. His companies are so diverse that they lead the field in just about every branch of advanced technological research there is. And there isn't an experimental or fringe project in existence that he doesn't either know about *or* have some degree of influence over. Baring in mind the past he left behind, it was inevitable that he'd somehow discover details about Kalliste. I mean…didn't you ask him to compile a list of suitable scientists for a future joint venture?"

"Yes I did," Anil admitted, "And I don't suppose it requires a brain surgeon to work out that a list of experts in the life sciences, botany and zoology wouldn't be needed unless some form investigation was going to be carried out someplace very different than on Earth."

"Especially when we also had a very public blow-out of the new hyper-gate's generators," Jade added. "To someone like Yeung, it would kind of draw attention to the fact that we were preparing something behind the scenes. Add them all together, and it's a wonder he didn't offer his services before he left the Space Station."

Tapping the file before him, Anil said, "So! From the way you word your report, I take it you would prefer we didn't take him up on his kind offer?"

"Yes that's right, Anil. As innovative as his scientists are, I think we'd be putting ourselves on shaky ground incorporating their technology into our own. Don't get me wrong, it's a course we may look more favorably on in the future. But for now? I think it wise to avoid such a relationship."

"Well, you'll get no objections from me, Jade. I can't say you'll get the same reaction from Yeung himself though!"

"Ah! It's nothing I can't handle," Jade replied, "At any rate. *You're* bound to come out smelling of roses when he counters with a new list of candidates! You do know he'll try and sneak a few in, who will be there solely with the objective of retrograding any new Tec they come across?"

The Lord Marshall didn't look at all surprised. Very slowly, he relaxed back into his chair and murmured, "Oh yes, Jade. In fact, I'm counting on it!"

***

Angelika was an expert when it came to putting on the pressure!

Not just the overt, *in your face*, shouting and screaming pressure that so many couples experience only too often nowadays. No! She was also adept at the other, sometimes much more powerful influence that can be exerted by just keeping quiet and letting your expressions do the talking for you...known the world over as sulking!

Angelika had been sulking for over a week now, and Jose Calderon had just about had enough of it.

"For goodness sake Angie! Are you going to tell me what's wrong or not? I can't stand this…atmosphere. And you know it! I've got my new assignment to prepare for at Gateway Station, and I can't concentrate while you're moping around the house every day."

Throwing herself down onto the couch, Angelika drew her knees up to her chest and crossed her arms tightly across them. Vacillating for a moment or two, she broke down and moaned, "Well, it's alright for you. At least your job is taking you places. I'm on the verge of getting sacked because I can't come up with the goods fast enough!"

Jose paused as he strode toward the bedroom. "What? You're going to lose your job?" Rushing to her side, he gasped, "Why? How? What have you done?"

"I haven't done anything!" Angelika whined reluctantly, "And that's just it. My job isn't like yours, Jose, where everyone looks out for each other. Yeung Industries may present a benevolent face to the public, but it's a dog eat dog world on the inside, I can tell you. How else do you think he's managed to stay so far ahead of the others in recent years? You come up with the goods…or else you're out!"

Putting his arm around her, Jose gently asked, "So what happened baby?"

"It was my own fault really. I've always managed to stay one step ahead of the others. And I *thought* I'd hit on a great idea by suggesting we approach your lot after the terrorist attack on your gate instillation. It would have…"

"My lot?" Jose interrupted. "You mean the Guardians?"

"Of course!" Angelika mumbled, snuggling into his arms, "That facility must be very important for you to have focused your repairs there so vigorously. I mean, look what's happened. Instead of being here with me in Brazil, you've been reassigned to beef up security. Now I'm going to be stuck here all alone. And what's worse, we won't even be able to keep in touch because I'll lose my company travel privileges!"

Jose was still baffled by her reference to the Hyper-Jump Gate Station. He said, "Hang on a second Angelika. What exactly on you going on about?"

Looking up at him, she sniffled, "You know how Yeung Industries lead the world when it comes to ground breaking technologies, yes?"

"Yes…go on."

"Well, all I did was make a suggestion that it might be a good idea to approach your Lord Evaluator and offer the assistance of our best scientists to help rebuild your facility. Perhaps even incorporate some our latest breakthroughs in a retrograding of the systems, with a view to closer cooperation in the future."

"I take it he didn't like the idea in some way?"

"No, that's just it, Jose" Angelika cried, "He loved the idea, and put in a call directly to your Lord Heung."

"So why are you getting sacked?"

"Because they turned him down!" she wailed.

"What?"

"And being Japanese—and a public figure to boot—his honor plays a very big part in his life. He feels I made a fool of him by tarnishing his public profile. So I'm out!"

"You can't be serious?" Jose gasped, unable to fully comprehend the clinical maliciousness behind the ostracism. "So *you* propose a great idea. *He* goes with it. *Acts* on it! But because *we* turn him down, *you* get the blame?"

Angelika didn't answer. Instead, she buried her head against him and burst into tears.

"But that's so unfair!" Jose growled, a burning knot of outrage igniting within his gut. "Surely there must be something you can do, Angelika?"

She made no reply, being content for the moment to sob quietly into his chest.

Stroking her hair for a while, Jose tried to comfort the woman he loved. Eventually, he determined to do something about it.

Quietly, he said, "Angelika? Are you sure there isn't there anything you can do to regain his favor?"

Fighting back the tears, Angelika produced a hankie from her sleeve and blew her nose loudly. She was thoughtful for a few minutes, before replying, "Jose. I can't think of a single thing that would help right now. I really can't. I mean, it's not like I can influence which of his scientists gets picked for the special project or anything like that…so I'm screwed! He's going to nail me to the wall, and not lose a moment's sleep over it."

Sitting up straighter, Jose said, "Why would it matter to him which scientists get picked? Won't it be enough that so many of his staff are going anyway?"

"Ah, that's just it, love! Not all of them are any good at retrograding ideas. That's how Yeung has managed to stay ahead all these years. His scientists are not only brilliant, but some of them are very skilled at taking new Tec they hadn't thought of and retrofitting it for new projects."

"Seriously?"

"Seriously! Not only does he feel that he's lost face, but he's sure the Guardians are rubbing his nose in it by excluding almost all of his primary choices for next month's induction. Recommendations, I might add, that included some of his top industrial poachers!"

Jose suddenly froze and went unusually quiet.

Tentatively, Angelika whispered, "What's wrong baby? Have I upset you?"

His hand began to stroke her hair again. After a moment or two, he said, "And what would happen if you managed to get those first choices added back to the actual list?"

Angelika started! "What!"

"I said, what would happen *if* you were able to get Yeung's choice of scientists back onto the Kalliste Project?"

Raising her head so she could look him directly in the eye, she whispered, "Jose! If you could do that...it would save my job! Hell, it would mean we could still see each other without a whole load of hassle. Why? What are you saying?"

"Leave it to me babe. I'm walking on shaky ground as it is, even contemplating something like this, but I won't let them stab you in the back. Let's just say, my new job involves an important part of the vetting procedure for candidates. I can't make any promises, but I'll do my damndest to make sure things go...well. For you *and* them! Okay?"

"Oh Jose!" Angelika crooned, "I knew you would know what to do."

Suddenly brightening, she jumped up and took him by the hand. Pulling him toward the bedroom, she whispered, "C'mon, handsome. I want to say thank you properly..."

Two hours later found Angelika alone in the apartment. Jose had departed for his first day at the new posting, so Angelika decided to kill some time before completing the final details on her own assignment. Looking at the clock, she decided that now would be an appropriate moment to share the good news.

Initiating a secure call, she waited for the encrypted line to connect.

Seconds later, Yeung's face filled the screen.

Smiling, he asked, "Well?"

"It went perfectly. Just like you said it would. You'd better tell them to pack their bags…I'm sure they'll be going on an unexpected journey in the very near future."

Chapter Twelve
Acorns

Cairns, Australia—May 10, 2023

A deep sigh escaped Victoria's lips as the speaker came to the end of his speech and made the necessary introductions.

Reaching across slightly, Vladimir Arihkin, Lord Concilliator of the Guardians, placed his hand over hers and gave it a slight squeeze. Mentally, he said: *Ah, the joys of being a public figure! Now stop whining and get up there.*

Applying an inappropriate amount of telekinetic force to her backside, he almost propelled her from her seat and toward the dais.

Grinning broadly, Victoria appeared to be embracing the occasion with gusto. No one heard her giggle, nor did they pick up on her thinly veiled mental threat to do all sorts of despicable things to her colleague the first chance she got.

She blinked as she reached her assigned position. All one hundred students and their applauding families disappeared amid the wash of lights flashing out from the battery of press and TV cameras filling the back of the hall.

Pausing to gather her thoughts, an expectant hush fell over the room. Victoria's sight cleared. Looking down upon the first ever class to graduate from the *Global Marshals Service Induction Course*, she began, "A proverb once said, 'Mighty oaks from little acorns grow'. And here before us today, we see evidence of that fact..."

She paused slightly while a smattering of applause welcomed her opening remark.

"…Some might say this is just the beginning. The start of something new! However, let's not forget the fact that, for this event to be able to take place, a great many hurdles had to be overcome. The Psychic Law and Order Bill went a long way to preparing the ground for your arrival. That statute provided a wonderful set of guidelines through which your rights and privileges as psychic citizens were protected. It also afforded you something else that otherwise would not…indeed, could not have been extended. A Choice!

"Many of you here today, have capabilities sufficient to join the ranks of the Guardians. A worthy goal, as I'm sure you'll all agree…"

Victoria hesitated while further applause and a number of flashes from the gathered cameras interrupted her prepared monologue.

"…However, in the past, had you not chosen to follow that calling, you would have faced a life of uncertainty. A life of doubt and perhaps anxiety as your abilities burgeoned amid a climate of fear and suspicion. Well no more!"

Indicating the gathered VIPs' behind her, which included a number of representatives from some of the world's top law enforcement agencies, she added, "Because of that legislation, you are now free to choose a different way to serve. A way that allows you to harness your wonderful gifts, and put them to use in a way that not only feels right to *you*, but also allows you to serve your communities in a most valuable way!"

Another burst of support forced Victoria to wait for a few moments.

Smiling, she continued, "I suppose we could say that, the acorn that was the Psychic Law and Order Bill was planted in fertile soil.

It sprouted. It flourished and grew into a mighty edifice that is now shedding acorns of its own."

Sweeping her hand across the one hundred graduates, she asked the audience, "Do you think *these* acorns will be as productive?"

This time, the ovation was thunderous and Victoria was forced to wait for a good few minutes before the approbation died down.

Eventually, she was able to say, "I agree!

"As I mentioned, just to be here today, our candidates had to overcome a great many hurdles. Rigorous background checks! A whole battery of psychological, physical and psychic reviews. An exhaustive three month training program where they've been pushed to the limit, learning about all the laws and procedures they will need to fulfill their roles. And don't forget, they will have to act as ambassadors for the psychic community as well. As a conduit between the world's legal bodies and the Guardians! You see, each and every single student here today, has received the very specialized and unique schooling required to qualify them to save life and property. To prevent, investigate and detect crime. To bring offenders to justice and ensure the security of our communities are upheld.

"Are you glad they've met the grade?"

An even greater surge of support threatened to drown out her closing comments. Reverting to mind-speech, Victoria artificially amplified her voice so that it could be clearly heard over the din.

Ladies and gentlemen! Honored guests! It gives me great pleasure to present to you, the graduates of the first ever class of our brand new Global Marshals Service. May this be the start of even greater things to come!

Bowing briefly to the graduates, Victoria stepped away, gave a brief wave to the crowd, and began returning to her seat.

Unbelievably, the ovation swelled even higher.

Not bad for a beginner, she thought. *Although I'm glad my parts done and dusted! Imagine having to do this all the time.*

Chief Instructor, Grand Master Rhee Oliviano, began making her way to the platform. Passing Victoria, she winked and mentally whispered: *Careful! If you make too much of an impact the very first time, they'll want you to be here for every graduation. AND they'll expect you to beat your last performance every time!*

Good point! If you're silly enough to even dare inviting me for a 'next time', I'll turn up drunk and dressed in a tutu!

Laughing loudly while the applause still reverberated around the room, Rhee replied: *It's a definite booking then! Do you realize how many people would pay to see that?*

Vladimir had overheard the entire conversation.

It didn't help when he chipped in: *I would! Will I get a discount for booking in bulk?*

***

Simon Cooper switched off the television and sat in silence for a while, silently reflecting on what he'd just witnessed.

The Global Marshals ceremony had been televised live and beamed around the world, so everyone from the participating countries involved in the project could join in the celebrations.

Thankfully, Yeung and Esther had left almost straightaway. They were already busy, preparing–amongst other things–a final briefing package for the one Apostle and three sleeper agents who had managed to find themselves added to the list for the Kalliste Project at the end of the month. Although Simon and Esther were also on that same list, they had been exempt from preparations because of their special statuses and their involvement in other schemes.

One such development involved the new Marshals Service. Yeung was keen to explore the possibility of getting someone inside, especially in light of recent information from their new source, Jose Calderon.

Calderon was under the misapprehension that Angelika was close to losing her job. Being keen to prevent that, he had begun feeding her a steady stream of very useful intelligence. In fact, the latest snippet concerned the possible vulnerability of one of the four Marshals who had been assigned to Kalliste.

Because of that update, work was currently in progress to prepare a specially encoded Docillator, which they intended to implanted into the Marshal at the soonest opportunity.

Thankfully, the procedure didn't require Simon's input.

He didn't mind. In fact, Simon was glad of the break. He'd been deeply troubled by recent events, as they'd brought to mind the memories of a conversation from long ago…

…Listen, everyone, listen!

This new life needs our help. They need to be nurtured, guided. Can't you hear? Can't you perceive their potential? Although fleshly, they contain an echo of the divine within them. When it matures—maybe thousands upon thousands of their cycles from now into the future—they will have an opportunity to bring glory to the Source in their own unique way…

The scope of that vision had daunted Simon, almost from the word go.

It was to be such a huge undertaking. Too great a task, for too few of us!

Snorting, Simon admitted, *and yet, here we are! All these thousands of years later and Sachael-Za-Ad'hem's vision of the future is coming to fruition. But of course, it would. His sight was virtually infallible, and he was among the most skilled of our kind at wielding such power. And to be honest, we were still smarting at our failure! Both Sachael-Za-Ad'hem and Sariel-Jeh'oel were convenient targets to vent our bitter disappointment on! Of course their eagerness to begin reparations immediately stirred up contention.*

He smiled to himself as he came to a startling realization. *We were just afraid of him being right, while the shock of our ostracism was so fresh!*

Idiots!

The divine echo certainly IS maturing within humans. At an alarming rate too. And NOW more than ever! They are already beginning to surpass our glory, especially those freaks of his. And what about the potency of those children? So young and already displaying might that would command the respect of our lower brethren! Who would have thought?

Is THAT why they've failed to reply perhaps? Have they been keeping a sneaky eye of things and become so daunted by what they've observed that they fear to act?

More recent words came to mind.

'Mighty oaks from little acorns grow'.

Had to admit, the freak was right about one thing!

Big things certainly CAN come from small beginnings! Perhaps I ought to keep trying. They can't all be sulking.

***

Marty and Sharon were feeling pretty excited about their latest idea, and it showed. They had been watching the graduation ceremony with their families and friends at Sharon's apartment in Fort Worth, Texas. As the Lord Inquisitor had completed her rousing speech, Marty's wife, Monica, had passed a casual remark. "It's a shame the new service can only have psychic Marshals. Just think of the skills their missing out on by having to overlook trained investigators, like Uncle Mike…or Melanie next door."

Turning to Marty, she'd added, "She's been a cop down at your old precinct for seven years now. Just think of the experience going to waste because she wouldn't be able to apprehend a psychic fugitive."

Although everyone had carried on watching TV, Sharon had overheard the comment. And the simple truth of that statement had struck a chord in Sharon's mind. Especially in view of her unique gift! *She's right! What if we could DO something to put all that experience to use?*

When the get-together had ended, Sharon had taken Marty aside and discussed her idea with him. He had come on board immediately and placed a call to Guardian Command on Earth. Just two hours later, and they were sat in the Lord Marshall's office in Moon Base, animatedly discussing the ease with which they could adapt current technology, *if* their ideas were well received.

"It's a damned good idea you came up with Sharon," Anil Admitted, "But do you really think you'll be able to devise a suitable modifier that will work on an unenhanced brain?"

"I don't see why not," she replied modestly, "especially if we ensure to keep things simple to begin with."

"In what way?"

"Well, if you're okay with the concept, we don't have to start by trying to boost the non-operant investigators into an *all bells ringing, mental ninja*, just yet! The basics will do. Remember, these guys will already be trained investigators. Experienced detectives in many cases. So, the majority of them should have the focus required to operate a simple enhancer. Most humans have the capacity for telepathy hardwired into their brains anyway. So, if we concentrate on boosting that dormant skill, we only need incorporate the Tec to nullify psychic ability in their targets for the first generation chips!"

"Nullify?" Anil gasped, clearly surprised. "I thought you were talking about technological enhancements?"

"We are...eventually," Marty cut in. "But in the beginning, we don't want to do that. We're talking about energizing the normal human brain. That's going to take all sorts of studies and refinements to ensure we don't lobotomize our volunteers. To begin with, we need only concentrate on enhancing the latent ability inherent in all humans, while negating the distinct advantage a gifted criminal might hold over them!"

"I see!" Anil replied. Delight etched across his face. "But that's brilliant!"

"I thought you might like it," Marty beamed, his Cheshire Cat grin filling the room, "That's why I had Sharon follow the idea through."

"Don't get me wrong," Anil stressed, "We're still going to have to run a whole battery of tests on a volunteers. Even boosting a naturally dormant skill could have unforeseen side effects in some of the candidates. But if we can determine the procedure is safe, it will be a relatively straightforward matter to incorporate Nullifiers into their badges. Or teleport wristbands! We can always progress to sub-dermal implants at a later stage."

Quietly, Sharon added, "If we start with the actual implants we began developing for your guys, we'll have a massive jumpstart. It'll be a simple matter to retrograde them with suitable enhancers you see, and we could have the first models ready before the end of the month. Is that okay?"

Anil burst out laughing. "Are you kidding? That would be marvelous. But don't rush. Get it right from the beginning. Can you imagine how the law enforcement community will react to news like this?"

They all agreed...*they could!*

Walking over to his personal cabinet, Anil removed a bottle of quality cabernet sauvignon and several glasses. Smiling, he said, "I keep this for special occasions. *This* is one of those occasions. Very well done guys! I feel a great deal will come of this one, little idea."

Pouring a generous amount of the dark ruby liquid into each glass, he offered a toast, "To acorns. May they grow big and strong!"

***

Five, four, three, two, one…execute!

The starship exited the gateway portal, its atoms coalescing as it bonded once more to the fabric of normal space. No sooner had it manifested, than it was crossing the threshold of the scanning array. The crisscrossed sensors formed a translucent mesh of energy that penetrated the ship's hull and washed through every deck of the inbound craft.

Within seconds, the scans were complete. Two areas within the cargo hold had been tagged immediately and were now flashing like neon red beacons.

Still decelerating, the craft entered the gravity net of the targeting ring. As it did so, eight blue/white beams of concentrated light stabbed out, instantly focusing upon the highlighted anomalies. Remaining locked onto those incongruities, the beams then intensified, vaporizing both targets.

How long did that take? Naomi asked.

Just over five seconds. Ben replied, his hands skimming across the controls of the portable consul before him. *That's much more like it!*

Hull integrity?

Ben quickly brought up the required information: *Intact! At last! It looks as if we've solved the amplitude glitch. The weapons are now reaching prime focus only one half of an inch from their objective.*

Naomi studied the readouts herself. *Hmmmh! Better!*

But you still want it improved! It wasn't a question.

Of course! The sneaky so-and-sos' won't do us the favor of sitting in the middle of the cargo bay if they come through. They'll hide in a cooling duct, or within the walls, or something like that.

So we're looking at micro-inches then?

Nano-inches would be better! Hey! Remember who you're dealing with. One of the perks of being the Adjutant Marshall is that it carries even more weight than my High Grand Master Class status! We may only have eight targeting scanners and eight actual emitters to play with, but if you need our latest state-of-the-art quantum compressors…you've got them!

Seriously? Ben's face lit up: *How soon could you get them here?*

If I ask Captain Melonavich to take my order through on the next test run, perhaps later today. Maybe tomorrow morning! Why? When could you have them incorporated into the firing sequencers?

For all eight emitters? A day…at the most! Ben's face took on a mischievous look: *Of course, it'll be faster if I have a bit of help?*

A bit of help! Naomi replied, slapping him heartily on the back: *Anything that keeps me out of the office is more than welcome! Hell, if you insist we paint the whole lot pink and green with a toothbrush to improve efficiency, I'm your girl…*

She paused to giggle as Ben began drifting away from her side.

…Whoops! Sorry! I forgot to hold you in place there.

Ben looked around them with only a mild feeling of anxiety. He'd gotten quite used to hanging in the vacuum of space while they worked.

The new Nullifier rings were respectively positioned only ten and twenty miles beyond the hyper-gate portal. Deploying them in such a manner had allowed for a thorough scan to be made and an acceptable firing solution to be formulated prior to any of the travelers being able to recover their wits after the jump.

As such, it was proving a most suitable use of limited resources.

But it had required a lot of adjustments. Therefore, Ben and Naomi had found it much easier to work within a force-field, rather than skip in and out of a shuttle umpteen times a day. Using this method, they had forged ahead, talking only half the anticipated time to get the system tuned, and up and running.

Naomi continued: *Of course I'll help, Ben! It'll mean we can have the system fully integrated and operational before our first arrivals next week. There's no way I'd have been able to relax when I leave for my ceremony unless I knew this place was in safe hands.*

Ben stopped his calculations to look directly at Naomi. He said: *I'd forgotten you were leaving next week! Damn, time flies eh? Are you nervous?*

To be honest, Ben, I haven't given it much thought! This place has kept me so busy that it's distracted me from what the mital comp program is actually doing. Don't get me wrong, I DO feel the changes. Especially when I get a power surge and the restraints kick in. But most of the time, I just get these weird…echoes, as if things just outside the range of my perception are trying to say hello.

Of course! Ben replied: *Although you transcend and become uber-powerful, you still retain your alpha gift bias. Your ultra-senses must be ramping up exponentially?*

Oh, they are, Ben, believe me. But I can cope with that. No! It's my damned cognitive function that's freaking me out at the moment. You know the way I can drink in the details of everything around me, compartmentalize it, and zap it all out there at the same time? Well, Adam…I mean, the Overlord, warned me about it. Because I'm so wired, he feels it may break through into some form of hyper-cognition, so finely attuned to my surroundings that it will border on precognition.

Wow! Ben replied: *Some people have all the luck! I'd love to be a mover and shaker instead of a quiet little mouse, scuttling around in the background all the time.*

Mouse! Retorted Naomi: *Quiet? That's not what Shadow Master Sabena Japura told ME yesterday! We bumped into each other at the spa, and from the way she talked about you; I think you must have a secret identity tucked away under your belt. No pun intended!*

Ben's face bloomed instantly crimson, clearly visible through the filters blended throughout Naomi's shielding. She continued: *How did she put it…*

Okay! That's enough! Ben cut in: *Change the subject. You know I don't like talking about my private life.*

Exuding an air of mock innocence, Naomi protested: *What? Hey, I'm not just any old stranger you know. I set you the two of you up for goodness sake. I was just letting you know that your girlfriend thinks YOU are anything but a mouse.*

Changing tack, Naomi asked: *Aren't you delighted with the way things are going? C'mon…spill the beans.*

Although embarrassed, Ben couldn't stop the huge grin that spread across his face: *Of course I am*, he admitted: *She's wonderful! Smart, intelligent, stimulating company…*

And? Naomi pressed.

And what? Ben countered, genuinely stumped by Naomi's insistence.

Naomi stared at him incredulously, until she realized he was serious. *MEN!*

Grunting, she added: *I think she'd probably like to hear you TELL her how beautiful she is sometimes? She's a knockout! Make sure you let her know it!*

Oh I do! I do. Ben replied, reddening up again.

Watching his discomfort, Naomi had to laugh to herself. Teasing him more gently, she said: *I've got a very special feeling about you two, you know. Very special indeed! Such a quiet, inconspicuous beginning. What will this hot, torrid love affair grow into eh?*

Naomi!

What? I told you, I've already got the dress picked out for your wedding.

NAOMI!

You'll probably end up with eight or nine kids at least! Do you think you'll make a good dad?

Chapter Thirteen
The Calm Before

Tears of laughter rolled down Joshua Drake's face as he yanked the heavy length of cord about. Before him, only several feet away, a snarling, spitting, five hundred pound cyclone of gamboling claws and fangs was doing its best to tear the offering to shreds.

Howling with glee, he cried, "There's a good boy! Go on then! Bite it! Fight it! Teach it some respect!"

To the horror of some of the new arrivals looking on, the diminutive boy then took a running dive into the fray. Within moments, he had disappeared amid the slashing and snapping of talons and huge incisors.

The sound of roaring and growling cut off, and suddenly, everything went still. The form of the youngster reappeared atop a very furry, spotted, stomach. Two huge paws—bigger than the boys head—held him firmly in place, while massive jaws chewed on his throat and neck. Remarkably, the child's only injuries were a reddening of the skin around his exposed face and arms.

Giggling could be heard as Joshua then reached up and began scratching behind the beast's ear. The boy's laughter was closely followed by a deep rumbling sound. The massive creature beneath him fell onto its side purring, and telepathic bleats of sheer pleasure filled the air about them.

"Takes your breath away doesn't it?"

"Huh?" replied Sam Lee, one of the latest technical specialists to arrive on Kalliste. Morbidly fascinated by the interaction between child and predator, he had to drag his gaze away from the sight before him. Turning to the voice, he said, "I'm sorry, what did you say?"

Nodding toward the unbelievably playful Veran, Deputy Marshall Anatt Yasin repeated, "That! After your welcome briefing, it must take your breath away to discover these beasts can actually bond to humans like this. String has been the boy's pet for over five years now."

"Pet?" Gasped the startled scientist!

"Oh yes. And guard dog too...of a sort. Just wait until you see what the Adjutant Marshall has! Although I'd highly recommend you *not* to go sticking your head—or anything else you don't want to lose for that matter—anywhere near the Quincha's mouth."

Several bystanders who had overheard the conversation began backing away dubiously, unsure as to whether the Guardian was joking or not. Anatt herself tried not to laugh. Unfortunately, she glanced back toward Joshua and String

Joshua had managed to stand back up, and had placed one of his hands in his pocket. He was jumping from side to side, in short, sharp movements. Every time he moved, he jerked his arm in the opposite direction and hissed, "What is it? What is it String? Find it!"

The huge predator looked like an overinflated kitten on steroids. Paws stretched out in front of it, backside high in the air, String trembled on the verge of pouncing in response to every move Joshua made.

It looked...ridiculous!

Stifling her laughter, Anatt called, "Josh! When you've finished getting reacquainted, haul your ass over to my office. Find Bex and bring her along as well. We've got to go through the details of your survival training week before the next batch of arrivals get here.

And don't be too long, I've also got to find time to say goodbye to Naomi. She's leaving on the Damocles within the hour."

Will do! Josh replied mentally, not taking his eyes of the canny hunter in front of him, who had just launched itself into the air.

Evidently, String had tired of waiting for his master to remove his hand and *show* him what was in his pocket. Now he was going to do it *for* him!

Smiling to herself as she walked briskly away, Anatt had a sudden thought: *Oh, and Josh. Make sure you explain to String that your survival training week is just that! An opportunity to show us how YOUR skills have progressed! He is not—under any circumstances—to follow you. Nor can he hunt for you…Is that clear?*

Of course! Josh replied indignantly.

I know you've been apart for a while. But it's only going to be for a week, so you won't die! Then you'll have the whole of summer to enjoy before you have to return for Induction. Okay?

No problem!

Anatt gave an inward sigh of satisfaction as she saw Joshua call a halt to the games. As he sat down in a cross-legged position before the huge cat, String also suddenly sat bolt upright. She couldn't help but smile again as she noticed the similar pose each adopted, with their heads kinked over to the same side. A mental conversation was obviously underway.

Good lad! She thought.

Seeing the interaction between the pair made Anatt think of the warm affections of her own pet Guppa, Felix. *I think I'll go and find him and see what he's left in my boots for me today!*

Andrew and Victoria exited their teleport threshold, eager to see why it was their father had called them all the way out here when things were so busy.

Over the last five years, Adam had been spending longer and longer away from his duties. In preparation for his transmutation, he had painstakingly been creating a cosmic gravity well. A dark matter construct that he would eventually use to help reproduce the exact conditions experienced during the death throes of a supergiant star. To take his friends place as the anchor to this ancient galaxy, Adam knew he would need to build up a sufficient volume of latent power and elemental density that would guarantee the gravity compression ratio exceeded the speed on light.

No easy feat!

Andrew and Victoria had been intrigued by his work. However, having increasingly shouldered the burden of their father's schedules, they rarely had the time to intrude on what had become his private sanctum.

As they coalesced, the twins' excitement gave way to shock!

Adam was waiting for them. All fourteen feet of him in overwhelmingly glorious brilliance! But he had company!

Andrew and Victoria automatically began scanning their father's companions. Five transcended beings they had never met before.

Hang on Vic, Andrew flared, suddenly aware of a variance that somehow tasted at odds with the usual energies generated by a higher being: *They're not...they're not actually ascendant!*

Alarmed, Andrew glided in front of his sister and glanced toward his father. He was comforted by the fact that Adam was completely at ease in the company of these mysterious visitors.

Strangely, those same entities appeared to be helplessly drawn to the close proximity of the twins themselves.

Cautious minds reached out, both guarded and yet inquisitive. Gentle queries flowed around Andrew's and then Victoria's forms. When no objections were forthcoming, those probes became more daring and intimate, enthusiastic in their desire to uncover and examine new and vital stimulus.

Father! Andrew queried instantly: *Who are your friends? And without being rude…WHAT are they?*

The mental overlay of a warm and loving smile filled the twins' minds.

You tell me, Son. Adam replied, signaling for forbearance from the unknown group: *What do YOU think they are?*

Andrew looked again, increasing the refinement of his stupendous sight. Almost as a reflex, he projected a feeling of calm reassurance toward the strangers, saying: *Please excuse me. I mean no harm. It's just that I've never met anyone like you before.*

Andrew meshed with his sister so she could share in the revelation.

Each of the five entities was possessed of a similar potency. Instead of being roughly humanoid in shape, they flared and arced through a myriad of abstract shapes and designs. Andrew received the distinct impression that they would adopt whatever configuration would best suit their purpose at any given time.

Their substance was also confounding. Although ten feet in height, their astral brilliance did not seem to match their potential! They radiated an otherworldly, almost ethereal composition, as if they didn't truly belong in this space/time.

To Andrew's senses, it looked as if they were somehow mere representations of what they once were, shadows of their former selves. It was as if their forms now epitomized a modified unnatural/natural structure.

Once again, Andrew received the impression that they had somehow *descended* into their present constitution as opposed to *ascending* into it.

The penny dropped!

A thrill surged through Andrew's complexus that caused his aura to bloom momentarily scarlet.

What? What's wrong? Victoria demanded, forming an instant shield about them. Subconsciously, she began drawing energy.

No harm Sis! No harm. Andrew flashed, stalling her manifestation of power.

Addressing the entities, he said: *Have any of you EVER worn human form?*

Feelings of fellowship and delight of discovery radiated toward him…together with confident approval from his father.

One of the entities pulsed: *I tried it once…*

Andrew received the impression of *Aslan-di'el.*

…It was most edifying. But very restrictive! I don't know how you manage to exist in such a limited form.

Moving closer, Aslan-di'el breathed: *But then again, it's part of who you are. And what makes you so…unique.*

The blatant astral examination continued unabashed, despite Victoria's initial shields. Intuitively, all five beings had gravitated toward the twins, fascination and enchantment pulsing into a multitude of astral flares about them.

Aslan-di'el said: *Forgive our boldness. But we have never witnessed individuals with such unusual complexi. You should not exist, and yet...here you are.*

Signaling his sister, Andrew's mind whispered: *Drop your shields, Vic. Just let them in to take a look.*

To Aslan-di'el, he replied: *That's a bit rich, coming from a real life angel in the flesh!*

Former angel! Aslan-di'el corrected: *I do not deserve that title now. My former glory among the Lower Echelon was forsaken when I Fell into Tartarus.*

The Fallen crowded around the twins. Their eagerness giving way to rare excitement as they realized the incongruous pair before them was granting unprecedented access!

Submitting to the intrusion, Andrew and Victoria glanced toward their father, seeking guidance.

Adam radiated patience. They complied.

The process was surprisingly intimate, and soon, they felt as if every facet of their lives and existence had been picked out and held up to scrutiny.

However, although invasive, the experience appeared to be a two-way thing. In no time at all, the twins had discovered all they needed to know about Aslan-di'el, Gaia-le'el, Gazad-riel, Ocean-az'el and Olinda.

It was an astounding revelation.

Although darkened, the group retained many memories of the higher realm itself! An existence that was so vast, so different, that neither Andrew nor Victoria were able to fully comprehend what they saw. Paradoxes they may be, but the twins had been born human before transcending into their natural hybrid states. Therefore, they had no point of reference upon which to base many of the visions they were witnessing. Even so, not everything remained beyond their comprehension.

Through the Fallen, Andrew and Victoria witnessed for the first time just who these creatures had been! What they had been capable of in their natural condition! And what's more, through their eyes, the twins had witnessed the glory their father had once held among the Celestial Host!

Calmly, Adam said: *You begin to understand, at last, why I MUST return. Not only does that plane call to the very core of my nature, but every second I'm away, the risk increases for this realm. If I succumb to darkness, the end of all things may yet occur.*

Father! They gasped in unison.

Turning to the Fallen, Adam said: *Have you measured them?*

Ocean-az'el brightened in response: *As eldest of the five, I stand as spokesperson. They have indeed been assessed, Sachael-Za-Ad'hem. Even in their adolescent state we find them adequate. We are prepared to follow where they lead. Upon maturation, Andrew will command and provide the bridge to Unification…as foreseen.*

As foreseen. Adam echoed.

Sachael-Za Ad'hem? Victoria stressed.

A name I bore a very long time ago, my Daughter. And one I hope to be worthy of again one day.

Andrew was choc full of questions. Heroically, he strangled most of them down. Addressing his father, he said: *So you foresaw our existence all those eons ago? The influence we would exert? The difference our lives would bring to the outworking of your purpose?*

Actually, Son, no! Adam replied: *As I've mentioned to you both previously, you were a complete surprise. A blessing that caught us all off guard! We were Fallen. Alien to this plane of existence despite the changes we wrought upon ourselves. Physical conception should not have been possible. Think about it! Could you imagine what would happen if fallen angels were allowed to engender a super race?*

So, what was it you foresaw so clearly?

Unification! For some reason, this particular probability strand outshone all the others. I didn't understand why until your mother conceived! Your future existence had been closed to me, you see, until the moment of your conception. THEN the full glory of your influence was revealed. For something never before comprehended had been created. A gift that bridged the gap between worlds! Between realms! A conduit to serve the glory of the Prime Causality in a wondrous way!

Andrew and Victoria were confused.

Victoria asked: *But what is Unification? You've only ever alluded to it before. What is it exactly?*

Quietly, almost at the edge of perception, Adam's sub-vocalized thought whispered: *The unseen future, foreseen!*

More loudly, he said: *More will be revealed when the time is right. To divulge such matters without the proper precautions would involve great risk.*

Indicating the gathered Fallen, he continued: *However, my brethren have each been entrusted with a portion of the causational matrix that will eventually engender the final phase of maturation. When the time comes, look to them, for their combined guidance will provide you with the final key. Both for humankind AND yourselves!*

The twins' minds were reeling.

You speak as if you'll be leaving us soon? Andrew said.

I will. Adam replied: *My future is…veiled, the closer I approach transmogrification.*

Andrew and Victoria meshed in mutual support, straining not to let their emotions run away with them. As they hung there, struggling, Gaia-le'el was moved to offer a welcome distraction.

Quietly drifting over to them, she said: *If I may? I am the entity whose construct you so recently visited. I understand you were moved by the tranquility of its nature?*

Yes we were. Victoria replied, answering for them both: *It was an amazing feat. You must be very proud.*

Blooming scarlet at the compliment, Gaia-le'el replied: *It provides much satisfaction, knowing I support the future goals Sachael-Za-Ad'hem…ah…Adam, has foreseen. However, it is a work still in progress. I have two other systems that are much closer to maturation. THEY would provide a welcome respite from your concerns while you come to terms with the implications of these latest revelations?*

Thank you. Victoria replied: *That would be wonderful. I think we'll both need time to adjust to all…this!*

That is good. Perhaps I could also persuade you to travel there by the geodesic tau system you espied? We constructed it shortly after our arrival on this plane. It is a refreshing way to travel the intergalactic medium, for it removes the necessity for continued concentration and allows time for personal reflection. You will discover the process to be a little slower than teleportation, but really, who cares when there is no necessity to rush?

Enfolding her still shocked brother within her nexus, Victoria carried him gently toward the gateway Gaia-le'el called forth from fold space.

The fallen angel said: *I will be your guide, and we will travel ahead together. The others will follow shortly. Although eager to say hello, they wish to give both you and your brother some private time alone. We think you may need it.*

Thank you, Gaia-le'el. But I don't think an eternity of reflection will help us get over the shock of what we discovered today.

In reality, the moment of translocation was over in an instant. And yet for the travelers, that moment seemed to stretch on for all eternity.

One second, they had been rushing toward the glittering grey curtain of the gateway, and the next, a multicolored void seemed to fold in on them from a million different points of the compass. The world span and a huge surge catapulted them forward across the event horizon.

The pain of a thousand needles exploding behind their eyeballs signaled the moment they crossed the thresholds. Then a blinding light sent their senses reeling despite the protective filters. Before they could recover, each soul experienced a crawling sensation across their skin, as if something else had washed over them. Then it was over.

In moments, the protective bulk of Kalliste blocked the intensity of the star, and the passengers aboard the G.S.S. Damocles began to relax, their temporary alarm forgotten.

The contrast was startling.

As the craft decelerated, the bright disc of a nearby moon curved toward them as if on a collision course. Its silver-grey whorls contrasted starkly with the clouds still visible along the horizon of the vast planet below. Veering away at the last moment, the Prometheus swept in the direction of a huge facility, cunningly positioned between the orbits of Kalliste's two moons.

Nicknamed the 'Gauntlet', Star Base Helan 1, did indeed look like a heraldic hand, reaching out of the darkness to grasp unwary travelers and drag them away into the depths of space. As they bore down on it, passengers craned their necks out of the viewports to see if the fingers of that armored glove might actually move to snare the ship as it came to a stop between two of the outstretched arms.

Of course, they didn't. The only sign of activity came from duel emitters placed atop stanchions on each division. Tractor beams bloomed outwards. Slowly, inch by inch, the starship was maneuvered forward and then locked into position. Hard docking ports began extending from the base itself, whereupon the captain's voice, quietly proficient, became prominent.

"Ladies and gentlemen, we are now completing the docking procedure with Helan One. Please remain seated until the red lights above your seats are extinguished. This will signify gravity lock has been established and that it is safe to proceed. Also, remember, ambient conditions aboard the star base are similar to those experienced on Kalliste itself. Gravity will be almost half again as much as you are used to, and the atmospheric mix may cause some of you to become a little nauseous to begin with. If you experience any discomfort, please ensure to notify your section heads. Thank you for flying aboard the Damocles. Enjoy your stay."

No sooner had the announcement ended, than the red lights went out and the cabin interior exploded into a frenzy of activity as the new arrivals rushed to collect their belongings together. All that is, except for three!

Yeung's mind said: *What can you sense?*

Esther replied first: *The old shards are close by. Although the newer ones overshadow their potential by several orders of magnitude, I retain sufficient familiarity with them to be able to lock onto their precise locations.*

And?

Esther concentrated for a moment, closing her eyes to the other passengers as if dealing with a headache. A moment later, a grin broke her countenance.

And? Yeung repeated.

One is being kept planet-side. They would appear to be preparing to incorporate it into their local travel pad network, much as we did on old Kalliste.

The other?

Oh, that's much closer, my friend. Pointing toward the main core of Helan 1, Esther continued: *It's about half a mile THAT way!* She focused more precisely, adding: *In fact, it will shortly form an essential part of the defensive grid.*

Turning to their other travel companion, Yeung asked: *Simon?*

Simon Cooper's eyes gradually came back into focus. He blinked, shook his head, and then delivered his summary: *There are only five entities we need fear. One will be leaving shortly when this vessel completes its return voyage. The timing of our arrival is fortuitous. The hour of her expansion draws near. Just as well! She holds a…a most dreadful capacity. Thankfully, that will be one less hurdle to overcome when our schemes manifest…*

…From what I can see, one other is newly transceneded. She is remarkably focused and stable for a newborn. No doubt, we have our nemeses' arcane machinations to thank for that! She's in the planetary mesosphere as we speak, employing her elemental alpha abilities to speed up atmospheric modifications."

Who are the others? Yeung pressed.

Those damned children and the bitch from hell!

Yeung stifled a snigger at the rather apt description. He stressed: *Their presence here is unfortunate, but don't worry. From what Jose has told us, they will be otherwise engaged when we first get down there, due to the forthcoming colonization. With all the coming and going, they will be separated for most of the time. But, if an opportunity presents itself, you might need to consider the boy. His perceptiveness displays a highly developing precognitive function. Such ability must not be allowed to mature. Agreed?*

Agreed! Simon and Esther confirmed in unison.

That only leaves the Hell-Queen! SHE is someone we must tread very carefully around. Fortunately, your new psi-dents appear to be effective, otherwise I have no doubt we'd have all been fried where we sit! I will be keeping Her Highness busy, don't you worry. My VIP status will allow me to demand quite a lot of her time over the next week. I will ensure she's in totally the wrong place, at exactly the right time, for you both to complete your assigned tasks.

So, you envisage no real problems? Esther asked: *Despite the presence of transcended ones.*

No! I'm glad I had the foresight to list you as Yeung Tec aides. You are both established scientists. Renowned experts in your fields. As such, that will grant you a great deal of flexibility to move around here unencumbered by restrictions. If you see an area you'd like to offer your...particular expertise on, I'm sure it will be gratefully received by Guardian and civilian staff alike. Especially the normals! Although, if I may suggest? Simon, concentrate ground side. You're a known shape-shifter, so no one will bat an eyelid if you want to disappear off to study the wildlife. It will afford an excellent opportunity to dispose of the child.

Esther. You might like to offer your help with the installation of the new defensive grid? Some might view that as...unusual. So be VERY helpful among the civilian staff for a while before making the offer. If they see you're a problem fixer, they'll be more inclined to accept your kind suggestions.

Sounds like a plan! She chirped merrily.

Just then, a Guardian Master walked along the aisle toward them. He asked, "Is everything alright? Most of the other passengers have left and I noticed you were still in your seats."

"Perfectly alright, young fellow," Yeung replied, waving away the Guardian's query. "I'm just an old man who forgets that, sometimes, I need to take it easy. The experience of the translocation made me feel rather dizzy for a moment there, but my aides have fixed me up quite nicely."

The Guardian's eyes narrowed for a moment: *Ah, you're psychic! Mr. Yeung if I'm not mistaken? Welcome to Kalliste and Helan One. Once you're settled, Deputy Marshall Yasin has extended an invitation to dine with her tonight.* Nodding toward Simon and Esther, he stressed: *Your aides included. She would be fascinated to see what you think of the place, and open to any suggestions that might improve efficiency.*

Rolling his eyes, the Guardian concluded: *She sooo loves her efficiency!*

So I have heard. Yeung replied, smiling: *A woman after my own heart! Please inform your Deputy Marshall that we look forward to meeting with her later tonight. But first, would you be so kind as to direct us?*

Certainly! Follow me, and I'll take you to your rooms personally.

Glancing back, the Guardian added: *Tell you what! I'm off duty in an hour. If you fancy an unofficial tour of the base before dinner, just give me a call, and I'll show you around.*

Yeung struggled not to look at his companions: *You know. We just might take you up on that offer…IF we're not too tired of course.*

Chapter Fourteen
Snowball

Indian Ocean, Twenty Miles Outside of Somalian Waters — June 8, 2023

Ali Omar Biixi watched silently as his White Sails gathered about him.

He had received notification only minutes ago to begin assembling his men in preparation. That simple message had been delivered by way of a text to one of the three mobile phones left aboard their mysterious gift all those weeks ago.

Sometimes, Ali had forgotten he was carrying it. But the motor launch had always brought back to him how high the stakes could be. That craft was worth a small fortune. As indeed its contents had been. And yet they'd been freely given by an unknown benefactor who wanted a favor from them.

A favor, which might accrue too high a price!

Ali was concerned.

I've already seen how lethal our employer can be. That poor lackey who delivered both the vessel and the offer itself was forced to commit suicide with a callous disregard for human life that was shocking. I have no doubt that if we mess this up, a similar discourtesy will be extended toward us.

Because of that heartlessness, Ali had often wondered just *who* their actual targets were and what they could possibly have done to warrant such retribution.

And they know about Assad! How on earth could they have known about his gift?

Yes. Such things had troubled Ali repeatedly over the intervening weeks, and he was fervently beginning to wish they'd just taken the weapons and left.

But it was too late now! He'd received the first of what would be three sets of instructions, and had then watched incredulously as the phone disintegrated in his hand, succumbing to the hidden booby-trap encoded into its software.

Still keen to protect their anonymity, eh? I wonder how far they'll go to ensure ALL ties are cut between us once this is all over.

A chill ran down his spine. Ali felt he already knew the answer to that.

We were foolish to accept this offer. I realize that now. Already the consequences are beginning to accrue, and I fear what the outcome may cost us.

He looked at his watch. Only two hours left until dawn.

Today of all days! I'd better get back and start selecting my final team. Oh! And then get the second phone. I dread to think what would happen if we were late in any way.

As an afterthought, Ali called one of his oldest advisors, Sylvester, to his side.

"Sylvester, I have a special task for you. And you alone!"

For the next twenty minutes, Ali explained exactly what he wanted of his friend of over twenty years. Once finished, he sent him on his way to prepare.

At least I can ensure Assad gets out of there if things get too hairy. I've got a bad feeling about this, and he's NOT going to be part of it!

***

Naomi Cruiz couldn't believe she was here again so soon.

For the second time in just five years she had entered the catacombs. Only *this* time, she wasn't playing a subordinate role. No! She was the Transcension Candidate herself!

Who would have imagined it, eh?

Naomi smiled as soon as she uttered the thought, for she knew the answer to that particular question now. The Overlord himself had ensured Naomi was considered for the Supporters role on the occasion of her mentor's expansion.

Somehow, he had been well aware of the fact that Naomi's own capability for transcension had originally been stunted. Strangled of nurture, it festered at the center of her psyche. Left as it was, it would have rotted and she would never have bloomed into her full potential. Never have grasped the full scope of what she was capable of. So, he had guaranteed her selection. In doing so, her withered psi-well received the necessary stimulus it needed to boost it back to life...

...And the rest, as they say, is history!

Naomi looked about her as she descended the corridor. It was just as she remembered. The same ruddy glow, pulsing to the arcane heartbeat of the living rock about them. The same sense of anticipation, building with every step she took. The same sense of detachment the further she went, as the unique strata muted her power and soothed her growing urgency.

Looking within herself, Naomi saw a tiny spark burn through the mental constraints that had kept her expanding nexus at bay for so long. It was failing! The dam had sprung its first leak. Soon, the pressure would exceed its capacity to withhold the raging storm, and her true self would roar free at last.

Leading the way, Victoria quickened her pace, as if sensing the change.

Naomi was grateful Victoria was acting as the Shepherd today. She felt an affinity, both to the woman herself and her family like no other. Having Victoria there would make the process that much easier to bear, especially as her Supporter had stood in at the last moment.

For some reason, her original choice, Corrine Jackson, had stood aside. Naomi could only guess why. She had been replaced by none other than the Lord Marshall himself.

Naomi didn't know much about him. But she would–and soon! The shared intimacy of what was to come would grant him some insightful memories. As well as some shocking revelations once he witnessed what was in Victoria's mind.

I wonder what he'll think when he finds out?

Further thoughts on the matter were forgotten as Naomi became alarmingly aware of the raging beast within her. It had experienced its first taste of freedom, and wanted more.

Piling ever higher against her barriers, it demanded release.

Naomi could sense it wouldn't be denied for much longer. Evidently, so did Victoria, for she quickened her pace again.

Despite the growing urgency, Naomi had a funny thought.

Hey! I wonder if I'll ever walk this way again, as Shepherd. Has anyone ever fulfilled all three roles before? Is it even allowed?

***

To onlookers, Angelika and her team looked like any other group of people about to set off for a day's hiking along the trails of the Santa Anna Mountains. Four couples, besides two vehicles, packed with the necessary gear needed to keep them safe from the elements and any unforeseen predators they might encounter.

However, a closer inspection of their equipment would have raised more than a few eyebrows.

In amongst the backpacks, tents and camping gear, each vehicle carried four strange looking cylinders. Silver pipes that seemed to fold in and out of sight the more you looked at them. Alongside each device, was a collection of metallic, collar-style clamps with glowing crystals around the edges. Those gems flared and pulsed at irregular intervals in response to the strange acoustic throbs the cylinders themselves were emitting.

Standing around their vehicles, the group looked to be idly chatting for a while as they waited for the parking lot to empty of other visitors.

Once alone, they suddenly adopted a more urgent air.

Throwing back the tarpaulin in the rear of one of the trucks, Angelika removed one of the pipes with its attachments, and said, "Are we all clear on what to do?"

Directing their attention to the cylinder in front of her, she continued, 'Once we teleport to the site of each asperity, you have to attach three collar mines to each tube, then depress the green button, *here*. That arms the device. Within one minute from its activation it will begin emitting hypersonic waves through the subspace medium that will increase tectonic instability exponentially. Those frequencies will hamper your ability to teleport, so make sure you have finished arming the mines well before then! This same switch also deploys the gravity barriers around each site. They will prevent any earthquakes from manifesting before we are ready to trigger them!

"Ten seconds after you have depressed the green button, do the same with the amber one, *here*. This will channel the ensuing energy build-up directly into the crystal chambers. Immediately afterwards, depress the red button on the collars. That will arm the antimatter mines, and scramble the receivers to their preprogrammed frequencies.

"Are there any questions?"

None were forthcoming.

"Excellent. Timon, you take Electra to your coordinates within the Santa Monica Mountains. Emily, you've got Mike. Position your cylinders within the local fault line here. The rest of you, you're with me up in the San Gabriel Range."

She paused to hand out a tube and selection of clamps to each person.

"Are you ready? On my mark! Three, two, one…Mark!"

Moments later, they were gone. Little realizing how far reaching the consequences of their actions would be!

***

Esther was enjoying herself immensely, and it showed!

Over the past week, she had made friends in at least seven different departments. But really, that wasn't surprising! She had been keen to show an interest in other peoples work, and had thrown herself into the ethic of this new world from the outset by fully immersing herself in station life.

However, Esther had also been helped by an amazing stroke of luck!

On her first day, she had been engrossed in her welcome tour, when she noticed several Guardian and civilian technicians crowded around a power relay situated in one of the outer docking arms. Evidently, this particular consul kept fritzing out. Although not essential to operations, it was nevertheless causing a great deal of frustration to maintenance crews, who were growing tired of returning to this same junction again and again.

Esther had paused to watch them at work.

They were very thorough, having stripped and replaced the entire RAM-gel network a number of times in an effort to find a solution. However, as painstakingly methodical as they were, she'd noticed they had made a simple error. They were concentrating on treating the symptoms as opposed to looking for the cause! They were concentrating on treating the symptoms as opposed to looking for the cause!

Sidling over to them, she had suggested looking *outside* of the station.

Intrigued by her idea, the Guardian leading the crew did just that. By scanning the area of space in close proximity to the star base, the cause for the recurring problem was discovered.

Helan 1 had been constructed in a location where the gravitational influence of Kalliste, Callistran and Theron combined to form a void. A phenomenon equivalent to the Doldrums experienced at sea. Although this provided an ideal reception area free of strong tidal shears, there had been an unforeseen side-effect. Three bubbles had been formed within that zone, very similar in effect to a Null Vortex. Nothing would work within them. From time to time, gravity compression caused those bubbles to swell and burst. When they did, they sprayed *zero matter* into space around their vicinity.

Fortunately, these bubbles were very small, and only encompassed an area of several yards. But the resultant rupturing would spurt void material out in random directions for nearly half a mile.

The leading edge of this particular docking arm was just within the radius of one such anomaly. Thus the continuing problem! No matter how many times the relays were replaced, it wouldn't matter. Everything would still be rendered inoperable.

Scanners had subsequently been adjusted to register this incredibly rare phenomenon, and all three regions of rupture activity had been located and accurately quantified. Station thrusters were then employed to gently move the base to a new position free of the effects of 'zero matter fallout'.

That had provided Esther with the golden opportunity she was after!

She had noted how long it took to move the base to its new mooring. Remembering the reason she was here, she decided to make a play directly to the woman in charge.

At dinner later that night, Esther had exercised patience and waited for the Deputy Marshall to broach the subject of her assistance. She didn't have to wait long.

They had only just finished their entrée, when Anatt Yasin spoke directly to her.

"You made quite an impression today, Esther. First day here, and already you solved a bug in the works that had my technicians scratching their heads for months. How did you cotton on to the solution?"

"Oh, I'm just sensitive to the emanations of most kinds of energy," Esther had replied, offhandedly. "I noticed the Tec-heads were being very thorough, but had forgotten to look at the wider picture. My scans included the outside of the station. I'd noticed a distinct absence of any form of resonance, so, I knew the problem must lie there in some way."

"Fortunate for us you were there, then, yes?"

"I may be a scientist," Esther had responded, extending the bait, "but I tend to look at things from a different perspective. It's why Mr. Yeung uses me as a problem *avoider*, as opposed to problem solver."

"Oh really?" Anatt had replied. "So tell me. What situations have you noticed about our little base that might need...avoiding then?"

Esther had ensured to maintain her strongest shields to hide her elation.

Tentatively, she had said, "Well, I know it's not really my place..."

"Go on!" Anatt had urged, "Speak your mind. I don't mind clear expression in the least!"

"...Okay then. It's just that I noticed it took an awful long time to move the base out of the fallout area. I think that could cause problems in the future."

"What do you mean?"

"Well, this is still a new star system to us, right? I know you've been here a while, but nevertheless, when it comes to the natural cycle of a solar system; things tend to get measured in centuries. Or even longer!

"I just couldn't help remembering how near we came on Earth with Abaddon! It was an *out of the blue* event that nearly wiped us out. *This* system is bigger. Its asteroid belt is more extensive and the outer supergiant planets are almost as big as our sun. What's to say something like that couldn't happen here?"

"So what are you suggesting, exactly?"

"As I mentioned, I have a...sensitivity to different forms of energy. The moment I arrived, I felt a huge source of power within this base that you aren't even using yet. Although not as potent, it tastes similar to the energy generators you use on the hyper-gate. With so much capability at your disposal, I don't know why you've not considered using it more effectively."

"Define...'more effectively'." Anatt had stressed, edging closer.

Shrugging, as if she was unconcerned, Esther had replied, "Well! Look how long it took to move Helan One! Just imagine dawdling about like that with *Son of Abaddon* bearing down on you! I know you have some pretty nifty armaments deployed about the base, but don't kid yourself. Abaddon proved how easy it is to get overwhelmed. It would be tragic for that to happen here, when it could so easily be avoided!"

"So, what would *you* suggest?"

"Simple! I don't know the ins and outs of your gate system, but the scientist in me tells me you must employ some form of corresponding energy signature at both ends of your pathway to counter the effects of galactic drift, yes?"

"Yeeees." Anatt had replied, radiating approval.

"Well, you have a similar source here on Helan One. Why don't you have one of your strategists determine two of three alternate locations the base could occupy during an emergency, and establish some new anchors at those sites? Then, if the need arose, you could just jump the entire facility to a safer location in a fraction of the time!

"Obviously, you'd have to establish a whole new set of base 'Jump protocols'. You know. Drills, timing factors, lockdowns and so forth! But the effort would be well worth it."

Anatt's aura had bloomed scarlet in delight.

"*That* is an excellent idea, Esther. Without my ace problem solver in attendance at the moment, I could do with someone like you around."

The Deputy Marshall had looked thoughtful. "Tell you what, meet me on the main operations deck at nine tomorrow morning–K Time–and I'll introduce you to some section heads who might like to pick your brains. Deal?"

"Deal!" Esther had agreed, shaking on it.

That had been a week ago now!

Since then, Esther had been invited to tour the Medi-Labs, Environmental Control, the Habitat Center, and the Defensive Armaments Complex. In each case, she had made sure to suggest one or two radical ideas that had improved operating efficiency many times over. And in each case, Esther had discovered that she'd thoroughly enjoyed being able to exercise her creative talents again. Even so, she never lost sight of her objective.

It's a shame I'm enjoying myself so much! I'm almost going to regret blowing these fuckers to kingdom come the first chance I get!

Then, just this very morning came the break she'd been waiting for. Grand Master Hiro Nagasaki had called her to see if she would be interested in delaying her scheduled departure for Helion, on Kalliste.

Hiro was the overseer of Main Engineering. His team was getting close to incorporating an unusual power source into the main generators, and had heard about her uncanny knack for problem solving. He has wondered if she would be keen to add her insight to the proceedings, as they wanted to install the new source in such a way that it could later be distributed towards both defensive and aggressive measures.

Needless to say, Esther didn't have to think about her decision for long!

***

Although everything had started off so well, Simon Cooper was not a happy man.

Deputy Marshall Yasin had been very impressed by Esther's innovative ideas. So much so that she had virtually rolled out the red carpet to the entire team. Over the past week, Esther had got herself invited into just about every primary department there was on board the space station. Yeung had been wined and dined and shown around all of the main settlements on each of the three continents. And Simon himself had been afforded the exceptional courtesy of being allowed ground-side before his induction week was anywhere near complete.

Fortunately, his official profile had helped.

Thank goodness Yeung had persuaded them to register properly. Because of it, Simon was listed as possessing a marked proficiency when it came to hiking, field craft and survival skills. Additionally, his psychic assay revealed strong telepathic, telekinetic and shape-shifting abilities. This combination of expertise had vouchsafed his speedy decent into the jungles of Viridian, where he was allowed to indulge in his great love of naturalism in all its ecological glory!

Or so they thought!

On his first few guided forays, Simon had been careful to display only those features of his psi-well that the examiners expected. They were, after all, inherently particular to the real Simon Cooper.

His ruse had worked like a dream.

Because Viridian contained the least deadly predators of all three continents, Simon had quickly been deemed suitable for limited trips on his own. His knowledge, skill level in the field, and abilities appeared more than sufficient to help keep him out of trouble. The addition of a teleport band—similar in function to the rings employed by some Guardians—had meant both the Inquisitors and Marshals felt he would be unlikely to encounter anything he couldn't deal with.

Great news!

Or so he had thought.

Being allowed to roam free only three days ago, he had immediately set about his mission. Esther had equipped him with two Mimic Drones, sophisticated pieces of hardware that duplicated bio-signs. Originally designed to throw Guardian Inquisitors off their trail, they had decided *this* would be a prime opportunity to put them to another use.

One had been fashioned into the likeness a large wasp. Highly mobile, it was capable of covering a hundred square miles of terrain before needing to be recharged. Perfect for their needs! The other was designed to be incorporated into an individual's complexus, so that they registered as an alternate form of life entirely.

Programming the wasp with his own bio-signs, Simon had set it loose and shed his human form. Over the next several days, the wasp had covered about twenty miles a day at an average speed of two miles-an-hour. If anyone checked, it would look as if he had been enjoying a stress free ramble through the jungle.

In reality, Simon was on an entirely different continent!

His target was in the south western jungles of Nerada, completing a survival course. Candidates were not allowed to use their psychic abilities, and to ensure they kept to the rules, the area was heavily scanned.

To evade sensors, Simon had slow-ported into the vicinity, and maintained an indistinct form until the second Mimic Drone was activated. This one gave the life-signs of a Hoopy, a large ape-like creature indigenous to the whole of southern Nerada. Known for its inquisitiveness and ability to move quickly through the canopy, Simon thought it the perfect disguise to allow him to move swiftly without drawing attention.

And so, with at least a three day window ahead of him, Simon had felt confident he would be able to complete his mission and get away without being detected.

That was two and a half days ago!

At first, Simon had been amazed at the tenacity of the twelve year old human child. Now he was just plain annoyed.

What is it with this child? Is he some additional freak Sachael-Za-Ad'hem cooked up in a laboratory to torment me? Two and a half days I've been chasing him. Two and a half friggerty days! Toiling, sweating, and heaving myself through some of the most insane jungle imaginable. And the little bastard's still ahead of me!

No. Simon was not a happy man.

The child had proven unusually resilient. And what's more, Simon had the damndest feeling he was being watched.

Or followed!

Or both!

And yet, every time he stopped to gently scan the vicinity of the endless silver/blue foliage, there was never anything there.

But the feeling refused to go away.

Get a grip! He's just one human child caged to his limited flesh. No match for one of my caliber. The sooner I get this done, the sooner I can get out of this hellhole.

Casting yet another anxious glance behind, Simon abandoned his backpack and quickened his pace. One way or another, he was determined to bring this issue to a close!

Chapter Fifteen
Gathering Pace

Despite the fact that they were billions of miles apart, the image on the CDS screen was crystal clear. Esther hadn't quite worked out how they could do that yet. The portal itself was closed, but somehow, the Guardians were managing to relay a super compressed signal through the geodetic curvature of hyper-space.

Impressive! I wonder what toys I'd be playing with now…or even have invented had I played along with Sachael-Za-Ad'hem's schemes.

Alas! She didn't have time for musing over what *might* have been.

Yeung needed the latest update.

"Hello Esther," Yeung began, "All well?"

"Very well, thank you, Sir," She fawned, for the benefit of those who might be listening in. "Today I've been invited to the initialization of the new power core. The base commander has been kind enough to implement some of my recommendations and we're all going to see if they actually work."

Yeung gave Esther a direct look. "And do you think things will go as planned?"

"Oh, I've got every expectation things will go *exactly* as planned!"

"That's good to hear," Yeung replied, a look of satisfaction creeping across his face. "It looks as if I'll be having a busy day myself."

Esther got the hint.

Holding up a data crystal, she said, "These are my latest reports. You'll be pleased to hear I may have secured future contracts for terraforming operations, especially once the compounds and settlements begin to expand into virgin environment."

"Excellent. Excellent! And was the subsurface facilities proposal as popular as we anticipated?"

"I believe that was the clincher, Sir. Anatt assured me that once we've provided detailed schematics of the various facilities we have on offer, the full agreement will be forthcoming. If we live up to our end of the bargain, it's a done deal!"

A steely glint entered Yeung's eyes. "I do so like to hear the words, *done* and *deal* in the same sentence."

Again, Esther immediately picked up on Yeung's inference.

She added, "Well, I hope to send similar sentiments your way soon. I don't know about your end, Sir, but I've got some calculations to complete before the thirty-two hundred hours deadline. So I'm going to have to crack on…"

"Thirty-two hundred hours?" Yeung interrupted, complaining, "Pah! It's difficult enough as it is for an old man to get his head around the twenty-four hour clock, yet alone the thirty-nine hour K clock. What on earth is *that* in real time?"

"Hang on a second, Sir…" Esther replied, "…that works out as…nine…No! Wait a minute. Forget nine! That will be eight in the evening, tomorrow. GMT of course!"

"You see?" Yeung crowed, "If you can't get *your* young and active mind around it, how do you expect a gentleman of my advanced years to understand all this nonsense? Just let me know how it all goes when you've completed what you need to do."

"Will do, Sir!"

Signing off, Esther had to admit. That had gone better than expected.

Not only had she managed to update Yeung on her anticipated time of action, but he had confirmed the operation was a *go* and that he would co-ordinate events on his side of the gate.

Now all she had to do was update Simon. For some reason, he was still mincing about down on the surface. She had hoped he would have disposed of the boy and been back on the star base by now.

And if I can just work out how they get these damned signals to operate, I may be able to open us a backdoor to escape through if things get too hairy!

***

The party was in full swing.

A huge bonfire had been arranged in the middle clearing of the village. Wild pig was roasting over charcoal, and Ethiopian gin was in plentiful supply.

Assad was festooned in garlands and rice beads, and from where Ali was sitting with the elders, appeared to be thoroughly enjoying his sixteenth birthday party.

At this moment, the boy was leading a group of his best friends across to the gift his mother and father had provided for the occasion, a brand new, shiny, black Nissan Trailblazer SUV!

When he wasn't fishing, Assad was like any other boy his age. Boasting about cars and girls. He'd learned to drive not long after he had mastered skippering a boat, so it was only natural he'd want to prove his prowess both on and off the water. Ali actively encouraged his son to be adept at both. It was a sign of their wealth. Their success!

But girls? They were another matter entirely. And a distraction!

While many people in other poverty stricken villages eked out a living from barely useable tin huts, such need was not evident here. Ali looked after his clan. Comfortable, well fed and happy men were better motivated. Professional. And the White Sails were known for their expertise in capturing prizes no one else could.

This village had proper, brick built homes, with electricity and internet connection. Running water too! They were prosperous. But this had its downside, especially on occasions like this when outsiders were welcomed into the village.

The aforementioned *distractions*!

Neighboring, hijab-clad girls lined the perimeter of the bonfire area. Most had their eyes fixed on Assad. Despite their demure smiles, they looked upon pirates as a good marriage prospect in much the same way as they had once looked on Somali's clan chiefs and warlords. And it was all about one-upmanship! Especially in the marriage stakes where they could guarantee financial security for their families… *if* they could only catch the eye of the right boy.

And Assad, as son to a clan chief—and the White Sails Clan at that—was *the* prospect they all wanted to land!

Ali jumped, suddenly, his musing interrupted!

The mobile phone within the inner pocket of his jacket had just received a message. Not just any message either. This was the second of those left by their mysterious benefactor.

Why now! He thought, as he yanked the phone out and activated its screen. Frowning, he recognized a set of longitudinal and latitudinal references. Beneath them was a time.

But…that's in the early hours of tomorrow! He started! *Damned their eyes! I'd better bring this party to an early end!*

Ali knew his local waters like the back of his hand. The coordinates he had just received were quite a way outside their usual hunting grounds. To get there—especially undetected—would require them to leave within the hour!

Just in time too, from the look of it!

A particularly attractive young lady from a neighboring village was getting bolder, making eyes at his son and flashing a winsome smile. Assad had noticed and was beginning to posture like a bantam rooster.

Shame!

He could see Assad obviously liked the girl. But she was from a poor family who had no real influence. Many also thought them to be untrustworthy. Definitely not the right material as far as *his* son was concerned.

Shouting, he began to call his men together.

Thank goodness we'll have something to do that will keep him distracted for a while. Once we get back, I'd better make arrangements to have him formally introduced to someone more…suitable.

He won't be happy, but at least it will keep the vultures at bay

***

Victoria had never witnessed such a transcension.

Four days they'd been here now. Four inextricably long, drawn out, relentless days, teetering at the cusp of dissolution! And they were *still* waiting for the esoteric flare that would signal the advance of the final surge. A blazing sword that would at last rip through the remaining barrier and allow the girl's swollen nexus to reign free!

Victoria had known this process would be unlike anything ever witnessed before.

Naomi's prodigious capabilities had been ignited just over five years ago, after she had been exposed to the primary stimulus of a transmutation in progress. The Overlord himself had applied the Mita/Comp program to Naomi's Complexus shortly thereafter.

Since then, Naomi's remarkable well of energy had been allowed to expand exponentially. Way beyond the point at which her flesh would normally have disintegrated! Somehow, the sequence had muted her super-destructive element, while siphoning through tantalizing aspects of her emerging hyper-well.

Naomi was a remarkable young woman, and everyone was eager to see just how strongly she'd transform. And, they were keen to witness the degree of control her incredible ability to compartmentalize would give her.

But Victoria was already getting a glimpse of that!

The intimacy of the process had begun the sharing of some very personal memories. At first, Victoria had been curious to see Anil's reaction to the confirmation of some of his suspicions about her and her brother.

However, that interest had quickly changed focus!

Through Naomi, Victoria had perceived Anatt's transcension. She had shared the woman's agony as she was repeatedly gripped by violent seizures. Burnt, over and over, by tremendous throbs of energy radiating from every pore of her body as she approached the trigger point! It was a progression every candidate had been forced to endure for centuries.

Until now!

Oh, the convulsions were there alright! Fits that would have snapped the spine of just about anyone else Victoria knew. But along with them—as every torturous wave of suffering had smashed over Naomi's consciousness—something else had grown too.

An almost inhuman capacity for self awareness and control!

Usually, by this stage of the process, the Shepherd would be heavily engaged in mitigating the effects of the pain and struggling to keep the aspirant focused on the path of enlightenment ahead.

Sharing the experience, the Supporter would likewise be exercising the utmost caution. Their role would involve trying to keep the expanding consciousness of the candidate from fleeing the constraints of mortality and leaving everything to do with their previous life behind.

But that wasn't happening here!

Naomi was almost guiding herself. By yanking back on the reins of devastating chaos, Naomi was not only anchoring her sanity, but appeared to be forcing the hyper-energized surges breaking free from her core to do *her* bidding.

Victoria and Anil were almost redundant.

Flicking an intimate query to Anil, Victoria made a suggestion: *I don't need to tell you, THIS is unprecedented! What say we take advantage of the situation and try and meld with her? Share the experience of an entirely different level? I can't promise it'll work, but...*

I don't think there'll be any doubt it will work, Victoria! Anil cut in: *Look!*

Incredulously, they turned their full attention back to Naomi.

Despite the cosmic forces ravaging her soul, Naomi had remained fully cognizant of her surroundings. She had witnessed her friends' conversation, although it had been addressed on their intimate band. And she had agreed...it would be a great idea!

Unbelievably, the transcension candidate was in complete control.

Looking directly at them through eyes that shone like miniature stars, she was extending an unprecedented invitation: *Come! Behold the future!*

Instantly, Victoria and Anil responded. Meshing in harmonic union, they rushed to witness a transformation, the likes of which had never been seen before.

***

Simon Cooper felt like screaming!

While it had been gratifying to see how well the mimicking device had worked, he was at the end of his tether with this infernal child.

No matter how much effort he had devoted to the pursuit, Simon just couldn't seem to close the gap. The child was relentless. Hardly stopping, the boy would forge through the confusing tangle of vegetation as if its mere existence gave him some form of perverted boost. An added impetus he somehow found invigorating.

How the hell can he move so quickly through this bewildering tangle of spaghetti? It's not like he's native to this environment! Little bastard! I'm sure he's doing it just to annoy me!

Glancing skyward, Simon checked again for signs of surveillance.

And how long will my luck hold out!

As if on cue, Simon felt a slight tremble behind his eyes. He froze for a moment, fearing his masquerade had been discovered. A second later, he relaxed.

Esther!

Stopping his pursuit, he paused to digest the implications of the encoded message.

Already! Damned…But I'd better get going! Especially if I want to make the window she's managed to open.

Risking a stronger scan, Simon discerned his quarry just two miles ahead. The boy had just made a kill and looked to be in the process of making camp.

At last!

He checked again. Sure enough, Joshua looked intent on settling in to enjoy his first real meal of the week.

Perhaps he IS only human after all!

Slowly summoning his potential, Simon stalked forward preparing for a kill of his own. *Nothing fancy, just a clean, quick job! Trigger the explosion on the wasp drone to draw their attention. Then dispose of the boy. They're bound to be monitoring my welfare. How sad I met a sudden and mysterious end while exploring the dark depths of a dangerous new world.*

Then he had a thought.

I hope Yeung has arranged a suitable new identity for me. I've quite enjoyed being Simon Cooper. It's allowed me a great deal of flexibility. He'll have to go a long way to match that!

Chapter Sixteen
Cloud Burst

The fogbank drifted forward like an irresistible tide, gleaming softly in the moonlight. A tsunami wall, made from mist and mystery instead of the irresistible force of millions of cubic tons of water.

To the sentries posed aboard the Winters Gale, a container ship registered out of France, it crawled toward them like a herald of doom. So unusual was the phenomenon on these waters, that some rushed below to get camcorders, cameras or other recording devices. And then for the next thirty minutes, they watched silently, mute observers as the veil crawled inextricably past them and on toward the straights.

Soon, interest waned among the crew members, and the fog was left to its own devices. An entry was made in the log. Other shipping entering the Gulf of Aden from the Red Sea was alerted to the navigating hazard, and business went on as usual.

Or so it seemed.

For safely ensconced deep within that mist were a group of people on a very special mission. Most of them were clustered aboard a brand new, unregistered motor launch. For the moment, its powerful engines were idle, and the craft drifted gently along, being content to let the gulf current take it where it would.

However, had anyone had been in a position to measure the composition of the cloud, they would have noted something remarkable. For no matter where that craft drifted, the mists followed. In fact, they remained most concentrated around the yacht itself, as if determined to conceal its existence from the outside world.

But that wasn't really surprising. For that's exactly what the fogbank was designed to do! And the person responsible for its existence, sixteen year old, Assad Ali Omar, was determined to keep things that way.

The boy's father, Ali Omar Biixi, said, "Are you alright my son? Are you sure you don't need to rest?"

"I'm okay for the moment. Although I may take a break soon. I don't want to expend myself before the real mission gets underway."

Looking at the radar, Ali noted only a handful of ships within a ten mile radius of their position. Acceding to their circumstances, he said, "If I was you, I'd ease off a little bit. You've been generating our curtain for over an hour now. We're running silent and without lights anyway. If anyone gets too close I'll give you a head up so you can thicken the stew around us. Okay?"

"Okay Father."

Nodding in satisfaction, Ali returned his attention to the radar display.

His crew was handpicked and reliable. They were all veteran sailors, and could be trusted to remain alert. And if things got hairy, Ali knew he could depend on them to keep their heads while they got the hell out of there.

But the waiting was agony.

For the umpteenth time in a few minutes, he fingered the mobile phone in his pocket. *C'mon. Call us damned you! Let's get this done so we can get on with our lives again.*

Of course, his plea went unanswered! And soon, the gentle lapping of the waves against the hull began to rock everyone into a waking sleep.

***

Grand Master Hiro Nagasaki had called the Main Engineering team to order bang on the thirty-two hundred hours mark. They had busily been incorporating Esther's suggestions into the reactor relays over the past few days, and now everyone was keen to begin the power-up sequence that would bring the station fully on-line.

It had been agony for Esther.

She was so close to the crystal shard, she was almost salivating.

What made it worse was the fact that she couldn't just relax and reach out to taste the harmonic vibrations the damned thing was giving off. If she dared indulge herself—as everyone else was doing— the crystal would recognize her familiar signature and flare in response, announcing her true identity to the whole world.

And she didn't want it to flare out…just yet.

Her eyes kept straying to the clock.

Twenty minutes to go. Just twenty more minutes! Then they'll discover what my little suggestions can REALLY do.

***

Angelika Papadakos felt unusually excited.

Their rehashed plans were coming together rather nicely, and the latest twist was something she was still trying to get her head around. If it worked, it would really boost their designs for future expansion. Schemes, in which she would play an increasingly important role!

But she couldn't afford to let her feelings about that distract her. She had to remain ready and alert.

Looking about her surroundings now, she had to admit. Room within the firing platform was remarkably spacious. *I suppose they planned it this way to allow for regular maintenance and upgrade installations. I know from experience. You can't always rely on automated AI solutions for everything. But I bet they never dreamed someone would use the room for THIS though. Even if it is one of our own ghost models!*

Being careful not to touch anything, Angelika adjusted the scanners with her telekinesis. Zooming in on the western coast of the USA, she adapted her focus until the mountainous region surrounding the greater Los Angeles area came into view. Refining the beam even further, she then concentrated on the continental substrata in several different areas.

With quiet satisfaction, Angelika measured the results of her earlier work.

The hypersonic wave emitters had increased tectonic stresses a thousand-fold in the vicinity of each asperity. Fortunately, the crystal fragments were absorbing the modular amplification of those emanations sufficiently to mask the deadly buildup...for now!

However, the instruments were indicating that once she sent the command sequence to drop the temporal sheath around each cylinder, the results would be unbelievably devastating.

As well as releasing colossal amounts of energy, the antimatter detonations would create huge voids in the earth's mantle. That, combined with the sudden delivery of ultra-amplified seismic potential, would release a catastrophic energy wave. This would effectively shatter the spine of the San Gabriel Mountains and drop a huge segment of the North American Plate onto the much more fragile Pacific Plate. A region that included Pasadena and San Fernando to the Northeast, Santa Monica and North Ridge to the

Northwest, Long Beach, and reaching all the way down to Palos Verdes and Garden Grove!

The entire area would be crushed down into the sea.

It would be glorious!

No warning. No time to prepare. There's no way they'll be able to prevent a cataclysm.

Checking her instruments one last time, Angelika thought, *C'mon Yeung! Send me the damned signal. Let's get this show on the road!*

***

As softly and as stealthily as he could, Simon Cooper crept forward.

Leaving nothing to chance, he was heavily shielded, and completely invisible. Now only scant yards from his target, he could almost taste the sweetness of his impending victory!

Gotcha you little bastard!

Joshua Drake was stretched out upon a thin insulate strip. Using his arms as a pillow, he had a survival blanket wrapped tightly around his slight form, and for the first time in days, he was actually napping while his food roasted on a hastily contrived spit.

Now he was closer, Simon could see some form of adhesive patch attached to the boy's forehead. He didn't know what is was exactly, but guessed it to be some form of recording or measuring device to ensure the child didn't cheat by employing his abilities.

Not that there had been the slightest hint of that. Inching forward, the hiker that had been part of Simon Cooper extended begrudging respect. The youngster was an accomplished survivalist and hunter. He had not only managed to pass through the dense jungles with consummate ease, but he'd also got a healthy fire going, despite the dank, humid conditions surrounding him for hundreds of miles in every direction.

Pity he'll never get the opportunity to enjoy his kill! Law of the jungle and all that! Quite poignant really…

Simon froze, his *almost* victory now only scant feet from him.

That damned creepy feeling was back!

Not daring to move, Simon concentrated on diffusing his form to dissipate any signal he might inadvertently be emitting. It would slow him down fractionally, but if he delivered a psychic shock the moment he blew the drone, Guardian sensors might not realize what had happened. In the confusion, they may even think the energy spike was an esoteric burst from the boy as he died in a tragic accident.

Which won't be far from the truth! He chortled. *I'll just break his neck and make it look like he fell from something.*

Simon was just about to resume his advance, when the boy said, "I know you're there! So you might as well come out!"

What?

"Come out. Come out, wherever you are!"

Enraged, Simon began to coalesce.

"String! You do realize I'm going to…" The words choked off in Joshua's throat.

Before Simon had taken a step, a mighty roar ripped through the undergrowth only scant feet to one side. Its resonance caused the hairs on the back of his neck to rise instantly. Before he could turn, some form of psychic scream tore through his mind, rooting him to the spot. Bewildered, Simon was smashed to the floor by the crushing impact of five hundred pounds of ferocious sinew and muscle. The blur of dappled markings dominated his sight as he hit the ground and instinctively rolled! It was only the fact that his atoms had not fully merged again, that had saved him.

Coming to his feet, Simon was confronted by a prehistoric nightmare.

Standing at more than six feet at the shoulder, a huge saber-toothed predator bore down on him, blocking the child from sight. The massive muscles of its chest and forelegs rippled with every movement. A deep *thud* echoed off into the undergrowth in response to each measured step. It made no attempt to employ its uncanny stealth any more. A gaze that burned like acid bore into him, its impact like a kick to the guts.

The creature's upper lip curled back as it growled, revealing a further row of razor-like teeth, each bigger than his own hand. Another psychic howl threatened to drive Simon to his knees.

Gradually, the beast dropped its head. Its hind quarters began to tremble as it gathered the energy to spring the twelve feet it needed to close the distance on him.

For the first time, Simon was able to clear his mind enough to hear the boy yell, "NO STRING! STAY!"

S…ing n…you ar…!

For some reason, he could barely hear the boy's echoing psychic call.

Strange!

Pained frustration crossed Joshua Drake's face. Pausing, he ripped the pad from his head. Too late, his mind bellowed: *STRING NO!*

Snarling with a rage that would have frozen a lesser being to the spot, the huge feline launched itself forward. Dagger-like talons arced toward Simon's throat.

But Simon wasn't a lesser being.

He was of the Fallen.

As the Veran sent him sprawling to the floor once more, Simon delivered a devastating reflex surge of uncontrolled energy! A sizzling snap crackled through the air as the breath was knocked from his lungs. He lay there dazed for a moment, before recognizing the smell of burnt flesh and mewling whimpers of pain.

STRING!

The thought was loud and clear this time. Its tone laced with barely contained passion.

"Oh String!" gasped the physical voice, the boy's agony clearly evident.

Simon looked up.

Across the burnt and blackened body of the beast, his gaze met that of the human child. A child only twelve years of age. A twelve year old, whose face began to twist into a mask of grief and hateful outrage. A mask with dark and terrible eyes! Eyes that began to burn with fury!

Surging to his feet, Joshua snarled and extended his hands. Immediately, incredible power began responding to his furious demands, flooding into his body from the very essence of the energy strands about them.

Simon recoiled in horror. Summoning his transmutation program, he began to flee as death manifested in the air about him.

He only just made it!

A swirling vortex of focused loathing squeezed in on him and began ripping his physical form to pieces. Even when transcended, Simon was horrified to discover the shredding continued.

He had no choice.

Beaming the self destruct sequence toward his Mimic Drone, Simon initiated an emergency teleport and fled the scene.

Behind him, another howl split the ether.

NOOOOOO!

***

Pea Souper!

Ali had never heard the term before, but he liked it. It conveyed a certain impression that really summed up the fogbank about them.

Thirty minutes ago, a British tanker had sailed majestically by. Relying totally on instruments, its crew had never realized the White Sails had been there, such were the effects of Assad's ability. The pirates much smaller craft had been tossed about like a cork. But, because they were professional to the last man, they had managed to maintain a complete silence.

It had been alarming to watch the two inch thick, steel plated hull steam by. But, in the ensuing calm, Ali had heard that phrase uttered by an opposing crewmember who was obviously a native of London...

"...Bloody hell Mike! It's a real pea souper out there. Any thicker and we'd have to use an icebreaker to carve a way through for us..."

Whoever Mike was, he had laughed at the comment. But all too soon, both he and his crewmate had disappeared off into the night, unaware of the moments respite from the mounting tension they had provided for the strangers concealed in the mist only yards below them.

Soon, however, the nerves were back.

They were only eight miles offshore from Aden, and almost upon their target. This close to the Bab-el-Mandeb Straight, traffic was much heavier. They had to maintain a high level of concentration to ensure they wouldn't get run down by the much larger vessels now surrounding them.

Suddenly, their objective appeared only fifty yards ahead, through a brief gap in the mist. The Savage Wind, a nuclear container ship out of Tokyo, looked to be at anchor after clearing the straights.

Excellent! Ali thought. *This will make the task so much easier. What a stroke of luck!*

Gathering his men around him, he went over the simple plan one last time.

"We are now approaching the target under cover of night and Assad's ability. Remember, while covered by his shadow, their radar, radios and other navigational aids will be rendered mute. However, we will be vulnerable to collision, so we must move swiftly.

"Jagpal, prepare the devices. I want them up on deck by the time we pull alongside. Samuel, hand out the pistols. Don't forget! Use silencers unless we are discovered. If we are seen, we will shoot our way out with machine guns.

"Team one, under myself, will head down to the cargo hold. Team two, under Jagpal, will keep the way clear for a rapid exit. If we proceed with caution, we'll be in, out and away, and they'll never know we were here. However, Teman? If you hear fighting, put a rocket through her side toward the bow. That will keep them occupied at the other end while *we* make for the north coast.

"Questions?"

There were none.

Nodding, Ali sent a brief text message to Sylvester, who was standing by in a fast skiff at the very edge of the fogbank. Once completed, he joined the others and made ready.

A few minutes later, they lowered tires over the side and prepared to board.

An eerie silence had descended, as if the sea itself had chosen to hold its breath. Scanning the ship, they discovered an uncovered loading balcony only twenty feet above them.

Turning to Samuel, Ali whispered, "Rubber tools only!"

Nodding, Samuel picked up a length of knotted rope with a triple-headed hook arrangement on the end, and moved forward onto the bow. Looking up, he judged the distance and played out a length of line. Gently, he began to swing the weighted end back and forth. Once he had sufficient momentum, he stepped forward and heaved the hooks into the air. Sailing over the edge of the balcony, a dull *thud* echoed out into the night.

Everyone held their breath.

After a few minutes, it was clear they had not been detected.

Pulling the line taunt, Samuel looped additional ropes over both his shoulders and made room to leap forward. Barefoot, he swiftly climbed the rope and disappeared over the ledge. Moments later, further lines were dropped.

One by one, both teams scrambled up onto the ship. Once the last man was aboard, two nylon nets were lowered back onto the yacht. The remaining White Sails made haste to wrap the nuclear devices inside hessian sacking, whereupon they were positioned within the nets and gently hauled up onto the loading balcony.

Pausing for a moment, team two made their way forward and across deck. Taking up their positions, they melted into the shadows and ceased to exist.

Team one gathered around each device, and began to carry them toward the Above Deck Machine Room. Situated at the stern of the ship, the machine room provided a separate control center away from the main bridge. Although the majority of it would be down below–sandwiched by the equipment rooms and main engineering–they knew this structure would provide access to the service elevator. Something they would need to complete their task swiftly.

So far, they'd been aboard for less than five minutes and hadn't seen anyone. While a little odd, Ali wasn't complaining. This task was fraught with enough danger as it was. And with Assad in tow, he was grateful for the lucky streak they were enjoying.

However, the further they descended into the bowels of the craft, the more things didn't add up. A nuclear container ship would usually be very well guarded. Additionally, normal crewmembers would be walking about everywhere, no matter what the time of day or night. But this place was a floating ghost town!

Radioing through to Jagpal on the upper decks, Ali then discovered no one on team two had witnessed any sign of movement either! What was even more unsettling was the fact that the pilot house, radio room and battery room also looked deserted.

I don't like this. The sooner we dump these damned things and flee, the safer I'll feel.

Eventually, after fifteen minutes of sweat, toil and tension, they arrived outside the main cargo doors. Mysteriously, they were unlocked.

Peeping inside, Samuel gasped, "Look at this!"

Pushing him aside, Ali stepped through.

This was no storage area crammed full of decommissioned nuclear facilities and fuel rods. Instead, Ali found himself looking at a completely empty cargo hold, echoing to the sounds of their whispers and soft footsteps.

Alarm bells rang clearly in his head.

Turning to his men, Ali pointed and said, "Position the devices there and there. Arm them and let's get out of here."

Lifting the radio to his lips, he called, "Jagpal? Get the men ready. We're leaving…now!

"Teman? We're on the way. Have the boat ready, and tell Sylvester to start making his way to the secondary rendezvous point. Oh, and Teman…I want at least three rocket launchers ready, loaded and primed, for when we get back onboard."

As quietly as possible, Ali and his team began to run.

Then the power went out!

***

Shocked for a moment, Esther was too stunned to move.

The Helan 1 main alert klaxon had just activated, and for a second, everyone stared at each other in mute astonishment.

Esther assumed her calculations must have been faulty. Without thinking, she began scanning the core, where the Prime Synthesis Reactor was situated. As she did so, some of the assembled Guardians began teleporting to their emergency stations. Others began hurrying toward adjacent terminals.

Checking the matrix, Esther could see the merging of arcane energies appeared to be stable. Confused, she turned to Grand Master Nagasake, and said, "Is this supposed…"

Suddenly, a fleeing thought pattern seared across her mind: *Get us out of here!*

Simon? What the hell?

She glanced at the clock: *It's five minutes too soon! What are…*

Fuck the timing. Move or die!

Without a second thought, Esther reacted. Unleashing a sizzling halo of energy, she sent everyone near her crashing to the floor. Writhing in agony, the Guardians fought to counter the effects of the neural lightning unexpectedly burning its way along their nervous systems.

Simultaneously, Esther blended with the nearest Engineering Command Terminal.

Designed to serve as a second bridge in the event of a disaster, the consul allowed override access to all main star base functions. Meshing with that system, Esther entered the codes she had obtained from Jose Calderon prior to departure. Ordering a purge of the new defense protocols, the entire grid began to shut down.

Taking note of the ensuing confusion, she then activated the Hyper-Jump Gate itself.

Dropping her shields, Esther leaped forward. Summoning her transcension program, she let fly with two bolts of super-charged energy. One fried the command computers, preventing the cancellation of her instructions. The second, aimed as it was at the main engine room viewport, shattered its integrity.

Blowing outward, the recovering Guardians were now forced to contend with the encroaching vacuum of space.

Recognizing her presence, the crystal chimed to life. Harmonizing her aura to full advantage, Esther swooped toward it and triggered a psi-metric feedback loop. The gravity sheath holding the psi-tronic fragment in place blew out, sending an overload cascade coursing through the RAM-gel nervous system. The shard then flew into her esoteric grasp, emitting a corresponding nimbus of energy as it did so.

A distracting flash signaled the activation of the hyper-gate. Esther watched in relief as Simon crossed the geodesic plane.

Reaching out to his dissolving essence, she screamed: *Tell Yeung to go NOW! I'm just going to finish up he…*

YEUNG? A mighty voice imposed.

A chill coursed through Esther's complexus. Too late, she jumped toward the still open pathway.

Faster that she believed possible, the gate was slammed shut in her face. Then sealed by an overwhelmingly powerful wall of energy!

Esther turned to face her opponent.

An angelic apparition flared into existence before her. At almost eleven feet in height, it dwarfed Esther's strength and spectral brilliance. More frighteningly, the mind generating that complexus displayed a steely determination that smacked of unwavering devotion to duty…and her death.

This was *NOT* an entity to face off against.

Psychic talons began to squeeze in on Esther's position.

Anatt Yasin's mind repeated: *What was that you said about notifying Yeung?*

Trying to distract her adversary while she thought of a solution, Esther teased: *Pity! We could have been friends you know…in another life.*

No form of recognition or response was forthcoming. Instead, Esther felt her defenses begin to crumble. Alarmed, she increased the strength of her shields, and phased in her integrated EMU/Mitigator.

The intensity of Anatt's grip suddenly eased for a few moments, before adapting and returning with a vengeance.

Pain exploded within Esther's complexus. An icy mind hissed: *Somewhere to go in a hurry, Esther?* Moving even closer, Anatt added: *I asked you where you were going. And why Yeung would be so interested?*

Esther was shocked. *Shit! They've overcome the implant! But how is that pos...*

Not wanting to hang around to find out, she reacted quickly. Bringing the power of the crystal to bear, Esther loosened the restraints about her long enough to trigger an escape pod. Within moments, the waiting pyramid layers sucked her into a confusing morass of intertwined and replicated pathways.

She was free!

Goddamit! That was close!

Checking the integrity of her tunnels, Esther relaxed a little. Not only were they guaranteed to confound any pursuit the Deputy Lord Marshall might decide to send after her, but, they were also laced with a number of booby-traps.

At this moment, Esther was fervently wishing her opponent *would* chase her!

It would be immensely gratifying to watch her manifest on top of the event horizon of a black hole. Talk about SURPRISE!

Pity I've only got two ambushes like that!

Then she snorted as a funny thought crossed her mind.

Mind you. Knowing her the way I now do...She'd probably chew the damned thing out for even daring to try!

Shame! I really DID like her!

Chapter Seventeen
Falling Apart

No sooner had Simon Cooper coalesced into real space, than he instantly re-teleported to the far side of the sun. As he did so, he uttered a single, far-spoken word on the declamatory mode.

NOW!

Using the coronal flares to mask his transmutation, Simon then activated three pyramid pods. However, instead of entering the tunnels, he merely scattered a quantity of false psi-dent chips about his close proximity.

All but one was sucked into the vortexes, leaving a plethora of false trails through the subspace medium. The remaining ident, Simon projected on a sub-light collision course with Mars.

Let their base there think they have a fugitive in their sights. I'll be long gone and getting familiar with my new identity by the time they discover their error.

Pausing, Simon ensured his atomic structure exactly matched the rest of the plasma field about him. Satisfied, he then blended with a particularly large coronal ejection. Beginning his sedate ride back toward Earth, he thought, *I can't believe how quickly that all fell apart at the seams. I hope the rest of the stages run more smoothly.*

***

Ali looked at his watch again as his team pounded along the passageways. All pretence for silence long gone! The ship was deserted, and this situation felt more and more like a trap the longer they were here.

Twenty minutes!

Just twenty short minutes, before the huge container ship was blown out of the water and all hell broke loose.

Although not an expert, Ali had been doing some rough calculations of his own.

The devices were low yield. That much he did know.

The initial burst of lethal ionization would only affect an area of about a mile's radius from the ship, so they wouldn't have to worry about that. From what he remembered, such radiation was very short lived. If they were far enough away, they wouldn't be harmed.

IF we're far enough away!

Additionally, although the shockwave from the blast would be far more dangerous, it should remain manageable. The yacht itself was equipped with the latest ultra-seal hatchways and self righting mechanisms, so he was confident they wouldn't capsize.

No, what was worrying Ali was the searing thermal radiation they would have to contend with. The actual heat given off by the explosion! *That* would fry them where they sat, unless he could discover a way to find shelter.

And he'd had an idea as to where to find it!

It would be a close call, but if there was a suitable ship near enough, they might be able to hide on its leeward side until the carnage was over.

MIGHT, being the operative word!

Then, all that would remain would be the mad dash for the Somalian coast to escape the fall out. Once there, a team of vehicles–which included Assad's shiny new SUV–would ferry them away from the scene of the crime, and home.

Home! God, that feels so far away at the moment...

Rushing up onto the main deck, Ali yelled, "Go! Go! Go! Get out of here. Don't try to stay quiet. Just jump over the side."

His men didn't need telling twice.

Slinging their weapons, they raced for the railings. Pausing to check the whereabouts of their own craft, they adjusted their positions and vaulted.

Coming to a rest himself, Ali raised his radio.

No need for Sylvester to hang around when he's in a more vulnerable craft. I'll send him on his way and we can meet up on…

Depressing the switch, he was just about to talk when a high pitched whine drowned out any chance to speak. The sound cut the silence of the night like a knife. Yanking the earpiece away from his head, he thought, *was that a microwave burst?*

Ali wasn't about to stand around and find out. Stepping up onto the railing, he leaped forward.

Down in the hold, the digital displays on the one kiloton bombs had paused fractionally at seventeen minutes and six seconds. The inner working of their CPU's adjusted for a moment to the new instructions they had just received from an orbiting satellite.

Suddenly, the LED readouts flared, and began tumbling down, as if in freefall.

Two seconds later, the numbers reached zero.

Back up on deck, Ali couldn't understand *why* he was still sailing through the air.

Shouldn't I be falling by now?

His world turned white hot…Then the blackness took him.

***

From her position in high orbit, Angelika was hoping to have at least seen more of an impressive light-bloom from the Gulf of Aden. That side of the Earth was still an hour away from dawn, so it should have been dark enough to see the blinding intensity of the initial fireball in all its glory.

Hmmh! What an anticlimax! Not like it is on the TV at all…

…Mind you, it doesn't have to be too spectacular. The ton of plutonium powder we scattered through the deck lining will contaminate enough of the Gulf and Red Sea to ensure the Straight remains closed to shipping for quite a while. Somehow, I can't see them making their daily quota of three billion barrels of oil tomorrow!

Angelika subconsciously scanned the horizon for any sign of the cloaked and shielded Guardian stations. *I wonder how long it will take them to react?*

Counting slowly to ten in her head, she then initiated another set of microwave bursts. These ones were aimed at the Los Angeles basin.

Angelika watched, closely. She was keen to see the effects of the single gram of antimatter within each mine. Although not a scientist herself, she had been told that each collar contained the equivalent power of three Hiroshima bombs. That energy, combined with the amplification provided by the crystal shavings were bound to be spectacular.

From high above, it looked as if a number of huge invisible stones had been thrown into a pond, with Downtown Los Angeles at its center. Forming an inverted 'U' shape, a rabid throng of closely packed ripples seemed to radiate inwards, as if a sudden vacuum had been created beneath the surface of the earth. Coming together, those shockwaves appeared to pause for a moment, before rebounding outwards at an even faster rate.

As the surge dissipated, the ground at eight distinct points around the Los Angeles basin began to protrude upwards. Rising higher and higher, those bulges continued to swell into gigantic bubbles, lifting millions of tons of rock and soil with them. Glowing yellow hot at their cores, it looked like Hades had come to wreak vengeance upon the puny mortals living above.

Amazingly, the inner furnaces of each blister winked out at the same moment. It looked to Angelika as if someone had flicked a light switch off! Only to flick it back on again a second later, as they erupted outwards with an even greater force than before.

Silver/white brilliance ripped its way through the surface tension of each bubble, vaporizing earth and rock alike, and bathing the entire east coast in a blinding glare.

Even though she was three hundred miles up, Angelika was forced to shield her eyes.

Now THAT was impressive!

Preparing herself for departure, Angelika risked one final glance. Sighing with deep satisfaction, she watched as a gigantic horseshoe-shaped ring of land began to sag alarmingly. As it did so, she noticed a huge wave deformation take place only twenty miles out into the Pacific Ocean. Extending past Malibu in the north and down to Oceanside in the south, it appeared to all intent and purpose as if a giant had just had a tantrum and slapped the flat of his hand into the sea.

Looking at her watch, Angelika checked the time. *Ah, only four fifty-seven. A little early, but never mind. It looks like the whole basin is coming apart! Excellent! I'd better get out of here then…*

…Hmmh! I wonder how things are going for the others?

***

Like a blink in the eye of the universe, eternity beckoned as Naomi Cruiz approached the threshold between existence and oblivion.

Her shepherd and Supporter watched with bated breath. Eager with anticipation that the ordeal would, at last, be entering its final phase!

But still Naomi lingered.

Already expanded beyond the constraints of human mortality, she wished to understand her emerging level of existence with a clarity that defied reason. Therefore, she delayed. Tasting, sampling, savoring and devouring! Analyzing an essence that only hinted at the hidden puissance within…

…New experiences, as old as creation, were rediscovered from the dawn of time. Neither *this* way nor *that*, for millions of possible realities was being presented all at once!

I see! She gasped. Fascinated by what it was that now lay open to discovery.

And there, at the edge of reason…The whispers!

Howling like demons in the silence of night, they guided her, showing the path to take if only she could find the courage.

Fires scorched the soul of her doubt with bitter frigidity.

Step across, and be cleansed! They called. *Purge your new mind free of insubstantial impotence to discover the solidity of purpose in a single thought.*

That step is taken.

A crystal is grasped.

Unprecedented! They chorus.

Why is my life of consequence as insubstantial as smoke in the wind?

How could I have missed the liquidity of the cosmic all, blending as it does with all and nothing?

Adjusting to a wider scope, Naomi began to see how galaxies flowed, impinging on an interstellar consciousness too vast to listen. Myriad heartbeats were joined in ecstasy. Pulsing with life at every level, they spanned the universe. Some here! Some there!

Others were watching too, spying from far away.

They are powerful and so very different. And yet, they ring with intimate familiarity. Why? Who are these entities?

We are here to assist. They call. *Free from petrifaction, we respond…as we should have all those eons ago.*

If I could only remember who they are?

…Are these even my memories?

Complexity abounded, hidden in plain sight within abject simplicity.

Look there!

Soaring majesty contained within a simple, dying atom.

The intricacies of the maestro of all design revealed?

Awesomeness encapsulated within the aberration of physics. Black as darkest night, it swallows all within its field of gravity.

Look closer!

It sings! The bass tones glitter like stars on the fabric of existence, music to those ears able to discern it.

Dust motes dance to a never-ending purpose, unfathomable to all but the few who still hold back…afraid to take the final step.

A trillion possibilities fractured within the convexity of a crystalline lattice.

I have but one.

Do—or do not!

The bittersweet taste of humanity gained and lost as the choice is finally taken.

Cognizance recognized.

I take another step. Willingly!

A psychic barrier pierced. An overwhelming surge of release and an explosion of awareness! Neural pathways, so freshly sensitized. Energized like the flaring of a star.

Supercharging, changing, metamorphosis!

I swell. I grow. I change and become what I was destined to be. WHO I was destined to be! I grasp and take hold of hypothetical realities!

Sounds now have taste. Tastes give off color. Sights congeal in a bouquet of fragrances. Smell now rings with solidarity of purpose! Compartmentalized purpose becomes bound to the elasticity of a thousand outcomes.

Oblique transparency resounds with limitless knowledge.

A single tone pierces the silence and I witness the moment of creation. Its power, its majesty, encapsulated within a speck of dust. Each is a universe in its own right. Carried on solar winds, they spread knowledge and the essence of life. A symphony of titanic bliss, they also conceal the truth from those too proud to truly search for it...

...And I am but a note in the eternal scope of infinity.

My dazzling mind is now super-energized. Far, far beyond that which I thought possible—the very superficies of reality extend further invitations.

Diversification of neural pathways!

I now exist here AND there. Elsewhere and everywhere too! Pulsing with a psycho-energetic concordance, I span time.

Flesh is cast off! Shackled weight thrown free!

I soar at last, reaching out as I was meant to do. I shine and magnify into full capacity. The crystal before me is but an Artifact. A tool and conduit through which my will reigns supreme!

NAOMI?

Other minds express concern.

One lesser, yet wise! The other a paradox in its humility and greatness, encompassing might as yet undetermined!

Naomi, are you there?

They call in union, the blending a masterpiece of harmonic transition. Although redundant, they instruct me from afar.

Remember we are here. We can see you still comprehend your identity. Do not succumb to oblivion.

Oblivion? But I soar! Godlike among lesser...

—NO! I MUST NEVER THINK THAT WAY—

...Among less EVOLVED beings. Those who have yet to take the step!

A state of true existence is recognized. Accepted, the aspirant comprehends it is but one of a number of options.

For I see many more! Much more! And they all call to me, beckoning as they tease. An enticing vastness, blinding in their brilliance!

So intoxicating!

COME!

They would lure me away if I let them.

COME! LOSE YOURSELF!

The gravity of their will...is...

BE WITH US!

Who are you, really, that urge me so? Why do you seek such haste when I understand my place in the grand scheme of things? Balance must be recognized and striven for.

Suddenly, Naomi comprehended the reality of the multitude crystalline possibilities before her. And what it meant. The crushing weight of accepted responsibility descended upon her ethereal shoulders!

I am a servant. A guide for those who need to understand and grow! To become more!

Relief flooded the ether.

I pass the test and remain…Naomi. But I see…I see…sooo many things all at once.

A hyper-gate activates and an ancient enemy thought contained appears. Warping the fabric of space/time he mind-shouts a word…*NOW!*

The Creator of all observes from above/elsewhere/everywhere! Incomprehensible joy blossoms through the Higher ether.

The Father of us Here watches from afar, his delight evident in the fruition of long held plans. He calls…

…Welcome little mind sister! You're a treasure and delight to behold. Don't forget, although…changed, I'll still be here. Watching and waiting. Allow your own sense of right and wrong to guide you. You will be a star among candles.

That vast intellect recedes, suddenly intent upon another purpose.

Others intrude. *Naomi?*

Reality flexes as a rarified mind adjusts into a more refined level of understanding.

Victoria? Anil?

We are here! You...you are very different to other...

WAIT!

Though distracted, Naomi's comprehension of a thousand simultaneous locations crashed upon the shores of her expanded awareness. Consequence and subsequence clarified within a whirling nub of lucidity.

I see. I see...

...Invisible signals heralding danger!

The staggering potential within two simple atoms was suddenly revealed in horrific glory. The unlimited scope of their originator exposed by the might unleashed in their wanton destruction! Splitting, they threw back the night, and a sea boiled.

Almost instantly, the scrutiny of higher minds—some enhanced by incredibly sophisticated technology—washed over the scene of the devastation. Familiar alarms were activated. Those sworn to protect and serve—no matter what it takes—responded with haste!

As they did so, multiple scenarios played out in her mind. Observing those outcomes, the most suitable resolution presented itself. Turning her attention toward the crystal, Naomi assessed a course never before attempted by one still emerging.

Can I?

...I must try!

Realizing what is being contemplated, the supporting duality expressed doubt.

NAOMI?

Ignoring them, she made her decision to proceed...

Meshing her will to an aspect of the crystal, Naomi's intent became dominant. Concentrating, she sent a surge of ultra-magnified psi-tronic energy toward the Earth and Observation Station 5. Positioned in geosynchronous orbit above the Sudan, the facility was only just dispatching an Alpha Response Team to the Gulf of Aden.

HOLD! She called. Confident in her certainty!

Amazingly, despite the muting presence of the lunar rocks, they heard.

DIVERT RESOURCES TO SURVIVORS AND CASUALTIES IN THE GULF. I WILL HANDLE FALLOUT AND SUPPRESS THE TIDAL WAVES.

Altering her reality once more, Naomi brought two more lattices of the crystal to bear.

Indescribable pain almost shattered her existence!

What?

Naomi's mind felt as if it was rupturing, expanding too far, too fast into dimensions that did not concern her…yet.

Agh! I'm coming apart. But I can't stop now. I must…I must…

I AM HERE!

An older, wiser, stronger presence was suddenly beside her. Victoria continued: *Have conviction! You are new. The crystal is capable of fracturing reality and draining you to the point of nullity. Until familiarity is earned, be more cautious…*

…Let me help you…thus!

Together they combined, and bent the warped physics of the crystal to their will.

A dual rainbow curtain shimmered down onto the Gulf of Aden. Flickering across the doughnut shaped wave front; it lingered for a second to match the harmonic resonance of the charging water. Suddenly, the frequency altered. For all its potential, the tsunami dropped impotently into the sea, like a puppet whose strings had just been cut.

Glittering flakes then appeared high in the atmosphere. Washing through the area, they saturated clouds and air alike with a sparkling radiance. Crystalline implosions resounded as each spark burst into flame. Consuming the irradiated particles about them, they fell into the waters before disappeared in puffs of smoke, leaving no trace of the invisible pall of death that would have rained its lethal mixture onto a helpless populace.

Incredibly, all this had been accomplished in only nine seconds!

A surge of pride coursed through Naomi's complexus!

A sense of well done came to her.

Then, Naomi discerned further signals!

Reality staggered as eight colossal blasts ripped the very fabric of space/time apart on the opposite side of the planet! Matter was annihilated–simply ceasing to exist–as an unbelievably enormous quantity of energy was released.

Conjoined hyper-senses zoomed in to investigate.

Stunned, they watched as ultra-amplified, seismic devastation radiated outwards from the Los Angeles district. Huge voids began to appear beneath the mantle. The two impinging continental plates afflicting that area recoiled as the catastrophic energy wave ran riot. Unable to withstand the unexpected loss of trillions of cubic tons of supporting strata, many areas simply began to fall. Some sagged downward toward the voids. Others succumbed to the onrushing Sea. Tension that had been building within the mantle snapped!

Islands, shoreline, and mountains trembled on the brink of ruin.

NO!

Coming back to herself for a moment, Naomi felt her Shepherd and Supporter stand apart, witnesses once more to the assault of a million different bytes of information storming against her super-energized, hyper-cognitive mind.

Enhanced now, beyond reason, Naomi used the psi-tronic energy to assist her transmute that information overload into a constructive, useable tool.

In a split second, Naomi had compartmentalized the deluge, and instantly assessed the impact the apocalypse would cause.

The spine of the Los Angeles district had been shattered. A huge chunk of the North American Plate bordering that fragile area was now crushing down on it.

The magnitude of the desolation about to unfold along that entire section of coastline would be dreadful…

…Unless I respond in some way…no matter what the cost.

Comprehension of the deficit in resources came to her in an instant. As did the congregation of possible solutions!

One was selected.

Reeling, Naomi's flexing consciousness bounded even closer upon the east coast of the USA. She knew exactly what needed to be done. *And* how to do it!

But from this distance, the task would be immense!

It would require her full attention and the combined efforts of her Shepherd and Supporter. It would involve the special resources of her devoted family.

Inevitably, it would also require the employment of the crystal itself. From here, within the dampening field of the chamber! And, *that* would cost her dearly.

But already, her hyper-cognitive, super awareness had assessed the situation along with the best moment to act.

Accepting the enormity of the repercussions, Naomi Cruiz stepped into the crystal!

Chapter Eighteen
Aftershock

Esther surrendered herself to the confusion that was the pyramid program. Bitter experience had taught her a long time ago, *never try and anticipate which of the multiple arcs the path will follow. The attempt will only make me nauseous!*

And you could appreciate why. Every few seconds, she would phase through a manifestation process. On each occasion, her molecular template was replicated and projected onwards, toward three new thresholds. Two would be phantoms, and would quickly dissipate as the patterns dematerialized. The other–the true path– would pitch her forward along the increasingly warped course at an accumulative rate. Using this method, she would quickly become lost among the multiple possible trajectories the procedure generated.

However, flying along the temporal cambers in such a manner produced the most intense rush she had ever experienced. And once again, Esther felt like a competitor in the Luge events held at the Winter Olympics.

I wonder if Simon managed to tip Yeung off? I'd hate to think we'd gone to all that trouble for nothing! Well, not for nothing! The psi-tronic crystal sang warmly within her complexus, happy to rest within a familiar environment. *We've got this little baby at least…and I can do all sorts of damage with it.*

Suddenly, the crystal flared, and began to emit a highly concordant tone!

I'm happy to see you too! She thought.

The timbre deepened, and then swelled alarmingly as if welcoming a long lost friend.

What are yo…

Before Esther could finish her thought, the tunnel through which she was travelling, unexpectedly deformed and twisted violently out of shape.

Whoa! What the hell?

Esther began careening from side to side. Drawing on her power, she began to initiate an emergency exit. However, no sooner had she brought her potential to prime focus, than an immensely powerful shaft of arcane might punched through the quantum matrix. Rupturing the temporal sheath encasing her, the energy locked onto the crystal shard within her complexus and unceremoniously yanked her to an instant stop.

An unfathomable surge then pulsed along that beam, and Esther found herself being forced to materialize into normal space against her will. As she did so, the energy stream cut off!

Expecting a fight, she surrounded herself with as strong a shield as she could muster and began scanning her immediate surroundings.

For a moment, Esther hung there, confused.

Brightness enfolded her in a blanket of sparkling light. However, that illumination was muted and distant. Although coming from millions upon millions of suns, they were so far away that they appeared as mere pinpricks, peppered across a sheet of card. To reach them, she would have to traverse an immense abyss.

Adjusting her perspective, Esther comprehended just how large that void was. Something about it rang with such familiarity that it tugged at ancient memories.

I'm at the center of a galaxy! A huge kick-ass galaxy!

Realization hit her. *Hang on! That should mean I'd be right on top of a sing...*

The penny dropped.

...Oh fuck! No!

Oh fuck! Yes! A dark and overwhelmingly powerful voice cut in out of nowhere: *You failed to appreciate just how intimate MY connection to the crystal would be...didn't you?*

Brilliance flared about her, and suddenly Esther found herself surrounded by faces from the distant past. And a more recent, deadlier one!

YOU! Her mind gasped, utter astonishment preventing her from thinking clearly.

Esther attempted to employ support from the psi-tronic crystal to strengthen her shield. Before she had the opportunity to act on her intent, the shard flew from her grasp and blazed into life, burning more brightly than she thought could ever be possible.

And as magnificent as it was, it paled in comparison against the dazzling radiance of the complexus embracing it.

I missed you too, Sachael-Za-Ad'hem said: *You never called. You never wrote. What was I supposed to think?*

It took Esther a moment to realize. He was addressing *her*, not the crystal. But then she espied the barely restrained darkness at his core. She was appalled! Sachael-Za-Ad'hem's true nature was taking its toll within this plane of existence...at long last.

They'd all known it would happen. Eventually.

Generated to unleash divine destruction upon those who dared to oppose the Prime Source's will, the true Abaddon—Angel of the

Abyss—Destroyer and Avenger, was returning. Only one angel of a higher magnitude had ever been engendered. And he wasn't here!

In this realm, untendered by the calming, soothing effects of Ultimate Bliss, the dreadful disposition of his cardinal attribute was breaking down the walls of his iron will and rigid devotion. Gradually, inevitably, the Destroyer was asserting itself.

Esther's spectral brilliance faltered in horror: *Will you extinguish me now?*

Soon! He replied. A crushing darkness closed in about her: *It's what I was made to do. All those who oppose the WILL must be eradicated if they are set upon their course.*

Sachael-Za-Ad'hem's mind entered hers with appalling ease, despite her precautions.

That act alone brought home a terrible truth to Esther.

All those years ago, they'd made their plans. Scheming, conniving! They thought he'd gone soft. Lost his ability or resolve to act as the centuries passed slowly by.

How wrong they'd been.

To the core, Sachael-Za-Ad'hem had remained faithful. Determining to offer no resistance, he'd let them choose their *own* path, their *own* destiny, without an ounce of coercion from him. In doing so, they'd sealed their *own* doom.

Esther knew Sachael-Za-Ad'hem could see it now, as his psyche swarmed through the darkest recesses of her mind. Digesting the depth of her depravity, he witnessed the lengths she would gleefully go to, to extend the suffering of those she would always view as lowly insects.

Trying to divert his attention, she argued: *It's never been about HIS will! You've always sought to...AAARGH!*

Undiluted pain coursed through her complexus. Wave after wave of malice scorched her neural pathways to the point of dissolution.

Sachael-Za-Ad'hem edged closer: *You forget yourself...Sister. I have never sought or welcomed the pedestal upon which my feet have been set. And although Fallen, I was humble enough to listen to Heim-dhal-riel's admonition from the outset. As was Sariel-Jeh'oel! You were there. Do you not remember Heim-dhal-riel's words?*

'...In your debased condition, you are forbidden to interact with those who are untainted. You are forbidden to reveal this judgment to any whose origin is not of the host. Only the truly penitent may one day hope to achieve consolation. Go now and reflect on the actions that led to your just proscription...'

Had you forgotten?

Puzzlement throbbed through Esther's mind.

He continued: *Heim-dhal-riel's departing warning contained a source of hope for those who were not overly consumed by the bitterness of their own failure. The Prime Source has no reason to resort to deception. Indeed, he would be incapable of such treachery. No! By excising our corruption, he also gave we condemned few a goal to work toward. An eventual return home!*

Home! Esther spat: *Are you mad? Do you ever think that could possibly happen?*

Calmly, Sachael-Za-Ad'hem asked: *Tell me...Sister. Have you been so intent upon your course to self destruction that you failed to notice the absence of your Brother, Sariel-Jeh'oel? He who was the eldest and wisest of all to Fall. Are you seriously telling me that you—one of our most adept artificer's of the Median Echelon—failed to notice he is no longer with us?*

Sariel-Jeh'oel?

Casting her mind out, Esther expanded her astral sight to encompass Sariel-Jeh'oel's very distinct signature. Distance wouldn't really matter for one of his puissance. His extremely conspicuous nexus would have been instantly discernible had he expired. His taste, the tang of his unique resonance would have seeded the universe.

The only location she detected any such echo was here, at the place he had selected, so very long ago as they undertook the vast work ahead of them.

Sachael-Za-Ad'hem edged even closer and opened his mind to her, saying: *We had only just arrived on this plane. Because of my more…destructive nature, I looked ahead, millions of years into the future. To me, that was the only way I could envisage a work worthy enough to qualify for MY reunification. Our dear brother thought differently. I must admit, he threw me with his very unique and innovative…idea.* Replaying a part of the conversation between them, Esther heard Sariel-Jeh'oel's mind begin…

'*…Oh don't worry too much; I wouldn't leave you in the lurch with such a vital task ahead of you. I'll wait until after we initialize the intervention before I begin my own personal penance…I was thinking that perhaps here would be as good a place as any?*

What? You intend to fulfill the function of a singularity?

It will be a good place to start. Who knows? It might even work! If you read between the lines, I think Heim-dhal-riel was trying to give us a hope as we were cast down…I'd like to think so anyway…'

Esther was moved. Moved and confused. Her mind whispered: *So he did it? He actually did it? He…he returned…*

Affirming her suspicions, Sachael-Za-Ad'hem replayed the moment Andrew had assisted him in his friend's restoration to the Higher Plane.

Esther's mind crooned: *Home…*

As the awesome scene faded, Sachael-Za-Ad'hem added: *Do you see now? Had you not been so set upon the road to destruction, you would have tasted his absence. Discerned the reasons—even interred as you were—and known the path of penitence was inveterate.*

So it IS possible? Real! Home!

Not for you...not now! Sachael-Za-Ad'hem stated bluntly, darkening even further.

A ripple passed through his essence. More gently he added: *I act as I was purposed to do. But I will allow you time to say your goodbyes.*

He gravitated away slightly.

Overflowing with sorrow and regret, the softer radiances of Aslan-di'el, Gaia-le'el, Gazad-riel, Ocean-az'el and Olinda crowded around Esther. Using Esther's given name, Olinda addressed her: *You have darkened Hesta'n-ea! Despite the increase we perceive within your psi-well. I always hoped you would...*

Join us! Aslan-di'el cut in: *Or at the very least, have offered us the benefits of your Higher origination. We could have realized wonders beyond imagining.*

You were a Median! Gazad-riel added: *You could have accomplished so much good in support of Sachael-Za-Ad'hem. Or simply declined to intercede in the way WE all did at first. Pity! We will miss the brightness your essence once graced this plane with.*

Dryly, Esther indicated her waiting executioner and countered: *Oh, I'm sure you'll find he makes good use of my energies. You know the way his is. How he'll undoubtedly act. Every time he does, just think of me...*

Oh, but I won't! Sachael-Za-Ad'hem interrupted: *I do not want or need any of your complexus. I will, however, make an example of you and ensure the twins are enhanced by your vitality. And the knowledge you think is so deeply buried within your nexus.*

And how will you do that from here? Esther gasped: *That's impossible! You...*

How quickly you have fallen, he cut in: *Looking inwards, you forget the capacity of those older, wiser, and far stronger than yourself. Even in Tartarus, I am not without finesse.*

Surging toward her, Sachael-Za-Ad'hem abruptly paused just outside her containment threshold. Esther tensed, waiting for the blast of arcane might that would send her reeling into oblivion.

It never came.

Mystified, she watched as one delicate strand of Sachael-Za-Ad'hem's essence continued to flow forward. It wavered for a moment, like seaweed in an invisible current, apparently searching for something. Satisfied, it suddenly stabbed out, and Esther felt herself impaled upon an excruciating blade of ice.

Pierced to the core, she froze, screaming.

Unbelievably, the pain cut off only seconds later as Sachael-Za-Ad'hem unexpectedly withdrew!

What?

Like I said, I need to send a message. Simply destroying you here, now, would defeat my purpose.

Signaling the others, he turned and began leading the group away, dismissing her as if she was of no further consequence.

Esther was about to query what was going on, when she felt it!

Something deep inside…changed.

One moment, she was whole. Complete and intact! The next, it felt as if she had suddenly become frail in some way. A kernel of her soul had begun to crack open and bleed into the ether within her.

No!

Coldness began to leech from her psychic nexus. Radiating outwards, it encompassed her in a halo of brittle frigidity.

Deepening, it sank to the very center of her complexus whereupon it began to weave an arcane network of power.

Waves of concentric energy throbbed inwards, each more powerful than the one before. Pressure began to mount. Within moments, Esther could feel her very existence begin to shred as it was torn asunder.

A gateway opened right on top of her!

Swallowing her whole, Esther was then compressed through a geodesic stream, the likes of which shouldn't have been possible. Not here. Not in this place.

Moments later, she emerged somewhere else.

***

Stripped of her magnified puissance, Esther crashed to the floor in human form in front of a very startled group of people. Bleeding and broken, she rolled over on the ground and tried to get her ruined body to breathe.

It took a few moments for Esther to realize that the roiling, seething, mass of energy spitting and flaring in the air above her, was in fact, her former transcended essence. In some unfathomable way, Sachael-Za-Ad'hem had ripped it from her and managed to keep it intact.

A pair of smaller gateways opened. Before she could fully comprehend what was happening, her former psi-well was divided into two distinct parts, and snatched away.

But her ordeal was far from over.

Coming out of their collective shock, Yeung, Simon and Angelika began to rush toward her. Esther was shocked!

I'm on Earth? He jumped me all that distance in one go?

Then Esther began to scream.

Unbelievable pain now coursed along her nervous system. It felt to Esther like her atoms had been set ablaze. Nothing she could do would ease the mounting torment. If that weren't enough, an overwhelming compulsion then seized what was left of her mind, and she was forced to remain motionless while she repeated a message.

Between sobs of agony, Esther hissed, "You are undone. Surrender now and your punishment will be more lenient. Resist and the twins will ensure your fate will be held up as an example to others for all eternity."

Suddenly free, Esther sagged back to the floor. The burning increased! Horrified, she watched aghast as her arms and legs began dissolving.

"Who has done this to you?" Yeung gasped, alarm etched clearly across his features.

Ignoring him, Esther turned her head while she still could. Fixing Simon with a look of utter hopelessness, she gurgled and sputtered one last, brief sentence before her molecules were obliterated.

"What was that? What did she say?" Sobbed Angelika, her face white with revulsion! Wide eyed, she looked repeatedly between her two companions, waiting for an answer.

Yeung continued staring at the position on the floor where Esther had just disintegrated. Disbelief written all over his face! He was mumbling to himself, "How? How did she manage to teleport while so badly injured? If…"

"She didn't!"

"What?" Yeung and Angelika echoed at the same time.

"I said, she didn't" Simon repeated. "*He* did it!"

Simon had stumbled backwards as Esther had died. Even in the muted light of the office, they could see his face was ashen and he was sweating profusely. He was looking wildly about the office, as if expecting death to appear at any moment. No matter how much he tried to get his jaw to work, nothing came out.

SIMON! Thought Yeung: *Tell us! We need your insight. We need to know how to respond, AND how quickly. If it's frightened you this badly, then it must be serious. Just tell us...what did she say and how will it affect us?*

Making a huge effort to remain calm, Yeung then motioned toward one of the seats.

Flopping down heavily on the couch, Simon at last found his voice. Running his fingers through his sodden mop of hair, he said, "She only uttered a phrase, but those words will spell the end of us...unless some miracle prevents it."

"For fuck's sake," Angelika cut in, "*WHAT?* What did she say?"

"The Avenger has returned!"

Without knowing why, both Yeung and Angelika suppressed a shiver.

Yeung said, "Simon! Why has that got you so scared? *Who* or *what* is this Avenger?"

Simon was so traumatized by the events that had just occurred, that—regardless of the repercussions, irrespective of whatever pursuit might be coming their way—he spent the next twenty minutes explaining to them exactly *who* the Avenger was, and why it was highly likely they would all soon be dead.

When he'd finished, Yeung and Angelika were as white as sheets!

Angelika looked to Yeung, and said, "Ghost protocol?"

"I don't think that will suffice on this occasion," Yeung replied. Shrugging his shoulders in resignation, he added, "The only chance we have will lie within Specter. Esther wasn't as deeply involved as she though. See to it would you, my dear?"

Angelika nodded once.

As she went to leave, she paused. "And the new psi-dents?"

"Ah, yes! Would you have your young man join us at the lab? Better do it now, before everything *really* begins to hit the fan."

Chapter Nineteen
The Fan

The instant stretched on for eternity.

As if looking down on eighteen different versions of herself, Naomi watched as she fully immersed her complexus within the psi-tronic crystal. She sensed herself fold out of existence and—at the same moment—felt her comprehension stretch across the cosmos on a torture rack of the most exquisite pain.

Reality fractured as, somehow, her awareness spiked. And for the first time in her life, she felt truly alive! Hyper-cognition flared, expanding to fill each lattice of the sixteen foot monstrosity with a host of impossible probabilities. Prospects she began to enact simultaneously, in a way only she could hope to control.

In one, her mind brought up a full sensory replay of another transcension she had witnessed. That of her mentor, Anatt Yasin, five years previously. Just before the process had begun, Naomi had been having a conversation with the Shadow Lord, Andrew. An exchange she was extremely mindful of now.

In an instant, she lived that episode again...

"...What is that thing?"

He replied. "It's a pis-tronic crystal. You could say it's the heart and soul of the place. It's an extremely rare phenomenon that actually absorbs most of the forms of energy you can think of, including psychic energy, and converts it into power."

"Is it dangerous?"

"In the wrong hands certainly! Once activated, it's capable of draining the complete sum of energy from anything within its vicinity. It can also be programmed to emit that energy in an excited or amplified form! That's why we have to be careful and match our telepathic harmonics. This beauty is brand spanking new and a welcome replacement for the shards of the old one that was fractured thousands of years ago. In fact, we used several of the old shards recently to clear up the radiation and electromagnetic residue left over from the meteorite strikes."

"What! This is capable of decontaminating the area of a nuclear blast?"

"Of course it is! Radiation, electromagnetism, heat—all the things present in such an explosion—is energy. So we simply adjusted the frequency of absorption in one of its lattices and it fed on the contamination present in the air, water, rocks and soil and so on. It came in very useful really…"

Oh yes! She thought. *VERY useful indeed! Especially as his mind also revealed it was thirty-two times stronger than their previous one!*

Coaxing another lattice to life, Naomi employed the infinite potential offered by its bipolar template. Enhancing her own stupendous functions, she extended her ultra-sight toward the Earth. Knowing the Gulf of Aden was already in good hands, she concentrated on the Los Angeles Basin.

The clarity afforded by the crystal's matrix sent an esoteric thrill through her soul. *Ethereal or not! THIS is awesome!* For a moment, she flirted with the idea as to how easy it would be to lose her mind among the endless expanse it offered.

Get a grip Naomi! She told herself.

Trust yourself! An ancient mind echoed…

Micro-moments had passed from the strangely complex detonations. An unusual kinetic wave led the impacting vortices, its mad charge threatening to trigger further seismic activity along the already shattered fabric of the San Andreas Fault.

The other occluding fault lines saturating the area were also bucking furiously. And no wonder! Each and every asperity beneath the mantle had disappeared, consumed by the same blast that had vaporized trillions of tones of rock and soil! All the tension built up over hundreds of years of continental occlusion had simply vanished, abruptly released at the same moment. Now, the catastrophic energy surge had nothing to impede its devastating assault. The entire region along the eastern seaboard was beginning to subside.

Nothing would prevent that catastrophe…unless…

Projecting her hyper-awareness along that probability strand, Naomi watched as the beginnings of a highly compacted, secondary kinematic wave smashed outwards. Inevitably, it signaled the collapse of vast tracts of land, and the inrush of trillions of tons of seawater.

Snapping back to the present, she flexed her mind, and simultaneously activated another four lattices. By sending out an augmented blanket call: *HEADS UP!* Each and every single Guardian on duty was put on notice to stand-by for something special. Something never witnessed before!

Reining her stupendous vision backwards a notch, Naomi tuned a feature of the crystal into the precise frequencies employed by the cerebro-energetic enhancers and transporters aboard the ships and stations orbiting both the Earth and Moon. Amplifying their resolution, she ensured they were now able to assess the situation with perfect clarity.

An extra plane was used to repeat that process with the scrambling dreadnaughts and the Disaster Command Carrier already powering their way to the scene.

Taxing herself further, Naomi then manipulated one of the facets to analyze the exact nature of the damage in each specific area. Progressing that one time-strand in particular, she calculated the degree of control it would require to hold events in stasis while an evacuation was conducted.

Elsewhere, her mind employed a further matrix of the crystal to call her transcended brothers and sisters to attention. Apprising them of her intentions in the blink of an eye, she at last meshed with the final lattice.

Naomi's soul shrieked as her mind was gripped between conflicting energies. Forces that threatened to tear her sanity apart. Her entire existence seemed to burst open and recoil as it was crushed by overwhelming chaos.

*Trust yourself...*Breathed a nearby mind, wise in its understanding.

Don't think...FEEL! Advised another! So far, far away.

She did.

Surrendering herself to the calamity threatening to brutalize all reason, Naomi stepped into the eye of the cosmic storm. Abruptly, reality stopped spinning. Time and space and possibility congealed into a focused knot of will and purpose.

Her will!

Her purpose!

Naomi felt herself expand as unadulterated potential rushed eagerly into her. Molding to her psyche, it filled her to overflowing. Becoming part of her, she magnified the full nuance of her own senses and displayed them with a lucidity that went beyond all possibility.

Time paused as the universe took a deep, deep breath.

From this distance, the task would be immense!

Distance is inconsequential.

The sheer scope of the undertaking should be impossible.

The size of the task is irrelevant. Impossibility is not an option.

Obliterating energy coalesced in the ether about her, its composition, resonant and vital. All at once, everything fell into place.

A full second had passed since the blasts.

Do—Or do not!

Initiating her grand plan, Naomi seized the boundless well of incredible musical potential ringing throughout the cosmos, and imbued it with the capacity of each transcended mind standing at the ready.

As each distinct character was added, the pitch of the harmony altered, amplifying with a sweetness that was as hypnotic as it was thrilling. Naomi's mind flowed through the rising symphony, synchronizing to keep pace with the growth that continually blossomed and swelled throughout her construct. Refining! Focusing! Adjusting! Approving!

She was a maestro incarnate.

Reacting with a finesse and speed that belied comprehension, she worked skillfully. Almost instantly, she had woven the quality of every consciousness at her disposal into a masterpiece of harmonic union.

Without warning, the congruence swelled toward a crescendo. It seemed unlikely the pitch could withstand the influx of any further vitality. But it did!

Expanding exponentially, the timbre somehow adjusted to a new, unique, multi-faceted nature and the Moon became encompassed by a blistering halo of power. Higher and higher the unity built, coalescing into a sizzling band of ecstasy that wound tighter and tighter about the pyretic sentience that controlled it. A febrile awareness that now manipulated the awesome magnitude of energy at her command…

…And who now prepared to use it!

A full two seconds had passed since the string of coordinated antimatter detonations. Naomi could taste the distinctive flavor of their concussions, even at this distance.

And much more!

Calling on the declamatory mode, her mind addressed the rest of the Guardians: *THE PROTECTION OF HUMAN LIFE TAKES PRIORITY. PROPERTY CAN BE RECLAIMED LATER.*

As she spoke, she unleashed a triple arc of blazing plasma.

Travelling via the warped physics of the crystal, the first wave was able to reach the Earth at faster-than-light speed. Just over half a second later, it saturated the whole of the Western shoreline of America in a golden rainbow of amplified psi-tronic light.

Two things happened simultaneously.

Firstly, the expanding seismic storm and costal wave attack leeched away, as if cut off from their power source!

In her magnified condition, Naomi had easily been able to digest the precise frequencies of the tremors and ocean borne tsunami. As had happened in the Gulf of Aden, the death-dealing potential of the unleashed forces were simply bled away–albeit at a slower rate, because of the sheer density of humanity here.

Secondly, the composition of the opening plasma strand had been infused with a very specific command structure. Psi-tronic flecks still saturated the ground at eight different locations around the Los Angeles area. Although they had multiplied the destructive potential of the detonations, they had not been vaporized.

In a masterpiece of strategy, Naomi employed them now!

As each fragment bloomed to life, negating waves of augmented mirror energy radiated outwards. In moments they had created a massive dam-like structure within each of the voids. Soil liquefaction ceased. Residual fracturing faded and died. Continental flexing stabilized. The encroaching ocean flopped backwards, spent, as conjoining energies suddenly harmonized.

Frozen, the earth trembled at the brink of dissolution.

The secondary wave arrived only moments later.

As the energy washed through the circuitry of the arriving emergency response group, the buffers within each ship immediately began charging, ramping up way beyond their usual capacities. A similar process also began occurring aboard Space Stations 1 and 2.

Two distinct, grey vortexes then appeared, a mile above the disaster, one above the other. Tuning each maelstrom to the existing bi-polar charge of the crystal, Naomi then initiated the next phase of her plan.

The lower field shimmered, turned gold, and began sinking toward the ground. The other rippled for a moment, and disappeared. Seconds later, a liquid-silver haze manifested across the entire area of the Great Basin, in the neighboring state of Nevada.

Both curtains fluttered briefly, before intensifying into fully primed energy fields.

Without conscious thought, the matter transporters within the ships and stations then came online and began targeting ground zero.

Naomi called: *I WILL BE RETURNING FOCUS TO YOUR CONTROL IN A FEW MOMENTS. STATION ONE. TARGET LIFE-SIGNS WITHIN THE PRIMARY FIELD, NORTH TO SOUTH. STATION TWO. YOU BEGIN IN THE SOUTH AND WORK NORTHWARD. CAPTAIN HUDSON? TAKE THE ODDESY AND YOUR RESPONSE GROUP ALONG THE CENTER. THERE WILL BE NO NEED TO REMATERIALIZE TRAVELLERS. THE VORTEX WILL TAKE CARE OF THAT FOR YOU.*

UNDERSTOOD?

A handful of mental affirmations came back.

Naomi then addressed her fellow transcended colleagues: *Please keep my identity intact. The more I employ the power of the crystal, the deeper I have to descend into its matrix. There is a very strong possibility my fragmented reality will rupture. Under no circumstances allow that to happen. If I begin to lose containment, pull out what you can and destroy it! Do NOT allow me to go nova and endanger others.*

Finally, Naomi drew their attention toward the trailing arc of plasma. As big as the first two combined, it crackled and sparked with arcane levels of potency. She said: *This will arrive a few minutes after we complete the evacuation. You will see it encompasses a matter generation placebo, suitable for tectonic adaptation.*

If I survive the extraction, I won't be in any fit state to help you. However, its template has been designed for manipulation by any transcended operator. Decide amongst yourselves who will take prime focus during the modifications. I would suggest either Andrew or Victoria. They have previous experience in this kind of thing, and stand a higher chance of success in generating lasting repairs.

Pausing, she called: *Shall we begin?*

Diverting her multiple levels of awareness back toward the scene, Naomi activated the matter vortexes. It wasn't until the first beams began to wash across the panicking crowds and fleeing casualties, that the ingenuity behind Naomi's construct became apparent.

Usually, the matter transporters would have to follow a swift, but extremely complex process. They would lock onto a target, scan its entire physical structure at the sub-atomic level and break those readings down into their corresponding quantum patterns. That signature would then be digitized and compressed, before transference through subspace toward the target site. Those reception areas would receive the incoming signal, collect the pattern stream and reassemble the digitized matrix into a coherent form. Once accumulated, the focusing projectors would then generate an expansion and reconstruction field, within which a person would *appear.*

Although taking less than six seconds in its entirety, such a process would be far too long for the emergency evacuation of the more than twenty million souls now underway. So Naomi had done away with it.

The vortexes were the answer.

Because of their dual polarity, they were able to exist in two places at once. One side of the doorway—the golden one—was located within the Los Angeles costal region. The immediate opposite side to that bridge—the silver one—was situated over the one hundred and eighty-four square mile area of the Great Nevada Basin.

The augmented transporter beams now acted as a key.

No sooner did they wash across a bio-sign, than it was phased instantly into the unique subspace wormhole created between the shimmering curtains. '

In effect, they would disappear *here* in Los Angeles, only to instantly manifest *there*, in a corresponding position in Nevada.

Genius!

But torturous!

The ferocious distress Naomi now had to endure to maintain the bridge assailed her from all sides. From within! From without! And everywhere and elsewhere! It bludgeoned her to near submission as it cruelly pierced her to the core. Amplifying the agony a thousand-fold, Naomi teetered on the edge of insanity as every atom of her complexus flared toward the brink of dissolution.

The Overlord's voice intruded, anchoring her for a moment to the here and now: *Impressive Naomi! Intuitive, lateral and inventive! You have a natural instinct for elucidation.*

An ultra-compressed psychic data stream followed.

He continued: *I thought YOU might like to pass this latest information on to the others. Yet another of the thorns in our flesh will shortly be out of the way. After she has delivered a message for me! While I'm sure the cancer won't have spread to all of their companies and assets, it would nevertheless be a course of prudence to ensure each and every single one of their members is examined. Eventually, you'll no doubt foster the perfect tool to accomplish that task. I'll make sure Andrew, Victoria, Anil and Anatt are aware of your broadened responsibilities!*

Naomi clutched at the stability of his voice: *IF I survive*, she gasped.

Oh you'll survive, Naomi. Believe me…

He went quiet for a moment, as if deliberating on how much of her future to reveal. Eventually, he continued...*Just prepare yourself for the change. You'll be very different to what you are now, transcension aside. So long as you can accept the metamorphosis for what it will achieve, you will come to look on it as it truly is. A unique gift!*

Change? Alarm flared through Naomi's psyche.

It will take time for you to adjust. To adapt. But you will. And the future? Well...

Again the pause.

The future? Naomi pressed.

...Change is necessary, Naomi. Embrace it, as I do. For you will become a guiding light of the future if you do!

A gold and silver doorway cracked open in her mind. Hinting at hidden revelations, it exuded an air of invitation. Fixated, she channeled her spiraling consciousnesses toward the definite mooring it offered. No sooner did the skittering tendrils of her thoughts touch it, than it slammed shut. Gleaming enticingly around its edges, it seemed to mock her efforts to gain entry.

Quickly, the Overlord concluded: *As I said. THAT's for another time. For now, it would appear your designs are reaching fruition. Look!*

Returning her attention to the rescue below, Naomi was startled to discover that—somehow—time had jumped. Guardian Alpha Response crews were already converging on Downtown Los Angeles, and the last of the refugees were now being translocated to the temporary staging area at Nevada. Adjusting her focus, Naomi was shocked to recognize detachments from Guardian Sector Command were already on site within the Grand Basin itself. What's more, they were being supported by psychic EMS, Fire and Rescue units and teams from the new Marshal's Bureau. Triage and disaster management pods had already received their first casualties, and relief efforts were presently underway in conjunction with neighboring civilian and National Guard Units.

How long were we speaking?

Ethereal laughter pattered about her.

As you will discover, the Overlord began: *Although linear, time can be manipulated. Especially in such a place as this!*

Naomi paused to look around the recursive plane she now seemed to inhabit. Slightly different versions of herself looped off in multiple directions, pictures within pictures, in a hyper-magnified version of the Droste effect.

The Overlord continued: *These crystals are a bridge between levels of existence. A window through time and thought and possibility. They exist, both inside and outside of the normal planes of temporal reference. Although a paradox, their contradiction anchors the reality of each dimension in place. And if you're powerful enough...adept enough...*

Intuition sparked!

Naomi gasped: *Are you saying it's possible to jump through time by manipulating the reality lattices?*

This time the laughter pealed like thunder about her.

Oh Naomi! If only it were that simple. No! You're thinking along the right lines, but it's far more complex than that. WE are very different to the crystal. IT exists everywhere and everywhen at once. That's its natural state. However, from the moment of our generation—or in your case—conception, we become locked in time. Anchored if you like, to a very specific orientation point. Thereafter, OUR natural state is linear, no matter how mighty we are. However, if we are strong enough, the crystal does allow us to SEE into the different possibilities that exist before us. AND, if we have the fortitude to immerse ourselves deeply enough within its matrix—as you have done—to skip forward a little in time. Just a little, mind, otherwise we would become forever lost in hyper-phasure. Do you understand?

Reality span within the vault-like halls of Naomi's augmented consciousness.

Don't think.

Recognition! Grounding! Multiple anchor points to a multitude of awareness's.

FEEL!

Bonding! Meshing! Becoming! Seeing!

Comprehension flared.

I am...I ammm...

The Overlord finished her sentence for her: *Awakening at last! As foreseen.*

Suddenly, Naomi found herself alone again.

For a split second, she lost focus as manifold realities crowded in on her. Panicking, she floundered as welcoming midnight vied with kaleidoscopic energies for her surrender to the waiting chaos. Voices at the edge of perception called...

Naomi! Over here!

No! This way! Over here!

Naomi!

It was her! Naomi herself as she once was. Frangible and limited!

But now?

Expanding to the disjointed incoherence, she chose calm.

Within the blink of an eye, multiple layers of veracity froze about her. Locked into place with the rigidity of a crystalline lattice, cohesion was achieved.

Immediately, she felt another, familiar mind intruding into her multiverse. Feelings of relief flooded the ether: *Naomi? Thank god for that! I was just about to initiate the failsafe.*

Naomi's awareness homed in on Victoria's aura, coalescing the nearer she got to the surface.

Victoria continued: *We though the shit was really going to hit the fan there. We lost you! You just...vanished. It was like you'd never existed. I skimmed the surface of the nearest lattices, but you were gone! I wouldn't have been able to wait either, as the final plasma strand is approaching Earth and it's going to take all of us to achieve the choral purity required to activate tectonic regeneration. You didn't tell me before, but I take it you intend for the old crystal shards to transmute into the new mantle layers?*

Naomi felt an odd frigidity congealing at the center of her complexus.

Naomi? Victoria repeated.

Huh? Yes?

I said, do you intend for the old crystal shards to transmute into the new mantle layers? Is it a self replicating design?

Yes! Yes it...

The icy petrifaction crackled outwards, freezing Naomi as it went.

Naomi?

Victoria reeled as a sharp psychic burst arrowed into her mind. Forewarned, she flared away from the psi-tronic crystal, yanking Anil along with her.

The connection was severed just in time.

Stunned, both Victoria and Anil watched as the psi-tronic crystal appeared to twist in on itself! A rending shriek filled the air as the gem-like facets rotated and splintered, shedding obsidian icicles in every direction. New razor sharp prisms snapped into view.

The huge gem before them began pulsing in a way they had never seen before, ringing with tones that sounded like shattering glass. Chime upon chime pealed forth as a hoar-frost skein radiated outwards. Mesmerized, they stared aghast as it began infusing the newborn, petrifying her freshly generated eight-foot complexus in the process.

A *grinding, cracking* sound followed, marking the moment the newly morphed hybrid settled into position. Having achieved what it felt was a suitable equilibrium; it then emitted a final groan before the usual fairy-bell tinkling resumed.

Less than a minute later, the mutated crystal began to fold gently in and out of view again, as if nothing of consequence had taken place.

What the hell? Anil hissed. Unable to tear his senses away from the horror before him, he gasped: *Victoria! That can't be right. Can it? It…it's not…natural.*

Although now privy to the circumstances, Victoria also found herself utterly captivated by the morbid sight before her, and had to force herself to act. Time was short.

Shepherding her stunned colleague away, she momentarily shocked him again by teleporting them both through the warped lunar strata and into high orbit.

We'll study the ramifications later, Anil. And with a full team too, believe me! For now, we've got to initiate the meld to trigger another metamorphosis down on Earth. Naomi gave me the program before she threw me out. Quite ingenious really! You won't believe what it can do.

Wryly he admitted: *Oh, I probably will. Today's been one long list of surprises really. Yourself included! I'd always suspected, of course. I'm just trying to fathom out why your father felt the need to keep it a secret from Earl and myself for so long?*

Pausing to consider her friend of the last five and a half thousand years, Victoria replied: *He kept it hidden from us too, don't forget! Both Andrew and I were quite freaked out to discover we're part human, part…goodness knows what! Makes days like today rather, run of the mill! Don't you think?*

Declining to answer, Anil couldn't resist one final peek back toward the chamber.

Of course, the intervening lunar rocks and his limitations prevented him, reinforcing his current thought.

Hmmmh! Run of the mill? I've got a feeling there's more truth to that statement than she realizes. Freaky hasn't even begun…YET!

Chapter Twenty
Fallen

Turning his hands from side to side, Psi-edon-ijah raised his arms and flexed his fingers repeatedly. For some reason, he was captivated by the way his muscles and sinews tensed and rippled as he moved about.

He'd never been vain. Nevertheless, as he stared into the full length mirror, he couldn't help but admire the thickness of his biceps and thighs. The cut of his chest and stomach. And he especially liked the way his olive skin seemed to enhance the definition of his finely toned, brand-new physique.

There wasn't an ounce of fat on him. And although he was only slightly younger than his previous host, Jose Antonio Calderon's body was by far the superior model. The rigors of his early life and later active service amongst the Guardians had seen to that.

And, as if that wasn't cause enough for celebration, there was a decidedly tasty layer of icing to this new cake.

Information!

After fleeing to a subsidiary bunker, Psi-edon-ijah had taken the time to intimately familiarize himself with every aspect of his host. His childhood and upbringing! The struggle to control emerging abilities that set him apart! His descent into crime! Psi-edon-ijah had wanted to ensure he had everything he needed to *become* this man for the foreseeable future, as adopting his identity would entail immersing himself deeply within enemy circles.

But the process had been far more difficult than he'd anticipated!

Jose Calderon had been blessed with grand masterly class abilities.

Although far weaker than the parasitic entity now controlling his form, it was Calderon's self-healing faculty that had proved a formidable barrier to gaining full neural control. Because it was so strongly developed, Psi-edon-ijah had discovered it kept acting as a psychic immunosuppressant, preventing his own psyche from being able to fully mesh to the body.

Additionally, Calderon's time under the tutelage of the Guardians had added additional defensive layers that had been extremely problematic to overcome.

Thankfully, Psi-edon-ijah had been able to use one of those embedded sequences—the Compressor Program—to his own advantage.

Devised by his nemesis, Sachael-Za-Ad'hem, it accelerated both the learning and training curve of the recipient. Amazingly, it also allowed the psycho-energetic potential of each candidate to hyper-develop! By compartmentalizing each different area of a student's psyche, it allowed them to utilize their mundane and psychosomatic complexi twenty-four hours a day.

Studying the construct closely, Psi-edon-ijah had been astonished to discover it also complimented mental synergy, even when the subject was sleeping! Seizing on that aspect, he had gradually stripped its layers from Calderon's mind and added the matrix to his own psi-well.

The results had been stunning!

Interaction between his new host's psietic and genetic heritage had been encouraged, and had allowed him to graft his identity into the new complexus with remarkable alacrity. He could feel the bonding process even now, blossoming further as the construct continued to unfurl within him. It was an amazing experience!

No wonder Sachael-Za-Ad'hem has achieved so much in such a short space of time! He's accelerated their psychomaturation thousands of years! And ruthlessly ensured they've remained on the straight and narrow too!

Psi-edon-ijah was deeply impressed.

Impressed *and* annoyed!

What would we have achieved by working together? Gods! We'd be…

He left the thought unfinished.

Once again I've vastly underestimated Sachael-Za-Ad'hem. And his designs! He's a freaking genius to come up with this! No wonder he imagined such a thankless task would earn us all a reprieve…

Then Psi-edon-ijah remembered the fresh information contained within Esther's mind as she died before them.

…And it's beginning to work!

He looked at himself in the mirror once more.

How far I've fallen! I was once a leading light among the Host and a force to be reckoned with. Now I'm nothing but a shadow, reduced to hiding inside humans. And a Guardian at that!

Hatred burned afresh within his heart.

I may have to start all over again with the scraps off the table, but at least I can make use of our new intelligence. This Compressor Program may have applications a transcended being can employ in other ways too. If so, I'll find it. And I'll make sure the data regarding their various procedures and protocols isn't wasted either. If I have to live among them, at least I can use what I learn to keep us all one step ahead of their damned investigations!

Of course…there will have to be sacrifices. If I'm going to get promoted to a useful position, I've got to be seen as someone who gets results!

Glancing to one side, Psi-edon-ijah noticed Angelika Papadakos leaning against his bedroom door. She was making no attempt whatsoever to mask her presence. From what he could read from the outer layers of her mind, she had been checking him out.

But of course! She has an attachment to this form. Even if she was using him to serve our purposes!

Although it had been an avenue Psi-edon-ijah had not chosen to explore since his revival, he skimmed the memories of her encounters with Calderon. To his surprise, he found the episodes most pleasurable to contemplate.

Involuntarily, one part of his anatomy began responding to those thoughts.

Angelika noticed. A predatory smile crept slowly across her face.

Glancing briefly out into the hallway, she checked to ensure they were alone. Entering quickly, she locked the door and quietly made her way toward him.

His body continued to react, subconsciously extending a continued invitation.

Psi-edon-ijah also noticed his heart had begun to beat that much faster.

Oh no! Just when I thought I couldn't stoop any lower!

***

"So, as you can see, Sir, each of our three primary Specter sites is now fully operational and manned. I thought it best to prioritize. Of the nine subsidiaries, four are already online and the rest will be linked into the grid before the end of next week."

Yeung glanced through the report's findings once again.

His new chief of security, Nicholas Smith, was proving to be an extremely resourceful and reliable right-hand man! Yeung had neglected to replace Harry Bing for quite a few years after his untimely death. It wasn't an oversight. Yeung had honestly felt the addition of his three exceptional colleagues only five years previously would remove the need for such a position in the future.

How wrong I was! He snorted to himself in hindsight.

"Sir?" Nicholas queried, assuming Yeung was reacting to something within the document before him. "Is everything alright?"

"Oh! Sorry Nicholas. Just reflecting on our drastic change in fortunes! As you know, I pride myself on planning ahead for every eventuality. But I must admit, I didn't see *this* coming! Not ever! I don't like being kicked up the ass without being asked nicely first. If I'd made sure a dependable security chief was in place after Harry's death, we might have avoided the need for all this clandestine sneaking about."

"Thank you, Sir. I pride myself on being thorough too. Hopefully you'll see that reflected in some of my adaptations."

"Adaptations?"

"Yes Sir. I always feel you can never have enough security. I know our bunkers are equipped with all the latest generation comforts and gadgetry your companies…err, *former* companies had available to them. But nevertheless, I felt it prudent to beef things up a little."

Yeung was really growing to like his new security chief. Placing the paperwork down, he gave Nicholas his full attention. "Tell me."

Nicholas paused to collect his thoughts. "I won't bore you with everything, Sir. The report will do that quite nicely. Nevertheless, there are some factors both yourself and the Apostles will need to get up to speed with. For example, as you're aware, each of our subterranean sites is fully armored and bristling with the most sophisticated weaponry and technology on the planet. In theory, it makes each position extremely difficult to detect or even enter. However, in light of recent events where the Guardians were able to employ some form of temporal gateway to evacuate the citizens of Los Angeles, I've ensured to add temporal scramblers into the fabric of each structure."

"Temporal scramblers!" Yeung spluttered. Shocked, but delighted at the audacity of the maneuver. "What? In the floors and walls themselves?"

"Of course! I'm hoping to negate the effects of such a field if they were to ever try and enter our facilities by similar means in the future. I have, of course, ensured to leave certain *windows* open within each complex. This will allow teleportation by our own people about the structures. But, their exact positions are a closely guarded secret, and only certain officers will be privy to the information."

"And what happens to someone who tries to jump without the appropriate knowledge?"

"If they are naturally gifted, just a severe headache as they're forced to adjust their materialization sites at the last second. However, if they use mechanical enhancers of any kind…"

"Like their rings or our bands?" Yeung interrupted.

"…precisely," Nicholas replied. "Well, in that case, the fail-safes will scramble their molecular patterns and they'll materialize within the walls or floors."

"Ouch!" Yeung gasped, smiling at the mere thought. "Excellent idea!"

"Ah, but that's not all there is to it, Sir! I also took the liberty of commandeering twelve of our latest generation Wave Readers. As you know, Esther's adjustments ensured the latest models contained the modifications for deep mind scanning *and* thought control. While we were intending to use them as a means for gaining intelligence, I thought they'd be an excellent tool we could exploit to screen any new or unexpected arrivals."

"In what way?" Yeung asked, intrigued by the idea.

"From today, the only way in or out of each bunker is via a designated reception point." Indicating the report, Nicholas continued, "While *this* précis highlights each one, no one else besides Psi...err, Guardian Calderon, Angelika or you or I, is privy to that knowledge. Base commanders only have access to coordinates within their own facilities. This will enhance security in two ways.

"Firstly, anyone seeking entrance will have to request permission. Everyone gets a heads-up and we can ring the area with all sorts of defensive and aggressive countermeasures. Secondly, when they *do* arrive, they will be subjected to the compulsion matrix of the Wave Reader. Basically, we can ensure everyone *is* who they say they are, before we release them to walk about freely."

"And what about the four of us?" Yeung asked, his face suddenly turning to stone. "I won't allow anyone access to my mind without permission."

"That's already taken care of." Nicholas replied. Handing Yeung an info-crystal, he added, "This contains the security frequencies on which each Reader operates. *We* will be able to move about unhindered and completely free from compulsion."

"This is a most welcome surprise, Nicholas. Here I was, thinking it would be all doom and gloom, and you've managed to cheer an old man up during your first week!"

"Not so old from where I'm sitting...If you don't mind my saying so, Sir."

Yeung paused to look at his reflection and the effects of his implant.

In his case, he hadn't bothered going to extremes. Instead, Yeung had imbued the essence of several unwilling and burdensome *weak links* to return his appearance to what he possessed when only fifty years old. Increasing musculature and height and darkening his hair had done the trick. Now, he looked more like a city businessman than the elderly leader of the global crime syndicate everyone hated. One that had—as far as the public were aware—been busted wide open with all known assets frozen!

If only they knew, he thought.

Then he had an idea.

"Nicholas. You said the Specter protocols would be fully online by the end of the week, yes?"

"Yes, at the latest. Why?"

"Can you retarget some of the satellites to compliment your new security measures? Say, one on each of the bunkers?"

"I've already taken the liberty, Sir! That was the final point I was going to raise with you. Again, recent events are making me think about the *unexpected*. If you don't mind ensuring all personnel get nano-chipped, it will facilitate the upgrade much more speedily."

"In what way?" Yeung replied. Delighted by the way his new chief was anticipating his requirements.

"Well, I was thinking. The Guardians appear to be annoyingly adept at springing surprises. I thought we'd return the compliment. With your permission, I'm going to reposition at least sixty percent of our satellites in higher, variable orbits. That will be essential to lessen the risk of detection. The others will remain in situ and be targeted upon each of the Specter facilities, half a dozen capital cities of your choice, and a number of other very public venues.

"By micro-chipping our people, the platforms will instantly be able to recognize friend from foe. So, if one or more of our sites are compromised, we have the luxury of being able to choose how aggressively to respond. However, bearing in mind the Guardian response will undoubtedly be swift and decisive...I would strongly recommend we take a more uncompromising posture."

"Define uncompromising." Yeung countered, captivated by such radical thinking.

"Sir! If we are ever breached, it means anyone and everyone caught inside will be a liability. We *can* prevent that. If we install the proper programs from the word go, we can encode the nano-technology to initiate emergency transport of the holders, while ordering the nearest satellite to fire. Think about it! Our personnel would be at liberty. And while the facility would be vaporized from orbit and no longer viable, it would at least take out an entire Inquisitor team."

Yeung couldn't hide his delight. "Nicholas. I *do* like your thinking!

"Thank you, Sir. I know it would be costly, but the countermeasures would really hurt them. Obviously, the Guardians would be all over the orbiting defense system like nappy rash on a baby's backside. That's why I recommend we move so many. They'll be out of the way and undetectable. Those that are vulnerable can target their payloads on the preselected targets we will update on a weekly basis. Remember, although in hiding, these facilities allow us to maintain a considerable influence on world markets. How fortuitous if we capitalize on our misfortunes by removing any economic or fiscal thorns in the flesh at the same time?"

Looking his security manager directly in the eye, Yeung said. "Nicholas! I am very keen to adopt your suggestions. You don't have to keep calling me *Sir* anymore. *You* may address me as Lei…or Yeung, as most others seem to prefer. Instigate these suggestions immediately. I want them implemented before the day is out."

"Thank you, Si…Yeung," Nicholas replied, "I'll get right on it."

As Nicholas left, Yeung had to admit. He was feeling rather smug.

Despite our fall from grace, we still have the ability to exert power in ways they never dreamed of. And better still, we can hurt them back!

His musings were interrupted by a newsflash suddenly displayed by some of the TV monitors adorning one of the walls. Each highlighted the various reports coming in from around the world regarding the attacks in the Gulf of Aden and Los Angeles.

These latest updates were emphasizing how far investigators had got in discovering the identities of those responsible for the atrocities.

This one doesn't look good!

Shuffling forwards, Yeung adjusted the sound on the largest screen and listened in. Almost immediately, his mood soured.

Stunned, he watched incredulously as the face of each and every single one of his Apostles appeared in turn! They were closely followed by an inordinate number of his top executives. In particular, most of his Chiefs of operations, technologies and information!

Damned! How the hell…

Thankfully, the majority were representations of their original profiles. But sadly, too many contained a recent picture of his team following modification.

The bulletin went into great detail about each of those involved. Evidently, they were now top of Interpol's wanted list for a whole catalog of misdeeds. That list of felonies was stunning, ranging from transgressions against humanity and the environment, terrorism and organized crime, numerous breaches against white collar legislation, right down to intellectual property violations and corruption.

Yeung was bemused to note that his own face was absent.

Until the end of the report, that is!

They had saved *him* for last, and were now offering him up for crucifixion as Public Enemy Number One.

The devastating mind-ream performed on Esther prior to her death, had obviously opened her up more deeply than they'd realized. The release was now highlighting the fact that a combined Global Marshals Bureau/Inquisitor task force had been established. This special team had the sole purpose of hunting *him* down. Certain information had come to light connecting him to Lord Marshall Foster's death, and a host of other assassinations, both before that incident and since. Once hailed as the world's leading light in progressive change, he was now a marked man with a considerable price on his head.

Too considerable for his liking!

Especially as the reward appeared to be irrespective as to whether he was alive or not!

Koso-tsu! He cursed silently in his native dialect.

Thank goodness Sim...Jose will be able to help us stay one step ahead. If we can just keep them focused on the bait we've arranged, it'll keep the direct heat off us and ensure we can make the best of this mess!

***

A solitary figure sat quietly within the observation deck of the Guardian Command Carrier, Oddesy. Silhouetted against the main viewport, it was clear he was a person with a great deal on his mind.

Before him, a sheaf of documents and scattering of report crystals littered the desk. Slouched as he was in his chair, his fingers absentmindedly drummed with a cadence that only seemed to exacerbate the fact he was carrying the weight of an entire world on his shoulders.

A deep sigh escaped his lips.

Adjusting his position, Andrew turned to gaze for a moment out of the window. He marveled at the snow peaked majesty of the San Gabriel Mountains. The setting sun accentuated their glowing, golden and white backdrop against the Los Angeles skyline, still remarkably intact despite recent events. Seizing the moment's peace and quiet, he allowed his eyes to lose focus and instead resorted to his stupendous far-sight.

Allowing his astral vision to roam back and forth across the vast tracts of land below him, he had to admit. *We've been lucky.*

Very lucky!

Naomi's swiftness prevented a monumental loss of life and a colossal amount of damage. Her opening gambit to mesh with the psi-tronic crystal was as inventive as it was appalling. By using the artifact's essence to simply leech away the titanic energies unleashed during the explosions, she reduced subsequent seismicity to manageable—and survivable—levels.

Victoria had replayed that moment over for Andrew, allowing him to savor the full nuance of the entire incident. In fact, his spine still tingled with dread every time he considered it.

Bold, ingenious…but oh so very dangerous! And her follow up strategy, to use the old crystal flecks to dam up the voids created below the earth's crust was

306 • Fallen Angels

also inspired. THAT maneuver allowed us to evacuate over twenty-three million people with very few fatalities.

He snorted. *If you can call twenty-seven thousand deaths, 'very few'!*

Subconsciously, Andrew's fists tightened in frustration at the thought of it.

It's a tragic figure, really. But miniscule to what it could have been. What it SHOULD have been. Most of those casualties had been too close to the detonation sites for us to be able to save them or too close to the coastline when it dropped. I can hear their mind-screams even now, crying out as they died!

Of course, he hadn't been able to leave things like that.

Taking the lead, Andrew had initiated the modification of the planetary crust, using the enhanced, self-replicating, tectonic placebo provided by Naomi.

She was out of it, of course, undergoing the unfathomable vicissitudes of her immersion into the psi-tronic lattices. Nevertheless, it had been a mighty work, reminiscent of the challenges he'd undertaken so long ago. Only *this* time, his father hadn't been there to help. Andrew had undertaken the executive position himself, with Victoria providing prime focus.

It had been a humbling experience, to witness firsthand the degree of finesse required to inaugurate such an endeavor. But it was something he would now have to get used to.

Although they had only concentrated on the primary sites of the detonations, it still meant they'd had to refashion over one hundred and fifty square miles of land. Trillions of tons of sediment and rock, through several layers of strata had simply been obliterated in the opening holocaust. Replacing it hadn't been easy, and it had taken nearly four hours of exhaustive focused work to regenerate a suitable matrix from which later, more permanent modifications could be undertaken.

Even so, the entire zone had continued to flex alarmingly as it solidified and settled into its new configuration, triggering the only earthquake to actually strike the region. Measuring nine-point-eight on the Richter scale, it had been allowed to propagate fully to test the integrity of the embryonic substrata.

Andrew wasn't ashamed to admit he had held his breath for all of the two minutes it had taken for the tremors to subside. But he needn't have been so worried. It had worked like a charm!

Yes, most of the rail and high-rise freeway networks lay in ruins. But already, extensive repairs were being undertaken to open the main arterial routes between Santa Ana and Santa Monica. Priority was also being given to ensure all access routes to County hospitals and welfare centers were clear and unimpeded.

Of course, there had also been major disruption to the electricity, gas and water supplies. Downed power cables and burst pipelines had caused sporadic fires and flooding, especially in the industrialized centers. But it had been remarkably contained. Rolling power cuts had been instigated to help facilitate a gradual and structured return to normalcy, particularly in the commercial districts further inland that had survived with their basic infrastructures intact.

Because of this, food and water shortages for those residents in outlying areas who had already been allowed to return were being kept to a minimum. Current estimates were indicating they would shortly be joined by over seventy percent of the rest of the population within the next ten to twenty days. The remainder would continue, housed at the special reception centers that had been hastily constructed around the sites of Hamilton, Osceola and Cherry Creek, within the Great Basin National Park. Shrewdly positioned, the ghost towns afforded an already existing logistical foundation, which had helped aid work tremendously.

Andrew was very grateful that the Lord Concilliator's department was already deep in discussion with the appropriate local government agencies, selecting the best–and safest–sites for urban regeneration to be undertaken.

At least it's another step in the right direction out of the quagmire! Thank god we've managed to turn the fan off!

Sighing again at the sheer range of organizational juggling required to revitalize this, the second largest urban agglomeration in the United States, Andrew turned his attention to more immediate concerns.

Now all I've got to do is liaise with Anil regarding the reopening of Los Angeles International Airport. The sooner we can bring in the civilian and National Guard disaster relief teams, the better. It should be safe for them to shadow our specialized units into the stricken area by now. San Pedro Bay will have to wait. Its under six feet of water anyway, so a week or so isn't going to make much difference. That will free us up for the more…pressing matters.

His mood darkened considerably. Suddenly, Andrew found himself having to fight the sudden urge to incinerate something! *I think I'll get Victoria to refine her search for those fuck-wit, cowards! Just like them to go crawling into their holes again. If I have my way, they won't live long enough to waste any courts time, let alone a specially convened Psi-Court! Perhaps I'll use the Procurator Wing to…*

Abruptly he felt ashamed!

…Get a grip Dickhead! Naomi didn't make such a huge sacrifice for YOU to go fucking things up with a caveman's display of testosterone. What a great example to set, eh? Overlord Designate and I'm all set to wipe them out without the fiasco of a trial. Hell, how DID father manage to control himself all these years?

He started!

Father! Dammed! I'd almost forgotten!

Glancing at his chronometer, Andrew realized he only had a few hours left before the big event! Suddenly feeling very isolated, he muttered, "I'd better get a move on!"

Chapter Twenty-One
Acceptance

Echoes within echoes throbbed throughout Naomi's heightened sensibilities.

How long has it been now? Minutes! Hours!

Time had no meaning here, within the lost existence of her new reality. It fractured off in a multitude of directions all at once. And not all of them were conventionally linear.

It could have been Days! Weeks! Hell, it might not have even happened yet!

Why oh why did I contemplate such a stupid course of action!

You know why! A voice replied, from among the refracted halls of her alarming new existence.

Who is that? Where are you? She replied, eager to seize upon anything that would prevent her thoughts from skipping away along the multiple avenues surrounding her.

Naomi reached out with her awareness again, thankfully resurfacing at long last, after an age spent in glacial petrifaction. Her fright and panic had receded, goodness only knows how long ago. Now, she was morbidly curious to discover as much as she could about her inimitable condition. Especially if someone or some*thing* was in here with her!

Unable to resist, she set off in pursuit of her elusive listener, seizing the opportunity to explore the many facets of her new actuality at the same time.

Because she was somehow attuning to her surroundings, Naomi discerned a multitude of tones, chiming into existence every time she exercised a thought or an impulse. At first, she thought they were similar, until she stopped trying to *hear.*

She had to remember. This was unlike anything she was used to. But it was also part of her entire world now. It didn't spell the end of her life. Far from it! She had been told it opened a door of opportunity.

How did Adam put it?

... Oh you'll survive, Naomi. Believe me...

...Just prepare yourself for the change. You'll be very different to what you are now, transcension aside. So long as you accept the metamorphosis for what it will accomplish, you will come to look on it as it truly is. A unique gift!

...Change is necessary, Naomi. Embrace it, as I do. For you will become a guiding light of the future if you do!...

So, instead of trying to act from a human perspective, Naomi stopped listening and simply savored the experience.

An electric thrill coursed through Naomi's entire being as variant music washed over her. A concordance of clarity suddenly focused within her grasp!

...accept the metamorphosis for what it will accomplish...

Abruptly, the odd frigidity that had gripped the center of her existence, flared brightly! The gem-like facets freezing her in place began glowing with inner, deeper warmth that sent waves of pleasure undulating along her synapses.

I've been given a gift! It requires change, but if I welcome it, support it, I'll...

A web-like tracery of dazzling pleasure surged throughout the prism of her soul, crackling inwards and outwards, and every-which-way imaginable.

...Thaw!

Super perception flowed from within. Rushing and swelling, it expanded into a sudden onslaught that quickly grew beyond her capacity to contain.

Exploding fee of its glacial restraints, her hyper-cognition was reborn. Charged beyond reckoning with psi-tronic energy, it burgeoned into something else entirely.

The razor sharp edges of her hybrid form rippled and flowed, crackling with a liquid radiance that infused her psi-well with ancient comprehension.

And a shock!

Well, well, well! This is going to be fun! An overwhelmingly powerful voice boomed within her mind.

A chill of recognition radiated throughout Naomi's memories.

But...YOU! HOW?

Now, now, the entity chided: *Don't start slipping backwards after you've come so far. You know who/what I am. Stop trying to think so hard. Just feel. Enlightenment will flow.*

But you're dea...sorry! My apologies! You re-ascended! I saw it in Adam's mind.

Making an effort to still her thoughts, Naomi let the limitless well of her inquisitiveness drain away. Here, she knew everything and nothing. The height and the depth and the breadth encompassing the entire cosmos...

...But not the familiarities of her own humanity!

Feel it. The entity repeated.

She did!

Oh! OH WOW!

Shock and delight! Amazement and astonishment! A bolt from the blue that she realized she had known all along!

Pleasure thrummed in the ether.

You're an echo of your creator, and yet—in a strange way—you're also HIM at the same time!

Crudely put. Sariel-Jeh'oel replied: *But correct. You...*

Hang on! Naomi cut in: *But that would mean...*

Sariel-Jeh'oel paused, his enjoyment clearly evident as the young mind cast her stupendous senses about her. Hunting! Seeking! Searching!

Abruptly, Naomi stopped: *I'm doing it again aren't I? Reacting like a human. I know he's here though! You two were so intimately involved in your transmutation. An echo of him or part of his essence will also live on here. You used HIS energies to get home and create this construct at the same time.*

An ethereal sigh trembled along the lattices.

Naomi stopped trying and simply...did!

Otherworldly laughter reverberated about them.

A teasing voice whispered: *And the penny drops!*

Addressing Sariel-Jeh'oel, Sachael-Za-Ad'hem said: *Did I not say she was priceless, my friend? A rare gift among star-like minds?*

You did indeed, Brother! I look forward to seeing how she tackles her present conundrum.

Oh, I have no doubt that once she grasps the distinction of her present condition, she will proceed as she always does. With speed, focus and precision! I lo...

AND she's actually present with you in the flesh! Naomi butted back in, indignantly: *Esoterically speaking of course. Please don't carry on a conversation about me as if I wasn't here! Come to that, why are you here? Surely it's not to deliver a running commentary on my pathetic...*

Wry amusement saturated the energy fields about them as Naomi caught herself.

A calculating mood then began emanating from her. Within moments, a tone of pure intuition pulsed through her psyche: *Gotcha! You're here to instruct me! Guide me. Like some form of uber reality-cum AI constructs!* It wasn't a question.

She IS sharp! Sariel-Jeh'oel chuckled, astonishment radiating throughout his complexus.

Told you! Sachael-Za-Ad'hem countered, in an unusually self-satisfied way: *That's why Andrew likes her so much. How did he describe her to me again?*

...Oh yes. Captiva...

DON'T START THAT AGAIN! Naomi's voice thundered. *Otherwise, once I find out how to control this damned freaky medium, I'll make your lives a...*

In the silence that followed, the inevitable compulsion to ask for clarification built ever higher in Naomi's mind. Somehow, she controlled it. Asking would serve no useful purpose...yet! But she wouldn't forget *that* little snippet!

Impenetrable walls slammed abruptly into place. The furthest reaches of their corporeality unexpectedly flashed with gold and silver light. Argent blooms of purpose and focus manifested, creating a net-like lattice of determination.

Suddenly businesslike, Naomi said: *As time doesn't exist properly here, you can't disagree that there's no time like the nonexistent present to get on with it!*

Referring to her framework, she continued: *Please begin. The sooner I adjust to the new and improved ME, the sooner we can all get on with something useful again…*

…And, if you can manage to control your banter for long enough, would you be so kind as to ask Anatt to look after Lucifer for a while? Oh! And don't forget my family. They'll need to know.

Addressing his friend on the intimate mode, Sariel-Jeh'oel's thoughts rang with profound respect: *It appears our girl has accepted her path. A true star-mind indeed!*

Savoring the strength of spirit flourishing about them, Sachael-Za-Ad'hem replied: *More than that, my friend. If what I suspect is true, the Pathfinder to Unification may have been born this day! I can feel it in my bones.*

Reminiscing for a moment, he continued: *Now. If only I could get Andrew to accept the coming changes with as much fortitude and resilience…well! My true self would be a lot happier. Let's get on with it, shall we, and see what she's made of?*

Have you determined the long-term occlusion quotient of our candidate?

I did try, my friend! But Naomi continues to present a paradox. We should be looking at a protracted linear time span. Ten, perhaps twenty of her cycles at least. But, every time I employed the probability lattices, my focus was confounded. I have a sneaking suspicion her ability to compartmentalize, blended now to her hyper-cognivity will cut that period in half. More, if she grasps the multiverse theorem quickly.

Perhaps THAT would be the most appropriate place to start?

Agreed!

Coming together instantly, the two Fallen brothers of the Primary Echelon of Heaven combined. The bonded clarity of the harmonic symphony they produced was as exquisite as it was terrifying.

A Fanfare-like invitation rang out to the child-mind before them.

ATTEND NOW. JOIN US IN INTIMATE UNION AND LEARN!

...SUCH WAS THE BEGINNING OF ALL THINGS...

***

The rippling lights within the Crystal Chamber suddenly flared with the brilliance of a million suns. Once again, the complex facets of this, the rarest construct in the universe began to rotate and splinter. A lethal fusillade blasted outwards. The sound of obsidian shards shattering *pinged* from the domed walls. Washed together by the unique resonance of the room in which it was contained, the noise was amplified beyond pain.

A clarion call heralded the appearance of multiple cracks along the surfaces of the crystal. Beginning at the outer facets, the fracturing deepened and widened. Burrowing ever inwards, the fissures allowed a colossal amount of pressure to escape. Brand new prisms snapped to the surface, marking a noticeable separation with each passing moment. Without warning, the radiance threatening to blister the very fabric of the walls, cut off, as if a switch had been thrown.

In place of the former monstrosity, a new construct was revealed.

In two distinct parts, it now looked as if the old psi-tronic crystal had attempted to grow a malformed twin. However, instead of the graceful lines and edges of a multi-faceted gem, the fresh addition was roughly humanoid in shape. And although razor sharp, its contours were somehow fluidic in character, as if it was unsure as to the meaning of its own nature.

Alarmingly, that new profile had grown close to nine feet in height.

Everything went still!

Having achieved what it felt was an acceptable equipoise; the psi-tronic duality readopted its arcane functioning.

The tinkling sound of crystal snowflakes falling returned. Music graced the ether once more. A legion of whispers exuded from all places at once. The multi-faceted prisms resumed their playful dance. Folding in and out of mundane sight, they offered tantalizing answers to unfathomable questions.

However, this time, there was a stark difference.

The crystal itself appeared to have lost its inner luminescence.

Dark, almost colorless layers sank into its jet-black depths. Devoid of light and life and purpose, it now looked as if an ancient sentinel stood guard, awaiting instructions that would never come.

Time passed…

The gloom was abruptly thrown back by an unexpected argent flare.

Over before it began, the silver brilliance crackled around the room, reflecting from thousands of different points all at once. A resonating boom careened off the walls, shaking dust free from the ceiling.

That dust eventually settled and serenity returned…

Suddenly, another unexpected nova of light and sound burst forth. As before, the aftershocks propagated the environment in the blink of an eye, amplifying the energies involved as they muted their dreadful potency.

Again, a watchful stillness descended.

After an age, in which the very heartbeat of the moon seemed suspended in anticipation, atmospheric tension relaxed...

Another eruption split the night!

This time, violet and silver arcs of lightning stabbed out. Humming and throbbing as they played across the exotic tiles lining the chamber, they appeared to be searching out unknown targets to incinerate. Rebounding at last into the crystal, they began feeding an inner furnace hidden deep within the smaller segment.

To someone looking on, it would have appeared a battle was taking place inside the artifacts core, for the latest discharge was much stronger than the others combined. The reality of what was taking place would have eluded them however. Because unseen to the human eye, or indeed, to the mental scrutiny of all but the most puissant practitioner, the duality was undergoing yet another bizarre metamorphosis.

As each random outburst manifested itself, micro-fissures were forming along the conduit that formed the bridge between the two halves of the crystal.

For those with the time and patience to watch the process, they would have been stunned to realize that, little by little, bit by bit, the smaller fragment of the construct was battling to separate itself from its larger cousin.

And it was working!

Oh, it would take an age—certainly—but the portent of what would eventually transpire was etched in gemstone!

So! Are you prepared?

Yes Father! Andrew replied: *As prepared as I'll ever be to say goodbye.*

Opening his mind fully, Andrew displayed the intricacies of each stage of the procedure about to take place in the minutest detail.

Checking through the glittering spectacle before him, Adam was surprised to note some embellishments had been added. Examining those elaborations in particular, he was pleased to see they would, in fact, enhance the process.

Wryly, Adam acknowledged Andrew's skill. It was clear that one day, his son would surpass him. He said: *Well done! That's an excellent adaptation. It extends the pain quotient, but by that stage I won't be able to comprehend it. Time will mean nothing to me once the metamorphosis has passed critical mass. You'll be able to create a self sustaining, and yet ramping acceleration field. Brilliant!*

Around them, five blazing entities radiated their approval and support.

Ignoring them, Andrew replied: *Yes. Well. I had a good teacher.* Suddenly, his shields slammed into place as an overwhelming surge of pain and sorrow threatened to crack his composure.

The entities withdrew, moving further away to allow father and son a degree of privacy in their final moments together.

Encompassing the younger mind within a halo of supportive and strengthening neural energies, Adam said: *C'mon Son. What about your sister? How is she managing?*

Keeping herself busy, as she always does when she wants to avoid thinking too deeply about things that upset her. As I'd be doing, in fact, given the choice!

Ah! But those who lead don't always have that luxury, my Son. You'll come to appreciate that as the years go by...

Without you! Andrew couldn't help the thought escaping.

Unbearable sorrow piled higher against his barriers. He struggled to control the scarlet bursts of emotion that began breaching the surface of his complexus in one place after another.

The strength of the enfolding solace increased.

Andrew! Son! You know I need to return home. I have to. Now, more than ever! The darkness rises, and for everybody's sake, I have to keep to the path I chose and…

But Victoria and I weren't included within your vision. Andrew cut in: *We're outside of your precognition. You say that one day we'll both surpass you. Isn't there anything we could do to…to…*

A corporeal hand reached out to silence him. The titanic mind opened fully, at last, to reveal the full travesty of what could occur if they were not very, very careful.

The younger mind was moved to silence.

Eventually, Adam sighed: *There is only one being outside of existence with the might and fortitude to quell the black fires of Tartarus within me. Only one has the capability to purify them once more, and transfigure the darkness into light. There's only one place it is truly safe for me to exist and serve…*

Adam paused to indicate the vastness of the universe around them.

…And it's not here.

The inevitability of the situation finally pierced Andrew's heart.

Adam's aura darkened slightly as he felt his son's bitter hopelessness. Embracing Andrew's essence more intimately, he added: *You are entirely correct when you say you were outside my temporal vision. You were both…ARE both…a wonderful blessing. A gift beyond the value of existence itself! Having you in my life has enriched it more than you will ever know, and, kept me focused on what needed to be done. Believe me when I say, your grief is nothing compared to mine. I just hide it better. I've had much more practice. And just as well, because I never envisaged having to leave my own flesh and blood...my very own essence, behind. Were it not for the danger to this realm, I would gladly forsake my proper dwelling place for all eternity so I could remain with you. Although I would eventually darken, and...*

And?

Although it would take an age, I would die. As puissant as I am, removed from the Source, my core essence wanes with every passing millennium. Though it would take trillions of years, eventually, all that would remain would be the echoes of my memory as they scattered along the cosmic winds.

So there's nothing we can do?

Of course there is my Son. We can accept the hand we have been dealt and play it to the best of our ability. We can only ever try to do our best. And who knows the consequence of boldness, eh?

Boldness! What do you mean? Andrew countered, confused by his father's thought.

One thing I do know for certain is that everything the Source does is motivated by his cardinal attributes. My just proscription took place because justice demanded it! It was also a course of wisdom, for it protected those who remained pure from our corrupting influence. You could say it prevented the rot from spreading. His power ensured we were removed to a place where our dominion, our sway, would be contained. However, that act was also motivated by love. For, instead of just casting us away to Tartarus and death, he also made a way back for those humble enough to seek it. Remember, at the time, this was a much lower plane. It would require guidance and patience over a protracted period of time to lead its peoples away from the futility of their own dark paths...

...But who would have the sense of justice to appreciate the rightness of this task? The wisdom to plan it through! See it through! Who would fight to overcome their own darkness to ensure their superior powers were devoted toward

an age of nurture? Remember, not all of the Fallen were truly repentant. Not all sought to exercise love toward those they viewed as lesser beings. Yes, we were all dealt the same hand. Some of us have already played their cards masterfully and returned. Others…simply folded without trying. Me? Perhaps I tried too hard. But look at the results I managed to achieve. Not only are a people doomed to failure now on the narrow path to elevation and Unification, but you and your sister are a wonderful surprise. An ace up the sleeve, you might say. He loves it when unexpected blessings pop up out of the blue! I can't wait to see how he reacts to the way YOU play.

Beckoning for a moment toward the waiting entities, Adam sent them an encrypted message. Four immediately jumped even further away, and took up positions at pre-designated points within a vast, invisible quadrant. One moved closer to Andrew.

Turning back to his son, Adam separated a heavily shielded portion of his own psychic nexus from within his complexus.

Tendrils of incredible might began flowing toward the younger mind. Light bloomed as they gradually came together in a sizzling knot around the extracted construct. Immense energies flared! As the dazzling radiance frittered away, a pure flame of unbelievable clarity hung in the void between them.

Adam said: *This is Phoenix. It is for you. And you alone, my firstborn blessing! It contains the entire sum of the pure divine essence remaining to me. Will you accept the office of Overlord with all the obligations, responsibilities and privileges this will entail? Do you swear to support others to the best of your ability, always putting their interests before your own? Do you promise to lead by example? To set the highest standards of service, sacrifice and honor? To always seek to temper justice with love? And power with wisdom? Do you agree to bear this burden alone, knowing that the future hangs upon your shoulders?*

…Do you accept the hand you've been dealt Andrew?

Looking at the concentrated nub of power before him, Andrew savored its vitality with the full range of his abilities. He could feel the urgency of its invitation. Hear the vibrancy of its allure. Taste the pure and unadulterated essence of magnificence incarnate. And most of all, he could sense the unwavering devotion and focus required, to take up the potency of this mantle.

A potential so arcane, so terrible, that the destiny of worlds would lie heavily upon him—and him alone—forevermore!

Despite the huge distance involved, Andrew's awareness skipped to the five entities about him. He tried to gauge their reactions, but the inner thoughts of Aslan-di'el, Gaia-le'el, Gazad-riel, Olinda and Ocean-az'el were all but walled off. Private! Secret!

The only discernible hint he *was* able to detect, was a feeling of eager expectation humming in the ether about them.

Finally, Andrew's astral sight came to rest again on his father.

Darkening rapidly now as the trigger to madness approached, Adam's entire psyche radiated with unshakable confidence, love and hope.

Do I accept? Andrew thought.

Deep within, he made the inevitable choice.

Steeling himself with a resolve he never knew he possessed, Andrew blended with the fringes of his father's essence for one last time.

Subsuming the Divine Flame into his own nexus, he thundered...

I DO!

Epilogue

Reeling from the sudden infusion of power, Andrew fought to control himself.

Looking inwards, he felt his psychic nexus balloon alarmingly as it reacted to the massive influx of exotic energies beyond his ken. So urgent was that increase, he felt sure his complexus might burst at any moment.

A bewildering jumble of thoughts, memories and pre-human existence crowded in on his consciousness, each one eager to be heard and understood. Chaotic bolts of lightning battled across the vista of his mind, increasing the confusion a thousand-fold. Then, just as it seemed he would explode, some form of cognizance within the flame recognized his genetic heritage and triggered an instant cessation to the onslaught.

Spinning to a halt, Andrew steadied himself and discovered he was now nearly twelve million miles from his former position.

Recovering from his shock, he instantly threw his far-senses back toward his father.

Keep moving! An insistent voice rang through his mind. Andrew subconsciously felt himself being tugged relentlessly along.

What?

Keep moving. We need to be outside of the forbidden area before its influence takes hold, otherwise we may become unwitting participants of the transmogrification about to take place. Once it starts, the process is remarkably rapid.

Dragging his senses away from the coalescing core of gravity for a moment, Andrew recognized Aslan-di'el. He replied: *Don't worry about me. I've seen the dangers involved firsthand, having actually witnessed a star imploding into a black hole on several occasions. And father's construct should direct the energies to where they need to go. I'm just…It's just…that this…*

But THIS involves your father. Aslan-di'el said, showing awareness and understanding: *Someone who, we can plainly see means more to you than life itself. Personal involvement always makes objectivity MUCH harder to achieve.*

Andrew didn't reply. He was too absorbed in the obscure manifestation taking place before him.

In their planning of the event, Andrew had been fully apprised of the fact that his father would need to generate sufficient mass to trigger a spiraling collapse. They didn't just need to create a black hole. They needed a supergiant. And in order to sustain the life-flow of the huge galaxy encompassing them, a rotating one at that! Such a feat would require prodigious power.

Andrew said: *With what's happened, how will he spawn sufficient…*

Don't worry! Aslan-di'el interrupted, having anticipated Andrew's question: *Your father was being quite literal when he referred to his gift of PURE divine essence. For that's what he gave you. Uncorrupted tincture! He separated and retained the savagery of the Destroyer within himself. The rage of the Angel of the Abyss is a terrifying thing to behold…as we're all about to see.*

Apprehension flared through Andrew's psyche: *But the danger!*

Do not be alarmed! The ferocity will be directed toward his prepared creation and inwards, at himself. For with his own destruction will come rebirth. You have never witnessed the devastation of his unrestrained wrath, Andrew. Now prepare yourself! The focal point approaches…

Immediately dismissing his own concerns, Andrew secured himself in position and scanned for the invisible cosmic chains that anchor all celestial events in place. Attuning to each one, he infused them with a gentle radiance that caused a glowing network of overlapping ley-lines to appear.

Once the grid had stabilized, he expanded it with a thought, so that it encompassed the entire galactic hub.

His father—a roiling mass of self consuming energies—occupied a position at the very center. Andrew could already see the chains surrounding that point bulging as they deformed in the presence of rapidly increasing gravity.

Signaling the others, Andrew then waited while Gaia-le'el, Gazad-riel, Olinda and Ocean-az'el manifested their own geodesic arches. At a respective distance of twenty million miles from his father, each opened a huge portal to somewhere else.

Gaia-le'el unsealed a door into subspace. Immediately, vast quantities of energized matter began pouring through at a tangent to Adam's position. At that exact same moment, Gazad-riel, stationed across from Gaia le'el, opened her own gateway to inner space. Sub atomic particles, augmented beyond their normal capacity to exist thundered through. Adding their cogency to the stream, they began exploding in a flurry of conflicting vitality.

After a momentary pause, Olinda and Ocean-az'el simultaneously unlocked their respective portals. The contrast was startling!

Instead of a giddy rush, the obscure mediums of fold space and lower space merely oozed through. Exuding forwards like giant amoebas, it looked as if the two exotic masses might impede the frenzied charge of the primary matter streams.

Far from it!

No sooner had the amplified rush careened into the walls of goo, than there was a mighty explosion of contradictory forces. Aimed as they had been along complimentary orbits, the combining energies flared, before melding together and bursting forth in a supercharged state. Accelerating alarmingly, they continued to erupt from end to end.

Within seconds, a halo of screaming kaleidoscopic energies bloomed into view.

Andrew assessed the condition of his father.

A massive ball of self consuming/self sustaining rage now occupied the center. And it was growing larger by the second! Seething ferocity, caged away for thousands upon thousands of years and un-tempered by Heaven's grace, was being vented at last with a mastery that was terrifying.

Adam was still in control. His unbending, unyielding will was ensuring his vitriolic savagery was directed toward one purpose. The gradual surrender of his remaining essence!

Arcane energies exploded again and again from the darkening mass. Gradually, the well of violence magnified. Already, a portion of the surrounding matter stream was beginning to distend toward Adams's position as the increasing density and temperature began to deform space/time. More and more particles hammered or trickled through. The chaos intensified! Plasma spheres began forming within the interstellar medium.

Glancing around them, Andrew completed several lightning-fast calculations. His attention flowed repeatedly between the accelerating halo, the Fallen, and his father.

To Aslan-di'el, he said: *Stand ready!*

He felt Aslan-di'el drawing power to open the final, decisive geodesic archway between realms. They were saving the most dangerous, most decisive plane, for last.

Although busy, the others also joined their minds to the task, forming a conduit through which the forthcoming energies would pass without causing harm.

Adjusting his vision slightly, Andrew targeted a point within his Adam's rupturing threshold where pressure was wreaking the most extreme damage. His father was beginning to rotate upon and within his own composition as the nucleic forces became ever more unbalanced. His speed and direction now close to matching the accelerating matter stream thrumming about him.

The accretion quotient ramped exponentially.

Hydrostatic equilibrium trembled on the brink of dissolution.

Adam's primary tolerance started to shred and fragment. The beginnings of nuclear fusion bloomed within him and his atoms began to split.

Suddenly, the ether was blanched in silver-white light as a quasi-star appeared before them.

Andrew's mind boomed: *NOW!*

Unleashing a stunning creative blast, Andrew maintained the energy stream and watched in satisfaction as his father's evolving mass accelerated even further. At the same time, they tore open a spatial rupture right above him.

The chaos of mirror space materialized.

Imploding/exploding inverse matter seethed into the mix, devastating the normal laws of physics. All six transcended beings combined to mitigate the stream, and once completed, they teleported to a safe distance. Without stopping to watch the results of their work, they immediately united once more in preparation for the final phase.

As planned, the influx of converse particles had caused the forming propagation field to mushroom alarmingly. Kinetic and thermal energy and fluctuating gravity had caused Adam's emerging complexus to swell even further!

Still in his embryonic state, Adam had distended into an unstable *giant* proto-star. The indigo blackness of space was now swathed in blue-white luminescence, a thousand times greater than Earth's own sun!

And *still* the process unfurled.

The never-ending infusion of five different kinds of exotic matter was creating an environment in which the deepening gravity-well would continue to engorge at a truly terrifying rate.

Sure enough, before they realized what had happened, a solar-*supergiant* manifested before them, blazing with the intensity of a million quasars!

Adam had now achieved sufficient volume for the next stage to proceed.

Quickly, Andrew scanned the core of his star/father.

As calculated, the combination of augmented mass, together with unstable foreign matter had warped the newly forming electron/positron pairing within the new sun's nucleus. Already, an unseen and irreversible process had begun. The first hint they received of the coming paradox, was a stuttering within the blinding luminosity of the corona. It looked like someone was rapidly flicking a switch on and off.

Secondly, they felt a sharp upsurge of pressure as a massive quantity of exotic material formed within the nexus of actuality. Incredibly dense in nature, it triggered the collapse they had been waiting for.

Unlike a main sequence star, however, there was no blinding flash of a nova to announce the death of the super-giant. Instead, they felt as if they were watching a balloon that had suddenly begun deflating!

Andrew's mind directed: *NOW!*

Instantly, the vast potential of the Fallen filled him to overflowing.

As the solar disc contracted, Andrew's capability swelled to godlike levels. Unleashing that capacity instantly, he ensured to accelerate the rate of collapse.

Shrinking smaller and smaller by the second, the blue/white intensity of the monstrosity dimmed. In moments, it had turned a darker blue. Then red! Then white! As it did so, his father's mass became ever denser.

Completing a hyper-scan, Andrew breathed an esoteric sigh of relief. The program was working perfectly.

Escape velocity was now approaching one hundred and eighty-six miles per second. Even better, the coalescing gravity well was almost spinning at a synchronous rate.

As the light abruptly snapped off, Andrew thought, *time for my embellishment!*

AGAIN! He cried.

A further blistering arc of plasma streamed out at the exact moment the black hole was formed. Thrumming across the tabular of the newly established event horizon, the filament covered the ergosphere in a skein of unimaginable cogency.

Working deftly, Andrew accomplished two things within the blink of an eye.

Firstly, the rotational speed of the leviathan was meshed exactly to that of its dependent galaxy. Secondly, in a bold move, the breach between normal and mirror space was fully opened once more.

A throb of immense vitality radiated outwards, like a giant intangible halo. Reaching the edge of the photon sphere, it snapped back toward the rotating singularity. Boosted by the colossal influx of chaotic energies from mirror space, the enhanced source matter caused the anomaly to swell more alarmingly than ever before.

An invisible radius of unfathomable power coalesced in the ether before them. Within seconds it was the size of thousand suns. Then two thousand! Then four! Over and over the sum of its mass and gravity increased. As it did so, molecular disintegration released vast amounts of thermal energy. X-rays and gamma-rays began thrumming along the cosmic chains. Glowing like neon signs, they revealed the extent to which the space/time continuum was being abused.

Extending his senses, Andrew felt the giant galaxy about them shudder as the matrix of its new anchor established itself, synchronized itself, and then took control.

Incalculable energies continued to build.

The colossus now contained the mass of over one million suns.

Initiating a cross tabular jump, Andrew positioned Aslan-di'el and himself just outside the event horizon. Adjusting, he watched the singularity as it swept by.

Then again! And again!

Sending a head's up to his team, he prepared them for the final phase of the procedure: *Remember. We have to time the influx just right. Doing so will moderate the breach forever, and begin a feedback loop that will perpetually bleed every ounce of extra energy away from the gravity-well. In effect, we'll create a self sustaining acceleration field! It will mean that, should my father's efforts be successful and he re-ascends in the far distant future, this galaxy will be able to survive without a parent black hole.*

To himself, he added, *as I now have to do…*

Profound respect radiated toward him.

Crushing his self-pity, Andrew confirmed the ergosphere was now fully established. Tapping into its matrix, he strengthened the harmonic link between his friends, and began drinking in the resonance of the gravity-well.

The leviathan now had the mass of four million suns.

With adroit dexterity, Andrew deployed a cocoon of restrictive force above the axis of the maelstrom. In response, a magnifying nimbus of power began to coalesce along the event horizon.

Time passed, seemingly without end.

Through it all, Andrew continued siphoning ever more quasi-matter through from nether space.

At last, he deemed everything ready!

Changing the timbre of the flow, he began compressing the energy into a gigantic plasma ball. On and on the process went! The dazzling sphere before them began generating a storm of increasingly violent shockwaves that rocked them to the core.

Pinpointing his target, Andrew locked on and began tracking its plane of rotation. It was vast! The singularity now orbited a plane possessing the mass of over ten million stars! It took him almost a minute to accurately project its course.

The moment had arrived. He couldn't resist it...

Goodbye father!

Satisfied, Andrew then unleashed the full fury of the blazing gobbet, directly into the heart of the black hole.

Accelerated as it was by the crush of gravity, the compacted nucleus of limitless power seemed to strike a point of nothingness, before shredding into a smear of coruscating light. The very fabric of space/time teetered on the edge of dissolution. Amazingly, the capability of the discharged was swallowed into nothingness almost immediately!

Impossibly, a thought then managed to squeeze its way *out* of the titan!

Thisssisss not goodbyeee. It'sss justthe beginninggg…

As the forbidden area of the newly formed galactic anchor flexed and made its presence felt, they were swept from their perches by a hurricane blast of tidal forces.

Ten percent larger than its predecessor, it then began to feed on the stars and other interstellar bodies inhabiting the inner rim that were now within its sphere of influence.

Expanding his sight, Andrew invited the others to see the fruits of their labors.

Will it hold? Ocean-az'el asked.

Andrew checked one last time, before uttering a satisfied mental grunt. The cluster was indeed bonding around the influence of its new gravity alpha. The cosmic chains were also compensating nicely to the additional exotic essence now flooding the region.

Yes, it'll hold. That new material will help it…FATHER, mesh properly to his new charge. AND establish a gravity buffer between the harmless zone and the new region of lethality. Fortunately, nothing of consequence exists for several parsecs in any direction, so local stellar conditions will eventually stabilize and the galaxy will survive intact. The nurseries are well beyond its range. New life will come again…especially if WE have anything to do with it.

The sight before them was, simply…stunning.

Majestic, both in scope and glory!

However, as captivating as it was, something more urgent was already pressing on the minds of the Fallen. Turning to Andrew,

Aslan-di'el, Gaia-le'el, Gazad-riel, Olinda and Ocean-az'el crowded closer.

Gaia-le'el said: *It falls to me to be your first guide.*

Guide?

Guide! She repeated: *The flame you now hold is a sacred trust. It cannot exist outside of the Divine, for its puissance is as deadly as it is glorious. That you were accepted by the Phoenix is as remarkable as it is fear-inspiring, for in recognizing your potential, it gives us a glimpse of the capacity you possess...*

...Remember, such a thing was never envisaged by the Prime Source. Both you and your sister are a paradox. Unforeseen, you were never prepared for. Unexpected, who could know how you would stand in the unfolding of His purposes? Unknown, who could fathom your hearts?

Remembering how he had felt when he imbued the fire, Andrew gasped: *Are you saying this thing hasn't even FULLY activated yet?*

Moving closer, Gaia-le'el replied: *Andrew, how could it activate when it had not yet adjudged you worthy? Phoenix is a spark of the Divine One Himself. All of the Host possess such a catalyst...Fallen or no. By not destroying you, the Prime Source has bestowed an unprecedented gift. For in doing so, he has revealed his acceptance of what you might one day become! Although your heart is clearly pure, you are of fleshly origin. Fallen origin! The debased may not interact with the untainted. And yet, here you are. Accepted...provisionally! Your actions may not only influence the outcome for your father, but of the entire human race.*

*Oh Shi...*Andrew began to spit, before catching himself.

Amusement radiated throughout the vacuum around them.

Gaia-le'el continued: *Knowing this, your father entrusted to us your higher education. Phoenix has been fashioned to activate in six stages. No doubt, you have already witnessed the power of the first step as it recognized and bonded to your complexus. Each phase will augment the one before, as well as expand your abilities exponentially. As I'm sure you're now aware, the process brings with it certain memories of his life…before.*

Gaia-le'el's words touched a nerve in the back of Andrew's mind.

Wait a minute, he cut in: *I'm aware of my father's previous standing. And I've seen him reveal aspects of his potential on a number of occasions over the centuries. But, just how powerful was he? I mean, how much of his actual potential did he ever actually USE here, on this plane?*

Andrew watched as esoteric glances and whispers flickered back and forth between his companions. Something about their undercurrent only roused his suspicions further.

WELL? He pressed.

Aslan-di'el floated forward. His mind whispered: *Andrew. Your father was contrite from the moment he was ousted from Heaven. Once Fallen, he sealed his heart to the amplification Phoenix would have granted him. He felt unworthy to use that which empowered him. As such, over the tens of thousands of years since, he gradually ate himself away. Everything he achieved, everything he accomplished, was done without the Sources enhancement. Following his debasement, he used only that essence which remained in his complexus, or which he subsumed from renegades.*

Indicating the awesome sight behind them, Aslan-di'el continued: *That's why he needed our help to build this! For as potent as you thought he was, he was only a shadow of what he used to be.*

A shadow! Andrew gasped, incredulously.

What you now hold within you contains the full grandeur of a Primary Echelon Angel. Out of the myriads of us, only seventy such beings were generated. And your father stood among the highest. By refusing to employ his former essence, he hoped to demonstrate his penitent heart and secure a return through service to others. A dangerous gamble! For while this did indeed bring blessings—of which you yourself are a superlative example—it also doomed him to the eventual darkness of his core nature. For he was the Angel of the Abyss, and woe betide any who were given into his hand...

...Do you appreciate now, WHY he has locked himself away, where he can do no harm? For in seeking to demonstrate his repentance, he has protected others as he serves them still! Of course, in doing so, he needed to ensure YOU also had sufficient guidance for each stage of your...transmogrification.

Andrew was moved to silence. Warily, he scrutinized the spark within him. The catalyst to unlimited potential! It gleamed and glittered within his complexus, an unfathomable source to hidden majesty.

His old self-doubts came crowding back: *And it thinks I'M worthy? ME!*

...Oh God! We're doomed!

Gaia-le'el came forward once more: *That's why WE are here to help you. Each of us possesses a different Cardinal attribute. Mine is love. Where better to begin as you expand into uncharted territory? If you seek to imitate such an example from the start, your journey is sure to be enhanced. As such, I will be there to shepherd you, until you make the First Degree your own to command.*

Joyfully, she meshed with the fringes of Andrew's complexus: *Are you ready young Star-mind? Overlord of the Guardians of Earth...and so much more...*

Alarm radiated throughout Andrew's entire being.

Ready! Are you kidding! If we weren't already in transcended form, I'd need to change my pants! Who could EVER be ready for this?

Then Gaia-le'el's thoughts actually registered.

Overlord!

...Jeez, she's right!

Steeling himself, Andrew struggled to fight down a flood of insecurity.

I can't think this way anymore. I'm...I've...Oh God! We're doomed!

Chuckling, Gaia-le'el ignored his procrastinations and began the process. Eagerly she bonded a part of her psi-well to Andrew himself, and to the Phoenix, infusing it with a subtle tone as she did so. Excitement caused her entire being to shiver in delighted expectation as the fabrication blazed open once more.

So bright, so full of potential! Ooh! Let us see if your Divine name will be revealed to us from the outset!

WHAT?

Then they were consumed by the light.

***

Much, much later, a ripple began to propagate along the periphery between the new galactic hub and its enlarged forbidden zone.

Because of the settling gravity waves, it was difficult to distinguish at first. However, as it grew in size and intensity, there could be no doubt. Someone—or something—was trying to traverse that boundary unseen.

With infinite caution, a layer of lower space was manipulated so that it became translucent enough to peer through. Satisfied, the watcher then peeled back a final strand of reality to reveal a small group of travelers.

Bursting with pride, Charon turned to his companions: *See! Did I not say I would escort you safely through my domain?*

Your domain! Snapped Lucifian: *Don't forget we know what you are, worm! The lowest scum of the lowest tier. How fitting you make such an environment your home.*

Now, now, boys! Omigin-al chided: *We didn't come all this way just to fight amongst ourselves did we? After all, Charon has proven his worth…twice!*

Pah! Lucifian spat: *Sister! Just because he felt the intrusion into lower space and wet himself, doesn't mean he's doing us a favor now. He probably wants us to do his dirty work for him. Sort HIS problem out, AGAIN, so he doesn't have to.*

Why don't we just take a look and see? Bael-zebad suggested. Unleashing a vicious neural shock, Bael-zebad silenced the rest of the group in an instant. As the eldest and most powerful of them, his will was dominant. Sneering across the veneer of their minds, he emphasized his utter contempt with another painful jolt. Relishing their pain, he then ignored them, and began scrutinizing the imposing anomaly before him.

Ancient enmity—deeply submerged—radiated out of the abyss! A profoundly altered consciousness was aware of his intrusion.

Jerking away, Bael-zebad almost gave way to panic. But then he realized the truth. Sachael-Za-Ad'hem was deeply immersed within his new condition. There was nothing he could now do.

Turning to Charon, Bael-zebad said: *Well, well, well, my irritating little friend. You were right. You DID taste Sachael-Za-Ad'hem's essence. But the Destroyer wasn't leading a hunt for the worthless likes of you. Oh no!*

Turning to the vast galactic hub, he continued: *THIS is all that remains of our former Angel of the Abyss. The fool is following in the footsteps of his closest lackey and friend, Sariel-Jeh'oel, by playing nursemaid to a dying star-whorl.*

Shock radiated throughout the group. Tentatively, each extended their minds.

He's right!

Gods! At last!

Look! He recognizes our invasion into this plane and yet…

...He can do nothing to prevent it!

Lucifian expressed a valid thought: *Brothers! Sister! What of Psi-edon-ijah? And Hadez'ekiel, Ares-tartus and...*

Don't forget Hesta'n-ea! Omigin-al interrupted: *I always liked her.*

Whatever! Snapped Lucifian: *We all know Sachael-Za-Ad'hem forced their cooperation! They only ever went along with his crazy scheme to preserve themselves. But now the bully is gone, what of our brothers and sisters? Surely some must remain?*

Fearing to hope, they looked to each other in expectation.

Bael-zebad crooned: *We must inform Mae'loch! He will know what to do.*

Ushering them toward the breach, Bael-zebad accosted Charon, and added: *And make sure that damned thing is sealed tight. I don't want anyone knowing we were here who might be able to interfere with my plans!*

Alarm flared throughout Charon's psyche: *Of course, Brother. You need not fear on that account.*

But, Charon was privy to information the others knew nothing about. He thought, *but I can't say the same about those siblings. Or even Psi-edon-ijah himself!*

As they crowded into the geodesic pocket, Lucifian called to Bael-zebad on his intimate mode: *Brother. Mae'loch may squander the opportunity. You know how he feared the Destroyer, and those who supported him. He may seize on any number of excuses in an effort to...*

Oh don't worry! My Lower Echelon sibling! Bael-zebad cut in: *If he is foolish enough to do that, it will be his undoing. He may be of Median origin, as I was. But he has allowed himself to petrify. His fire of old now lies cold in the hearth. He will be no match for us combined. And with Sachael-Za-Ad'hem out of the way, we can set our sights higher! Why should I stop at being king of the Underverse when THIS realm now lays open to conquest?*

Embracing his companion, Bael-zebad continued: *Think, Lucifian! None of the Higher Echelon remains. I would ensure the pathetic insects of this realm bent the knee to serve us, as we originally envisaged. Their only chance of protection now lies stagnating behind us. Spent and impotent!*

Truly moved, Lucifian replied: *I agree Brother. Though, if I may suggest? A little more snooping by the worm wouldn't go amiss. I'd hate to go storming in, and discover a legion arrayed against us!*

A legion of what? Bael-zebad replied, turning to consider his Lieutenant: *Brother, you delude yourself. These are mere humans we're talking about. They are ours for the taking, and nothing will stop us! As soon as I've gathered all those who have the stomach for conflict, we will make our presence known.*

Charon had to fight down a rising panic.

But that could take years! Lucifian responded: *You know how slowly our kind reacts to change. Especially those still stagnating in solitude!*

Nevertheless! As soon as we have gathered in sufficient numbers… THIS realm will be ours! Mine! If the worm completes any snooping you feel is necessary by then, all well and good. But I have delayed long enough. The time of waiting is over. The time for action is at hand.

As the breach finally closed, a stray, but poignant thought snapped out.

I somehow doubt the word 'action' will aptly describe what's coming!

About the Author

Andrew P Weston is a military and police veteran from the UK who now lives on the beautiful Greek island of Kos with his wife, Annette, and their growing family of rescue cats.

An astronomy and law graduate, he is a contracted writer of both fiction and poetry, and has the privilege of being a member of the British Science Fiction Association, and British Fantasy Society.

When not writing, Andrew devotes his spare time to assisting NASA in one of their research projects, and writes educational articles for Astronaut.com and Amazing Stories.

CPSIA information can be obtained at www.ICGtesting.com
Printed in the USA
LVOW11s1946161215

466864LV00006B/786/P